THE TRAVELLER'S STONE

THE TRAVELLER'S STONE

S. J. HOWLAND

SILVERWICK
PRESS

First published in 2019 by Silverwick Press

Cover by Cakamura Designs

ISBN 978-1-9161662-0-2

for Tom, who always had faith,
with all my love and gratitude

CHAPTER ONE

The events which change lives, forever dividing time into before and after, seldom announce themselves, line up gently or offer the choice to decline. That would probably be easier. No one had asked Alexander King whether he wanted to be thrust into a reality where shadows did not remain tamely in their places, but instead massed into terrifying ranks to pursue him, or where the laws of physics could apparently be suspended at will. There was not a single hint when he woke up to warn him this would be the last morning of his former life.

It had begun in the usual way. He had breakfast alone perched on a corner of the cluttered kitchen table, with odd thuds and muffled exclamations coming from his mother upstairs as she got dressed for work, and the morning hum of London traffic outside. The only indications that today might be any different were the jeans and shabby green jumper he was wearing, even though it was a Friday in term time. He had almost finished his first piece of toast when he heard a plaintive call from over the banisters.

'Have you seen my bag, Xander? I know I brought it upstairs last night –'

Xander didn't even bother to roll his eyes.

'No, you didn't, Mum. It's here in the kitchen,' he called back.

At the age of fourteen, Xander had come to the reluctant conclusion he had grown *older* than his mother in most relevant ways. Not that she was stupid; Xander knew – because many people had told him – she was a genius. She had been one of the youngest people ever to achieve a triple-doctorate and her work was apparently re-writing the textbooks on geophysics. It was just a shame she couldn't always be trusted to put her shoes on the right feet.

'Oh, thank goodness.'

Mrs King dashed down the stairs and snatched up her bulging satchel with a sigh of relief. Xander's mother was thin because she often forgot to eat unless someone, usually Xander, reminded her and her crinkly brown hair was tied back in an untidy knot, with a pair of sunglasses holding her over-grown fringe off her face. Mrs King saw Xander glance quizzically at her head and then out of the window at the grey sky and steady drizzle.

'I couldn't find any hair clips,' she explained.

'Cunning,' said Xander, straight-faced and then looked more closely at her. 'Mum, your cardigan is on inside out.'

'Is it really?' Mrs King poured a glass of orange juice, glancing vaguely down at her clothes. 'I'll probably be a bit late back. Did you hear about the seismic activity last night?'

Only his mother, Xander reflected, would assume that everyone else followed each random convulsion of the earth's surface.

'We'll be pretty busy – I mean, this activity is extraordinary. The last significant activity in that area was over ten thousand years ago –'

Xander paid little attention as his mother rattled on; he knew more than most normal people would ever want to about seismic activity already. Finally, she glanced at her watch and said, in what she obviously assumed would be reassurance, 'Don't worry, I put something for your supper in the fridge.'

Xander just shrugged. He was under no illusions that whatever she thought he could eat for dinner would be either edible or advisable.

'It's all right, Mum. I'll be fine.'

This vague assurance seemed to satisfy Mrs King, and she put down her orange juice, having forgotten to drink any, and headed towards the door.

'Breakfast,' said Xander firmly, pressing a piece of toast into her hand. His mother took it with a smile and then spotted his clothes for the first time.

'You have school today, don't you?' she asked, looking rather confused.

Xander glanced down at his jumper.

'Yeah, but we've got a trip. I told you last night.'

'Oh yes, I remember,' Mrs King said, blinking. 'Do you need any money?'

'You already gave me some,' Xander reminded her.

'Good.' She crammed the piece of toast in her mouth and then bent to kiss him. 'See you later, then. Have a good day.'

'You too,' said Xander, brushing toast crumbs from his forehead.

Just as his mother opened the front door, Xander heard her say, 'Morning. I'm just off.'

Xander leaned forward so he could see into the hallway.

'Mum, your top's still –'

The front door banged. A moment later a stout woman in a voluminous blue apron rolled into the kitchen, carrying a tub of cleaning paraphernalia and a huge handbag. She beamed at Xander.

'Was your mother wearing her cardigan –'

'Inside out? Yeah.' Xander shrugged. 'You know Mum. It's not like anyone at work will notice – they probably all wear

3

them like that.'

'And the sunglasses?'

'Don't ask.'

Xander got up and put his plate in the dishwasher. His thick brown hair fell into his eyes as he leant down and he shoved it back. Although it annoyed him sometimes, he preferred not to cut his hair shorter; it was useful to hide behind. Xander was used to disappointing people's inevitable expectations of him, since they always presumed that he would have inherited his mother's academic brilliance. He was tall for his age, which drew enough unnecessary attention, but it was something his mother told him he had inherited from his father. Xander thought this was grossly unfair. He would have preferred to get at least some of her genius, rather than just large feet and a gangly build.

The stout lady was now rummaging in the depths of her handbag, although she glanced up when Xander began wiping up toast crumbs.

'Don't you worry yourself about that,' she said, emerging brandishing a large plastic tub. 'Here you are. Stick this in your bag. You said last week you had your trip to the museum today, so I made you a wee box of fudge.'

Xander's face lit up.

'Awesome. Thanks, Mrs Mac,' he said, pulling off the lid and stuffing one of the generous chunks into his mouth. 'This is amazing,' he said thickly.

Mrs MacLeod was the best cook Xander knew, although admittedly his field of comparison was rather narrow; his mother felt anything that was not actively black and smoking was a culinary success.

Mrs MacLeod just winked at him, then reached once more into her bag and brought out a squashy lump wrapped in cling film, which Xander knew would be a large egg sandwich to eat with her cup of tea at eleven o'clock. She took it over to the fridge and opened the door, then stood and stared, clucking her tongue in exasperation. Xander had a good idea of the cause but walked over to confirm his suspicions.

A plate sat in the middle of the mostly empty fridge, with a scrap of paper on which was scribbled 'Xander – supper'. On the plate were two green peppers, a small lump of parmesan cheese and a can of baked beans. Even by his mother's standards, this was fairly bizarre.

Mrs MacLeod shook her head in disbelief.

'Your mother may be a genius in volcanoes or whatever, but in everyday life she ought to have a keeper. Green peppers and baked beans indeed.'

'Don't worry,' said Xander. 'I have loads of takeout menus.' He was on first-name terms with most of the delivery drivers.

Mrs MacLeod put her sandwich in the fridge next to Xander's plate and shut the door. Something seemed to occur to her, and she reached for her bag again.

'Do you have enough money for that?' she asked, pulling out her purse.

Mrs MacLeod had been cleaning for the King family for the last five years and during that time she had adopted a maternal attitude towards Xander, on the basis that *someone* ought to. It was Mrs Mac who had rectified the situation when Xander's mother had provided him with a pack of girls' blouses instead of white school shirts, and she again who had come to many of Xander's junior school plays and concerts.

'Masses,' said Xander. 'It's okay. I'll be fine.'

Mrs MacLeod touched his cheek affectionately. 'I know you will, laddie,' she said. 'But you're going to be late if you don't get moving.'

A glance at the clock told Xander that she was right. He stuffed one more piece of fudge into his mouth before shoving the box into his schoolbag.

'Bye, Mrs Mac. See you next week,' he called over his shoulder as he headed for the door. 'Thanks again for the fudge.'

'You're very welcome,' she called back. 'You take care now.'

Xander waved a hand in acknowledgement before he banged the front door behind him.

Three hours later, shuffling at the back of a straggling line of his fellow victims, Xander wondered whether you could actually die of boredom. There are some people who are born to teach: effortlessly holding their students' attention, they inspire, amuse and inform. Unfortunately for the pupils of Park School, Adrian Tubner was not one of those people. His voice, both nasal and droning, had long since cleared the upper gallery of the British Museum of all but the hearing impaired. Xander had stopped listening some time ago, but he knew there was little chance of being caught out – part of Mr Tubner's charm as a teacher was that he didn't appear to care whether his pupils were actually taught.

Finally, the only words Xander had been listening for percolated through the fuzzy haze in his head.

'Onwards, class, onwards.'

All morning, that phrase had preceded entering a different area of the museum, all of which had appeared promising until Mr Tubner managed to reduce it to the sum of its dullest parts.

Xander wondered vaguely whether there was a guidebook he had missed at the entrance, *'The British Museum for the Terminally Boring'*.

'D'you think if I gnawed off my own leg, he'd let me off for lunch?'

Xander grinned sideways at Will Nicholson, his best friend and fellow-sufferer, and shook his head.

'Better not risk it. I bet he knows lots of boring facts about losing a limb – you'd bleed to death before he actually let you leave.'

Will grimaced in response.

'Have you got any of that fudge left?' he queried hopefully, but Xander shook his head.

'Nah, we finished it while he was talking about 9th century glazing techniques, remember?'

Both of them winced in memory of that half hour.

The long string of boys passed once more through the central atrium, a great circular space in the heart of the museum where soaring stone walls rose to an intricate glass roof. Xander lagged behind, enjoying the brief respite from Mr Tubner's monotonous voice. He glanced around idly and found his gaze following a tall, white-haired man who strode through the hall, weaving through the crowds, a huge black dog padding at his heels. A dog had never been possible in their rented accommodation, but Xander had always wanted one and this big black animal with its plumy tail was very close to his ideal. Xander watched it with longing and he nudged Will to draw his attention.

'Look at that dog.'

Will looked over reluctantly. He had been eying the cakes in the cafe area with an almost palpable yearning. 'What dog?' he asked, giving a cursory glance around before turning back to the double-chocolate muffins.

Xander twisted around to follow the dog with his eyes as they crossed the atrium. It did not appear to be a guide-dog but he realised that none of the museum staff were paying any attention to it, even though it didn't have a lead, nor even a collar as far as Xander could tell. The tall man paused a moment, staring at something just out of Xander's view and it struck him that this man did not seem as if he needed a guide-dog of any description. He radiated alertness and tension, and appeared to be listening intently to something.

As if drawn by Xander's wistful gaze, the dog suddenly looked around; its stare hit Xander like a blow. Its eyes were not brown, as he had expected, but pale, shining and filled with intelligence. They evaluated him for several seconds before the dog turned and followed the man off into the crowd. Xander let out a breath he had not known he was holding.

'Wow,' he breathed, and then was struck by the silence in his vicinity. Glancing around, he realised that he was standing alone and hurried to catch up with Will and the other stragglers who were passing through a large archway to the cool marble halls where the Egyptology section lay. Will was glowering now he had been removed from the food and Xander heard him muttering darkly under his breath, but the only words he could make out were 'carrot cake'.

Xander himself looked around with interest. Several years before, his mother was invited to a conference in Cairo and had decided that he could come. She had described with great enthusiasm the myths and monuments of the ancient civilisation by the Nile and he was fascinated. Of course, as usual, something had come up and the trip was cancelled. Xander remembered this without bitterness, despite his disappointment at the time; he was used to constantly changing plans. However, his interest in all things Egyptian had remained.

His first thought on entering the echoing hall was how incongruous it seemed, these vast and ancient pieces of stone standing under fluorescent lights, thousands of miles and centuries away from where they began.

He leaned closer to what looked like a giant stone bathtub and looked at the neatly carved hieroglyphs on the side, wishing he knew what they meant. Some seemed so sharp in relief, while others were more worn and Xander began to notice many repetitions of the same symbols.

With a quick, guilty glance around, he reached out in defiance of all the signs and brushed his finger over a hieroglyph depicting a man sitting at a desk, then onto the vivid image of a bird.

'What're you doing?'

Will's grumpy voice made Xander jump, and jerk his hand away.

'Nothing,' Xander shrugged. 'Just wondering what they mean.'

'Hmph,' said Will, prodding the base of the stone with his shoe. Despite his lanky build – Mrs MacLeod called him a 'string bean' – Will was one of those people who needed regular feeding to maintain a pleasant disposition. Xander was well aware his friend's mood was veering rapidly from bad to completely foul. It appeared that the close encounter with the cakes in the atrium had pushed him over the edge.

Gazing around for something to distract Will from his stomach, Xander spotted some large stone tablets displayed on the wall, protected by thick sheets of perspex. He shot a quick look over at Mr Tubner, who was gesturing ponderously towards a tall marble statue, quite oblivious to the pained looks he was inducing in innocent members of the public.

'Let's dump Tubbers for a bit,' suggested Xander. 'He'll never know, he's busy butchering perfectly good history. Some of this stuff is actually quite interesting.'

Will growled something that Xander took for agreement and, with another quick glance over at his teacher, Xander walked over to examine the stones on display. He wandered down the row of exhibits, reading the labels mounted on the wall next to each one. The last tablet was cracked, with the top left portion missing, but the clarity of the carved symbols on it belied the damage the stone had suffered. According to the sign, it was found in one of the smaller tombs in the Valley of the Kings, but experts could not decipher the hieroglyphs on it.

Xander leant closer to examine the symbols; they did seem subtly different to the others he had seen. All of a sudden, like an electrical current run briefly through a light filament, several of the symbols glittered. It happened so quickly that Xander wondered if he had imagined it and he reached out to touch the perspex over the hieroglyphs.

His fingers passed straight through the glass as if it didn't exist and pressed against cold stone. Instantly, the symbols blazed into white light and his stomach was wrenched sideways. Xander yelped and yanked his hand back, then stared around in bewilderment to see if anyone else had seen, but no one was looking. When he turned back to the stone it was once more dormant behind its perspex protection. Xander stared at his fingers in confusion, but they didn't look or feel any different.

'It's your hand, mate. You've got two of them.'

Xander jumped again as Will appeared behind him, and his friend gave him a curious look.

'Bit twitchy today, aren't you?'

'Sorry,' said Xander. He hesitated and then pointed at the

stone on the wall. 'Do you see anything weird about that?'

Will stared at the stone intently for several seconds.

'I give up. What's weird?'

Xander shrugged, trying to seem nonchalant.

'Nothing, I s'pose.' He felt strangely reluctant to describe what had happened.

'Well, that was a fun game,' said Will. He turned away, scanning the room for the rest of their class. 'C'mon, they're not here. We'd better go find them. It shouldn't be too hard; we just need to follow the smell of hopelessness and despair.'

Xander followed Will in silence. He glanced back once over his shoulder at the stone as it hung innocently on the wall and then stiffened. It was glimmering again with that elusive light, but none of the people wandering past it seemed to have noticed. Xander looked away with a shudder. This place was seriously weird.

Finally, they tracked down the rest of the class, penned up in a small room. Mr Tubner gave no indication that he'd even noticed they had been gone, as they slipped into the back of the group. He had at least stopped talking, although Xander suspected the relief was only temporary to allow him to surreptitiously tidy the thin black strands of his comb-over.

Will nodded towards the teacher and sniggered.

'Who's he trying to impress?' he asked.

Xander shrugged and wandered over to examine the only object in the room, the stone frontage of an ancient temple. The bright lights overhead threw the shadow of the building on the pale marble floor in sharp relief and Xander winced. His stomach still felt distinctly uneasy. As he walked around the side of the temple, Xander realised the shadows on the floor were wavering, as if the light that cast them was flickering, and a faint sound of static hissed in his ears. He glanced up in irritation but the lights shone steadily.

'What's the matter with this place?' Xander muttered under his breath. Fury flamed through him, the surge of aversion shocking him rigid. 'I've *had it* with all this. I need to get out.'

The words burst out of him in a near shout, drawing startled glances from the surrounding people.

Mr Tubner looked over in vague surprise to see Xander glaring at him, and then glanced at his watch. 'Lunchtime,' he conceded with a reproachful look, which was wasted since Xander was already halfway through the door.

As soon as he was back in the cool atrium, in the soaring space filled with natural light and normality, relief rushed through him. He scrubbed his hands through his hair, waiting for the rest of the class to catch up and feeling foolish. He tried to rationalise what had happened, that he had obviously been hungry and fed up, and had imagined things. A memory of smooth, cold stone flashing into light tingled for a moment in his fingertips, but he repressed it ruthlessly.

Will hurried through the doorway, ahead of the rest of the group, his concerned face lightening as he saw Xander waiting self-consciously.

'You all right?'

Xander shrugged and grinned sheepishly.

'Yeah, fine. Just low blood sugar or something.'

'Come on then, or we won't get a seat,' said Will, dismissing Xander's odd behaviour as perfectly normal if it was hunger-related. He marched off to the large grouping of seats on the far side of the atrium, and Xander followed him after an apologetic grimace at Mr Tubner. Ten minutes later, with his sandwiches eaten and a large iced bun in his hand, Xander was quite sure he had imagined the whole thing.

Without warning, the raucous sounds of his classmates faded abruptly, as if they had been muted, and were replaced by a soft buzzing noise, disorientating and disturbing. At the same time, the light in the atrium dimmed into a strange twilight, turning the people into faded versions of themselves, moving in slow motion.

Xander stared around wildly, his stomach sinking, and it was across this curious monochrome scene that he first saw them.

They strode across the atrium, the faint glow around each figure throwing them into sharp relief in the dusky light. There were five of them, four men and a young woman whose bright red hair seemed like the only colour in the whole place, and they came from different directions but were converging, Xander realised, on the hallway he had just exited – the Egyptian halls. They moved through the crowds of people as if they did not exist, and no one but Xander seemed to have noticed the half-light or the silence.

Xander was halfway across the atrium before he even realised that he had moved, in time to see a sixth person appear, striding over to join the others. With a small shock, Xander recognised the tall man with the black dog. He spoke briefly to one of the figures, a man with cropped dark hair, and his terse voice travelled across the distance to where Xander stood, frozen – 'There's shade-trace. It'll hit in twenty-four hours'. The tall man walked through the archway, but the dog paused on the threshold and then turned; its cool stare cut across the pallid people in the atrium and burned into Xander's eyes, challenging him. The dog's head tilted in unspoken invitation before it turned and disappeared through the archway.

Xander looked back at the mysterious figures, only to meet the narrowed gaze of the crop-haired man. Xander returned the stare, struck by the coiled tension in the man, whose hard muscles were revealed by the rolled up sleeves of his light shirt, and the long scar – obviously old as it had faded to silver – running down the man's right cheek. The man made a slight movement towards Xander, but then his head jerked towards the Egyptian halls, as if something within had urgently captured his attention. He signalled to his companions and they all strode through the doorway; the man did not waste another glance on Xander. He was the last through and, as he passed, Xander saw him make a quick gesture with his left hand. The marble doorway glowed a brilliant blue, fading almost immediately, by which time all of the strange figures had disappeared.

The world around him lurched back into light and sound, but Xander stood immobile, staring at the doorway across the atrium and completely unaware of the irritated looks of the people whose paths he blocked. He heard Will's familiar laugh back at the table but felt oddly dislocated. The light was too bright, the colours clashed and he could not get enough air in his lungs. The logical part of his brain was scrambling to provide a rational explanation but unfortunately it was failing. Xander could not look away from that now innocent-seeming doorway.

'Don't do it. You don't want to know,' Xander muttered. He had never been prone to flights of fancy – someone in his family had to stay in touch with reality – but he did have a wide streak of natural curiosity, and he wrestled for a moment with the urge to walk through the archway and see what would happen. Uncertain, he glanced back at the tables where the rest of his class were still eating lunch, the normality of the scene making those brief moments of dislocation seem like a strange dream.

'This is ridiculous,' Xander said, out loud. Things like this just did not happen. His mind made up, he turned away from the Egyptian halls and resolutely walked back to the table and real life.

✕

Xander was still determinedly not thinking about it as he turned his key in the front door and pushed it open. He hung up his coat, damp from the continual drizzle, in the narrow hallway and kicked off his shoes, before heading into the kitchen to grab a handful of menus. He flicked through them, unenthusiastic despite his empty stomach, and threw them back onto the cluttered tabletop. The kitchen was dark and silent, the overcast sky outside allowing little light to come in through the narrow window. Xander shivered, then flicked on the lights and reached for the remote to turn on the television. The room seemed more cheerful immediately and Xander remembered that he had baked beans and cheese, which would at least be quick and filling. He pulled open the fridge door, and paused in surprise.

The note on the plate holding the green peppers, cheese and beans now had a large 'NOT' in Mrs Mac's neat handwriting above the words 'Xander-supper' and on the shelf below was a large, foil-covered bowl that had definitely not been there that morning. Xander pulled the foil back to reveal a generous portion of homemade lasagne and a huge smile spread over his face.

Five minutes later, the rich, cheesy smell filled the kitchen, making it feel warm and cosy. Xander ate the generous portion in small bites, so it would last as long as possible. Finally he scraped the last remnants from his plate and sat back, feeling rather overfed but contented. He dumped his plate into the sink and wandered through into the sitting room, where he curled up on the squashy sofa and flicked through the channels on the television, full up with good food and comfortably dozy.

Xander woke with a start, feeling disorientated. It was dark outside and he squinted at his watch, which showed that it was half-past ten. Surprised that his mother arriving home had not roused him, he rolled off the sofa and walked out into the blackness in the hallway.

'Mum?' he called, but there was no reply. He flicked on the lights and went partway up the stairs, looking through the banisters, but his mother's room was dark and empty. Back downstairs, he glanced into the kitchen but everything was just as he had left it earlier, only a faint smell of lasagne lingering. Xander retraced his steps and slumped down on the sofa. It was not the first time that Mrs King had returned late but today the house felt particularly empty to Xander. He steadfastly refused to wonder why that would be the case.

As if on cue, the picture on the television screen broke up with a brief sound of static. Xander felt a swift, crawling sensation down his spine at the sound, then shook his head as the picture returned to normal.

'Don't be stupid,' he admonished himself. He would not let his imagination run wild again. Deciding to get a drink from the kitchen, Xander walked across the hallway, only to freeze as the sound of static assailed him once again. The picture on the television in the kitchen was rolling over and over and then, even as he stared at it, the signal vanished altogether, leaving the screen fuzzy.

With a quick, convulsive movement, Xander lunged forwards and turned the television off. For a moment there was total silence, then a faint buzzing began; it seemed to come from the air itself. Out of the corner of his eye Xander saw movement by the fridge, as if the shadows were shifting by themselves, flickering and wavering on the floor. A memory of the strange temple from the museum crawled at the base of his skull and Xander's breathing quickened and his skin prickled, though his feet felt rooted to the floor.

The brash sound of the telephone ringing cut through the oppressive atmosphere and Xander, in the release of tension, dived into the hallway and snatched it up.

'Hello?' he gasped.

'Hi Xander.'

The sound of his mother's voice, sounding as normal as ever, filled him with relief.

'Mum,' he blurted. 'Where are you?'

Despite his best efforts, his voice was shaking a little but his mother did not appear to notice anything wrong.

'I'm still at work,' she said brightly. 'We've had a bit of a breakthrough and since our deadline is coming up soon, we thought we would just carry on while it's going well. I just thought I would make sure you were okay at home. You don't mind, do you?'

Xander glanced around, trying to figure out how to explain why he did mind and it was not okay. It all sounded very unlikely as he groped for the right words.

'Xander?' she prompted, as he remained silent. 'Are you okay there?'

Xander let out a breath. 'I'm fine,' he said carefully. 'It's just – it's been a bit weird today and the TVs have all got static.'

'That's just the rain,' his mother interrupted. Xander heard a voice in the background calling her name. 'I have to go, so don't stay up late and I'll be back tomorrow. Sleep well.'

'Mum?' said Xander, but the ring tone showed that she had already hung up. Slowly, Xander put the telephone back and then went into the sitting room, where the picture on the television was now rolling in and out. He picked up the remote control and turned it off.

'Just the rain,' he repeated, but it did not sound convincing, even to him. He shivered. There was a distinct chill in the air and a hint of movement in the corner again. Xander found that when he looked straight at them, the shadows on the floor and walls appeared still, but his peripheral vision clearly showed them shifting and flowing together, puddling in dark masses. The television stood blank in the corner, but the faint sound of static hissed in his ears. His heart now thudding painfully in his chest, Xander was shocked to see his own breath hanging in the air before him in the sudden, penetrating cold which had invaded his home.

A surge of fear galvanised Xander into action. With a terrified yelp, he grabbed the lamp from the side table by the sofa and the tall standing lamp by the door, his hands shaking as he fumbled with the plugs. He bundled them under his arms and raced up the stairs, stumbling in his haste as he caught the unmistakable signs of shadows massing in the hallway. He snatched up another little lamp from the upstairs hallway, before retreating into his bedroom and slamming the door shut. Hastily, he switched on his desk lamp and bedside light before setting up the other lamps around the small space to ensure that no area remained unlit. When he had switched them all on the whole room, and particularly his bed, was bathed in brilliant light. Xander checked to make sure that there were no shadows which might start moving in inexplicable ways, then pulled his curtains shut and dived into bed where he lay with his heartbeat thumping in his ears.

'This is insane,' he muttered, but he could hear the quiver in his own voice. He lay awake for a long time, his fingers stuffed in his ears to block out the intermittent hiss of static and his eyes fixed on the gap under his door, where he could see the ebb and flow of shadows shifting strangely in the hallway beyond. Finally, exhausted, Xander fell asleep. Outside his door, the darkness moved and swelled until the dawn drove it out.

When Xander woke up, his head was groggy and he blinked in surprise to see most of the lamps in the house surrounding his bed and trained on him. A faint headache left him confused for a few moments until remembrance swept over him and he sat bolt upright in bed, pushing his hair out of his eyes. Daylight filtered around the edge of his curtains, the shadows on the floor remained firmly in their places and downstairs he could hear the faint sound of his mother's voice, evidently on the telephone to someone. Everything seemed quite normal. For several minutes, Xander tried to persuade himself that it must all have been in his imagination, but the ring of lamps around his bed stood as silent witnesses to the strange and frightening occurrences of the previous night.

There was the sound of light footsteps on the stairs and then a tap on the door. It opened and his mother's untidy head poked around it.

'Good morning,' she said brightly. 'You must have been tired. It's almost lunchtime. I'm making some beans on toast, if you're hungry.'

She beamed at him and shut the door again.

Xander looked around his room wryly, wondering what it

would be like to live with a mother who might notice that her son had brought every lamp in the house into his bedroom. He clambered out of bed and turned off the lights one by one.

Down in the kitchen his mother had turned the television on again, and a weekend news programme with a perky, rather over-enthusiastic presenter blared out; the picture and sound were as bright and sharp as normal. It would have been all too easy for Xander to convince himself that he had imagined it all, were it not for the cold feeling in the pit of his stomach.

'Mum?' he said, perching on a chair and balancing the plateful of singed beans on toast on his knee, since the table was once again covered in piles of files and papers. He hunted for the right words. 'Have you ever had something weird happen? You know, something you just can't explain?'

Mrs King glanced up from the papers she was reading while nibbling at a forkful of blackened toast.

'Everything can be explained, Xander. You just have to find a rational explanation.'

She smiled vaguely and returned to her work.

Xander ate a few more mouthfuls, turning this over in his head. A rational explanation sounded very much like something he would like to find. All of this strangeness had started yesterday in the museum, with that odd stone on the wall, and then the temple room when the shadows had first moved in bizarre ways. He vividly remembered the smooth, cool feel of the stone under his fingers before it had flared into impossible life. Perhaps there was something on the stone, Xander reflected. He'd heard of funguses which could cause hallucinations and it was possible, in fact he thought it was quite probable, that something like that would be on a stone tablet from an ancient tomb deep underground. That would mean that all the strange things he had seen and heard were just caused by a reaction to whatever had been on the stone. He was chasing the last few baked beans around his plate, congratulating himself for having identified a scientific explanation so quickly, when his inconvenient memory reminded him he had only touched the stone because his fingers had passed straight through the thick, protective perspex sheet fixed over it.

'There has to be a reason for all this,' Xander muttered, mutinously.

'Hmm?' said Mrs King, without looking up from the papers on which she was scribbling.

Staring down at the empty plate in his lap, which was not providing him with any answers either, Xander suddenly thought about the unusual group in the atrium. He would bet they knew what was going on in the museum and he frowned a moment, trying to recall the words of the tall, white-haired man. He had said something about shadows or shades and mentioned twenty-four hours.

With a quick glance at his watch, Xander made a decision. He would return to the museum. If he saw those people again, he would ask them to explain what had happened and, more importantly, how to make it go away. Most likely however, there would be nothing to see, everything would be entirely normal and he could officially put this whole experience behind him; just something weird he had imagined. Much happier now he had a plan, Xander stood up and put a hand on his mother's arm to make sure she would actually hear him.

'Mum? I'm just going back to the museum to check out a few things.'

Even as he spoke, Xander felt better; decisive and definitely on the way to a rational solution.

His mother looked up and nodded, her eyes not quite focussing on him. 'No problem. Have a good time.' She smiled distractedly, her hand already reaching for another file.

After pocketing his keys, Xander headed out to catch the bus back to the museum. In his haste, he did not notice the shadows shifting behind him in the hallway, sliding down towards the door he had just slammed shut.

It was still lunchtime when Xander stood once more in the atrium. The lofty space was teeming with people but still was not crowded. He was in the same spot as before, where he had witnessed the odd little group passing into the halls beyond, through a doorway illuminated with blue light. In a conscious repetition of the day before, he turned and looked over his shoulder at the cafe area where his class had sat, oblivious to the bizarre turn of events which Xander had witnessed. Today, the tables were full of strangers: families with small children in high chairs, grey-haired couples and groups of tourists with bright-coloured backpacks.

'It's now or never', he told himself. He turned back towards the doorway and barged straight into an unassuming brown-haired man, who had been trying to walk around him.

'Sorry,' Xander blurted out, embarrassed.

The man gave him a strange look before walking off without a word and Xander wondered whether he had been talking out loud to himself like a crazy person. He rubbed his shoulder where it had knocked the unsuspecting passerby and walked over to the entrance to the Egyptian halls.

As he drew closer, he saw a faint lattice of blue light criss-crossing the doorway, and had a sinking suspicion this would not be the uneventful re-visiting on which he had been pinning his hopes. The lattice was so faint as to be almost invisible, but

Xander could see occasional shimmers of blue along the fine threads. He hesitated, uncertain whether it would be safe to walk through this glimmering barrier. As if in answer to his question, a couple of tourists, chatting unintelligibly, walked straight through it and past him into the atrium. They were both clutching maps of the museum and appeared completely unaware of anything out of the ordinary.

For just a moment, Xander wished fervently that he could still believe that a mysterious fungal infection had caused all this, but the impossible barrier still hung there, barring his way. The image of a beautiful black dog with pale challenging eyes flashed up in his mind's eye, its head cocked at him. He took a deep breath, telling himself that he wasn't doing this because he had been dared to by a dog, squeezed his eyes shut and plunged forward through the doorway.

After three or four steps, he stopped and opened his eyes. The first thing he saw was a little girl, staring at him and giggling. Xander grinned back. Obviously he had looked ridiculous, leaping through the doorway with his eyes screwed shut and tensing as if he expected to be blasted back out again. When he looked back, he noticed the lattice was still visible from this side, but even fainter. The disturbing static sound was back, now he was on this side of the barrier, buzzing in his right ear. With an uneasy shake of his head – which drew another laugh from the small girl avidly watching him – Xander began to follow the sound.

He made slow progress at first, his way impeded by crowds of people, all of whom appeared to be heading for the atrium. Eventually, Xander gave up the unequal struggle of trying to force himself against the tide of people, and just stood back against the smooth marble wall to wait for them to pass. It was only when his way had cleared that he became aware he was the only person left in the halls. The abrupt change to echoing emptiness was unsettling and, for a moment, Xander considered turning back, but his curiosity drove him onwards.

As he walked through the doorway into a small chamber, the buzzing noise rose to a sharp pitch and he immediately recognised the frontage of the small stone temple. He had barely set foot in the room when he heard the ripping noise of a furious snarl. Spinning around, Xander saw the huge black dog, standing less than five feet from him, its hackles up and long white teeth exposed. Xander froze, but the dog wasn't looking at him; its snarl was directed at the blank stone on the side of the temple. It was the exact same place where the shadows had been flickering so oddly the day before and Xander's stomach lurched. He wasn't sure how, but he was quite certain that something very bad was about to happen.

'What are you doing here?'

Xander started. In his preoccupation with the dog, he had not noticed anyone else in the room, but now he looked around to see the same mysterious figures from the atrium, angled around the stone building and looking tense. The man with the cropped dark hair stood closest to Xander, his cold blue eyes staring at him with mingled surprise and exasperation. It was clear he was the one who had spoken, his voice hard and resonant.

'How did you resist my ward?' he demanded.

Xander hesitated. The dog's rumbling growl was a continual counterpoint to the man's words and he could feel the *wrongness* rolling off the temple wall. Xander swallowed hard against the queasiness rising in his throat.

'I dunno,' he faltered. He assumed the man was referring to the strange barrier. 'I just walked through, I suppose.'

The man gave him an irritated look and opened his mouth

to speak again but –

'It's coming.'

The red-haired woman's voice was sharp and the man swung back around to face the temple wall, his hands rising as if to repel something. Xander saw that all of them wore large, crystalline stones set into bands on their wrists, which were glowing with a clear light.

'Get out. Now!'

The man snapped out the command to Xander but his attention did not waver from the wall of the temple which, to Xander's horror, was flexing like it was made of some fluid material. The air before it was shimmering, as if in a heat haze. All of the figures had their arms outstretched now, extended towards the temple, and light was flaring from each of their wrists. The air itself seemed to crackle and the buzzing noise rose to a screech. Xander backed uneasily towards the door, but it was already too late; in a heartbeat, the world turned upside down.

The side of the temple exploded with a noise that hit Xander like a punch, but no flying stones, heat or light accompanied the blast. Instead, fluid blackness flowed out of the temple, dropping in snakes and tendrils to the pale marble floor, where it oozed and coalesced like shadows turned liquid. Cold sweat broke out over Xander's body and the only part of him that was not rigid with sudden terror was his frantically beating heart. His experience the previous night was nothing to this. Every ancient fear of what lurked in the darkness was realised in this heaving mass of shadow, so black it seemed to draw light from the rest of the room. The temperature had plummeted and Xander could see his breath coming in short, panicky pants.

'Don't let them coalesce. They're more dangerous when

they're corporeal,' snarled the crop-haired man, sounding as though he was speaking through gritted teeth.

Without warning, a black column rose out of the mass on the floor and swayed for a moment, before lashing out with blinding speed at the slightly built woman. She defended instantly, a barrier of white light flaring to existence before her and repelling the blackness with a sharp *crack*. As Xander stood, transfixed, two more columns rose. A hand grabbed his upper arm and threw him back towards the doorway.

'Run,' growled the crop-haired man. 'Go back to the atrium.'

Head pounding, beyond reason, Xander turned and fled. In his blind panic he was no longer sure which was the way out and, as he raced past stone friezes mounted on the wall, he knew he had not come this way before. He skidded to a halt in a large hall, searching frantically for a sign for the atrium. With a sudden chill he saw the familiar row of stone tablets mounted on the wall, behind their protective perspex; the nearest tablet was cracked and missing the top left corner.

'Great, Xander,' he muttered. This was the last place he wanted to be. Desperate, he looked around the room, seeing many entrances and quite unable to remember which one would take him back to safety.

Shouts and loud cracking noises came from the distance and Xander made an instant decision, dashing towards the farthest doorway, but even as he ran the buzzing sound rose again and the air chilled. The light in the room dimmed and faded to that ominous monochrome. Xander stopped, his heart hammering as the shadows lying on the floor beyond the doorway twitched and oozed in that now familiar flow towards him. He spun around, towards another doorway, and froze. A black column had risen from the floor and was blocking the way out. Gazing around in wild terror, he realised that he was now trapped. Mist was forming in wisps along the wall, as the temperature plunged.

Unable to breathe, with cold sweat prickling down his back and on his shaking hands, Xander began to back slowly against the wall. He flinched as he saw the tablet which had started all of this trouble hanging right next to him. It was quiescent now but he cringed away from it, trying not to even brush against its frame. His mouth opened wide to shout for help but, like a nightmare, he could not make any sound come out. The shadows slid along the floor towards him, the edges of each separate flow merging silently. Xander watched, horrified, as a column rose before him, knowing he was helpless.

'Hang on,' shouted a female voice, as an arcing lance of light instantly vaporised the swelling black column. Xander's knees shook with relief as he recognised the red-haired woman running towards him, her small, pointed face full of concern. 'Stand still – they react to movement.'

Xander grimaced. This advice was fairly redundant since he wasn't sure his legs would carry him. The woman stopped on the edge of the heaving black mass, blasting three more rising columns with casual ease. With a quick frown, she raised her hands and directed two streams of blue-white light into the mass on the floor, trying to clear a path through to Xander as he shrank back against the wall. There was a violent explosion.

The woman was thrown backwards across the chamber, against the giant stone bathtub Xander had examined the day before, while the shadow-mass seethed, creeping inexorably forward across the floor. It was only ten feet from Xander now and he tried not to imagine what would happen when it reached him.

'Well, that didn't work,' the woman said and Xander could

hear the anxiety in her voice.

'Ari!'

Both of them turned at the urgent shout. The crop-haired man and his other companions burst out of the corridor lined with friezes, and his jaw dropped as he spied the boy pinned against the wall. He recovered himself almost immediately and his eyes narrowed.

'I thought I told you to get out of here?' he snapped.

Xander's temper finally flared. It was almost a relief to find that there was room beside the terror in his mind for anger.

'I was *trying* to get out,' he shouted back. 'Those – those – *that* wouldn't let me.'

Ari had scrambled to her feet and hurried to the man's side.

'D'you really think this is the time for lectures, Flint?' she asked pointedly. The darkness was seeping backwards and forwards, as if distracted by so many targets, but Xander was relieved to see it had, at least temporarily, ceased its flow towards him.

'Don't over-react, Ari. We'll just lift him out.'

Flint gestured and the stone on his wrist flared. Suddenly, Xander felt weightless and, looking down, was stunned to realise that he was already several feet off the floor. Several things happened at once: a forest of black columns snaked up and lashed out at Xander's rescuers, and Xander's feet slammed back onto the ground. He staggered but managed to catch himself before he tumbled face first into the shadows. He pressed back against the wall, his heart trying to burst out of his chest.

Flint picked himself up off the floor and then offered a hand to Ari, who had skidded several feet further backwards. He scowled at Xander as though it was all his fault.

'Who are you, boy?' he demanded. 'You're like some kind of a shade-magnet. Where do you come from?'

'I'm Xander King,' Xander returned, his voice shaking. 'I came here on the bus, from my house.'

Flint stared at him as if he was mad.

'This is obviously going to be harder than I thought,' he muttered. He looked perplexed as well as irritated now. 'I've never seen shades react this way before.' He frowned at Xander, who glared right back at him.

'I didn't do it,' Xander's voice was embarrassingly close to a wail. 'How do I get out?'

'There's a Stone right there on the wall,' said a different voice. The tall man with white hair eyed Xander, as if he was an interesting puzzle to be solved, while the dog rumbled defiantly at the seething dark mass. 'Luckily it's still operational so he can use it to get out.'

'What?' Flint and Xander both spoke at the same time.

'He activated it yesterday,' the man responded, his calm voice reassuring.

'How is that possible?' demanded Flint, eying the tablet while Xander himself just gaped. 'That thing is literally a museum piece, not to mention broken. How could the kid operate it?'

The black mass gave a sudden lurch in Xander's direction and he cowered back. Amid his terror, the part of his mind that was not petrified with fear could not help wondering why the shadows were moving so sluggishly. He had seen them strike with lightning speed before, but now they seemed almost reluctant to move further forward, as if they were being repelled.

'Possibly the 'how' is less important right now than the 'what to do'?' suggested the tall man, in his quiet voice.

The shadows lurched again and Flint's hands lifted involuntarily, but then stopped; he seemed to come to a decision.

'Can you use that Stone?' he demanded.

Xander hesitated, warily eying the tablet hanging dormant on the wall beside him.

'I touched it yesterday. My fingers – they went *straight through* the glass on it, and then it lit up and yanked at me.' He stared at Flint, looking for a normal, sceptical reaction to what was clearly an insane sequence of events. Flint just nodded in a matter-of-fact way.

'That's right,' he said, while Xander blinked in disbelief. 'See the top of the Stone? There's a symbol there, on the right, which you can use.' He sent a meaningful look to the tall man, who grimaced before leaving the room at a run through one of the now-cleared doors, the dog loping at his heels. Flint continued on with his terse instructions. 'It'll pull you out of here, just relax and let it take you. When you get there, *do not move*. Someone will come and meet you. I'll come as fast as I can but we still have all this to deal with.'

Xander stared blankly at him. This was most definitely not the rational explanation he had come to the museum to find. He squeezed his eyes shut, in a desperate hope that all this lunacy and horror would just disappear and he could find himself back in the sensible, logical world he had thought he lived in. With a deep breath, he opened his eyes again.

He had only a split second of warning. With an ominous hiss, a pillar of blackness, wreathed in mist, rose into the air with blinding speed in front of him. Xander's hands seemed to move of their own accord, one thrown out in front of him in a vain attempt to fend off the attack while the other reached unerringly for the stone tablet. His fingers passed through the glass again as if it did not exist, and the symbols on the stone blazed with sudden fire as he touched the one Flint had indicated. As his fingertips pressed into the stone, the light flared into incandescence and his stomach was once again wrenched sideways. This time he did not resist and, for a moment, he felt as if every part of his body was exploding, even as the hand held up in front of him burned with sudden heat. The last thing Xander saw was the darkness detonating before his eyes and, behind it, Flint's stunned face.

CHAPTER TWO

The world shattered into fragments of whirling colour. After an endless instant, Xander felt a sharp lurch and found himself standing in a small, dusty room with his fingertips pressed to another stone tablet, this one whole and seemingly a part of the wall. As he snatched his right hand back, pain bloomed in his left and he turned it over to see that his palm was oozing with blood. His vision started to swim, his heart-beat roaring in his ears and he swallowed hard, twisting his hand away. Xander had always had a weakness for the sight of blood and now he took several deep breaths, trying to control the visceral reaction.

Attempting to distract himself, he stared around the room. It looked old, with blank stone walls and floor, and could plausibly be in the museum. This impression was strengthened by the stack of wooden storage crates and the piles of worn, carved stone blocks, some standing upright while others were leaning against the wall. Most were broken. He noticed a door, but hesitated as he recalled the man's urgent warning to stay where he was. Instead, he walked over to the single window, injured hand awkwardly held behind him, and rubbed at the smeary glass. It was a wasted effort; when he had cleaned enough to see, the only view was onto a small courtyard, empty but for a few bins.

Xander had just turned away in frustration when he heard running footsteps. The door banged open with enough force to make it rebound off the wall, almost hitting the tall boy who had burst in.

'Move,' he snapped without preliminaries, gesturing towards the door. Xander hesitated and the boy muttered what sounded like a curse under his breath, before grabbing Xander by the arm and shoving him towards the doorway. Xander instinctively pulled back. He was getting very fed up with being yanked around today.

'Get off me,' he snapped, jerking his arm away and glaring at the figure standing over him. The boy appeared to be a few years older than Xander, in his late teens, but the strangest thing about him was his face. It was oddly blurred so that Xander could not make out his features, although there was a hint of vivid eyes. The boy made another impatient noise and turned his obscured face away from Xander's scrutiny.

'I don't have time for this,' he snarled. 'If you want to meet Flint, come now. Otherwise, I'm out of here.' His blurred face twisted with contempt as he said the name and he barely waited a moment before turning away. 'Your choice.'

Xander hesitated for only a moment, and then chased after him.

'Wait,' he called. 'I'm coming.'

Charging through the doorway, he almost fell headlong down a flight of stone steps, spiralling downwards. The boy scarcely turned his head to acknowledge Xander following but, with lightning-fast reflexes, he threw out a hand to check Xander's fall. Xander noticed a twisted silver ring on the middle finger of the hand which gripped his arm for an instant.

'Where are we going?' Xander panted.

'Out,' was the terse reply.

The staircase was both steep and worn, and Xander was concentrating so hard on keeping his footing he stumbled again when they reached the bottom, and he was on level ground. When he looked up he saw a long hallway with many doors opening off it, currently empty of other people. The boy stopped and pulled Xander around to face him, his eyes running up and down, evaluating. Xander stared back at him, blinking as he tried to penetrate the strange blurriness of the boy's face.

'You'll just about pass,' the boy said curtly, although his gaze lingered with a frown on Xander's tatty old trainers.

'Pass for what?' asked Xander.

The boy ignored him, crossing over to a small wooden door at the end of the corridor. He glanced around and then undid the bolts at the top and bottom with a furtive air. When Xander just stood there, the boy waved him over with an impatient look.

'Out here, I'll shut it after you.' He glowered at Xander, hostility in his whole demeanour. 'And you can tell Flint from me he can clean up his own messes in the future.'

Xander still hesitated. 'Is this the way out of the museum?' he asked.

'Wait out there. That's all I know.' The boy glanced over his shoulder, as if he had heard something. 'Out,' he snapped.

He gave Xander a sharp shove, which sent him tumbling through the doorway, and slammed the door. Xander heard the bolts being drawn again, and then silence.

Uncertain, Xander stood in the dim alleyway, still shaken enough not to appreciate its deserted air. He noticed several more doors, all closed; some were larger than the one he had exited through and one was unfeasibly small. He edged backwards against the solid stone wall and tried hard not to imagine movement in the shadows further along the alley.

'This is ridiculous,' he told himself after a few minutes, sternly and only a little shakily. He was skulking in an alleyway which was probably right next to the British Museum. The events of the past day were so unbelievable that Xander began to doubt his own sanity. With sudden decision, he shoved away from the wall and marched up the alleyway towards the puddle of sunlight at the end. Stepping out, the bright light was momentarily dazzling and he paused, blinking until he could see again.

Opening out before him was a wide square, bounded by enormous, stately-looking buildings built from a golden-white stone which shimmered in the afternoon sunlight. Large ornamental trees, covered with flowers, stood around the square and in the centre was an ornate fountain, sending jets of water high into the air before splashing back into the pool below, a thousand rainbows glistening above it. The sky was a deep, cerulean blue and the air itself seemed to sparkle. There were people everywhere, walking alone or in groups, or sitting on the intricately-wrought white benches. Many of them would not have drawn a second glance in London; others, however, would have caused a riot.

Xander stared wide-eyed as some of the flowers launched themselves into the air, swirled in a kaleidoscope cloud of vivid colours and darted past him; flashes of tiny forms with streaming long hair and fine, gauzy wings. Two huge figures, at least twelve feet tall with wild bushy hair and craggy faces, crossed the pavement in front of him, their rumbling voices resonating in Xander's bones; following behind them lumbered a stoop-backed creature with rough greyish skin and a vacant expression. Xander heard a rushing noise in his ears and cold sweat broke out again down his back, as he stood stock-still and gaped.

'Are you all right, mate?'

The harsh voice came from the level of Xander's waist. He dropped his gaze slowly, until he met the concerned brown eyes of a small, bearded man; a groan of disbelief escaped Xander's mouth. Clearly visible amidst the man's curly hair were two little horns. Xander backed away, his shaking hand clamped over his mouth.

'I only asked,' growled the man, offended. 'No need to be rude. Don't know why I bothered – *your* kind are all the same. Typical. Just asking a question, showing concern –'

The little man marched off indignantly, his grumbling voice fading as he moved away. Hanging out of the man's coat, and swaying as he walked, was a short, tufted tail.

Xander backed into the relative normality of the alleyway, his legs shaking. Maybe he was having a nervous breakdown. Or else he had tripped over and hit his head during the school trip and had hallucinated everything; that was a more likely answer. Probably he was lying on the floor of the museum right now, unconscious, while Mr Tubner lectured the class on how first aid had advanced through the centuries. Xander hoped that someone had called an ambulance and that it would get there soon. Leaning back against the cool stone wall, he closed his eyes and banged his head, twice.

'What are you doing now?'

The hard voice was only too familiar and Xander's eyes flew open to meet the accusing stare of the crop-haired man, Flint. He stood in front of Xander with a look of suspicion on his face.

'Trying to wake up,' replied Xander in a shaky voice. 'I'm hallucinating, I think.'

'Hallucinating?'

'Aren't I? I saw what's out there,' Xander said, gesturing wildly towards the square. 'There are flying things and – *tails*. I must have hit my head, or else I've lost my mind.'

Flint eyed him for a moment, his face looking like he was having an internal argument. Finally he sighed and shook his head with a rueful expression.

'You really don't know about any of this, do you?'

'NO!' It came out in a near-shout, all of Xander's fear and confusion expressed in one desperate word. He pressed back against the wall as if it was his only refuge and his injured hand throbbed; drawing in a long, shaky breath, he stared at the ground. He had spent far too much time in the last twenty-four hours backed up against walls as reality lost its mind.

'This is no hallucination, kid. It's very real.' Flint's voice was still abrupt, but there was a tinge of sympathy in his tone which brought Xander's gaze back up to his face.

'Where am I, then?' he demanded in an unsteady voice.

'London,' Flint responded. At Xander's disbelieving look he shrugged, and conceded – 'in a manner of speaking.' He nodded towards Xander's left hand. 'You're hurt.'

Xander held it out, keeping his eyes averted. He felt Flint take his hand, turning it so he could examine his palm.

'This needs treating,' he said. 'Where we're going they can take care of it.'

'Going?' Xander looked up with a surge of panic. 'Where are we going? I just want to go home.' His voice wobbled and, right at this moment, Xander did not care.

Flint shook his head, his expression closed. 'After what we saw back there, it's not safe to send you back right now. There's something odd going on and, until we get to the bottom of it, you're staying here where we can keep an eye on you.' His tone indicated that there was no further discussion required.

Xander disagreed and opened his mouth to argue, but Flint had turned away with guarded relief as two people appeared at the top of the alleyway. Xander recognised the small redheaded woman from the museum; standing next to her was a stocky boy of Xander's age with tousled, sandy-coloured hair.

'Stopped for a picnic, Ari?' queried Flint, a sarcastic twist to his voice.

Ari smiled back at him, unflustered. 'Got held up by the old shrew at the Halls while I was springing Ollie.' She walked straight over to Xander, her hand outstretched in friendly greeting. 'Hi. We didn't get a chance before to introduce ourselves. I'm Ariel.' She grinned, her freckled nose wrinkling. 'My mum was a bit whimsical about names – she called my sister Calypso, so I suppose it could have been worse.'

Disarmed by her warmth after so many unpleasant shocks, Xander reached out to shake her hand. Her grip was surprisingly firm for such delicate fingers, and it was impossible not to respond to her infectious friendliness.

'Xander,' he said, feeling tongue-tied but Ari just turned to wave over the boy, who had been standing eying Xander's trainers with a puzzled expression. 'This is Oliver Stanton. Ollie, meet Xander.'

The boy held out his hand, with a look of mingled awkwardness and curiosity, but his clear blue eyes were friendly and when Xander shook his hand, his face relaxed into a cheerful grin.

'Always happy to skip out of the most boring lesson of the week,' he said genially. 'So thank you for that.'

Xander felt a quick smile pull at his lips, thinking of Mr Tubner.

'You're welcome, I guess,' he replied.

While the two boys spoke, Ari and Flint had been exchanging a few terse words, and now Flint nodded and gestured peremptorily to the two boys.

'We'll head out,' he told Ari. 'You go to the debriefing and I'll join you when I can.'

'Do I mention –?'

Ari glanced at Xander, who stiffened. Flint shook his head.

'Not in public for now. That's why we're going to Woodside. I'll fill in the Wardens later.'

Ari nodded and then winked at Xander. 'I'll be seeing you,' she said with that quirky grin. 'Try to stay out of trouble.'

Before Xander could respond, she had walked jauntily out of the alleyway and disappeared around the corner into the square. Xander eyed Flint.

'Where are you taking me?' he demanded. 'And who *are* you people? You don't understand – I need to get home.' His last words had come out sounding rather unsteady, so he took a deep breath and glared at Flint.

Flint was entirely unmoved. He eyed Xander and then spoke in an even voice. 'You detonated shade-strike with your bare hand, the moment you left the museum all of the shades disappeared, my ward had no effect on you and, to top it off, you travelled here with no training and using a broken and obsolete Stone. Until I get an explanation for all that, you're staying right here.'

Xander gaped at him. Out of the corner of his eye he could see Ollie, his mouth also open in stunned surprise. Flint's intimation that those terrible things in the museum had been targeting him sent unease crawling over his skin.

'I don't know about *any* of that stuff,' he said in desperation. 'I just want to go home – my mother will call the police if

I don't turn up.' Xander tacked on the last part purely as a threat. He strongly suspected that he could be gone for quite some time before it occurred to his mother that she hadn't seen him for a while.

Flint seemed undisturbed by this. 'No, she won't. You're not missing,' he replied coolly. Xander stared at him in disbelief but Flint made an impatient gesture with his hand. 'Whether or not you understand, the fact remains it's not *safe* for you to return.'

Xander felt his arguments drying up as he remembered what he had been running from. Correctly taking his silence as acquiescence, Flint nodded.

'This isn't the place for discussing this, anyway,' he said curtly.

Eying Xander's pale face and with a quick glance at his injured hand, Flint jerked up the sleeve on his left arm, revealing the metal band on his wrist that Xander had seen in the museum, with a large clear crystal set in it. The band itself was a dull black metal, with no obvious joins; Xander wondered how it came off. It was the first time he had seen one of the strange stones close up and he noticed that there were odd flickers deep inside it, like contained lightning. He swallowed, but could not help a surge of the same curiosity that had got him into this trouble in the first place. Idiot, he told himself.

'We're going to jump. Take my arm and don't let go,' Flint cautioned.

The boy, Ollie, stepped forward and gripped Flint's arm with the ease of familiarity. Xander noticed he also wore a band around his wrist but narrower, made of a grey, pitted metal. Unlike Flint's band, this stone was a dull opaque yellow and there was no life in it. Xander realised that both Flint and the boy were staring at him, waiting; he hesitated, and then reached out to put his hand on Flint's outstretched arm.

This time, there was no explosion. It felt like missing a step while running downstairs – an instant of disorientation and a lurch of his stomach, over as soon as it began. He had automatically closed his eyes and when he opened them again, he was no longer in the alleyway.

They now stood on the edge of another open place amidst tall buildings, but that was where the similarities ended. Running through the centre of the space, looking like nothing so much as the displaced cloisters of a giant cathedral, were two long lines of linked stone arches, each row curving at the end to meet the other. The arches were not of a uniform size, some much larger and others smaller but the weathered grey stone hinted at their great age. All of this Xander took in with wide eyes before he realised that he was still gripping Flint's arm. He took a step backwards.

'How did we get here?' he demanded.

'Jumped,' Flint replied. 'There are limitations but it's useful. I thought you could do without further exposure to flying things and tails.'

He raised an eyebrow, making Xander flush, before turning and striding towards the arches with Ollie at his heel. Xander took a breath and then followed them.

He had gone only ten paces when he froze, staring in disbelief. He would not have supposed, if he had stopped to consider it, that this day could bring him any more shocks, but the sight of two people materialising out of empty space under one of the arches was still enough to leave him incredulous. Xander understood that he himself had twice been dragged inexplicably through space, but it was quite another thing to see it happen before your eyes and in such a casual, everyday manner. The two women, chatting unconcernedly, crossed the street and disappeared, in a more prosaic fashion, down one of the many side-streets. Xander stood rooted to the spot, his eyes fixed on the archways. They looked much more threatening now that he suspected Flint intended to make him go through one.

Flint glanced over his shoulder, then turned back, clearly annoyed to see Xander standing rigid in the middle of the street. He gestured sharply, and Xander edged forward a few more steps.

'Could you try not to draw unnecessary attention to yourself?' Flint snapped, his eyes flicking around the many windows overlooking them.

Xander glowered at him. He felt his behaviour was quite reasonable, given that his strongest desire currently was to continue banging his head against a wall until he achieved that concussion.

'What are those?' he asked, with suspicion.

'These are just the South Gates.' It was Ollie who answered him, his voice reassuring although he looked puzzled by Xander's confusion. 'That's how we get places, since the rest of us can't just jump around the place.'

'I already told you, that has limitations. Travellers often use the gates too, as you should well know,' interrupted Flint. 'Now, if you two have finished your little chat, do you think we can go? We can finish this conversation later.'

Without waiting for an answer he strode off, leading them along the nearside row until they reached one of the smaller arches, where he clasped Xander's shoulder in a firm grip. Xander was not sure whether this was for reassurance or to prevent him bolting. As they stepped forward together, Xander glanced up at the apex of the arch and saw, carved in deep but worn lettering, the word 'Wykeham'.

He felt a slight chill run over his body as he took the first step through the archway; his second step took him out onto soft grass. Before he could react, Flint tugged him away from the gate, then let go of his shoulder. Xander spun around and stared at the small stone arch, looking even more incongruous rising out of what appeared to be a neatly-tended village green. As he watched, Ollie appeared and strolled forward to join them.

'Where are we now?' demanded Xander, looking around as if clues might be hanging in the air. It was a very disconcerting feeling to have no idea where two footsteps might have taken him.

'Wykeham,' said Flint. He caught Xander's confused expression and relented. 'It's near your Winchester.'

'Winchester!' Xander did some hurried calculations. 'But that must be almost fifty miles.'

'Sixty-one. Now let's go,' Flint said, clearly intending to pre-empt any further questioning. He marched away across the grass. Xander took one last look at the arch and noticed that on this side the word 'London' was carved into the apex. Shaking his head in disbelief, he turned and followed Flint.

The green was surrounded on three sides by quaint-looking cottages with wildly blooming front gardens behind low stone walls. Xander eyed the blossoms warily as they passed, in case they suddenly transformed into impossible flying creatures. The fourth side was bounded by a small river which bubbled briskly along, crossed by a low stone bridge, while ducks and swans paddled serenely on the water. The appearance of calm normality did not comfort Xander in the slightest; he stared down into the water as they crossed and wondered darkly what might be looking back at him from the depths.

Flint led them along past more houses, some larger with big gardens while others hugged the lane, until the road began to rise and the houses thinned out and then disappeared altogether. Glancing back, Xander realised that the place was bigger than he had assumed; it spread out to fill the small valley, cut in half by the little river. Flint strode on without looking back and turned down a narrow, tree-lined track at a pace that discouraged any conversation, until they reached a high, thick-leaved hedge blocking their way forward; set in it was a tall, grey wooden gate, with the name 'Woodside' across the top in wrought-iron letters. Without hesitation, Flint swung the gate open.

Before Xander stood a rambling grey stone house, set within wide gardens and embraced by thick forest, which appeared to curl around it protectively. The house was large, its many windows shining in the afternoon sun, and covered with wisteria and ivy, softening the high walls. At the front, a great door stood wide-open in a welcoming manner. Xander tensed as he saw movement around the abundant blooms in the front garden, but it was just brightly-coloured butterflies swirling between the flower beds. The air was filled with the drone of busy insects, the faint piping of birdsong from the woods, and the rich scent of growing things. Flint shut the gate behind them with a click of the latch and headed towards the open front door. A sharp chiming noise cut through the air and he paused, glancing at the stone on his wrist. He turned and gestured to the two boys.

'Go on ahead,' he said brusquely. 'Tell Thea I'll be there in a moment.'

Ollie didn't hesitate, glancing sideways at Xander. 'I live here,' he said, breaking the awkward silence. 'Come on, I'll take you to meet Gran.'

Ollie walked through the wide front door, Xander trailing behind him. It was cooler inside, with a stone-flagged floor and a great wooden staircase rising to the next floor, while the hallway itself cut straight through the centre of the house. There were several doors opening out on both sides of the hall but Ollie headed straight for the heavy-looking wooden door at the end. It was closed, but from beyond it came a nasal, whiny-sounding voice, ranting away. Ollie pushed open the door without hesitation, but Xander hung back. He was not at all sure he wanted to meet the owner of that unpleasant voice and so hovered just behind the doorway, out of sight.

'Hi, Gran,' Ollie's voice was cheerful, as if he couldn't hear the furious tirade. The carping voice stopped mid-word.

'Don't you 'hi, Gran' me.' A different voice answered, far more pleasant than the previous one, although with a distinct edge of annoyance. 'Did you walk out of the academy in the middle of a class? Just listen to this message.'

The disagreeable voice started up again.

'-graceful behaviour. I would have thought Oliver would appreciate the opportunity for further study, given his,' there was the sound of a throat being cleared maliciously, '*difficulties*, rather than disappearing with that delinquent. I suppose that we should be grateful he bothered to turn up, which is more than can be said for his cousin who didn't deign to grace us with her presence at all –'

The voice cut off again.

'Well? Whilst I was thrilled to get this message from Pri-milla Pennicot, of *all* people, it would be nice to know just why you saw fit to give her another excuse to criticise you. And where, by the way, is Len?' There was a slight pause and then – 'Where are you going?'

Ollie's face appeared around the doorframe and he gestured for Xander to come into the room. 'Quick,' he whispered, with a conspiratorial grin. 'Before she really hits her stride.'

Still wary, Xander stepped through the door. The room beyond turned out to be a large kitchen, welcoming, sunny and reassuringly normal. His eyes were immediately drawn to a smooth, silvery panel set into the wall, showing a woman's pinched, haughty-looking face. Her rabbity mouth was open and she was obviously mid-word. Given the unpleasantness of her expression, Xander guessed that she was the sender of the message that had so annoyed Ollie's grandmother.

To one side of the room was a long wooden table and standing in front, dominating the space, was a slender lady. Her silver hair swept back elegantly from her aristocratic face and her apron was immaculate; not even the smear of flour across her nose diminished her air of distinction. She exuded exasperation.

'Gran, meet Xander,' said Ollie, clearly enjoying wrong-footing this formidable woman. 'Xander, this is my grand-mother, Althea Stanton.'

Mrs Stanton blinked, and then held out a welcoming hand, her innate good manners overriding her desire to demand an immediate explanation. 'Hello, Xander,' she said, taking his hand and drawing him further into the room. 'Welcome to our home. I don't think I've heard Oliver mention your name before?' She glanced over at Ollie, her delicately arched eyebrows rising in a clear question.

'He's with Flint,' Ollie explained, somewhat incoherently. 'He said he'd be here in a moment to explain and he sent Ari to fetch me – I wasn't bunking off.'

'I see,' said Mrs Stanton tartly. 'So Ariel was your delin-quent friend. I might have known. Is this why Len isn't there?'

Her expression was sharp and Ollie flushed, looking uncomfortable.

'Dunno,' he said, avoiding his grandmother's penetrating gaze. 'Maybe.'

'Hmm,' she said, and then her attention swung back to Xander. 'So, dear, where are you from? How do you know Ben Flint?'

Xander felt pinned to the spot and unsure of how he should respond. He met Mrs Stanton's expectant look and swallowed.

'Um, London. But not the one here –'

His voice trailed off as her eyes widened in sudden understanding. At that moment, the kitchen door swung open again and Flint walked in; Xander found that he was actually relieved to see him. Mrs Stanton swung around, an appalled expression on her face.

'He said he's not from Haven and that you brought him here,' she said without any preliminaries. She looked as if she wanted Flint to contradict her but he didn't answer her, instead turning that now familiar look of irritation on Xander.

'Didn't waste any time broadcasting it, then?' he queried sarcastically.

Xander glared right back. 'You didn't tell me not to. In fact, you haven't told me anything,' he muttered.

'An *outlander*? Really, Ben, what were you thinking?' Mrs Stanton pulled out a chair and sat down, her hands lying limply on the table before her.

Flint just let out a huffing breath. 'Don't overreact, Thea.' Yanking out a chair of his own, he gestured to Xander to sit. Xander complied reluctantly, cradling his injured hand under the table, while Ollie took the chair next to him.

'There was another incident but it didn't originate on our

side, so we went over to deal with it. *He* saw us,' Flint jerked his head towards Xander, without looking at him. 'There was a breach, as we thought, and the place was crawling with shades. We were trying to tackle it but the kid seems to be a magnet for them.'

As Flint was outlining the events in the museum, Xander felt an elbow nudge his ribs. Ollie leant over to him.

'Seriously? Did you actually see shades?' he whispered, with evident fascination.

Xander nodded. 'Saw them, was chased by them, nearly got caught by them,' he muttered back. 'Still don't know what they are, though.'

'Wow,' said Ollie, looking impressed. 'When I was little I used to think Gran invented them to scare us when we were playing her up. I've never seen any.'

Xander shook his head over Ollie's enthusiasm. 'Believe me, you don't want to. They're pretty horrifying.' Just thinking about the rearing black shadows sent shivers running down his back.

'So, are you a Traveller too, then?' Ollie leant further forward in his interest. 'I didn't know they had them on your side, or are they called something different.' He eyed Xander with eager curiosity but Xander was struck by the sudden silence in the room. Glancing up, he realised that Flint and Mrs Stanton were looking at him, both waiting for the answer to this question.

'How should I know?' he asked, feeling helpless. 'I was just on a school trip to the museum and that's apparently when the world decided to go mad. I don't know anything about glowing stones that break every law of physics, or terrifying black things that appear out of thin air, or Travellers, or any of the insane things that have happened to me in the last day. I just want everything to go back to normal.' He finished out of breath and with a burning sensation in the back of his throat.

Mrs Stanton's eyes softened but Flint leant back in his chair, his expression unmoved.

'The world hasn't gone mad – you're just seeing it clearly for the first time,' he said coolly. 'As for the shades, people have always feared the dark but they've long forgotten what really lies within it, and so blinded themselves to the truth. Deep down, you know this. You have names for what you saw in the city square, don't you? The things that sent you fleeing back into that alleyway.'

Under Flint's intent stare, Xander gave a reluctant nod. The names burned through his mind; an insistent litany of lunatic words like 'fairy', 'giant', and 'faun'.

Flint smiled grimly. 'Ask yourself why you know those names, when according to *your* world, such things don't exist.'

Xander was aware that his mouth was hanging open and he probably looked an idiot, but he couldn't seem to string together the right words to ask the question that would make sense of this. He noticed that none of what Flint had said was a surprise to Ollie or his grandmother, so he supposed that either they both believed all of this, or else they were in on the joke. Xander tried hard to pull himself together. This all seemed a bit far-fetched for a joke but even so, it was still rather – far-fetched.

'What are Travellers?' he asked.

'People like me and the others you saw at the museum,' Flint replied. 'We can cross over using the Stones, as you saw, and we're responsible for keeping watch on the border between Haven and your side. We also have some other – abilities.'

'Like using those things on your wrist to blast the Shades?' A thought struck Xander and he looked over at Ollie's band, just visible under his sleeve. 'Can you do that too?' he asked him.

Ollie just laughed, shaking his head.

'No way.'

'They are called orbs,' corrected Flint. 'They're not just worn by Travellers, although ours are different.' He did not elaborate any further on that and Xander got the sense that Flint was choosing his words with care, controlling how much information he was letting slip.

Xander finally asked the question that had haunted him since he had first seen the darkness shift and mount its terrifying pursuit of him.

'What would have happened if those shadow-things had got me?'

'Disfigurement, madness or death,' replied Flint. 'Depending on the type of exposure.' He touched his cheek absently and Xander eyed the silvery scar there. 'Just one of them can have a dire effect on you mentally or physically but when they mass, it's usually game over for the unprotected.'

Xander swallowed. 'Oh.'

'Which makes it all the more curious,' continued Flint, 'that you blew one to smithereens using apparently only your bare hand.' He gestured at Xander's left hand, still concealed under the table. 'That's one reason we came here. Thea is a healer and we need to deal with that injury of yours without any awkward questions in the wrong places.'

'He's hurt?' Mrs Stanton rose from the table with an awful majesty and hurried to Xander's side, throwing an outraged look at Flint. 'You didn't see fit to mention that first, before launching into this little interrogation? For Haven's sake, Ben, where are your wits?'

Even the obdurate Flint flinched under her withering look.

'I was getting to it,' he muttered but Mrs Stanton ignored him, leaning down next to Xander and reaching out her hand.

'May I see?' she asked him. Xander lifted his still-throbbing palm from where he had tucked it under the table and offered it to her, averting his eyes again as she took it in cool, gentle fingers. She examined it for only a moment. 'I have a dispensary here, Xander. Is it all right if I treat this for you?'

When Xander nodded, Mrs Stanton led him over to the end of the kitchen, where a door led into a small room. It was lined with rows and rows of shelves full of bottles of bright-coloured liquids, crystalline phials and neatly-stacked tubs filled with more familiar medical supplies. A white work table stood in the middle of the room and Mrs Stanton sat Xander down at it, before busying herself with gathering what she needed and lining the things up along the table. Xander laid his hand, palm up, on the table and looked away from the raw, seeping wound. Mrs Stanton smiled at him over her shoulder, her eyes understanding, as she washed her hands in a little sink.

'You don't like blood?' she asked as she returned. 'Don't worry, it isn't as bad as it looks.' Even as she spoke, her quick, gentle hands were at work and then Xander felt something cool being spread across his palm; the throbbing faded and then ceased entirely. Risking a glance, Xander saw a thick layer of pale gelatinous ointment covering his skin, before Mrs Stanton topped it with gauze and then swiftly bandaged his hand. She looked up at him with a reassuring smile. 'All done,' she said. 'I'll redress it tomorrow but, barring any complications, it should heal up well.'

'Thank you,' said Xander, tentatively flexing his fingers to test the efficacy of the apparently miraculous painkiller. He smiled in relief at Mrs Stanton, who was restoring the room to immaculate tidiness.

'You're very welcome,' she replied with a warm smile, and then ushered him back out into the kitchen where Flint was pacing restlessly. He swung around as they re-entered the room, his gaze flicking to the pristine white bandage swathing Xander's hand.

'All right?' he asked.

'It is now,' Mrs Stanton said tartly. 'I'll want to monitor it though; there's a fair amount of abrading on his palm.'

'Fine,' said Flint. 'I'll just leave him here for the time being then.'

Without a glance at Xander's wide-eyed face, Flint turned towards the kitchen door only to find himself impaled on Mrs Stanton's accusing glare, her eyes narrowed ominously.

'And?' she demanded.

'And – what?' Flint said, but his tone was somewhat wary now. He was clearly not immune to the force of the Stantons' formidable grandmother.

Instead of answering, Mrs Stanton turned to Ollie. 'Please show Xander your room, Oliver.' It was not a request and Flint winced as she added, 'Don't hurry.'

Ollie jumped to his feet and headed towards the exit – evidently he was well aware of the right time to make a break for it. Flint's eyes followed him, looking as though he wished that he could leave as well, but Xander lagged behind. It was clear whatever they were going to argue about concerned him and his future, and he wanted to know what it was.

Once outside the heavy kitchen door, which Mrs Stanton closed after them with a foreboding thud, Ollie wasted no time in heading for the stairs.

'Come on, quick,' he threw over his shoulder. 'Or we'll miss it.'

Perplexed, Xander followed Ollie as he dived up the stairs,

two at a time.

'Miss what?' he panted.

Ollie sent him a knowing grin as they reached the top of the stairs and turned off to the left.

'Well, I assume that you want to hear what they are saying in there?' he said. 'Adults only ever throw you out when they are talking about something interesting, and probably about you.'

Despite his worry, Xander grinned back. Obviously some things did not change no matter what reality you found yourself in. Ollie led the way along a wide hallway and then down a short passage, to a large bathroom with antique-looking fixtures. Xander eyed him in confusion, but Ollie put his finger to his lips and pointed at a vent set into the wall by the floor. He beckoned Xander forwards.

'Gran never remembers you can hear every word from the kitchen through this old vent,' he murmured. 'But the sounds will go both ways, so don't speak when it's open.'

Xander nodded and crouched next to Ollie. With another warning glance, Ollie slid the vent open.

'– need to prioritise this, Ben.'

The words rang out, appearing to come from the middle of the room. Xander jerked around and stared behind him, then saw Ollie shaking with silent laughter. Xander shot him an embarrassed smile.

'I said that I'll look into it, but there are other pressing issues right now. The boy'll be fine here for a while. Just keep him out of sight until we find out what the deal is with these breaches – what's causing them. When that's fixed, he can go back and hopefully no-one the wiser.' Flint's voice was impatient.

'And his ability to use the Stone, or hold off shade-strike

with his bare hand?' Mrs Stanton demanded. 'Are you no longer curious about that? It seems pretty noteworthy to me.'

There was a pause.

'Of course it's strange but the kid is hardly a threat to us and these breaches certainly are. That has to be our main concern, not some oddity turned up by chance. I don't have time for this right now, Thea.'

'Make time,' snapped Mrs Stanton. 'Oddity, my eye! People are not just things, Ben, to pick up or discard when it's convenient.'

'Are we still talking about the boy, Thea?' Flint asked coldly. There was another meaningful silence and then, 'Fine, have it your way.' Xander could almost see Flint rolling his eyes as he ground out the words. 'We'll get on it. Happy now?'

'Ecstatic,' replied Mrs Stanton, drily.

'Just keep the kid out of trouble and don't let him go wandering around. The less he sees, the better.'

'I'm not putting him under house arrest, Ben. He'll be fine with Ollie and Len. We'll just say he's a friend of the family come to stay.'

Mrs Stanton's voice was breezy, now she had got Flint to capitulate.

Ollie closed the vent. 'We'd better scram before she realises we were listening. Come on, I'll show you my room. You can share with me while you're here.'

Xander followed Ollie in silence. He felt thoroughly perplexed, particularly by the assumption that he could just stay here. He almost bumped into Ollie's back as the boy halted and then opened a door, standing back to allow Xander to go in first.

It was a big room and there appeared to be two beds, an armchair and a wide desk under the window, but it was hard to tell anything else because every available surface and most of the floor was covered in mess. Crumpled up clothes, balls, papers, odd-looking racquets and general debris was strewn everywhere, along with what looked like a short and colourful surfboard propped up against the wall. Ollie glanced around as if seeing it for the first time, and pulled a face.

'Sorry, it's a bit messy,' he conceded. 'It kind of gets away from me sometimes. I s'pose I ought to clear the other bed if you're staying.' He picked his way over the floor to one of the beds, swept all the clutter on it up into his arms and looked around for somewhere to put it; with a quick shrug, he threw it into a corner. 'There you go.'

Xander stood rigid by the door. 'I can't stay here,' he burst out. Somehow he had to get this concept across to *someone*. 'Seriously, my mother will go mental if I just disappear. Even she will notice I'm gone eventually.'

Ollie eyed him in concern but a bellow from downstairs saved him from having to answer.

'You'd better tell them that,' he said. 'But I warn you, Gran is pretty stubborn...immoveable really...rocklike. She cannot be reasoned with. You're welcome to try though.'

Xander straightened his back as he followed Ollie back down to the kitchen, and began to speak as soon as they walked in through the door.

'I appreciate the concern but I need to go home. My mother will freak out if I just go missing. She'll call the police. It'll be on the news.'

Mrs Stanton and Flint were standing rigidly at opposite ends of the table. They both turned to look at Xander as he made his dramatic entrance. Mrs Stanton looked concerned at his words but Flint just eyed Xander with a narrow smile.

'No, she won't,' he said coolly, 'because you're not missing.

Everything is quite normal, as far as she is concerned.'

Xander gaped at him.

'How am I not missing, if I am in fact here?' he demanded.

'You're right, you are here. But you're also there,' Flint replied, without expression.

Xander felt that surge of temper rise again; the man was being deliberately aggravating. He opened his mouth to snap at him, but Flint pre-empted him.

'When you cross over the border using a Stone, particularly when you are inexperienced, you can leave a reflection behind. We call it a shadowself. It's a facsimile, the idea of you that belongs in that reality. It will last some time before it fades, and it's certainly enough to prevent people from noticing that you aren't there. When you are more experienced it doesn't happen by accident.'

He eyed Xander, as if expecting a comment or argument, but Xander just gaped at him.

'It's even possible to access your shadowself, so you can see through realities. There are limitations, of course, and you can only observe. To affect a reality directly, you have to Travel.' He made an impatient movement, as if he had let slip more than he had meant. 'However, that takes aptitude, plus a great deal of time and training. It's not relevant here.'

There was a brief silence.

'So, no-one knows I'm gone,' said Xander, in a small voice. The idea that he wouldn't be missed was strange, and unsettling.

'Precisely,' Flint said. 'And now, I really need to head out.'

Xander felt like his head was spinning. He was aware of Ollie looking at him with concern, but he ignored him. This shadowself thing was just as crazy as the rest. Acting on an impulse he began to focus deliberately on the idea of a different part of himself, to reach out to it. As he expected, nothing happened and he was about to give up when suddenly he felt light-headed; pins and needles prickled all over his skin. For just an instant, before his vision went black, he was standing on the front steps of the British Museum, looking up as soft, drizzling rain fell onto his face. There was a dislocating lurch and he was back in the kitchen, crumpling sideways. He slumped onto the floor, feeling sick and dizzy.

Flint had spun around at Ollie's sharp exclamation and he was by Xander's side in two swift strides, lifting him up. He tightened his grip as he felt Xander stagger.

'I was there,' Xander choked out. 'I was right outside of the museum. It was raining.' He touched his face with a shaking hand. It was dry.

Flint gaped at him for a moment, speechless. 'Obviously *not* so much time and training,' he eventually muttered. He glanced over at Mrs Stanton and grimaced at her pointed look.

'I feel sick,' said Xander, thickly.

Flint lowered him into a chair and pushed his head down. 'If you're inexperienced it can cause disorientation. Take deep breaths, it'll pass in a minute.' He shook his head, looking perplexed before he noticed Ollie watching him; his unguarded expression changed to neutral. He looked back as Xander's faint voice came from between his knees.

'Well, there's one good thing,' he said. 'I have a chemistry test on Monday – I hope my shadow-thing enjoys it.' He laughed, and even he could hear the hysterical note.

A sudden hubbub of cheerful voices, brisk footsteps and general bustle broke into the awkward silence that had followed Xander's last words, and then the kitchen door was flung open.

'Hi, Gran. Are there any biscuits?'

Two little girls, perhaps six or seven years old, bounced

into the room and the smaller of them, pony-tail swinging, flung her arms around Mrs Stanton's waist.

'Evvy's come for tea and we're both starving.'

Mrs Stanton laughed, even as another voice came from the doorway.

'Katie! Give Gran a chance to draw breath before demanding food the moment you set foot in the house.'

A woman walked in, a wry smile on her face as she exchanged amused looks with Mrs Stanton. She was petite, with the same sandy-coloured hair as Ollie, and was carrying an armful of bright blue pots, full of little seedlings sprouting up vigorously. Ollie himself jumped up and hurried over.

'Let me grab those for you, Mum,' he said. 'Where'd you want them?'

'Just outside the –'

A high-pitched voice cut off her answer. 'Who are you?' demanded Katie, staring at Xander as he sat in his chair, bandaged hand on his lap.

'Katie!' exclaimed the blonde woman, even as Mrs Stanton said, 'Is that how we greet visitors in this house?'

Xander shifted uncomfortably as every eye in the room fixed on him. Mrs Stanton came to his rescue. 'He's a friend of Ollie's, come to stay for a while and his name is Xander,' she said, in her calm voice. Her eyes flicked over to Ollie's mother, telegraphing without words that she would explain later. Ollie's mother rose to the occasion. Surrendering her armful of pots to her son, she beamed at Xander and came over to shake hands.

'Hi, Xander,' she said. 'Do call me Jenna.'

'Hello', he replied, rising awkwardly.

He noticed Mrs Stanton glancing around with an exasperated look, and realised that Flint had taken advantage of the sudden influx of people to slip away. The door was opened yet again and a man walked in, his eyes skimming the room and settling on Xander.

'Hello, Xander,' he said and then, as Mrs Stanton's eyebrows shot up in surprise, explained, 'I just saw Flint outside.' His voice was cheerful and friendly but his expression was cautious, and his gaze flicked down to the bandage on Xander's hand. 'I'm James Stanton.'

Xander smiled shakily and took the proffered hand. 'Hello,' he replied, not knowing what else to say. He felt out of place and wished he could just retreat into a corner, unobserved, until this whole mad mess resolved itself. Mr Stanton eyed him perceptively.

'All a bit much?' he asked, and the quiet sympathy in his voice brought an unwelcome lump back to Xander's throat. 'Don't worry. Things generally have a way of working themselves out. You're safe here and you never know, sometimes it's the unexpected that turns out for the best.'

James glanced over at his wife, who smiled back at him, her eyes twinkling. Xander could clearly see the resemblance to her son.

'Sit down and relax,' she said kindly. 'It's a bit chaotic when we all get home but I promise it does calm down. I'm just going to make some tea – would you like some?'

Xander nodded and subsided back into the chair. James patted his shoulder, and then went over to kiss his mother's cheek.

'Busy day?' he asked, as he helped to pull mugs and plates out of various cupboards.

'Reasonably,' Mrs Stanton replied, swiftly slicing up a large loaf of bread. 'A few patients this morning and then home visits. Old Mr Herbert is bed-ridden again but he still refuses to listen. That man has never met a sweet pudding he won't eat but can't see the connection with his sore stomach.' She rolled her eyes in exasperation, but her son just laughed.

'Good luck with that,' he chuckled. 'See, that's why I work with animals – less arguing.'

'Indeed,' she said, and then her gaze fell on the two little girls, who were surreptitiously reaching for a plate full of biscuits. 'Katherine Stanton – I see that! No biscuits before tea. You two can wash your hands, and then help lay the table.'

Xander sat in his place, watching as the family fell into what was obviously a well-accustomed routine of preparing the meal. He was handed a large mug of tea and the table gradually became loaded up with plates and platters of fresh bread, hams and cheeses. Jars of pickles and relishes appeared and a large, steaming tureen of soup; Xander's stomach reminded him he had eaten very little that day and he hoped no-one else had heard the insistent growling.

In a remarkably short time, everyone was sitting at the long table, and food was being pressed upon Xander from every side. Ollie had shot into the chair next to him and was eating at a pace which drew his mother's attention.

'Hungry?' she inquired, but a smile tugged at the corner of her lips and she passed another tray of cheese to his end of the table. Ollie grinned back, his mouth too full to respond.

Xander ate more slowly, listening to the buzz of chatter and savouring the home-cooked food. It tasted wonderful and he reflected that it was a huge improvement on burnt offerings and take-away menus. Katie and her friend had begun their meal with many sidelong glances at him, followed with whispers and giggling, but after Jenna had sent a firm look at them they had subsided. No-one asked him difficult questions or treated him like an outsider and, for the first time in twenty-four hours, he felt the tight knot of tension in his stomach ease.

As he glanced up from his plate and stole a few quick looks at the people around the table, he noticed that the adults wore those narrow bands on their wrist, although with crystalline stones of different colours, while the little girls did not. As he ate, he thought of Flint's insistence that these were not the same as his orb and wondered about their purpose.

The meal was almost over when the kitchen door opened again. Mrs Stanton looked up.

'And where exactly have you been?' she enquired.

Xander twisted, looking over his shoulder, and saw a girl wander in, an expression of cool unconcern on her face. Her chin-length hair, the palest shade of blonde that Xander had ever seen, hung untidily over her face, and a pale purple streak was clearly visible at the front.

'Out,' she replied evasively, sliding into a chair at the table and reaching for the bread. She looked over at Ollie and pulled a face; he just grinned back in obvious amusement.

'I realise that, Len,' replied Mrs Stanton tartly. 'The question is why you weren't at the academy, where you should have been. I got yet another complaint from Primilla Pennicot about you.'

The girl glanced up at the screen where the image of the sharp-faced woman was still frozen mid-word. 'So I see,' she said unrepentantly. 'Great pose – it really captures her sweetness and charm.'

Mrs Stanton swung around, flipping her hand at the screen. It went blank for a moment, silvery-smooth, and then Xander noticed smudges of colour gradually blooming across it like ink drops in water. The colours twisted and merged, forming vague flower shapes that grew and blossomed, before fading away to make room for new ones. It was oddly engrossing.

'Don't change the subject,' snapped Mrs Stanton, refusing to be diverted. 'Why weren't you there?'

The girl bit hard into her sandwich and glowered right back. 'Seriously, Thea, what's the point?' she demanded. 'In what way could I possibly participate?' She brandished her arm at Mrs Stanton in what Xander thought was a rude gesture before he realised that her wrist was bare; she did not wear a band.

Mrs Stanton looked rather discomfited.

'You were supposed to be there, Len,' she reiterated, but without her earlier conviction. 'And don't call me "Thea".'

Len shrugged, clearly feeling that this argument was already won. She reached for some cheese. 'Did you have to put that on?' she asked, jerking her head at the slowly blooming panel on the wall. 'It's gross.' She still hadn't acknowledged Xander's presence at the table in any way – a fact that Mrs Stanton did not fail to notice.

'It's a famous piece of art, whether you appreciate it or not,' she said firmly. 'More to the point, do we not greet guests in this house anymore? Honestly, Len!'

Len rolled her eyes but twisted to look at Xander, pushing her silvery pale hair off her face impatiently. He noticed that her eyes were also a light colour, not blue or green but a shade in-between. She was saved from looking completely washed out by her skin, which had a faint golden tinge. She paused, considering him, and then abruptly stuck out her hand.

'I'm Len,' she said.

'Xander.'

As his fingers closed around hers, he felt her hand jerk and she snatched it back after the briefest of contacts, her eyes wary. She said nothing else for the rest of the meal, although Xander felt her gaze resting on him from time to time, considering.

After everyone had finished, she helped to clean up and then disappeared without another word.

Xander might have wondered why she was behaving so oddly but he was distracted by another effect of his recent experiences. Now that his stomach was full and his initial panic had receded, the night of terrified sleep deprivation followed in rapid succession by one shocking event after another had caught up with him. The dark heaviness of exhaustion seeped insistently into every part of his body. Sounds, movement and the hum of voices in the kitchen faded as Xander felt his head nod forward; he caught himself with a jerk.

Mrs Stanton did not miss a thing. A moment later, she was leaning over him, her cool fingers brushing across his forehead.

'Are you all right?' she asked. 'You're very pale.'

Xander looked up, trying to focus his eyes on her face. 'Just didn't get much sleep last night,' he said blearily. 'All the shadows outside my room and weird noises. Then today –'

His voice faded away again as he lost track of what he was trying to say.

Mrs Stanton exchanged a look with her son, who crossed the room and slid his arm around Xander, lifting him to his feet. 'Up you come,' he said, his voice a kindly rumble from above Xander's head. 'You'll feel better after a good night's sleep. Let's get you upstairs.'

He was as good as his word and with no further discussion, Xander found himself tucked up in the spare bed in Ollie's room, while Mrs Stanton drew the curtains to block out the early evening light. Within seconds, sleep had rolled relentlessly over him.

✕

Xander woke abruptly, blinking in confusion and wondering what had roused him in the middle of the night. The sound of soft breathing from across the room made him freeze in confusion before, once again, recollection swept over him and he let out a long breath. Darkness pressed in on him but it felt quite different to the terror of shifting shadows the night before and, after a few moments, his eyes began to adjust. There was a small gap in the curtains and faint light from the moon glanced in, allowing Xander to make out the shape of the other bed, and of Ollie sprawled out across it. An owl hooted outside and was quickly answered by another from further away. Xander felt a smile tug at his lips. Owls were not something he had ever heard from his home on a busy London street.

As this thought flittered across his mind, it brought with it the image of his own bedroom and a sudden urge to reach out again, to find that elusive reflection that Flint had called a shadowself. He hesitated for a moment, remembering the sick dizziness of his previous attempt, but, impulsively, decided to go ahead. Flint hadn't said it was dangerous, just difficult, and Xander reasoned that at least if he was already lying down he couldn't fall again. Taking a deep breath, he closed his eyes.

It was easier this time. Almost at once Xander's body prickled with pins and needles, and he felt that surge of lightheadedness. Cautiously, he opened his eyes again. All around him were the familiar sights of his bedroom, bathed in the orange glow of the streetlights just outside his window; he could even hear the faint sound of a television from downstairs. Everything was normal, and for a moment Xander wondered whether he had dreamt the entire thing. As if in answer to this question, the room lurched and he was once more lying in soft moonlight in a different bedroom, with a queasy feeling in his stomach. He lay breathing slowly in and out, and heard the owl hoot again like a welcome back.

Xander had wondered whether seeing his home would make things worse, reminding him how far away he was from everything that was familiar and safe. Strangely though, being able to see it when he chose brought the two sides of his reality close enough he felt he might be able to bridge the gap. As he thought back to his arrival in Haven, he remembered the hostile boy with the blurred face and realised that he had not passed on his message to Flint. He punched his pillow into a more comfortable shape and rolled over. He would tell Flint when he saw him next, Xander decided drowsily and grinned as he imagined Flint's likely reaction to the rude message; within a few moments, he was asleep again.

CHAPTER THREE

As it turned out, Xander didn't have the chance to ask about his unfriendly rescuer or pass on the message, since Flint did not turn up the next morning. There were plenty of other things to distract him, however. He woke up from a sound sleep to someone prodding at his arm and opened his eyes to see his new room-mate hanging over him, with a friendly grin on his face and a halo of wildly dishevelled hair.

'Morning,' said Ollie as Xander scrubbed at his eyes. 'Breakfast-time.'

Sitting up, Xander realised that while he had slept in his t-shirt, someone had taken off his shoes, jeans and jumper and they were now lying in a neat pile on the table next to his bed. He dressed, wondering what he would do about clothes since he couldn't keep wearing the same things. As Ollie led him downstairs, Xander could hear the faint sounds of people moving about the house, washing and getting ready for the day. There was no sign of the family when they reached the big kitchen, although he noticed that someone had already laid the table for breakfast.

'What d'you want to drink?' asked Ollie hospitably.

Xander did not answer. His attention had been caught by two tiny figures, barely knee-high, edging along the skirting board at the far side of the room. They moved with exaggerated care, their huge black eyes transfixed on something by Xander's feet. Intrigued, Xander turned his head to take a closer look and at once both of the figures froze, one of them blinking worriedly, while the other stared at the ceiling. Before he could do anything else, he felt a sharp nudge and Ollie leaned in close.

'Don't look at them,' he hissed.

Xander turned away and out of the corner of his eye he saw both of the odd little figures heave sighs of relief.

'What are they?' he murmured to Ollie.

Ollie leaned even closer, so he could speak into Xander's ear.

'They're brownies and they're invisible.'

'No, they aren't,' blurted Xander in a louder voice. 'They're right –'

His words were cut off as Ollie's hand covered his mouth.

'Do *not* say it unless you want to be the one to explain to Gran why they've left.' His expression was serious and Xander nodded to show he had understood. Ollie let his hand drop, leaning forward again to whisper in his ear. 'They like to visit people and help around the house, cleaning and stuff, but you have to pretend not to see them because they believe they're invisible.'

'But you *can* actually see them?' Xander whispered back.

'Course,' replied Ollie promptly, with an amused look. 'These two are called Brolly and Spike, and they've been coming for years. Gran just says it's important to respect their culture.'

Xander turned this over in his mind, while covertly watching the two little figures as they continued their stealthy progress across the room, using chairs and handy table legs as cover. He frowned as a flaw in this logic occurred to him.

'If they believe they're invisible, why are they tip-toeing and hiding?' he asked, as the brownies made a break from the thick wooden leg of a side-table to the relative security of the big squashy couch sitting against the kitchen wall. They ducked underneath the trailing ends of a long blue throw and paused for a moment, the material bunched up around them and their small brown shoes poking out.

Ollie looked surprised, as if the answer was obvious.

'Just because they're invisible doesn't mean you couldn't hear them. They don't want to draw attention to themselves.'

Both boys watched the conspicuous bulges inch their way along the base of the couch, until they were only a few feet from where Xander was standing. There was a second's hesitation, and then two heads emerged from under the throw. Xander stood very still, trying to look in the other direction whilst peeping at the brownies. Both of the little figures had thick brown hair – one with wild curls while the other had spiky tufts sticking out in every direction – through which the tips of sharply pointed ears were clearly visible. Xander noticed that one of them was clutching a bulging leather bag in its hand and that both of them appeared absolutely transfixed by something –

'Why are they staring at my shoes?' Xander whispered anxiously to Ollie.

'They like fixing all sorts of things but they have a bit of a – a thing about shoes,' Ollie explained. 'They've probably never seen any like that before and, no offence, but they're sort of a mess. Usually they do wait until the shoes aren't occupied though.'

The little creatures had edged their way behind Xander's feet and he could no longer see them, but he felt a tentative finger poke at the back of his tatty old trainers and heard a low murmuring in tones of wonder. There was a faint clinking noise as the bag dropped onto the floor and then the sound of rummaging; a moment later, Xander could feel a gentle tugging and prodding as the two brownies set to work.

Of all the weird things that had happened to him since his arrival in Haven, Xander was fairly certain that pretending not to notice as two little figures sewed diligently at his trainers was the oddest.

Breakfast was a chaotic affair. Unlike Xander's own home, where meals were often a solitary occupation, this house was bursting with people and activity. Racks of golden toast, without a hint of charring, appeared in front of Xander along with rich yellow butter and creamy scrambled eggs, which Mr Stanton conjured up in large quantities as he stood at the big stove, laughing at his daughter's attempts to avoid having her hair plaited by his exasperated wife. Len was leaning over a small screen in the corner, eating an apple with one hand while furiously typing with the other and Ollie was trying to persuade his grandmother that since he had a guest to entertain ('seriously, Gran, he'll get really bored on his own'), he should have the day off.

On top of all this, the brownies were hard at work in the kitchen and, as a consequence, were seriously underfoot. Twice, Xander had to choke back laughter when first Katie and then Mrs Stanton tripped over them, and then carefully pretended they had no idea what could have caused their stumbles. Finally, Mrs Stanton gave up the unequal struggle to manoeuvre herself around the brownies while feigning selective blindness and sank into a chair with a sigh.

'No, Ollie,' she said firmly. 'You already missed the extra coaching yesterday so you *are* going this morning. Xander will still be here when you get back and I'm sure we'll find something to amuse him.'

'But Gran,' began Ollie, but the fast-scrolling monitor screen had caught Mrs Stanton's attention.

'Len Stanton,' she said sharply. 'Please tell me you're not hacking into the academy system again.'

Len glanced up and took another bite of her apple.

'Of course not,' she said, deadpan. 'That would be wrong.' With a few more keystrokes, the screen went blank again. 'I was just updating my schedule.'

Mrs Stanton looked unconvinced but as she opened her mouth, there was a quick tap and Ari's cheerful face appeared around the kitchen door.

'Morning,' she said brightly to the room at large, before turning to Xander. 'I thought you might like some company, since I assume the others have class?' Her eyes took in Ollie's disgruntled expression with quick amusement.

'Perfect,' said Mrs Stanton in satisfaction, before directing a firm look at Ollie and Len. 'You two will be late if you don't get moving.'

Ollie heaved a long-suffering sigh and stood up. Len was already halfway out of the door when she was brought up short.

'Haven't you forgotten something?' Mrs Stanton asked, holding out a narrow grey band set with a pale yellow stone. Len's nose wrinkled in disgust.

'I told you, it makes me itch,' she grumped. 'And it's not like I can even use it.'

'It was made especially for you,' said Mrs Stanton firmly. 'And your teacher told me just the other day that he thinks you're on the verge of a breakthrough and you only need to apply yourself a little – and actually *wear* it.'

Len's face twisted into a furious scowl. She reached out and grabbed the band with extremely bad grace. 'I think you'll find what I'm *actually* on the verge of is a nervous breakdown,' she growled as she slapped the band around her wrist, and ostentatiously scratched beneath it.

Mrs Stanton just rolled her eyes, patently unimpressed with Len's dramatics.

'You finished?' Ari asked Xander, as she grabbed a piece of toast.

'Yes,' said Xander, standing up and adding, 'thanks very much for breakfast.' He reached out to clear some plates from the table but was waved away by Mrs Stanton.

'Don't worry about that right now,' she said, her eyes still resting on the balefully scowling Len. 'It's all under control.'

Xander grimaced sympathetically at Ollie, who was wearing an expression more appropriate to a condemned man than someone just leaving for school, and ducked out of the back door after Ari.

Bright morning sunlight bathed the garden, and the old stone terrace outside the kitchen was already warm underfoot, while its border of delicate lavender plants filled the air with their sweet scent and the faint hum of bees moving busily between flowers. Just in front of Xander, two broad stone steps led down onto a wide expanse of grass, while to his left he could see a small orchard where the trees were covered in blossoms. Everything seemed entirely normal.

Xander looked around at Ari, who was watching him with that quirky little smile on her face.

'Shall we head out?' she asked, offering him her arm. The stone on her wrist glittered in the sunlight, ice pale. Xander reached out cautiously; he was not sure he would ever get used to this mode of transport. This time, the lurch was much sharper than when Flint had taken them, and Ari wrinkled her nose apologetically as Xander staggered forward when they arrived.

'Sorry,' she said, grabbing his arm to steady him. 'I've never been very good with passengers.'

'S'okay,' replied Xander, although he still felt a little wobbly. Looking around, he realised that they were now standing in light woodland on a narrow track, hardly visible from lack of use, which wound ahead of them up a steep incline.

'Where are we?' asked Xander, in what he felt was becoming an all too frequent refrain.

'Not far,' replied Ari, leading the way up the track with her usual jaunty stride. She glanced back and smiled. 'I just thought you might want to sit and chat for a while.' She said no more until they had reached the top of the hill and the path, such as it was, had petered out entirely. There was nothing there save a few bare outcroppings of rock surrounded by scrubby grass, and a view which went on for miles.

'I used to like coming here when I was younger and wanted to think or have some space to myself,' said Ari. She hitched herself up to a comfortable perch on top of one of the taller rocks and leant back, her legs dangling down. Xander clambered up with slightly more effort and found a space for himself.

'Did you live near here?' he asked.

Ari shrugged. 'For a while. It's hard to keep track.' She glanced sideways at him, with a little grin. 'Travellers, right? It's not just a name.'

'So you never settle anywhere?'

Ari shook her head. 'Never. We belong everywhere and nowhere.' Her voice had taken on an odd lilt and Xander had the sense she was repeating some kind of creed.

'So, where do you live, if you're always moving?' he asked.

'I'll show you later,' replied Ari, turning her face up to the sun and closing her eyes. The freckles on her nose stood out in sharp relief in the bright light. Xander stared at her, wondering how much 'later' he would stay in this strange place.

'How does all this even exist?' he blurted out, as he had wanted to ever since he had found himself transported to an unfamiliar room, one finger pressed against an unreadable symbol on an old stone. 'The stuff here is only meant to be in fairytales – how can it be real?'

Ari didn't open her eyes, but her lips twitched in amusement and sympathy.

'Haven't you ever thought it was just a little bit odd that those old fairytales – the myths and the legends – are so similar, your world over? They may use different names but, fundamentally, the stories are all the same.' She turned her head and looked at Xander, one eyebrow raised.

Xander frowned. 'But that's because, well, people moved about and spread the stories, and made up fantastical creatures to explain stuff, you know, before science.' Even to Xander's own ears, this explanation seemed a bit lacking.

'Maybe,' allowed Ari softly. 'Or maybe it's because all those fairytales are true and always have been. Maybe the old stories and legends had a purpose, to pass on information and guidelines and warnings.'

'So it's all real then?' demanded Xander, a little shake in his voice. His entire worldview had been systematically stood on its head over the past couple of days and he wasn't sure yet how he felt about it.

'Mostly,' said Ari, and then she grinned mischievously. 'Not vampires, though. They're definitely the product of overwrought imaginations.'

Xander thought for a moment. 'So how come no one sees

anything these days? You'd think that if all these weird *things* were roaming around the countryside, somebody might notice. They'd have got a picture or some proof by now.'

He turned to look at Ari, having made what he considered to be a good point, but found her eyeing him with no trace of her usual humour.

'What?' he asked, uncertain what he had done to bring such a disapproving expression to her face.

'Each of those races has a history, a culture that goes back just as far as yours,' Ari said quietly. 'They are thinking, feeling beings. They're not 'things'.'

'I didn't mean it like that,' Xander protested, surprised by how serious Ari's face could look when not wreathed in secret amusement.

'Words are powerful, Xander; they frame your thoughts. When you name someone as less than they are, before you know it you start to think they *are* less.' She glanced at Xander and he was relieved to see her mouth quirk into that familiar smile, taking the bite out of her lecture. 'Our worlds are not really so different, more like two sides of the same coin. There have always been places where the borders are thin, and the old races could slip between. It was only the people who are fixed on one side or the other – for the most part, anyway; we Travellers have always been able to pass over.'

'Using the Stones,' Xander confirmed.

'Exactly.'

'You said the other th-, I mean the old races,' Xander corrected himself mid-thought and saw Ari's quick smile of approval. 'You said they could come across. Do they still?'

'Even if they could, I think they choose not to,' replied Ari thoughtfully, poking her chin idly with the tip of one slender finger. 'They have learnt to be wary of your people. Your world is growing smaller all the time – there are so few solitary places left, where your technology cannot reach.'

She stopped speaking, apparently lost in thought, and Xander hesitated before asking his most important question.

'What am *I* doing here?'

Ari turned and eyed him. 'Yes, that's the real question, isn't it? Honestly, I have no idea.' Her words hung in the air for a moment before she jumped down from her perch and brushed off her trousers. 'Come on,' she said.

'Where?' asked Xander, lowering himself to the ground rather more cautiously.

'You wanted to see where we stayed,' replied Ari, as she headed back down the faint stony track. The trail led sharply downwards into the trees, past where they had arrived, and onwards through the thickening woodland. Finally, it levelled out, and they stood on the edge of a wide open glade, surrounded by close-growing trees and filled with thick, scrubby undergrowth. On the far side was a slight, rocky incline covered with brambles and old leaves. Xander looked about in confusion, wondering why they had stopped here, and then caught sight of Ari, watching him intently.

'Okay,' he said. 'Why are we here? Did you used to camp here?'

Ari did not answer directly but instead just gestured to the clearing. 'First, tell me what you see,' she said.

Xander looked around again. 'Open space, trees, scrub, thorns. What I am supposed to be seeing?'

Disconcertingly, even as these words left his mouth, Xander was aware of an odd haziness in his peripheral vision, a blurring that reminded him of the hostile boy's face on the day he had arrived in Haven. It was annoying, and he shook his head slightly, as if to dispel it. Ari was watching him closely, and she smiled at this.

'Close your eyes,' she said, that secret amusement lilting in her voice again. 'Concentrate on seeing what is really here. You have to look past what your mind is trying to tell you.'

Xander shut his eyes and took a deep breath. He had always thought that if he could see something, that must mean that it was real. This place seemed to prove just the opposite. He focussed hard on wanting to see what was really there and then opened his eyes.

The scrubby undergrowth had vanished, revealing a broad swath of soft green grass starred with little flowers. Where the bramble-strewn slope had been there now stood a long, low-beamed building with rustic-looking windows, hanging lanterns and a large door, green-painted and standing ajar. Xander stared around, amazed at what had been concealed.

'Welcome to Mistleberry Lodge,' said Ari, her eyes sparkling. 'I knew you'd be able to see through the wards. Most people can't, you know. They're so convinced by what they believe must be true that they go blindly through their entire lives, with the truth literally under their noses.'

At her words, a stray thought darted through Xander's mind, the reflection that remaining oblivious might have been a more comfortable way to live. There was a small, fearful part of him that wanted not only to squeeze his eyes shut to this new and disconcerting reality, but to pull a sheet firmly over his head until it went away. Unfortunately, Xander suspected that there was no way back for him. Some things were just too big to be unseen.

'I stayed here several times while I was growing up. Mistleberry is one of the oldest Lodges,' said Ari, breaking in on his thoughts. She waved an airy hand towards the old building. 'It's a bit small and cramped really, a lot of it is in ruins, but I always loved it here. It's a shame to see it so neglected.'

Xander followed her across the grass as she walked over to the half-open door. Closer up, Xander could see that the bright-green paint was peeling and there were weeds growing by the door frame. Ari flicked disapprovingly at the bramble fronds hanging over the doorway.

'Is it just left empty if Travellers aren't here?' asked Xander.

'Sometimes,' replied Ari. 'But most Lodges are placed where there have been historical weaknesses on the border and traditionally we maintain a presence in these places, usually older Travellers who take up residence. Of course, for generations the border has been quiet, for the most part.' She glanced at Xander. 'Until recently, that is.'

Without saying anything further, Ari tugged at the heavy door. It scraped against the ground as it swung ponderously open. Xander peered inside, but all he could make out was a large empty space, with motes of dust floating and dancing in the shaft of sunlight. Ari walked confidently inside, her light boots thudding on the grubby stone floor.

'Hello?' she called, but only the echoes replied. After a moment Xander followed her inside, his eyes adjusting to the dimmer light in the entrance hall. Several doors stood ajar, but there was nothing to be seen beyond them except a few wind-blown leaves. Ari did not appear affected by the desolate air of the place, and she called out again. 'Hello, the Lodge.'

A door opened abruptly, spilling a flood of warm light into the hallway.

'Well, young Ari,' said a soft, creaky voice. 'Back again, are we?'

An elderly woman poked her head around the door, peering over the top of a pair of light spectacles. Her thin fingers clutched a thick woollen shawl around her shoulders, despite the warmth of the morning.

'Hello, Mrs Tavish,' Ari stepped forward to give her a warm hug. 'This is my friend, Xander. He's never been to Mistleberry before so I thought I would bring him over.'

The old lady stared suspiciously at Xander for a moment. Evidently he passed her scrutiny as she beckoned both of them to follow her as she hobbled, bent-backed, into the room and sank down with a sigh into a large, shabby armchair by the fireplace. Xander covertly eyed the hearth itself as he followed Ari into the room. It was piled high with what looked like clear pebbles, which glowed and flickered with warm light and threw off considerable heat, making the room with its thick, tightly drawn curtains quite stifling.

'Sit, sit,' urged Mrs Tavish, waving a hand toward the other chairs.

Ari took the seat closest to the hearth, for which Xander was very grateful. He wondered whether it would be rude to pull his jumper off, as small beads of sweat formed at his hairline. Mrs Tavish tucked her shawl closer and eyed them beadily.

'Did Atherton finally get around to sending someone to investigate?' she demanded peevishly. 'We've left word over and over again, but no reply. Forgotten about us here, they have. Forgotten about the old Tavishes, I reckon.'

'Sent word?' asked Ari, with a quick frown. 'I hadn't heard anything about that. Is something wrong?'

'Wrong?' snorted the old lady. 'I should think so. Why would we leave messages if nothing were wrong? It's all wrong here. Bad noises and then the cold; terrible cold, it is. That's why we sent the messages.'

'Noises?' Ari asked politely, as Xander surreptitiously blotted his forehead.

'At night, hissing like snakes, that's what. Terrible things moving in the dark,' Mrs Tavish said darkly. 'Alvin hears them. He can always hear them now.'

Ari nodded, her expression sympathetic. 'How is Alvin?' she asked.

'The same,' replied Mrs Tavish flatly. 'Nothing to be done, they say. He's out with Tavish now. They'll be back soon and you can hear all about it. You can tell Atherton to send some people over.'

'I'm not sure that Atherton will listen to me,' began Ari, but the sound of heavy footsteps interrupted her. Mrs Tavish sat up straighter in her chair.

'They're back,' she said. 'Now you'll hear.'

The door opened again to admit an elderly man, with white, thinning hair and deep lines on his face. Xander's gaze, however, was immediately drawn to the figure that shuffled after him. He appeared to be middle-aged, but it was hard to tell as his features were distorted and marred by a twisted web of silvery scars that covered his entire face and extended down his neck. One eye was shuttered with scar tissue while the other was dull and vague, looking indifferently upon the world. He paused in the doorway, clutching a large bag in his gnarled hand. While Xander was distracted, Ari had stood up to greet the older man, who nodded abruptly back.

'You're one of the Aldanes, aren't you? Young Ariel?' he asked gruffly, glancing at his wife for confirmation. 'So you're who Atherton and Wooten send, after all this time? You and this child?'

He looked disgusted as he walked forward to stand next to Mrs Tavish.

'Not exactly,' said Ari, with an apologetic grimace. 'I'm afraid I hadn't heard anything about your messages, although to be fair I'm not privy to the Wardens' communications.'

'They don't believe us, do they?' snorted Mr Tavish, as if Ari had not spoken. 'Don't believe the old Tavishes when they say there's a problem. Sending someone barely trained and a boy, just to shut us up, I reckon.' Ari shook her head, but Tavish ploughed on, his voice rising. 'Think it's my imagination, do they? Paranoid, am I?' He looked over his shoulder at the figure still standing silently, clutching his bag and staring at Xander. 'I've good reason, I would say.'

The bitter words hung in the air like something physical, until Mrs Tavish pulled herself up out of her chair. 'Come on in, Alvin love,' she said in a gentle voice. 'It's only some visitors, nothing to worry about. Let's get your coat off now.' Speaking encouragingly, she led the man through another door and shut it behind her. Ari's eyes had followed them, compassion clear on her face.

'Is there any improvement?' she asked.

'No' replied Tavish shortly. 'Nor likely to be. Shade-strike that bad, you don't come back from it,' Xander felt a sudden chill go down his back at the man's words but Tavish continued on, his face twisted with frustration as he turned to Ari. 'That's why the Wardens should listen to my warnings, instead of sticking their ears in the ground. The boundaries are not secure, they're failing, and if those horrors get loose in Haven there'll be no help for any of us. Alvin hears them. He says they're coming.' He reached out and gripped Ari's arm. 'You tell that to young Flint. You tell him to make the Wardens pay attention.'

Xander vaguely heard Ari's voice, answering in calm, reassuring tones, but all he could see in his mind's eye were those shifting, menacing shadows in his home and then again, massing in front of him in the museum. Nausea rose sharply in his throat. He had known instinctively that they were dangerous, but he would have been paralysed with fear if he had understood the truth of what he was facing. Staring down at the neat white bandage on his left hand and thinking of that terrifying pillar of blackness that had struck out at him, he wondered how on earth he had escaped with only a minor injury. Suddenly his wrist was taken in a firm grasp. The old man bent over his bandaged palm, his expression intent, before he looked up with dawning interest into Xander's face.

'That's shade-strike,' he said, before glancing at Ari for confirmation.

Ari nodded.

'How did you know?' she asked.

Tavish curled his lip contemptuously. 'D'you think I wouldn't know the taint of it? It leaves its mark. This though,' he sucked air in through his teeth, considering, 'it's not – quite the same.' He peered into Xander's face. 'How many, boy?' he asked.

Xander remembered the wall of cold, hissing blackness massing in the museum, rising up and striking at him. He swallowed. 'A lot,' he muttered, and drew his hand back to stick in his pocket.

Tavish frowned, eying him for a moment, but then turned abruptly to Ari. 'Just tell Flint to come and talk to me. Tell him I'm Watcher in this place and he needs to hear what is happening. He's one with his eyes open and his brain switched on, not like that group of pompous –'

He cut himself off, with a quick glance at Xander.

'I'll tell him,' Ari assured him.

'Hmph,' Tavish snorted. 'Fine time it is, when a Watcher has to plead for a hearing. Got too comfortable, those Wardens. Can't see? Don't want to see, I reckon. Well, off you go. No time to waste. That's the problem with young people these days – no sense of urgency.'

Ari smiled at him, lifting a hand in farewell as she drew Xander with her, out of the room. Xander noticed that Tavish's eyes followed him as he left, his gaze lingering on Xander's bandaged hand.

The deserted hallway was refreshingly cool after the suffocating heat of the Tavishes' sitting room, and Xander couldn't restrain a sigh of relief as they walked towards the front door. Neither of them spoke until they stood outside again. The sun was high in the sky, shining on the broad green clearing, and a fresh breeze lifted Xander's hair, sending the long grass and flowers swaying. It appeared to be a place shielded from darkness and fear, and yet Xander shivered as he recalled the Tavishes' warnings. He could not blot out the memory of Alvin Tavish's ruined face.

'What happened?' he asked Ari. She seemed to know exactly what he meant.

'It was a while back, about fourteen years ago,' she answered. 'The border failed, and no one saw it coming. We barely even trained for shade-strike. It had been generations since we'd had to face that, and people believed the threat was gone. Alvin and a couple of others were caught out alone and unprepared; he was horribly injured, but the worst effect was on his mind. The Tavishes tried to keep travelling, they thought having people around and keeping some normality for him would help him recover. It didn't.' Ari sighed and glanced back at the lodge. 'That's when they applied to take on Mistleberry as resident Watchers. It's out of the way and hardly used. I think they hoped that quiet living would improve things for him.' Her voice trailed off, and she shrugged helplessly. Clearly it had not.

'What happened to the others with him?' he asked.

Ari looked away, not quite meeting his eyes. 'They didn't make it,' was all she said.

All of a sudden, it became quite clear to Xander why Ari had brought him to Mistleberry. 'I can't go back, can I?' he said quietly. 'Those things were in my house and targeting me at the museum. I can't go home.'

'I don't think so, Xander,' said Ari, equally serious, with the twinkle missing from her eyes. 'Not until we know what's going on and why they keep showing up around you. You need protection.'

Without another word, she turned and led Xander back over the grass, away from the silent lodge. Xander was content to walk in silence. He was turning everything he had heard and seen over and over in his mind, trying to make some sense of it all. Primarily, he decided, he needed to find out why this was happening to him, and he realised that the answers were most likely to be found here, in Haven. As they passed under the first trees surrounding the clearing, he looked back at the glade and blinked. The ward was flickering in and out; one moment the green lawn sat serenely in the dappled sunlight, and the next, the space was a scrubby brown wasteland. Nothing in Haven, he reflected as he turned away to climb up the woodland trail, appeared to be really as it seemed.

Ari brought Xander back to Woodside after that, but she did not seem in any particular hurry to leave, and they strolled through the gardens together. Xander looked over at the old grey house, with its many windows reflecting back the morning sun.

'So the Stantons aren't Travellers?' he asked.

Ari shrugged easily. 'Well, yes and no,' she said, and then laughed. 'What I mean is, mostly no. Thea married a Traveller, which was pretty much unheard of for someone from a Founding Family like her, as well as being unusual for us; we Travellers rarely marry out. It was apparently quite a scandal at the time.'

She glanced at Xander and smiled at the baffled look on his face. 'Sorry,' she said. 'I keep forgetting you know absolutely nothing about Haven. This must all be very confusing for you.'

Xander nodded, with a wry grin for that understatement. Ari stopped walking and sank gracefully down into the grass, sitting cross-legged.

'Tell you what,' she said. 'I'll start from the beginning.'

'That would be great,' said Xander, joining her with a sigh of relief.

Ari plucked a daisy and began absently twirling it in her fingers.

'Way back in the mists of time,' she began, 'Haven's government was founded by twelve families, known as the Founding Families. Even now they're still the biggest landowners, and they each hold a hereditary chair on the Council of Haven, although these days they don't control all the day-to-day decision-making. The Families are all extremely wealthy and powerful, and so the Peverells were less than impressed when Thea Peverell fell in love with a Traveller, and announced she would marry him.'

'Why would they worry about that?' asked Xander. Having seen the Travellers in action at the museum, personally he thought that they were pretty impressive.

Ari wrinkled her nose. 'Our role has always been to watch and ward the border of Haven, and the law states that the

Families and the guilds have to give a tithe to recompense us for risking our lives on their behalf. However, it's been hundreds of years since there's been any real threat on the border, except for a couple of incidents, and most Travellers are more engaged in trading these days than risking our lives in defence of Haven. There's sometimes bad feeling about that,' she said, shrugging, 'but the law is quite clear. So far there's never been any real attempt to get out of the tithes, but the Families tend to look down on Travellers and think of us as free-loaders. Hence, they weren't thrilled when one of their own decided to slum it, as they saw it, with one of us.'

'Oh,' said Xander. Mrs Stanton did not strike him as a very likely subject for a star—crossed romance, but clearly appearances could be deceptive.

'Indeed,' said Ari, with a twinkle in her eye as if she guessed at his thoughts and they amused her. 'Anyway, Thea defied her family and got married, and they had two boys, Ollie's father James, who you've met, and Len's father, Jasper, who's the only one in the family to have inherited the Traveller abilities. Thea's old aunt, who was a bit eccentric, had a soft spot for her rebellious niece and left her this house years ago; this is where they have lived ever since.'

She leant back on her elbows in the grass and eyed him thoughtfully.

'Any other burning questions?'

Xander's eyes immediately dropped to the orb on her wrist, glimmering in the warm sunshine. 'How do they actually work?' he asked, voicing the question he had been dying to ask since first seeing one. 'Is it some kind of magic?'

Ari laughed and shook her head vigorously.

'No, it's not magic,' she said, her eyes sparkling in amusement. 'Travellers are born with certain innate abilities and the orbs simply allow us to draw on the energy generated by the deep earth, and to focus and direct it.'

Xander frowned. 'So how come Ollie and other people who aren't Travellers have orbs as well?' he asked.

Ari sat up again and held her wrist out to Xander so he could look more closely at the stone. 'Can you see any differences between mine and the others you've seen?'

Xander bent over her orb, examining it carefully. 'Yours is clear,' he said, watching with fascination as tiny points of light flickered deep within it. He frowned as he tried to recollect in detail the other orbs he had seen and then glanced up at her. 'And the other coloured orbs have something in them, some kind of silvery threading, although it's hard to see in Ollie's.'

Ari drew her hand back with a little smile. 'Yes, perhaps Ollie's orb isn't the best one to use for comparison. For some reason, he's incredibly hard on them, not to mention rather prone to exploding things.' She shook her head, laughing. 'Anyway, he wears a synthetic orb like most of the people in Haven. It's actually a fairly new technology, invented about twenty years ago, and they're not like ours, but the coding inside them does allow a limited draw on the power. Before the coding was incorporated, it took people years of training to use orbs, even in the limited manner of non-Travellers.'

She glanced over at his fascinated expression and her eyes twinkled.

'This is something that anyone can learn,' she said, reaching out to pluck several more daisies. 'Watch.'

Ari laid the flowers in a little heap on the grass. A moment later, they whirled up into the air, as if a tiny tornado was lifting them off the ground, swirling around just above Xander's head. As he stared up at them, one daisy spun down to tickle the end of his nose before shooting back upwards to re-join the circle. Ari grinned at him.

'This is actually quite good practice for fine control,' she said, 'which is why it's one of the first things we learn to master.'

'Could you lift yourself up in the air, like flying?' asked Xander, as the daisies began to weave in and out of each other in a complicated pattern.

Ari laughed at that and showered Xander with the daisies. 'That would be fun, but unfortunately not. I can lift things, but my feet need to remain firmly on the ground.' A mischievous expression crossed her face, and suddenly Xander felt that odd sensation of weightlessness again. His eyes widened as he realised that he was floating several feet up in the air. 'I can lift *you* up, however,' Ari said, smiling at his surprise, and then lowering him gently back down again. Before Xander could say anything else, a voice floated down the garden.

'Drinks, you two.'

Mrs Stanton was standing on the stone terrace, holding up a large jug, and Ari got up from the grass. She held out a hand to haul Xander to his feet, with a quick grin.

'Come on,' she said. 'I've got time for a glass of Thea's famous lemonade before I need to head out again.'

As they reached the terrace, Ollie came bursting out of the back door with a large folder tucked under one arm. 'Just in time,' he announced with satisfaction, as he spotted the big jug. He dumped the folder on the table and pulled a face at Xander's curious look.

'Apprenticeship options for next term,' he explained, as he poured drinks. 'Once you're fourteen, you choose two each term, and spend a couple of afternoons a week on each option. You have to rotate through the various guilds and they won't let you narrow it down until you're sixteen,' he grimaced, with a pointed stare at Mrs Stanton who was flipping through the folder, 'which means that at some point I'll be stuck over at the Textiles and Apparel Association learning about beading and buttonholes.'

Mrs Stanton just shook her head with an unsympathetic smile. 'I think you'll learn rather more than that, and it's good for you to broaden your mind. You never know what will spark your interest if you don't experience it.' Ollie looked sceptical, but Xander gazed rather wistfully at the battered folder as he accepted a brimming glass of lemonade; education on Haven sounded much more interesting than his own schooling. When he looked up, he met an amused expression on Ollie's face.

'You've got daisies in your hair,' he said with a grin.

Xander reached up and hastily brushed at his head, while Ari laughed. 'I was giving Xander a quick demonstration of how orbs work,' she explained.

Mrs Stanton glanced up at that. 'Speaking of which, Katie needs to get fitted for her training orb tomorrow. If you're interested, Xander, you're welcome to come along with us.'

Xander nodded quickly. 'That would be great, thanks,' he said, with a wistful look at Ollie's orb. It was unlikely that he would ever get a chance to try one but he needed to find answers in this strange place, and this seemed like a good way to start.

It was late afternoon before Flint appeared, shouting for Xander from the front hall. Ollie and Xander shot through from the kitchen in response to the terse bellow, while Len hung precariously over the banister from the first floor, looking curious. Flint was customarily taciturn and clearly in a hurry.

'I've briefed the Wardens about what happened yesterday and they want to see you,' he told Xander brusquely. 'They don't want to draw attention, so you'll come over tomorrow night.'

Xander stared at him, questions brimming up in his mind. 'What are Wardens?'

'Leaders,' said Flint. 'They're the authority amongst the Travellers.'

'Do they know why I'm here?' asked Xander.

'No,' said Flint. 'That's what they want to find out.'

That sounded rather ominous, but before Xander could ask any more questions, Flint began rooting in the capacious pockets of his sleeveless jacket and produced a metallic band. 'This is for you,' he said, holding it out. With a surge of excitement, Xander took it and examined the stone. It was just like the one Ollie wore around his wrist, a pale yellow crystal with faint silvery lines of coding glittering at its heart.

'People would wonder if you don't have one, and we don't want you standing out or drawing any notice, particularly as Thea insists that you be allowed to prance around all over Haven,' Flint's tone made quite clear what he thought of that idea. 'It's been deactivated, of course. You've no idea how to use one and we don't need any more explosions in this house.' His disapproving gaze rested on Ollie, who grinned unrepentantly and shrugged.

Xander ignored this by-play, disappointment smothering his anticipation of only a moment ago. He laid the orb across his wrist, thinking that Flint seemed determined to remove any possibility of fun from Xander's experience in Haven. Flint himself shook his head ruefully at Ollie, as Xander fumbled with the strap.

'At some point I really need to sit down with you and try

to get to the bottom of –'

He broke off mid-sentence in shock. Xander had succeeded in joining the two ends of the strap with a smooth click and, as soon as the band had closed around his wrist, beams of arcing light shot across the hallway, scorching the walls and ceilings. Len dropped flat to the floor just before a streak of crackling light sliced right through where she had been standing. Instantly, Flint grabbed Ollie's arm and dragged him down.

'Get it off,' Flint snarled. 'Get it off *now*.'

'I'm trying,' gasped Xander, struggling with the band with shaking fingers. Another huge beam exploded upwards, blowing a hole in the ceiling. Finally, Xander managed to detach the band and, panicking, threw it down the hallway. As soon as it was off his wrist, the streaks of destructive light stopped, but the stone itself continued to burn brighter and brighter, until it was too intense to see. There was an audible popping sound, and the blaze vanished. When Xander risked a look, the stone was wreathed in smoke.

For a few seconds, the only sounds in the hallway were the gasping breaths of the three huddled on the ground, while Xander himself stood petrified, staring at the stone lying in the middle of a scorch-mark on the floor. Flint was the first to pull himself to his feet. His voice was quiet and stunned. 'What did you *do?*'

'I –I didn't,' stammered Xander. 'I swear, I didn't do anything. I only put it on and it went berserk.' His voice trailed away as he took in the blackened marks on the wall. He felt sick.

Flint shook his head and cautiously approached the band lying, apparently quiescent, on the stone flags of the floor. He nudged it with the toe of his boot and, when there was no reaction, he bent and gingerly picked it up. Len and Ollie got to their feet, Len wincing as she saw the banister next to her neatly sliced through. Speechless, they stared at Xander.

'I am so sorry,' he blurted, feeling his cheeks burning. 'I don't know what happened.'

Unexpectedly, Ollie's face broke into an enormous grin as he turned around slowly, taking in the charred walls and the smoking hole blown through the ceiling.

'Now *this*,' he announced, 'is what I call a *proper* explosion.'

Len spluttered and even Xander's face broke into a tentative smile.

The front door opened, and Mrs Stanton walked in, a well-filled shopping basket on her arm. It crashed to the ground, sending vegetables and cheeses rolling in every direction. She stood open-mouthed, taking in the devastation, before her wide eyes shot to Ollie.

'Oliver! What did you do?'

Ollie grinned, delighted. 'Would you believe that it actually wasn't me this time? This is the work of a real expert.'

'It wasn't Ollie,' said Xander, shamefaced. 'I'm afraid it was me. I'm really sorry – I didn't mean to.'

'You, Xander? But how?' asked Mrs Stanton, bewildered.

'That is certainly the question,' said Flint, holding out the orb to Mrs Stanton's startled gaze. The band itself was charred and brittle-looking, and the stone was now grey, with black striations. The coding was completely burned out. 'You didn't try to re-activate it?' he asked, with a penetrating look at Xander.

'I wouldn't even know how,' Xander protested and Flint looked away with a frown.

'In the meantime, who's going to fix this?' demanded Mrs Stanton. 'If I wanted an en-suite to my bedroom, it wouldn't be the downstairs hallway.'

As it turned out, to Xander's relief, Ollie's mother was able to repair it all with relative ease. She had laughed when she had seen the destruction and affectionately ruffled her son's hair. 'Makes a nice change,' she said, with an easy smile at Xander. 'It's quite refreshing to fix the damage someone else's son has done.'

Ollie contented himself with pulling a face at his mother, and then disappeared upstairs before his grandmother could find something useful for him to do, but Xander hung around. He still felt guilty about the damage, not to mention very curious how the diminutive woman was going to repair the large and heavy looking beams in the ceiling that had been blasted into smithereens. The hole was at least four feet wide and, to Xander's eyes, looked fairly irreparable.

Jenna Stanton smiled at him reassuringly.

'Don't look so worried,' she said. 'I know it looks bad but really it's pretty straightforward. Do you want to help?' Xander nodded and Jenna pushed open the front door. 'Come on, then.'

She led the way across the garden, veering to the left until they were walking under the eaves of the great forest that surrounded the house. After a moment she stopped and bent down to pick up a large branch lying on the ground in front of her. She tapped it with her fingers and nodded in satisfaction before turning to Xander.

'We need about ten branches like this. These trees are hardwood, so they'll work, but we need the branch to be long and with no rot. This one is perfect, but we need more like it.'

Xander nodded and headed off under the trees, looking for likely wood. Within a short time, he had found several possibilities and carried them back to Jenna. Two were rejected, but the rest passed muster and Xander piled them with the ones Jenna had found.

'Perfect,' she said. 'And now to work.'

She walked back to the house, the branches tucked under her arm, and stood in the hallway gazing upwards. 'The technique I'm going to use is a trade secret common to two of the great guilds, the Agricultural Association and the Constructionist Guild. We in the A.A. believe that we pioneered it with our grafts of living wood, while the Constructionists claim it was their invention to meld beams and mend holes.' Her eyes twinkled at Xander. 'Obviously we are correct and they're not.'

Five of the branches, all different shapes and of varying widths, floated into the air and positioned themselves across the large hole so that each branch touched the shattered ends of the damaged beams. It looked ridiculous and Xander smothered a small smile. Jenna glanced over with a quick understanding grin.

'Now watch,' she said and lifted her orb-hand, her fingers moving in a weaving pattern.

Initially Xander's attention was caught by the orb itself and he watched, intrigued, as the silver lines of coding began to glimmer in rapid, repetitive patterns inside the amber stone, their flickering lights making the orb appear to sparkle. It was captivating and strangely beautiful, and for a moment Xander was so absorbed that he did not notice what was happening with the wood.

When he raised his eyes to look, his mouth dropped open. Each branch was changing, untwisting and straightening itself, and thickening to match the great beams on either side. They expanded in surges, with wood fibres sprouting along the branch and then weaving themselves together until they were as solid as the original wood. When each branch was as wide and straight as the beams they were adjoining, Jenna turned her attention to the ends, and sprouting filaments reached out to entwine with other fibres which extended from the original girders. To Xander, watching open—mouthed, it appeared that almost no time had elapsed until the additions were only discernible from the original wood by their paler colour. Jenna lowered her hand with a sigh of satisfaction and glanced over at Xander.

'What do you think?' she asked. 'Pretty good, huh?'

'It's amazing,' said Xander, awed. 'It's completely fixed.'

'Almost,' said Jenna. 'It only needs a coat of plaster down here and I'll need to fix the floorboards upstairs with the rest of this.' She nudged the other branches with her toe. 'I actually rather enjoy doing this – it's quite relaxing, but don't say that to Ollie. He doesn't need any more encouragement to blow things up.'

She smiled at Xander in a conspiratorial way and he laughed. Just at that moment a loud clanging noise erupted from the kitchen, and Xander heard two thuds from upstairs and the sound of pounding footsteps. Katie emerged through the kitchen door, swinging a large handbell with a gleeful expression, as Ollie and Len came racing down the stairs. Ollie was a shade behind and tried to catch up by swinging himself around the large stair post at the bottom, but only succeeded in tripping as he tried to avoid the large pile of branches.

'Honestly, you two,' said Jenna, exasperated. 'You're not five anymore, you know. And I think you might stop ringing that bell now, Katie, before we're all deafened.'

Her words were tart but her face lit into a sudden smile as she hunted them all into the kitchen. Xander shot into his seat at the table next to Ollie, laughing, while Katie squealed as her mother caught her before tickling her into her seat. As the rich savoury smell of the large pie which Mrs Stanton was serving filled the kitchen, Len passed Xander a dish piled high with buttered carrots and green beans while James Stanton put tall jugs of a clear sparkling drink on the table, and grinned at Xander and Ollie as he passed by them. Only a day ago, Xander had sat at this same table, exhausted, confused and feeling utterly out of place in this world. Now, as he filled his plate with food and handed on the platters, while Len pulled a face at him across the table, he felt unexpectedly the first tentative strands of belonging.

CHAPTER FOUR

After his disaster of the previous afternoon, Xander was fully prepared for Mrs Stanton to have changed her mind about taking him along to the orb fitting, but that thought did not seem to have occurred to her. She tapped at the boys' bedroom door the next morning and then entered briskly, with an armful of clothes which she deposited on the table by his bed after a swift, disapproving stare around the room.

'Here you are, Xander,' she said. 'You can't keep re-wearing those clothes, so Jenna picked these up for you yesterday. Put yours in the washing basket, if you can find it in all this mess.'

She fished a cushion out from under a pile of trousers on the floor and threw it with perfect aim at the top of Ollie's head, buried under his covers.

'Wha –?' he grumbled, peering out with his hair on end. 'What's that for?'

'This tip,' retorted his grandmother. 'I expect to see it cleared up by tonight, and I *will* be checking. How you can live like this, I just don't know. Goodness only knows what's under this mess.'

Tutting to herself, she left the room and Ollie sat up in bed, looking around him with an air of puzzlement.

'It's not that bad,' he said, after a full perusal. 'You can still see quite a lot of the floor.' He crossed to the door, hopping over various piles of belongings, and grinned at Xander. 'Could be a lot worse.'

After Ollie had shot off to the bathroom, Xander turned to examine the clothes Mrs Stanton had left for him. They were much like the ones he had seen Ollie wear, plain trousers in dark blue and green, and various shirts in neutral colours. A long, intricately woven belt curled on top of the pile, and there was also a collection of underwear and socks. Jenna had not provided any shoes but, after the ministrations of the brownies, his grey trainers looked better than they had since they were new. They had followed their emergency first aid in the kitchen with what had evidently been some in-depth work overnight, and the trainers were now neatly mended, clean and re-coloured. Xander shook his head in amazement as he examined them before getting dressed in his new clothes.

'Looking good,' said Ollie as he re-entered the room. 'No-one will guess you're an illegal outlander now.'

Xander laughed. 'Not until I open my mouth and show my total ignorance of everything,' he said.

Ollie shrugged.

'Nah,' he said. 'We'll soon get you up to speed and you're just a kid – it's not like people will be interrogating you.'

Xander thought rather uneasily about the upcoming meeting with the Wardens; that had sounded uncomfortably close to an interrogation to him, but he decided to worry about it later. Breakfast followed, with Katie bouncing with excitement and anticipation about getting her first orb.

'By supper time I'll be able to clear the whole table by myself and lev everything to the sink,' she declared to the room at large. 'I'll do it all for you every single day.'

'Lev?' queried Xander under his breath to Ollie.

'Levitate,' replied Ollie, before adding in a louder voice. 'It's not actually as easy as that, Katie.'

His sister brushed aside his words of caution with an airy wave of her hand and Len rolled her eyes, but restrained from saying anything.

A short time afterwards, Mrs Stanton and Xander were walking down the lane towards Wykeham as Katie danced along in front. It was another sunny morning with only a few wisps of clouds overhead, and the air was fresh and fragrant. Xander looked around with interest as they walked. The last time he had passed this way, he had been so tired and overwhelmed that it had almost seemed like a dream. This time, however, he could appreciate the countryside they walked through.

The lane wound between hedges, interspersed with trees, while flowers starred the grass on either side; yellow narcissus and buttercups, white daisies, pink mallows, dog roses and tall, swaying foxgloves all blended their scents together. Heavy bees, humming gently, were busy about their work and many-coloured butterflies flitted from bloom to bloom, while Xander caught the occasional flash of white from a rabbit's tail, doubtless startled by Katie's energetic dance down the lane. As they began to enter the more populous part of the track, Xander heard the odd, 'Good morning' called out from a window or a front garden. Mrs Stanton replied cordially, but did not pause to chat, leaving Xander to twist his head to try to catch sight of the inhabitants of Haven. He was still rather expecting to see more creatures from fable and legend, but the glimpses he caught were of perfectly ordinary-looking people.

Mrs Stanton did not let up her brisk pace until they stood once again on the green turf in front of the incongruous stone arch with 'London' carved into its apex, the worn letters showing its age. Katie didn't hesitate for a moment, passing under the arch and vanishing into thin air, and Mrs Stanton followed after her. Xander shook his head, a little incredulous that being propelled inexplicably through space was beginning to feel commonplace to him, and then took the two steps that would take him through the arch.

The great space filled with the cloisters of linked arches had been almost empty the last time Xander stood in it, but at this hour in the morning it was busier. There were crowds of people everywhere, passing through and emerging from the many arches. Here in the city, Xander finally saw more of the non-human residents of Haven, and his eyes were wide as he tried to take everything in.

A family of giants, father, mother, and two children who were bigger than many human adults, passed through one of the larger arches, while a group of small creatures with squashy features and large, long-fingered hands materialised through one arch, pulling large trolleys behind them, before turning and disappearing through another. 'Gnomes', supplied the voice of his childhood memories and he watched them in fascination.

Mrs Stanton had paused to wait for him, obviously concerned that he might get lost, and Xander turned and followed her, trying not to gape as they threaded their way through the crowds and headed for a wide street opening out ahead. A young woman walked past, her head bent to speak to the small children holding her hands, with bags of groceries bobbing behind her like ducklings following their mother. She must have sensed Xander's awed stare because she glanced over and Xander quickly looked away, realising that it would seem odd to gawk at something that was clearly so commonplace. Certainly no one else appeared to think there was anything odd about self-supporting shopping.

They entered the busy street where tall shady trees lined the stone pavement, and store fronts opened out between grand, official-looking buildings, some of which had elaborate name-plates. Slowing his steps, Xander could make out the words on several of them. 'Guild of Jewellers' stated an ornate sign next to a heavy-looking door covered with a wrought-iron grille, while from the building marked 'Musicians' Institute' swirling melodies floated down from the open windows, strange but compelling to Xander's ears. There was so much to see that Xander only belatedly realised that Mrs Stanton had stopped again, looking for him.

'Come on, Xander, keep up,' she called when she spotted him, although her smile was understanding.

Xander jogged to catch up with them. 'Where do we get the orb from?' he asked curiously. Given his experiences so far, he half-expected to be told that they were heading for some underground lair, where glowing stones were extracted by more mythical creatures from his childhood bedtime stories.

Mrs Stanton gave him a quick sideways smile as if she guessed what he was thinking.

'From the shop, dear,' she replied. 'Right over there.'

She gestured with her free hand, the other being clutched by an over-excited Katie, who was doing a funny half-gallop in her excitement. Xander looked over and saw enormous glass windows glittering with light, extending the entire width of a large and imposing edifice.

'Thorne Store,' he read aloud, looking at the tastefully glimmering sign.

'That whole building belongs to Thorne Industries,' said Mrs Stanton. 'It's all owned by Perrin Thorne, a grossly unpleasant man. He made his name by inventing the coding for synthetic orbs, which could be manufactured cheaply, and used far more easily than traditional ones. He revolutionised the market almost overnight and made a fortune in the process, then he married the only daughter of the Larcius family, one of the Twelve. No question what that match was based on, on either side,' Mrs Stanton sniffed. 'He calls himself 'Larcius-Thorne' now.'

Xander was only half-listening, mesmerised by the displays in the store window. Orbs of every colour glowed softly on glass shelves, the glitter of their coding subtly illuminated by strategically-angled lights. Many orbs were displayed unmounted, the most beautiful revolving slowly so that their inner facets sent shivering lights across the pristine white backdrops. Others were mounted, ranging from simple and utilitarian-looking bands to wonderfully ornate bracelets, so intricate that they were like pieces of jewellery.

Mrs Stanton smiled indulgently at the sight of Xander and Katie with their noses almost pressed against the glass of the shop window. 'You know, there are even more if you go inside,' she said, ushering them both towards the door, before laying a hand on Xander's arm. 'It would probably be safer if you don't touch any orbs this time, dear. We don't want any awkward questions, or explosions.' Her expression was sympathetic, but firm.

Xander nodded, suppressing a flash of disappointment, as Katie shot into the shop with an excited squeak. He held the door open for Mrs Stanton, who nodded her thanks as she swept through. Her air of unconscious distinction took no time to have an effect; almost instantly a smartly dressed salesman appeared at her elbow.

'May I help you?' he enquired, with a quick glance at Xander. He recovered himself at once as Mrs Stanton propelled the still bouncing Katie forwards.

'Yes, you may,' she said briskly. 'My granddaughter requires her first training band.'

'Of course,' said the man, smiling in a rather patronising way at Katie. 'Please come this way and we'll begin the fitting process.'

Xander trailed over behind them, curious as to what this entailed. The man handed Katie up onto a stool beside one of the gleaming glass countertops that ringed the store, and then reached beneath it, drawing out a smooth, silvery tablet. It had two hand-shaped indentations in the surface and when he tapped it on the side, it began to emit a blue glow. The man placed it on the counter in front of Katie.

'Please put your hands on the tablet, palms down, for the assessment process,' he instructed. Katie, looking very solemn and self-important, placed her hands as instructed and waited expectantly. As Xander watched, the man glanced over at him again and Xander tried to look bored, as if he had seen it all many times. Katie began to giggle, as the light bloomed around her fingers, swirling up and down.

'That tickles,' she said.

'Try to stay still,' cautioned the man, but he gave Mrs Stanton an indulgent smile, obviously not wanting to offend a customer. At last, the lights stopped pulsing and faded away, and the man glanced at a flat screen mounted under the countertop. 'Excellent. You can move your hands now.' He tapped twice on the tablet and it went blank. 'Your coding will be ready in just a minute,' he said, sliding the tablet back under the counter. 'The training orbs are on display over there,' he gestured towards a section glimmering with orbs in every shade of yellow, and then indicated more displays on the other side of the store, 'and you'll find all of our mounting choices over there. I'll leave you to decide but don't hesitate to call me if you need assistance.'

With another ingratiating smile at Mrs Stanton, he helped

Katie down off her stool and moved back behind the counter, to wait until they called him. Katie danced off towards the displays, beside herself with excitement. As they turned to follow her, Xander took the opportunity to whisper to Mrs Stanton.

'What does that tablet thing do?'

Mrs Stanton glanced back at the salesman to make sure he was not in earshot.

'I'm not familiar with all of the technical details, but in essence it analyses your own particular makeup to tailor the coding to you personally. Traditional orbs, like the Travellers use, are often passed down in families but the synthetic orbs are only useful to the person they've been coded to.' Her voice broke off as she spotted Katie, who had ignored the more utilitarian yellow stones and was staring, entranced, at a display of giant, gaudy pink orbs. 'I'd better head over. I think some guidance is required.'

'Look at that one,' Katie bubbled with delight, pointing at a mauve monstrosity on an ornate silver band, studded with what looked like little diamonds.

'Vulgar and completely unnecessary,' Mrs Stanton said and steered her firmly back to the training orbs.

After a few moments of watching Katie wrestle with the choice of colour, wavering between lemon yellow, tawny or pale straw, while Mrs Stanton tried to be patient, Xander wandered off to look around the store. He saw the salesman's eyes flicking over to him every now and then, but ignored the scrutiny as he looked through the different collections of orbs, each colour available in many different shades and sizes. They were all highly polished, sparkling with relentless intensity in the clean, bright lighting of the store and, as Katie continued to vacillate, Xander felt the faint twinges of an incipient headache.

He glanced out of the window, through the glittering display, and saw a little side-street across the road. A plain wooden sign hung from the wall on the right hand side, swinging gently back and forth in the slight breeze. Driven by a sudden urge to get out of the shop, Xander went looking for Mrs Stanton.

'Do you mind if I go outside for a bit?' he asked. 'I won't go far, just across the road to get some fresh air.'

Mrs Stanton nodded, looking fraught. 'Yes, do,' she said. 'We'll meet you in Fountain Square, to the right of here up the road.' She appeared rather as though she would like to escape along with Xander.

Xander pushed open the tall glass door and the sense of being suffocated began to fade as he breathed in the fresh air. After a moment's hesitation, he crossed the street and walked into the alleyway, heading for the little shop he had spotted from the store. As he approached, he was struck by the contrast to the place he had left, from the simple hand-painted wooden sign declaring 'Hob's Orbs' to the narrow timber-framed window. Behind the dusty glass sat a wooden mannequin of a wizened little figure with pointed ears and bright yellow eyes, slowly and jerkily twisting the dials of a peculiar metal contraption. Revolving in the heart of the machine was an unpolished, pale-coloured crystal.

Xander wrestled for a moment between curiosity and the certain knowledge that Flint would be annoyed with him for wandering into strange shops. Curiosity won, and he pushed the door open. He heard a bell ring in the distance, but paused in the doorway, wondering if he had made a mistake. There was no merchandise here, nor anything else to indicate that it was a shop. There were no windows, other than the one blocked by the mannequin display, but the room was cosily lit by lamps on the wall and the firestones glimmering in the hearth. Drawn up around the fireplace were several squashy-looking chairs, while the only other furniture was a large desk covered with strange implements and unevenly-shaped lumps of rock. Xander was strongly reminded of the office of a friend of his mother's, a professor of geology.

He was still hesitating by the entrance when a heavy, metal-clad door at the back of the room swung open, and a small figure emerged in a cloud of fine, white dust. Some of the dust came from the little man's oversized leather apron, which trailed almost to his feet and was secured by a wide belt wrapped round and round his waist, but most of it was billowing out of the open door behind him. The man had the same pale skin, ruddy cheeks and sharply-pointed ears as the mannequin in the window, and clutched in his small fist was the orb that Xander had destroyed the day before. Xander's attention was so transfixed by the strange little man that it took him a moment to notice Flint, standing behind the small figure with an exasperated expression on his face.

Xander opened his mouth to speak, but breathed in a lungful of the fine dust and immediately doubled over in a helpless fit of coughing and sneezing. When he had caught his breath and wiped his streaming eyes, the little man had removed his apron and was hanging it on a hook on the door to the back room. He locked the door with a grimace.

'Apologies,' he said in a cold, raspy voice. 'I always forget that the dust is unpleasant if you are not accustomed to it.'

Flint had folded his arms and leant back against the metal-clad door. He did not appear remotely affected by the dust. 'Is it a compulsion with you?' he enquired. 'This inability to actually stay where you're supposed to be?'

Xander shrugged, keeping his eyes trained on the burnt-out orb; he didn't think Flint really expected an answer. The little man glanced between them, and then looked more closely at Xander. He stiffened and lifted his head, the nostrils in his long, pointed nose flaring as if he was catching some elusive scent.

'*You* did this.' It was not a question. Flint made an impatient movement, but the little man ignored him. His eyes burnt into Xander, taking in every aspect of his appearance. It was an uncomfortable sensation and Xander shuffled his feet, glancing at Flint who remained still, his face impassive.

Xander nodded reluctantly. 'I didn't mean to, though. It was an accident.'

'Please?' The little man's eyes were gleaming as he gestured for Xander to sit by the desk. They were a darker shade of yellow than the garish painted eyes on the wooden mannequin, but still like no eye colour that Xander had ever seen before, and there was something else strange about them, something he couldn't quite identify. Unsure, Xander looked to Flint for some indication whether he should do as he was asked, but the Traveller had walked over to the fireplace and leaned casually against the wall, half-withdrawing himself into the shadows. Xander assumed that meant he should go along with the request, and sat down in the proffered chair. Once he was sitting face to face with the little man, Xander realised with a shock what had been bothering him. The pupils of the curious yellow eyes were not round like his own but slitted, like a cat, making the man's face seem suddenly predatory and irredeemably strange. Xander gave an involuntary shiver.

'You have not seen my kind before,' said the man, a slight smile playing about his lips which did not make Xander feel any more comfortable. 'Interesting.' There was a clear insinuation in his words and he glanced over his shoulder at Flint, who didn't react. 'We are hobgoblins, the most powerful of goblin-kind. Orbs, and the mineral cores that power them, originated in our knowledge of, and our connection to, the deep earth. But of course, as a child of Haven, you would know this.' The implication was stronger now, and Xander flushed. 'You may call me Hob. And what shall I call you?'

'Xander. Xander King,' Xander replied. He watched uneasily as the hobgoblin repeated his name silently, his lips twisting as if he were tasting it.

'Hold out your hands, please. Palms up,' Hob instructed.

Xander was thoroughly unnerved now, and he suspected that was exactly how the hobgoblin wanted him to feel. He hesitated, and then thrust his hands out in front of him. He had wondered whether the hobgoblin would comment on the bandage on his left hand or react to the wound in the same way that Tavish had done in Mistleberry, but Hob simply reached out with his own thin hands and held them above Xander's palms, his face intent.

Xander frowned. 'Do you use those tablet things?' he asked. He wished he hadn't spoken when the hobgoblin's head snapped up, a contemptuous gleam in his eyes.

'Human props,' he growled, his voice like a rusty nail. 'My kind does not require such foolishness.'

He looked for a moment as though he might add something else, but then bent his head back down to concentrate on the almost-joining of their hands. For a moment, nothing happened and Xander wished he had the nerve to ask what was going on, but the silence was too oppressive. Then, in a rush of sensation, Xander felt a sharp tingling in his palms and a second later the space between his hands and the small hovering ones of the hobgoblin filled with a pale, pulsing light. The feeling was not comfortable and clearly nothing like the 'tickling' that Katie had giggled over. Xander shifted in his chair, looking up at the hobgoblin's face, which was twisted with the obvious effort he was expending.

'Remain still,' rasped Hob. He continued in a lower tone, as if to himself. 'You are difficult to read.'

The prickling in Xander's palms increased and then spread, the uncomfortable sensation sweeping up his arms to his shoulders and neck, then along his spine. It crawled on relentlessly until it reached the base of his skull where it halted, as if it could go no further. Xander held himself rigid, his teeth gritted as he battled the urge to snatch his hands away and itch them. Looking around for some distraction, Xander noticed Flint leaning forward, watching this process with a face almost as intent as the hobgoblin. Finally, just as Xander decided that he could not stand the crawling sensation in his neck any longer, it stopped and the hobgoblin withdrew his hands.

'Interesting,' he grated under his breath. When he glanced up, he seemed almost surprised to see Xander and Flint both staring at him.

'So?' demanded Flint. 'What's your assessment?'

He shouldered away from the wall and walked over to the table, towering over the diminutive hobgoblin. Hob looked up at him, his expression closed and unreadable, and then moved to the other side of the table. His hand hovered over its contents for a moment before picking up an uncut crystal and stroking it.

'I think,' he said slowly, his eyes never leaving Xander, 'that I wish to consider this.'

Flint's eyes narrowed. 'That's not exactly helpful,' he growled.

For once, Xander found himself in agreement with Flint's irritation. He was growing very tired of being kept in the dark about things which obviously concerned him. The hobgoblin looked over at Flint, his eyes hooded and secretive.

'Helpful,' he repeated, rolling the word around his tongue as if it was distasteful. 'Speculation and unconsidered thoughts are unwise. I will speak no further now.' His tone was firm and quite final.

Flint opened his mouth but whatever he had planned to say was abruptly interrupted. The orb on his wrist flared with light, and began chiming frantically. Flint lifted his arm and brushed the glowing orb with his fingertips; the next moment, to Xander's surprise, Ari's voice rang out in the silent room.

'Flint, we've got a situation. I'm heading over now.'

'Where?' Flint was all business now.

'At the ford,' she said.

'On my way,' Flint snapped. The glow disappeared from his orb and he swung around to Xander. 'You, get back to Thea and stop wandering around before you get into more trouble.' Without waiting to see Xander's response, he turned to the hobgoblin, who had been silently watching. 'We'll continue this discussion later,' he warned, before his eyes flicked back to Xander. 'Why are you still here? Move.'

Almost before the sound of his last word faded, Flint's orb had flared once more and he disappeared.

Xander glanced at the hobgoblin, in time to catch him staring with a speculative glint in his eyes.

'Well,' he said. 'I'd better, um –'

He swallowed and gestured awkwardly to the door.

The hobgoblin nodded, his thin, callused fingers still stroking the stone in his hand with an odd gentleness. His cold, strange eyes never left Xander's face.

'Indeed,' he agreed, his voice a low rasp. 'You should go. Be careful, Xander King. This is a dangerous place for one such as you.' He turned away and sat down by the fireplace. It was clearly a dismissal.

Xander emerged, blinking, into the street, his eyes taking a moment to adjust to the bright morning light after the dimly-lit shop. Feeling rather unnerved, Xander decided that he had better heed Flint's instruction to rejoin Mrs Stanton. He turned into the main thoroughfare but, as he did so, he couldn't help wondering whether the hobgoblin had meant his last comment as a warning, or a threat.

Following Mrs Stanton's earlier instruction, Xander followed the broad street up to where it opened out into a large square. With a sudden shock of recognition, he realised that he was right back at the place where he had arrived in Haven only two days before, although in some ways it felt to Xander like a lifetime had passed. It was as busy as he remembered, and he looked around at the massive, stately buildings that bounded it, with their huge doors and ornate windows.

A moment later he started as a light hand touched his shoulder and turned to find Mrs Stanton behind him. Katie promptly held up her wrist with a proud smile, as she displayed a lemon yellow orb, and Xander quickly assumed an impressed expression as she twisted it so that the sunshine made it sparkle.

'It's beautiful,' he told her, as Mrs Stanton's eyes twinkled at him. 'I think that's definitely the best yellow.'

'Isn't it?' she said, in deep satisfaction. 'I'm going to practice and practice so that I can surprise Ollie and Len when they get home.'

'Excellent idea,' said Mrs Stanton. She turned to Xander and pointed across the square, drawing his attention to one of the enormous buildings, with a line of closed doors across the front. 'Speaking of which, that building over there is the Academy, Xander. If you ever want to meet Ollie from school, you just wait at the bottom of the steps there.'

She gave Xander a moment to look and then turned back to the way they had come. 'Time to head home now, however,' she said. 'I'm expecting a couple of patients soon and I also want to have a quick check on that injury of yours, Xander, and make sure it's healing up.'

'And I have a lot of practicing to do with my orb,' added Katie, importantly.

Mrs Stanton met Xander's eye again, with a suppressed smile, as they walked back towards the gates. As they passed the little side-street where the hob's shop lay, Xander could not help his gaze lingering on the gently swinging sign, with a shiver for the strangeness of the occupant and his foreboding words.

Back at Woodside, Mrs Stanton drew Xander into her little dispensary again, leaving Katie sitting at the kitchen table clutching her orb hand and staring fixedly at a teaspoon with a determined frown on her face.

Xander wrinkled his nose as the bandage came off, and risked a quick peek at his palm. The gel that Mrs Stanton had treated it with on his arrival was obviously remarkable, as he had not felt even the smallest twinge of pain since, but he wasn't sure whether the abrasion would still look as gory. The gel had turned to a faint pink but, as Mrs Stanton gently cleaned it off, it was clear Xander's palm had healed dramatically. His skin was still swollen and red-tinged, but there was no more blood and Mrs Stanton made approving noises as she examined it.

'Excellent,' she said. 'You obviously heal up well, Xander.

This doesn't even require a dressing now, although you'll need to be careful with it until it's fully healed.' She turned Xander's hand towards the window, and then smiled at him. 'You're going to have a rather interesting scar there, however.'

She released him and chose some phials of colourful liquids and powders from her shelves. 'I'll mix you up a salve to complete the healing process and I want you to dab it on your palm in the morning and before you go to bed, okay?'

She glanced over at Xander, who nodded in response before turning back to his own examination of his hand. Mrs Stanton was right; amidst the redness of the newly-healed skin shone a pale starburst of the same silvery scars as Xander had seen on the twisted wreck of Alvin Tavish's face, and running down the side of Flint's cheek. He frowned, remembering old Tavish's claim that he could sense the shade-strike, and wondered what Flint would say when he saw the mark.

He was still pondering on that when Mrs Stanton handed him a small pot of salve and they went back out to the kitchen, where Katie was now glaring at the immobile teaspoon lying inoffensively in front of her. As they watched, she lifted her wrist to examine the orb, and then shook it with a professional air, before squinting furiously at the spoon again. Xander heard Mrs Stanton choke quietly behind him. At the same moment, Katie swung around on her chair.

'Graaan,' she wailed. 'My orb doesn't work.'

Mrs Stanton exchanged looks with Xander and then took a deep breath, before pulling up a seat beside Katie at the table. 'It works perfectly well, dear,' she said calmly. 'It just takes concentration and a great deal of practice.'

Katie pouted and Xander grinned to himself, before heading out of the kitchen. He had a strong suspicion that this practise session would take quite some time.

'C'mon, you lot, we're leaving now.'

The loud voice from the hallway echoed up the stairs and Xander looked up from the reference book he had found on the floor in Ollie's room. After the uncomfortable scene with the hobgoblin earlier he had decided that it would be better if he tried to educate himself about Haven, so he would be less likely to do or say things that immediately identified him as an outlander. This book had seemed like a good start but he was still finding it rather jarring to read a scholarly tome that covered seriously such topics as, *'the role of pixie pollination in agricultural advancement'* and *'gnome economics'*.

'Where are we going?' Xander asked, as Ollie shoved his chair back from the cluttered desk where he had been dashing through his homework.

'Dunno,' Ollie replied. 'But it'll be better than doing this stuff. Who cares about the legal history of the guilds anyway?'

Xander grinned sympathetically, although privately he thought Haven's history was far more interesting than his own lessons with Mr Tubner.

The two boys thundered down the stairs and found Len already waiting in the hallway, her hair neatly brushed and a mutinous expression on her face. Mrs Stanton bustled out of the kitchen, shepherding Katie.

'Are you sure you don't want someone to come and fetch you later, Jenna?' she called.

Jenna Stanton poked her head around the door.

'That's kind but don't worry, Thea. I could do with a bit of peace and quiet to catch up on my paperwork.' Her eyes flickered over Ollie, Len and Xander standing in the hall and she smiled. 'Be good and enjoy the Gathering, kids. Don't forget to look after Xander, Ollie.' She disappeared back into the kitchen, leaving Ollie beaming.

'A Gathering tonight?' He turned to his grandmother to confirm. 'Awesome.'

'Hardly,' muttered Len. 'Can't I just stay here with Jenna?'

Mrs Stanton clucked her tongue as she swept them all along in her energetic wake. 'Of course not,' she said. 'Sitting stewing in your bedroom is not a healthy use of your time.'

Len's snort was lost in the shuffle of getting out of the front door, where Ari was waiting for them in the garden, her red hair ablaze in the low evening sun. Her freckles seemed more numerous than ever in the rich golden light and her eyes danced as she walked over to them.

'Ready?' she asked, in her lilting voice. She held out both hands towards them. 'Grab on then.'

Xander took a firm grasp of her wrist and screwed his eyes shut. He still found jumping unsettling, and he didn't like to think about what might happen if he lost his grip on Ari halfway through. When he opened his eyes again, staggering slightly, they were no longer in the Stantons' garden. Trunks of tall trees rose around them and the evening light filtered down through a thick canopy of leaves. In front of them, and looking quite incongruous in the middle of the forest floor, was an intricately-carved stone pillar, about waist high, from which a well-trodden path led away through the trees. Xander could hear the distinct murmur of many voices coming from that direction and a faint smell of wood-smoke wafted towards him. Ari headed for the path.

'Come on,' she said. 'We should clear out of the way. There may be other people trying to come through.'

Xander hurried to catch up with her.

'What was that stone?' he asked curiously. 'Is it like a Traveller's Stone?'

Ari glanced sideways at him, her smile flashing out again. 'I sometimes forget this is all new to you,' she said. 'That's just a way-marker. There's no power in it.'

'What's it for then?' asked Xander.

'It's a guide,' explained Ari. 'Did you see the carvings on it?' When she saw Xander nod, she continued. 'They're unique to the location. It means you can always find any Lodge, not to mention a convenient landing spot outside of the ward when you are jumping. Traveller kids learn the way-markers of every Lodge from when they are little, so that by the time they are capable of a jump they can always find their way. There was one at Mistleberry but it's so overgrown that you probably missed it.'

They broke out of the trees into an enormous clearing and Xander stopped to look around. It was like Mistleberry but much larger and without the air of desertion. The door of the main Lodge was thrown open, and the evening sun reflected off the many windows and the hanging lanterns between them. The grassy glade was full of brightly-hued marquees and tents, small and large, interspersed with many hearth-fires. Some of the hearths were metal braziers filled with the glowstones Xander had seen before, but a few of the bigger ones were burning real wood, sending pale swirls of grey smoke up into the evening sky and imbuing the air with a homely tang. People were everywhere, moving between the tents and the Lodge, sprawling on bright, woven rugs by the fires or sitting on low, carved wooden benches. Children raced about, bringing armfuls of branches and sticks from the surrounding woods to dump in piles by the bonfires, while others carried trays of food to the cooks bustling about long tables and braziers, from which the rich aromas of roasting meats were already rising. Glass globes, each with a glowstone inside, were suspended from the trees edging the glade and glimmered in pale gold and white, their illumination still faint in the summer evening light.

Ari was evidently popular among the younger ones, who called out cheerful greetings to her and beamed when she acknowledged them. Xander felt curious eyes observing him and hung back behind the Stantons as they entered the clearing, but Ari would have none of it. She grabbed his hand and pulled him forwards.

'You're with me,' she said firmly to him. 'It's fine. Come on, I'll introduce you.'

Xander allowed himself to be towed forward, and tried to ignore the stares and the whispering that grew in volume as he passed the various hearths. He finally looked up when Ari came to a halt by a large bonfire on the far side of the clearing. There were quite a number of people sitting around the fire, or standing chatting quietly. With a shock of recognition, Xander saw the white haired man from the British Museum standing near Flint and Ari headed straight over to him.

'Xander, meet Rafe,' she said, tugging Xander forwards, before releasing his hand. 'Rafe, this is Xander. He was at the museum, remember?'

The man smiled at Xander.

'How could I forget?' he said. 'It was a most memorable afternoon.'

Xander smiled somewhat uncertainly at him, not quite sure how to answer that. Ollie had already disappeared into the crowd but Len marched past him and sat cross-legged on a blue and yellow woven mat near the fire. Her expression was not particularly welcoming, but Xander saw the advantages of keeping a low profile and he joined her. A moment later he jerked as a feeling like soft feathers brushed his arm and, as he looked around, he met the cool pale gaze of the big black dog. It regarded him thoughtfully, one ear flicking towards him, a hint of the same challenge in its eyes that had drawn Xander to step into the unknown in the museum. Xander stared back just as solemnly and then smiled.

'Look what you got me into, dog,' he murmured to it. The dog ignored that, laying down beside him and resting its heavy head on his leg, before insistently nudging at his hand until he scratched behind its ears.

'Suse likes you.' Rafe was looking down with a little smile, but his eyes were thoughtful. 'That's unusual.'

He said nothing further but Xander felt obscurely comforted by the acceptance, even if it was only from a dog. Despite his hair providing some concealment as it flopped over his face, he could still see people out of the corner of his eyes, pointing him out to others or staring. Len provided no help as she sat glowering into the fire and Xander couldn't think of anything to say to her to start a conversation, so he bent his head lower and petted the dog's head. Several pairs of boots crossed Xander's eye line, and then stopped.

'There you are, Flint,' said a firm voice. Xander glanced up to see a tall figure looming over him, a couple of other men standing just behind. 'Wooten is looking for you. He wants an update on border security.'

Flint snorted. 'Really?' he asked, wryly. 'I thought there was no issue with security, or so he is maintaining, I hear.'

The other man laughed, his serious face lightening into a warm grin.

'You know Wooten. In his view there's nothing so bad that energetically ignoring it won't make go away,' he replied flippantly. 'However, old Tavish has been in his ear again and even Wooten can't stand up against that level of complaining.

Anyway, he wants to talk to you.'

The man glanced down, catching Xander watching him. His gaze flickered over Xander, quick and piercing, then back to Flint. 'This is the kid I've been hearing about?' he asked.

Despite his preference of avoiding attention, Xander disliked being talked about as if he wasn't there. He got to his feet, standing as tall as possible. The man had an aura of power and command about him that made Xander feel rather insignificant, but he lifted his chin and straightened his back, trying to look more confident than he felt. Flint's lips quirked as he glanced back and forth between the two of them.

'Meet Xander King,' he said. 'Xander, this is Kirrin Ledger, one of the Wardens of the Travellers, which makes him a very important person now.'

Ledger stuck out a hand. 'Ignore him,' he said, in a deadpan voice. 'I'm newly appointed to my position, as Flint will doubtless inform you; but, to be fair, he's always had issues with authority.'

Flint snorted derisively again but a grin tugged at his lips. Xander decided to ignore this by-play and shook the proffered hand, then the man looked intently at Xander's other hand.

'May I see?' he asked.

Silently, Xander held his left hand out and Ledger gripped it with both of his own, tilting it to examine in the light. The silvery, starburst pattern was becoming even clearer now that the redness and swelling were subsiding further.

'Shade-strike,' said Flint, laconically. 'But, as you see, not the usual result. Apparently, he managed to shield to some degree but he doesn't know how.'

Ledger released Xander's hand and eyed him with new interest. 'Unusual,' he agreed. 'Hopefully we'll be able to get to the bottom of that and why the kid is a shade-magnet, or so I hear.' Flint made a non-committal noise and Ledger gave him a straight look. 'There are questions being asked, of course,' he said coolly. 'It's very curious that an outlander kid has abilities only ever seen in Travellers. Do you have any family from Haven?' The question was abruptly shot at Xander, the man's gaze sharp and penetrating.

'No,' replied Xander. 'I never even heard of Haven before I came here.'

'As I said, curious,' said Ledger to Flint, and Xander got the impression that more was being silently communicated.

'There you are.' Ollie almost fell over Len's legs in his haste to reach Xander. He was also precariously balancing three plates piled high with food and might have tipped the lot over Len, if Flint had not reached out to balance him. 'I got us food. What are you doing hanging round here?' His voice tailed off, as he looked around the group, taking in the fact that he had clearly interrupted a serious conversation, and he flushed.

'Sorry, sir,' he said to Ledger, awkwardly. 'I didn't see you there.'

Ledger nodded, with a gracious smile. 'No problem,' he said. 'We're finished for now. You kids head off and eat.'

Relieved, Xander smiled weakly at him and, with a quick glance at Flint who was frowning at Ledger, he took the opportunity to escape.

'Bit awkward, that,' said Ollie, once they were safely out of earshot. 'What did the Warden want?'

'I don't know,' replied Xander, uneasily. 'He said that questions were being asked about why I can do things like Travel and asked if I have any family from Haven.'

'I s'pose it's only natural,' Ollie allowed. 'They're probably freaked out it's another case of the Olympics. That happened thousands of years ago and it's still held up as a cautionary tale among the Travellers.'

'The Olympics?' asked Xander, but Ollie just thrust a plate towards him. Len had followed behind them and reached out for her own, with a quick smile for her cousin.

'Feeling under-fed?' she queried, as she took in the large quantities of food piled up on the plates.

'C'mon,' Ollie said, ignoring the dig. 'Everyone's over here.'

He turned and headed towards the tree-line, over to another of the bonfires which was almost under the branches of the trees. There was a small crowd of shadowy figures sitting around it, and Xander realised that they were all around his own age, mostly boys but with some girls scattered through the group.

'Budge up,' said Ollie, as they approached.

'Hey, Stanton,' said one of the figures. 'Is this him?'

Xander resisted the urge to tip his head down, letting his hair conceal him from all of the eyes which seemed to be boring in on just him.

'This is Xander,' Ollie returned cheerfully. 'Xander, this is Zach, Milo, Tomas –'

His voice trailed off as he glanced around the crowd of figures. 'Well, anyway you'll never remember all the names at once. This is everyone.' He waved a nonchalant hand at the group, and then pulled Xander to sit down beside him. Xander smiled round weakly, feeling thoroughly uncomfortable under the intense scrutiny.

'So you're really an outlander?' asked one boy. Xander thought he was the one Ollie had identified as Zach. He just nodded, not sure what to say or how much to share about his background. As usual, he thought, Flint hadn't exactly given him any guidance.

'We've not been outside yet,' chimed in another voice from a thin, blond boy. 'They don't let us Travel until we're of age. You're not eighteen though.' His voice was faintly accusing and Ollie hastened to swallow his mouthful of food.

'That's not his fault, Milo,' he said. 'He was being chased by shades. Flint and Rafe said he had to use the Stone to escape and even then he still got shade-struck.' That got everyone's attention and the blond boy, Milo, looked slightly more impressed.

'Seriously?' he asked. 'Where'd they get you?'

For the second time that evening, Xander held out his palm for inspection. There was a moment's silence and then Milo frowned. 'That's not bad,' he said. 'I've seen way worse than that.'

'That's because he shielded,' retorted Ollie. 'The Wardens themselves can't figure out how he did it.'

'Really?' said the first boy, Zach, his expression mildly ribbing. 'Up on the inner workings of the Travellers, are you Stanton?'

His voice was not unkind but Xander was suddenly aware that there was an undercurrent of difference between these young Travellers and Ollie, who was as much of an outsider in his way as Xander. Ollie, however, seemed to take it all in good part.

'Yeah, yeah,' he said easily. 'Keep your secret Traveller mysteries – I just come for the food.' He took another enormous bite and, cheeks bulging, pulled a face at Zach who laughed.

'Did the Wardens speak to you yet?' asked the boy who Ollie had named as Tomas, staring pointedly at Xander. He was smaller than the others, with short dark hair and a sharp, inquisitive expression. 'I heard they thought that the rules had been broken again.'

Xander shrugged awkwardly. 'One of them just did,' he answered. 'He wanted to know if I had any family from here.'

'Do you?' interjected Zach.

'No,' replied Xander flatly. 'Not that I'm aware of, anyway.'

'What about Greece?' demanded Tomas quickly. When Xander shot him a confused look, shaking his head, there was a swift round of sniggering from the younger Travellers around the fire.

Ollie rolled his eyes and then turned to Xander.

'They're talking about the Olympics,' he began, but was immediately overridden by Milo.

'I'll tell it, I'll tell it,' he said insistently and Ollie shrugged, sitting back and letting Milo take centre stage. The blond boy lowered his voice, as the flickering light from the fire played over his face.

'It all happened thousands of years ago, but it was so terrible that we still speak of it in whispers to this day, and one of the Wardens' main jobs is to make sure it *never* happens again.'

'Melodramatic, much?' muttered someone, and there was another outbreak of laughter.

'Shh,' Milo said firmly, before continuing in a more normal tone of voice. 'Anyway, in those days there were far fewer controls on how often Travellers crossed the border or how long they stayed, and there was no proper supervision over what they were actually doing there. Today, we have strict rules on concealing ourselves with wards and never openly using power, but back then it was pretty unregulated. And that was how a group of Travellers got away with effectively living over the border and using their orbs to scare the outlanders into serving them and doing whatever they wanted.'

Milo looked at Xander with a foreboding expression, giving the impression that very dark things were going unsaid, but Xander just stared back at him without commenting, so the blond boy continued with his story.

'Apparently it went on for nearly six years before rumours began to reach the Wardens and they sent people over to investigate. It was a *massive* scandal and Zeus de Silva, Apollo Atherton, Aphrodite Edwards, Hera Hinxton and Ares Rolleston were all dragged back to Haven before a Wardens' tribunal, and had their orbs confiscated. They were banned from ever crossing the border again and thrown out of the Travellers, but unfortunately the damage was already done in terms of all the rumours started amongst the outlanders.'

This time Milo got all the reaction he wanted. Xander's mouth was hanging open, his eyes wide.

'Zeus and Apollo? You're talking about *the Greek gods*,' he gasped. 'The *Greek gods* were actually out-of-control Travellers?'

'You've heard of them?' asked Tomas, looking intrigued.

'Are you kidding me?' said Xander. 'We learn about them in school, although we're told that they were mythical.' He shook his head in bemusement.

'Wow, how weird,' said Milo. 'Anyway, the other rumour was that maybe they got a little too involved with the locals, and that there might have been children born who could have inherited Traveller abilities. They all vehemently denied it but still, that was the worry; hence the query about you having any relatives from the Mount Olympus vicinity.'

Xander gaped at him.

'How on earth would I know that? You're talking about thousands of years ago.'

'So, what happened to them after they were thrown out?'

asked Ollie curiously.

'Don't know about all of them,' said Milo. 'Ares Rolleston got involved with the Constructionist Guild, and ended up pioneering some new type of metal working. And, according to the stories, Aphrodite Edwards, who was stunningly beautiful, married into one of the Founding Families. Supposedly, it was the Melvilles and they have been anti-Traveller ever since because of her resentment about how she was treated.' He glanced over at Xander, a wicked smile dancing around his lips. 'So, no sudden and inexplicable urges to hurl lightning bolts, then?'

Before Xander could respond, a dark figure loomed up behind them. 'Xander? The Wardens want to see you now.'

Xander scrambled to his feet, as Ollie took his plate. Flint eyed the younger Travellers thoughtfully and then turned away without a word, leading Xander back between the various hearths and through the gauntlet of whispers, and sharp looks. They walked straight over to a hearth set up to the right of the Lodge, softly lit by lanterns hanging from the branches overhead, as well by as a metal brazier full of crystalline glowstones. Standing or sitting around the hearth were several shadowy figures, who all looked up as Xander followed Flint into the circle.

Xander recognised the tall figure of Kirrin Ledger, who gave him a quick nod, before Flint gestured towards a small, wooden stool. Sinking down onto it, Xander swallowed his nerves and tried to meet the eyes of the seven people he assumed were the Wardens. Next to Ledger was a big, rather jovial-looking old man with wild white hair and a florid face, who beamed at Xander, but the others regarded him with a mixture of curiosity and concern.

One of the older Wardens, grey haired and with piercing

blue eyes, spoke first. 'So you're the young outlander we've been hearing about who can use our Stones and defend against shade-strike.' He looked Xander up and down with a faintly sceptical expression, as if he had heard these things but personally considered them very doubtful. 'You also apparently claim no knowledge of the origin of these abilities or indeed of Haven itself.'

Xander wasn't sure whether he was supposed to be answering any of these statements and so just nodded.

'Hmm,' said the Warden, pursing his lips. 'We are also informed that the shades appeared to be targeting you specifically. What can you tell us about that?'

His mouth snapped shut and he fixed Xander with an intent stare.

'I, um, I don't know about that,' stumbled Xander. 'They were all around me at the museum but I saw them before that as well, at my home the night before. I didn't know what they were though, just that they were pretty terrifying.'

There was a little stir amongst the group of Wardens, and some of them exchanged meaningful looks. The white-haired man looked sympathetic, while another Warden, also elderly-looking, pursed his lips.

'I don't know what things are coming to,' he said in a quavering voice, 'when we have outlanders involved in Traveller business. Where were the wards? That's what I would like to know.'

'Wards were used, Wooten,' said Flint quietly, from behind Xander. 'He wasn't affected by them at all.'

Wooten tutted, his watery eyes fixed on Xander with great disapproval.

'Most irregular.'

The Warden who had first spoken cut in, with an impatient look. 'Irregular or otherwise, we are where we are. Regarding the shades issue, there do appear to be some minor anomalies concerning the border at the moment and we will continue to monitor these, and intervene where it is appropriate to do so.'

Xander heard a soft snort from Flint behind him, even as the jovial-looking Warden leaned forward, raising a bushy white eyebrow.

'Minor anomalies, Atherton?' he said sceptically, shaking his head. 'Any potential defect in our border protection is hardly minor, I would say.'

'Oh, for Haven's sake, Bardolph,' snapped Atherton. 'Let's not get ahead of ourselves here. A few small glitches are no reason to flap and panic, or indeed push for extreme responses unwarranted by the current situation.' He glanced over towards where Flint stood, half in shadow behind the group, and then continued with cool certainty. 'We'll liaise with the hobs and with the authorities at the Nexus, and doubtless any malfunction with Haven's power infrastructure will soon be identified and rectified.'

'And the boy?' demanded Wooten.

'Best he stays where he is,' cut in Kirrin Ledger in his even, authoritative voice. 'At least until we can be certain that it's safe to return him. We're still looking into the circumstances surrounding his arrival here and he'll be safe enough with the Stantons, under our eye but without unnecessary exposure to Traveller affairs.'

'Agreed,' said Bardolph immediately, and there was murmured assent from most of the members of the group, although Wooten looked extremely put out.

'In the meantime,' continued Atherton, but he was cut off abruptly by the sound of running footsteps; a moment later,

Ari and Rafe burst into the circle.

'There's been a massive blow-out at the Nexus,' Ari panted. 'It's caused some power outages around the country, although apparently the secondary nodes kicked in pretty quickly and limited the damage.'

'We've also just had several reports in from Watchers about strange occurrences and border fluctuations,' added Rafe in his calm, quiet voice. 'They say it seems to have stabilised but want to know if there are likely to be any repeats.'

There was a short silence, broken by Wooten's quavery voice.

'Well, this is what happens when people mess around with things they don't understand,' he complained. 'It's Thorne's new-fangled synthetic rubbish causing this, you mark my words. Irresponsible nonsense to think he can supplant the hobs' Core that has supplied Haven's power for thousands of years and kept our border secure.'

Atherton cleared his throat irritably.

'We have no evidence of that and one can't simply stand in the way of progress for the sake of it, Wooten. Travellers don't draw power from the Nexus and so it's no business of ours how and where the Council and Guilds source their energy. Our *only* concern is if there is an impact on Haven's security and so we will need to examine that aspect.'

'They've shut down access to the Nexus for the moment, while they investigate, and won't let anyone in,' said Rafe quietly. 'They say they'll re-open by tomorrow mid-morning at the latest and expect to have answers by then.'

'Fine,' said Atherton, nodding in satisfaction. 'I'm sure they will be able to clarify the situation then, and there's no need for anyone to be running around ahead of the facts or causing a kerfuffle over nothing.' Again, his eyes flicked over to where Flint stood with Ari and Rafe. 'In the meantime, I suggest that we cease discussing Traveller business in front of this boy, and send him back to Woodside where Thea can supervise him.'

He turned away without giving Xander another glance and spoke quietly with a couple of the other Wardens.

Xander felt Flint's hand come down on his shoulder, indicating that it was time to leave and he jumped up, relieved to have got through the interrogation. Mrs Stanton had clearly kept half an eye on the proceedings, as she hurried over to collect Xander with Ollie, Len and Katie just behind her. She looked like she wanted to speak with Flint, but he held up his hand quickly.

'Not right now,' he said. 'I need to head out, but I'll pop by first thing tomorrow morning and we'll talk then, okay?'

Mrs Stanton tightened her lips but nodded, and Flint made a quick gesture to Rafe before turning away to join Ari, Kirrin Ledger and another of the younger Wardens, and disappearing into the dark woods surrounding the Lodge.

Rafe led them back across the grounds of the Lodge and this time people largely ignored their passing, as they leant in around their hearths and discussed the latest events in quiet tones, although Xander saw the gleam of several pairs of eyes following him. Once they had reached the way-marker, Rafe held out his arm to them and a moment later they were standing in the shadowy front garden at Woodside, warm light spilling out from the windows and the open door.

Rafe nodded courteously, and then vanished with just a quick glint from his orb to show where he had been. Mrs Stanton sighed and waved them all into the house, following behind Katie as she bounced down the hallway looking for her mother. With one accord Xander, Ollie and Len went straight upstairs, and then paused for a moment outside the boys' bedroom.

'So what happened with the Wardens, then?' asked Ollie. 'And why was everyone acting so strange afterwards?'

Xander bit his lip as he thought about what had happened. 'They asked me a few questions and then they argued about whether or not the anomalies on the border were serious. That guy Atherton seemed to think not but the one called Bardolph was disagreeing with him, and I think Flint disagrees as well. Then Ari and Rafe came running over and said that there's been some kind of power outage and problems with the border.' He shrugged helplessly. 'They were talking about a lot of stuff that didn't make any sense to me, honestly.'

Len eyed him thoughtfully.

'It's all political with the Wardens,' she said. 'Alwyn Atherton is the Senior Warden and he really doesn't like the boat to be rocked. Stavish and Wooten, the other older Wardens, are pretty traditional as well and Jory Bardolph tends to go along with them, although he's more open-minded. The younger Wardens like Kirrin Ledger, Jon Sefton and Con Kirkeby listen to Flint more, although they'll still tend to toe the party line.'

Ollie stared at her and Len tossed her head.

'What?' she said defensively. 'So I pay attention to what's going on around me.'

'What's the issue with them and Flint?' asked Xander.

'Flint thinks there's a bigger problem with the instability on the border and that the Wardens aren't taking it seriously enough,' replied Ollie. 'He thinks Travellers should train much more in defensive warding and dealing with shade incursions, while the Wardens think he's over-reacting about the risks.'

'It's not just that though,' said Len, with a wise expression. 'Flint has gathered a bit of a following among the younger generation of Travellers, and they train with him and look to him to lead them. The Wardens don't like that, hence the hostility from the older ones like Atherton. Ledger and Kirkeby are friends with Flint, but they were chosen as Wardens because they know when to get in line, while Flint goes his own way, more or less. As I said, it's all political.'

With a quick shrug, Len turned and headed off to her own bedroom, while Xander and Ollie looked at one another.

'Just another day in Haven,' said Ollie with a quick grin and Xander laughed. At this point, he reflected as they both turned into their room, he had no clue what could possibly come tomorrow.

CHAPTER FIVE

The next morning, Flint kept his promise and came over to brief Thea, but whatever he had said, it left her frowning in concern and sending worried looks over at the table where Xander, Len and Ollie were finishing their breakfasts. Finally, they walked towards the door and within earshot, clearly disagreeing about something. Xander kept his head down and listened intently.

'I need to head over to the Nexus headquarters,' Flint was saying with obvious irritation. 'I haven't got time for baby-sitting, Thea.'

'Well, that's too bad. I have to visit some patients and stock up the pantry, just in case these power outages get worse. I don't intend to leave this lot on their own and unsupervised until we know what the situation is at the Nexus. You can take them with you.'

Mrs Stanton's expression was steely, and Flint sighed and shook his head in resignation.

'Fine,' he grumbled. 'Have it your way.'

'I intend to,' Mrs Stanton said sweetly, patting Flint on the cheek while he glowered at her. She drew her basket over her arm and turned to the three still sitting at the table. 'Make sure you stay out of trouble, and no repeats of last time, please.' Her gaze rested on Ollie for a moment before she swept out of the kitchen.

'Baby-sitting?' remarked Len. 'That's fairly insulting.'

Flint grimaced unrepentantly. 'We'll see,' he said. 'Well, get your things. I'm in a hurry.'

'No repeat of what?' Xander asked Ollie as they raced to grab their shoes.

'Nothing really,' replied Ollie evasively. Xander heard Len's snort of laughter.

'Come on, you lot,' came Flint's impatient yell from the front door, so Xander's question went unanswered.

Flint set a fast pace down the lane towards Wykeham. He did not seem inclined to talk, but Xander suddenly realised that this was his first chance to ask the taciturn Traveller about the hostile boy who had met him on his arrival in Haven, and to pass on his message. Xander hurried to catch up, and Flint eyed him as he fell into step beside him.

'Flint, who was that person who came to fetch me out of the room when I first arrived here?' he asked.

'No-one important,' Flint replied dismissively. His face was expressionless, which was a cue that Xander was learning to read.

'He said to give you a message,' Xander persisted.

Flint did not react. 'Really?' he said, without interest. It was clear he was not going to ask anything further.

Xander sighed. 'He said to tell you from him that you could clean up your own messes in the future.' He watched Flint for his reaction.

Flint just snorted under his breath.

'Did he?'

Xander gave up and marched along in silence until they reached the little bridge onto the green.

'Aren't we jumping?' he asked, rather disappointed that Flint was walking towards the more prosaic gate. It was startling how quickly he had become accustomed to covering many miles in a couple of steps through an archway.'

'No, it's best to stay unobtrusive where possible,' Flint replied. He lifted an eyebrow sardonically at Xander. 'Something you might want to consider from time to time.' He turned back to the gate and Xander relieved his feelings by pulling a face. Len caught the tail end of it and smirked.

Flint led them through the Wykeham Gate but on emerging from it in the great cloisters he did not take the route towards Fountain Square. Instead he strode off to a narrow lane opening on their left, and then threaded his way through several winding streets, most of which were bounded by the backs of tall buildings or high walls. Xander was completely disorientated after the first five minutes and he dropped back to fall in beside Ollie.

'Where are we going?' he asked.

'The Nexus,' Ollie said promptly, and then comprehension dawned. 'Oh, you mean now? We have to go via the North Gates – this is just the quickest way to get there from the South Gates, where we came in.'

'Is there a gate for every place from the city?' asked Xander curiously.

'Not exactly,' replied Ollie. 'Wykeham has a direct gate because it's one of the oldest settlements, and so does the Nexus because they built it next to the hobs' Core, which is pretty ancient. Most of the main gates here in the city go to regional hubs, with other minor gates there.'

As he spoke, Flint led them into a space that was almost a replica of the cloisters they had arrived through and over to a soaring archway. It was one of the largest in the row, with the word 'Lodehill' carved into its apex, and there he paused, gesturing them through, before passing under the arch himself.

Xander found himself standing on a neatly paved path,

surrounded by beautiful landscaped gardens and looking at an enormous building that reared up ahead of them. The edifice had no battlements or towers, but still it was vaguely reminiscent of a castle with its thick walls, narrow arched windows and the pool that surrounded it like a moat. The pathway led forward over a little stone bridge and Flint marched forward without hesitation, over the water and up a flight of steep stone steps. The large and imposing entrance had heavy doors made of a grey, glistening material set back against the walls and Xander reached out to touch one as they passed by. It was smooth and cool, and gave slightly under his fingers, not at all like the metal it resembled.

'That's impregnate,' said Ollie, seeing Xander's gesture. 'It's a fusion of stone, metal and a sort of foam that the Constructionist Guild developed. It's pretty impervious to anything, which is why they use it here on the Nexus.'

Inset from the main entrance was a ten-foot-high revolving door, with clear glass panels. The segments were narrow enough to force them to pass through one at a time and, as Xander shuffled forward in his own section, he felt a light but intrusive touch shimmering over his body and tingling in his fingertips. It was instantly recognisable as a ward but unlike the previous wards Xander had encountered, this one had a strange metallic tang to it.

The feeling vanished as quickly as it had come and the next moment Xander stepped out into a huge vestibule, marble-floored and echoing. Several doors were set into the angled walls, all closed, and the only furniture was a large marble reception desk and two rows of stiff upright chairs set against the walls on opposite sides of the hall.

As Flint strode towards the reception desk, Xander leant over to Len, who was walking beside him. 'Did you feel that, as we came through the door?'

Len nodded, seemingly unconcerned.

'Of course. They're just making sure you're not bringing anything that's prohibited into the building.' She cast a wicked grin over her shoulder at Ollie who was trying, and failing, to look inconspicuous behind them. 'Surprising really that Ollie's not classed as prohibited yet.'

Before Ollie could retaliate, Flint called to them peremptorily from the desk and they shuffled forward. Looking around, Xander felt rather small and overwhelmed by this building, and he had the strong feeling that this was exactly the impression the vestibule was designed to create. As they lined up in front of the desk, the receptionist looked down his long nose at Flint, before his eyes fell with obvious disfavour on Ollie.

'You again,' he said sniffily. 'And only six months' recovery time from your last visit.' He stretched out a pale hand, palm up. 'Your orb, please. Let's try to limit this visit to uncomfortable, rather than catastrophic.'

Ollie, his face burning, fumbled with his wristband and then dropped his orb into the man's hand. The receptionist eyed the singeing and the dull stone with distaste, and then tossed the band in a box beneath his desk. He motioned impatiently to Len and Xander, and his eyebrows shot up as Len brandished her bare wrist with a sarcastic flourish. Xander hesitated, before following suit. Flint ignored this byplay and reached over, past the disapproving receptionist, and touched an indentation on top of the marble desk. It lit with a soft blue and Flint's orb flared once, tiny lightning bolts flickering in its depths. The light faded and the receptionist checked his terminal.

'You are cleared for access.' He did not sound very pleased by that, and pointed bossily at the rows of chairs. 'Please take a seat and wait for someone to come and escort you.'

Flint waved him off with casual authority and walked to the double doors behind the desk, gesturing for Xander, Ollie and Len to follow him.

'I know the way, thanks,' he said off-handedly.

Ignoring the spluttering of the clerk, he placed a hand on the panel beside the doors, which once more glowed blue. There was a soft chiming sound and a disembodied voice announced, 'Authorised. Please enter'.

The doors slid apart smoothly, disappearing into the walls on either side, to reveal a lift with dimensions as impressive as the vestibule it served. It seemed odd to Xander to see something so familiar and prosaic in Haven, where so much was strange. Len stepped in with a grimace.

'I really don't like this place,' she said, looking about her with distaste. 'It makes my skin crawl.'

'Level 3,' Flint said, paying no attention to Len's grumbles, and the disembodied voice confirmed, 'Level 3, stand by.'

Xander waited for the lift to move, but after a moment the doors just swept open again and his eyes widened in surprise. Before them was now a long hallway, white painted and sterile-looking. Xander stepped out, with a quick glance back at the lift that could apparently transport them with no sensation of movement whatsoever; it did not appear to have much resemblance to the mechanical lifts he was familiar with after all.

The corridor was full of people, working in the offices which opened out of it or walking along deep in conversation; a few wore white coats over their clothes, as if they were doctors in a hospital. Some people glanced at them with curiosity as they passed, but most ignored them. Flint headed straight for a set of double security doors at the end of the corridor, disregarding the sign stating 'Level 3A – Restricted Area.' The corridor on the other side appeared identical, except that now most of the people wore white coats. One man, with thinning dark hair and bright brown eyes, hurried up to them, smiling.

'Petros,' said Flint tersely, shaking his hand.

'I thought you would be over,' Petros said, before leading them down the corridor. He was a rather strange-looking figure, his white coat hanging on him as if it were several sizes too big. Xander noticed that his pockets were stuffed with pencils, most of which appeared to have broken points, while a large pad hung around his neck tied on with what looked like several frayed shoelaces. Despite his haphazard appearance there was something warm and engaging about him.

'We're trying to identify why this surge happened,' he said, as he hurried along. 'We think it may have originated in the hobs' Core and then impacted us from there, but you know how hard it is to get them to share information with us. It's not clear yet whether the border breach was an artefact of the surge or vice versa, but the fact that they occurred at the same time is not a coincidence, we believe. Reeve's down on the floor now but I warn you, he's not in the best mood. The surge last night immolated the new node he was bringing on line, so that's six months' work blown, quite literally.'

'How big was it?' asked Flint. 'The damage seemed fairly limited topside, except for the breach.'

'Really?' replied Petros, looking surprised. 'We're still calculating but it seems pretty large, and there's a strange signature which we haven't yet managed to decode. Maybe the damage was limited topside because the majority discharged internally. We've suffered a fair amount of damage to the system. Thorne was in here this morning, and he wasn't happy.' Flint nodded, tight-lipped as Petros glanced sideways at him. 'Reeve will want to talk to you,' he added but his eyes lingered over Xander, Len and Ollie. Flint followed his gaze.

'They need to stay with me,' he said firmly and Petros nodded in acceptance. He led them through more doors and down a short hallway to another lift, mirroring the one in the vestibule but on a far less grand scale. When they entered the lift, Petros said, 'Level 5, Sub-section C'. There was that pause again and then, 'That area is restricted to authorised personnel. Please confirm clearance'. Once again, a small panel glowed blue and Petros rested his hand on it. This time the pause was longer, and then the doors swept open. The others filed out but Xander stopped in the doorway, transfixed by the incredible sight in front of him.

The space was shaped like the nave of a great cathedral but about five times the size, with walls that soared up to a huge height. It was filled with enormous aisles of crystal, towering up in angular, asymmetrical shapes and glittering in pale blue and icy white. The entire mass glowed, lit internally by the intricate threads of metallic coding which wove through the heart of each crystal, a vast silvery web. The whole thing pulsed with a palpable vibrancy, leaving a perceptible buzz in the atmosphere.

Xander felt his scalp prickle, as if his hair was trying to stand on end. He was only recalled to an awareness of his immediate vicinity by the sharp jerking motion of the lift doors, denied the opportunity to close because he was standing in the way. He took another step forward and Ollie gave him a quick, understanding smile.

'Pretty amazing, isn't it? We came here a while ago on an Academy trip. There are six more like this here,' he said.

Xander stared. 'You're kidding?'

'No. The Nexus powers almost everything,' Ollie said.

'What would happen if it broke down?' wondered Xander.

Petros, who had seemed to be deep in conversation with Flint, turned around at this and shook his head with a confident smile.

'Not possible,' he assured Xander. 'They all operate independently and act as fail safes for the others, and each one is broken down into nodes, which can also be operated separately.'

He pointed to the strangely-angled aisles of crystal, then caught Flint's impatient expression and led them off to a long, gated platform just to their right. It had high safety rails but was otherwise open, giving them a wonderful view of the Nexus as it lowered them all down to the ground level. As they arrived, and Petros undid the safety gate, Flint sent a warning look at Xander and Ollie.

'Stay close. Don't touch *anything*.'

Ollie went red again, but it was on Xander that Flint's gaze lingered before leading them on after Petros' trotting figure. Within moments, Xander was completely lost as they wove in and out of the maze of glowing crystalline walls. It was cool in the Nexus and Xander wished that he had grabbed his jumper before they left. They passed quite a few people in white coats, who nodded to Petros and glanced curiously at his strange entourage.

As they approached a sharp right turn, Xander saw a pair of feet sticking out around the corner; inconsequentially, he noticed that they wore odd socks. As they turned the corner, Xander's eyes were drawn away immediately from the recumbent figure to the crystal walls and he stared, even as he heard gasps from Ollie and Len, and Flint's growled exclamation. This crystal was no longer smooth and clear but pitted and opaque, with thick black striations where the gleaming coding had been. Several of them were gouged and blackened, and scattered around them were the shattered remnants of the crystal that had been blasted outwards. Also on the floor was the owner of the odd socks, sprawled full length along the base of the wall and holding some kind of device. His trousers were as rumpled as his thick dark hair and he had bundled up his white coat into a cushion to support his shoulder. He was oblivious to their presence until Petros leaned down and gently shook his arm.

'Callan? Ben Flint is here.'

The man started and then twisted to look at the group staring down at him, his eyes still slightly unfocussed until they rested on Flint's concerned face. He rolled to his feet in an easy, practised motion. He was taller than Xander had supposed, his lean build half-disguised by the big, scruffy jumper he wore, which had holes in both elbows.

'I thought you'd be down,' he said to Flint, rubbing his hands through his hair.

'What in Haven happened here, Reeve?' demanded Flint. He reached out to touch the shattered stone, his eyes following the damage which continued down along the angled aisle as far as they could see.

Reeve shook his head, sombrely.

'That's what I'm trying to work out,' he said, his gaze wandering over to Xander, Len and Ollie.

'Thea wasn't comfortable leaving them unsupervised, given recent events,' Flint explained.

'I can understand that,' Reeve said wryly. The device in his hand bleeped and he looked down to check the screen. He made a frustrated sound and held it out to Petros, who leant over it with a frown.

'But I just recalibrated this one. It should definitely pick up something,' he said, shaking his head.

'Some kind of radiation being emitted, do you think?'

'Possible, but why wouldn't the sensors have picked up on it?'

The two engineers seemed to have forgotten their audience in their engrossment with the malfunctioning device. Flint cut across them.

'Do you have any theories about the cause? Any potential link between this and our border security makes this pretty serious, far more so than a minor glitch in people's power supply.'

Reeve did not appear offended by the interruption.

'Well, this level of damage is unprecedented but we are working to exclude any obvious possibilities. For instance, we are fairly certain that Ollie here is not responsible,' his voice was amused and Ollie went scarlet again, staring at the floor. Reeve continued in a more serious tone, 'We've only recently flushed the whole system, so that discounts build-up –'

While he was speaking, several other white-coated engineers gathered around, chipping in to offer their own opinions and debating with huge enthusiasm. Flint stood back, listening with a slight frown on his face, while Xander and Ollie exchanged glances and Len scuffed at the floor, her boredom quite evident.

Suddenly, a loud, domineering voice broke into the conversation.

'What's going on, then? Why are you all just standing around here when there's work to be done, eh?'

A short, stocky man, square-shouldered and bullish, marched into the centre of the group and glared around with small dark eyes.

'How's this supposed to get fixed if you're all just gabbing instead of doing? Mr Simm will be here shortly and there'd better be some answers for him.'

He snapped his fingers and several of the engineers backed away, looking harried, while Petros nervously broke the point of another pencil. Reeve however, just glanced over at him, unconcerned.

'Before anything can be fixed, Latchet, one has to first understand why it was broken,' he said calmly, before turning away to examine the striations again.

Latchet glared in impotent fury as Reeve continued to ignore him, then turned and stomped after the remaining engineers, barking out questions in a hectoring tone and sending them scattering in every direction.

'Idiot,' remarked Reeve, shaking his head. 'He hasn't got the first clue how any of this works, but of course making people run around like headless chickens will definitely solve it.'

Snorting derisively, he began to run another instrument over the shattered crystal, muttering what sounded like complex calculations under his breath while Flint stood next to him, waiting. There was a roar from Latchet in the next aisle and Petros jumped, dropping the device he held onto Xander's foot.

'Sorry,' he said quickly, squatting down to pick it up again. 'That man just shreds my last nerve.'

'S'okay,' said Xander, wiggling his toes experimentally. 'Who is he?'

There was another bellow and a pair of white-coated engineers fled past, looking harried.

'Alan Latchet,' replied Petros, after a wary glance around. 'He works for Lester Simm, the Council Liaison to the Nexus.' He lowered his voice. 'Latchet is living proof that a little knowledge is a dangerous thing and he makes everyone's life a misery; anyone who crosses him is gone. Thorne ought to kick him out, but Latchet toadies up to him and Simm, and gets him what he wants on the Council, so he turns a blind eye to his behaviour.'

Xander glanced over at Reeve.

'How come *he* gets away with talking back?' he asked.

Petros smiled. 'Because Callan's a genius and Thorne can't afford to lose him. He trained with the hobs, back when they still let humans into their Core, and there's no-one who understands the Nexus like he does. Latchet hates Cal but there's nothing he can do to him, and that drives him mad. He threatened once that if Cal didn't do as he said then he would destroy him, and Cal just laughed at him. I would have loved to have seen that,' he finished wistfully.

Reeve called Petros over to look at something and he left Xander with a quick smile, fishing in his pocket for an unbroken pencil.

After another fifteen minutes of trailing around behind Reeve and Flint as they moved down the damaged portion, conferring occasionally in quiet undertones, even the exotic nature of the Nexus began to pall. Len was sitting on the floor with a sulky expression, scratching at her hand, while Ollie slumped by one crystal wall, his hands shoved in his pockets, as if to advertise to everyone that he was not going to touch anything.

Xander himself was feeling some sympathy with Len's complaints that the place was making her itch. There was something about the crystalline structures looming on all sides, with their bright metallic coding and the sharp, blue-white light, that made him uneasy and his head ache, not helped by the chill inside the Nexus chamber. Flint had glanced over at them every now and again, and this time he followed the glance with a couple of quick words to Petros, who hurried over.

'You must all be really bored,' he said apologetically. 'We'll be a while longer but I thought you might want to sit down somewhere a bit more comfortable.'

Len scrambled to her feet as Xander and Ollie nodded. Petros led them down the shattered aisle, turned left and then right until they emerged from the walls of crystal to a space bounded by a smooth, dark stone wall, punctuated with several decorative alcoves. Near one of them and looking faintly incongruous in the wide empty space, was a table and a small pile of wooden chairs. Petros gestured towards them.

'We have a few seating areas scattered around. This one is a bit basic,' he said with an apologetic grimace. 'It's not much used all the way back here.'

Ollie shrugged with a quick grin. 'Better than sitting on the floor,' he said.

Petros smiled at them. 'I'll pop back and get you when we're all finished.' He turned away and then a thought seemed to occur to him. 'Don't wander off,' he warned. 'This place is a maze if you're not used to it.' They all nodded and Petros, apparently satisfied by their assent, disappeared back into the Nexus.

Ollie lifted three wooden chairs from the stack and pushed them towards the table. Sitting down with a sigh, he stretched his legs out in front of him. 'Well, this is pretty boring,' he remarked.

Xander squinted up at the towering crystal slabs and rubbed his eyes.

'I just wish they would turn the lights down in here,' he said. 'This place is giving me a headache.'

They all sat in silence for a moment, and then Ollie rummaged in his pockets, before pulling out a small packet with an air of triumph. 'I thought I had these with me,' he said. 'Fancy some cards to pass the time?' Without waiting for an answer, he began to deal out brightly coloured cards covered with strange symbols.

Xander leant forwards with interest.

'What do those mean?' he asked.

'Just give me a sec to get them sorted out. They're a bit messed up,' replied Ollie, swiftly sorting the cards into piles, but Xander was no longer listening. He was distracted by what was happening inside the nearest alcove. The plain, smooth wall within it, which had looked so solid, was starting to ripple, as if the stone had become liquid. Xander shoved his chair back noisily, his eyes wide. Ollie looked up, followed Xander's shocked gaze, and promptly dropped the rest of the cards on the table; a few of them slid to the edge and fluttered down to the floor below.

A hand, its fingers thin, white and elongated, emerged from the rippling stone and grasped the side of the alcove. It was followed by a face, chalk-pale, long-nosed and dominated by large, yellow eyes. In the bright light of the Nexus, Xander could clearly see the disconcerting, slitted pupils as its eyes swivelled towards them. It regarded Xander, Ollie and Len impassively, and then extended its white hand and crooked its finger at them, in a clear beckoning sign. As abruptly as it had appeared, the figure vanished back into the rippling wall.

They all stared at each other for a moment, speechless, before Xander abruptly stood up. He needed answers, however strange the source, and Flint himself had gone to the hobgoblins; it did not seem likely that they would kidnap him out of the Nexus, under everyone's noses. He hurried forwards before he could talk himself out of it and heard the other chairs moving behind him.

'Great,' Ollie grumbled as he got up. 'Follow the creepy, beckoning finger, kids. That's sure to end well.'

Xander paused by the rippling wall. He couldn't see anything beyond it, but he had the distinct feeling that someone was listening. 'You guys don't have to come,' he said, with a worried look at them. 'You could just wait out here for me.'

Ollie snorted derisively.

'Yeah, right,' he said. 'Let you follow the creepy finger on your own? That's not happening.'

Len eyed them both thoughtfully but just walked forward to stand with her cousin. Xander sent them both quick, grateful looks. The rippling wall looked rather daunting up close and he was privately relieved that he would not have to pass through it alone.

Ollie reached out and gripped the back of Xander's shirt. 'Let's stick together,' he said, and then muttered, 'and hope we don't become a cautionary tale for little children.'

Fervently hoping the same, Xander turned and stepped into the rippling wall, feeling Ollie's hand behind him, tugging on his shirt as the little procession followed him.

The bright lights of the Nexus vanished and Xander now stood in a dark, rocky corridor, lit with a faint light from the glowstone held in the pale hand of the hob who stood waiting for them. It was barely sufficient to illuminate his face, although the hob's eyes gleamed as he looked at Xander, Len and Ollie standing before him. Apparently satisfied that they would follow him, and without a word of explanation, the hob turned and walked away, holding the light low to the uneven floor.

Xander let out a deep breath and followed, reassured by the faint footsteps of Ollie and Len behind him. As they passed through the tunnel, the glowstone revealed faint sparkles of quartz, like tiny stars, glinting in the rock wall and then fading away. After a few moments of silent walking the hob halted at what appeared to be a dead end, then reached out and touched the rock in a stroking gesture. As Xander watched, the stone rippled away from the hob's finger, becoming translucent with a soft shimmering glow. The hob stepped forward and vanished, without a backwards glance, taking his light with him.

Xander hesitated again, looking at the glowing stretch of wall. He felt Ollie move forward to stand at his shoulder.

'We've come this far,' Ollie said, and Xander could almost hear the grimace in his tone, 'might as well follow the insanity to its logical conclusion.' Len snorted, her laugh sounding rather hollow.

Together, the three of them stepped through the translucent barrier and then stopped, gaping open-mouthed at what had been revealed. It was a huge space, similar in size to the chamber which they had just left and also filled with a vast crystal matrix, but it was radically different in all other ways.

Instead of standing in crisp rows of angular stabs, the crystal here appeared to flow organically, soaring up into archways and spires and then dipping down like sparkling waterfalls into basins on the floor. There was no glittering coding in these crystals and the light flowed in pulses and waves, a multitude of soft colours blossoming, shimmering and throbbing through the matrix. It was utterly mesmerising and Xander just stood and gazed at it, hearing the swift intakes of breath from Ollie and Len beside him. The hob waited in front of them, his face expressionless as he watched their reaction.

Finally, he broke his silence.

'Come,' he said, in a grating voice and then turned away to

lead them forward.

'It speaks,' muttered Ollie into Xander's ear, but his voice was still rather awed.

Xander himself could not stop staring about as they followed the hob. The crystal nodes in the Nexus were awe-inspiring in their raw power and size, but there was something different about this place; the crystals here seemed alive, glowing in their natural beauty and warmth as they pulsed with light. They passed under an archway made of two soaring pillars of crystal curving overhead and Xander was distracted, his eyes following the colours as they swirled and flowed upwards, so that when he looked down he was startled by what waited beyond.

The crystalline walls twisted into a bowl-like shape, and within it was a little outgrowth in the shape of a chair, glimmering softly. Sitting in the chair was a hobgoblin whose chalky face was lined with age and who had a distinct air of fragility, while surrounding him was a semi-circle of hobgoblins, all staring at Xander. Their erstwhile guide had evidently joined the group and was no longer discernible from any of the others, so similar were they all to Xander's confused eyes.

The hobgoblin who sat enthroned upon the crystal chair regarded Xander intently, his unnerving eyes running up and down over him, and Xander felt that same crawling sensation as when Hob had examined his hand in the shop. It was no more comfortable this time and Xander stiffened, resisting its insistent probe.

With a swift, decisive movement, the seated hobgoblin held out a hand and two of his entourage hurried to assist him down from his seat. They closed protectively around the frail figure as he approached, their alien eyes narrowed to warn of the consequences of any actions they considered threatening.

Xander was under no illusions as to his chances in that case and stood as still as possible, feeling Len and Ollie behind him doing the same.

The little figure came to within a few feet, and up close his face was cobwebbed with fine lines and wrinkles, and his pale hair was thin and fine. His eyes gleamed brightly, however, and Xander felt the weight of their gaze.

'So you are the one,' said the ancient hobgoblin, in a creaky whisper. Before Xander had a chance to respond, he continued. 'Or are you? We will see.'

He held out a claw-like hand, twisted with age. For a moment Xander held back, remembering how unpleasant the sensation had been in Hob's shop, but finally he thrust out his hand. He needed some answers and he suspected that the hobs might be able to give them to him; at least, he thought, as his eyes caught again in the hobgoblin's irredeemably strange ones, if they chose to share them.

The hobgoblin encircled Xander's hand in his own cold one, his clasp surprisingly strong for one so fragile-looking. The sensation was different this time, an odd pulling deep down in blood and bone, throbbing with his heartbeat. Startled, he realised that the crystal walls surrounding them were pulsing in the same rhythm, the colours blooming and shifting as if the whole chamber were beating time with his heart. The ancient hobgoblin lifted his head in an odd, flexing gesture, as his eyes took in the response, and Xander could see the flow of lights shift across his strangely reflective eyes.

Abruptly, the hobgoblin withdrew his hand and clapped. The pulsing ceased instantly and Xander felt a sudden sense of loss. The old hobgoblin smiled at him secretively, as if he knew exactly how Xander felt.

'It is there,' he said in his thin voice. His gaze was direct and knowing, and seemed to Xander like it was burrowing under his skin. 'The seed of the ancient blood, down through all the ages, come to us once more.'

There was a sudden stir among the group.

Xander stared back at the ancient hobgoblin. 'The seed of *what*?' he asked urgently. 'What does my blood have to do with anything?'

The hob shook his head with a mournful look, his eyes wary.

'It is not yet time to speak of it,' he said with finality.

Xander stared at him in disbelief. He very much wanted to speak about it, but before he could open his mouth to protest the hobgoblin turned and reached out a thin hand again. Immediately, a larger hobgoblin leapt forward and offered a supportive arm. It looked like a dismissal but instead the old hobgoblin turned his head and beckoned with his free hand. 'Come,' was all he said, but Xander felt his feet moving of their own accord, so commanding was the tone. The hobgoblins allowed Xander and his friends to follow, closing in all around them to keep a protective distance from the frail figure ahead; Xander heard Ollie's breathing, uneasy and as shallow as his own. This strange little procession continued through the twisting maze until Xander was quite certain he could never find his way out again without assistance.

The soft light grew dimmer as they walked and Xander caught glimpses of paler, more faded crystal through the flowing archways and pillars. The air had been pleasantly warm, especially in contrast with the distinct chill of the Nexus, but now the temperature was rising and it was becoming more difficult to breathe. Xander wiped at his face, trying to blot the beads of sweat that were forming on his forehead. Finally, the little procession halted and the old hobgoblin gestured to Xander to pass through a dully opaque opening in the crystal face. His eyes widened when he saw what lay beyond. Spread before him in ruined majesty was a shocking mass of darkened crystal, riven with fractures and exuding the same sense of wrongness that Xander had sensed before, at the little temple in the museum. He had to resist the strong urge to take a step back.

The hobgoblin shook his head, his face lined with deep sorrow.

'This was once the centre, the beating heart of our Core. Now our heart has been corrupted and the infection is spreading. We try to hold the canker at bay, to maintain what is left, but for how long?' He peered up at Xander. 'Did anyone tell you? Do you know what has befallen my people?'

His frail voice was accusatory, as if he held Xander personally responsible for what had happened. Xander shook his head, and the hobgoblin snorted.

'Of course not. Why should others care to speak of our tragedy?' His eyes narrowed. 'Over a hundred years ago sickness struck us with a brutal blow and we lost many of our most vulnerable, our Elders. We feared for its return but when it came back, it was with less force; while many would fall ill, no more died. It was an inconvenience, we thought, returning sporadically but with little ill effect. Then, fourteen years ago, it returned, but this time it came back like a lion. It ravaged through our people, unstoppable, cutting us down young and old, strong and weak; scarce one in a hundred survived the year's end. We were never a populous people, not like your kind, but there were enough, always enough, until the blow fell.'

The hobgoblin's creaking voice fell silent, and he shook his head mournfully.

'We are diminished and there are few now left. So much

knowledge lost, so many struck down in their prime. Maybe we will not even survive.' His voice trailed off as he looked around the small group of hobgoblins, still and impassive, before turning to Xander, Ollie and Len with glittering eyes. 'Perhaps your technology was always destined to supplant us but in this you sow the seeds of your own destruction, I think. The foolish humans do not sense the blight growing in Haven, a sickness that emanates from their own Nexus. They cannot heal it.' His gaze became penetrating as it rested on Xander alone. 'But you, perhaps, can.'

Xander stared at him.

'I don't see how,' he mumbled awkwardly. 'I'm not even from Haven and I don't know anything about – about this.'

The old hobgoblin did not relent. 'But an ancient Stone, long broken, answered your call and brought you here. Your speaking was also powerful enough to utterly destroy that weak counterfeit of Thorne's making.' The name was spat out with a twist of the lips. 'It still echoes in its shattered remains.'

The hobgoblin reached into a pocket of his thin robe and withdrew the blackened, broken orb which Xander had last seen at the little shop. He ran a spindly finger gingerly over the top of the stone.

'We have lost so much, so many memories, but this is not the first time destruction has threatened us. We still have fragments, pieces of lore given to help a remnant survive and we remember the truth of a bloodline who will return when the times are darkest.'

His creaky voice trailed away at the final word and he stood staring at Xander as if he expected him to wave his hands and fix everything on the spot. The silence grew too long and Xander saw Ollie eying him, looking worried.

'I'm really sorry that all this has happened to you,' he

began, although that seemed like a ridiculous understatement. 'The only thing is,' he said haltingly, 'I don't think I'm the one you're looking for. I mean, I'm just a normal kid, there's nothing special about me, honestly. Some weird things have happened over the last few days but I don't think I have any powers to fix things for you. I don't even know why I'm here – I don't belong in Haven. I'm an outlander.'

The hobgoblin's expression did not change.

'If you truly do not believe that you have this potential, then come here and place your hand upon our Core,' he said, waving at the ruined crystal face behind him. 'If it is as you say, then nothing will happen and the stone will be silent. There is no reason for concern.'

Xander felt privately that there was every reason for concern, particularly as that sense of wrongness was still rolling off the shattered crystal like a mist; however he could not think of a sufficient excuse that would get him out of doing what the old hobgoblin wanted. Biting the inside of his lip to control his grimace, he stepped forward and tentatively touched the crystal with the ends of his fingertips. Before he had even touched the stone, a flare of sickly yellow light bloomed hesitantly near his hand, and then sparked outwards as he hastily pulled away. The crystal face felt oily and he surreptitiously rubbed his hand on the leg of his trousers. There was a stir among the surrounding hobgoblins and the old one drew in his breath with an audible hiss; his eyes held a knowing gleam as he looked up at Xander.

'What did you do?' demanded Len in a plaintive mutter.

'Nothing,' Xander whispered back to her, with a faint tinge of panic.

'Again?' asked Ollie with a quizzical lift of his eyebrows and Xander flushed.

The hobgoblins were murmuring amongst themselves with many sideways glances being thrown at Xander. The old hobgoblin lifted a long, thin finger with great deliberation and ran it down the shattered crystal, and a sluggish hint of light bloomed again. He rubbed his thumb and forefinger together as if they were slippery. His eyes lingered on Xander, who wished deeply that they could just leave this creepy place before anything weirder might happen.

As if he had heard Xander's unspoken thoughts, the old hobgoblin gestured and the little procession made its way back through the dim maze. Xander tried to ignore the mutterings from their escort as they walked, but when he heard Len's sharp intake of breath he glanced around him; tiny sparks of sickly light were blooming tentatively in the crystal walls as he passed. Swallowing, he decided that the best course of action was to ignore it all, and he was ignoring his surroundings with such determination that only Ollie's swift grab at his arm stopped him ploughing into the backs of the hobgoblins. He stumbled back, and only then did he realise that the old hobgoblin was no longer among the group. Xander looked around in confusion.

'Where did he go?' he asked.

A hob brushed past him, ignoring his question and waving them onwards towards a blank rock wall. 'Come,' he said. 'You must leave now.'

He stroked the wall in that odd gesture and it turned translucent again.

Xander did not need a second invitation. He hurried forward, with Ollie and Len only a step behind him. Whatever the old hobgoblin had said to him about speaking to stones, he did not feel at all comfortable here. It felt utterly alien to him and he was suddenly desperate to get above ground again and to breathe cool, fresh air. This time the rocky tunnel which linked the Nexus to the Core seemed much shorter and the hob brushed past them to reactivate the exit. Xander felt like he should say something before leaving but could not think of the right words.

'Er, thank you,' he said awkwardly. It came out sounding more like a question.

The hobgoblin just stared at him with coldly gleaming eyes. 'We will be waiting,' he grated out.

Swallowing nervously, Xander plunged through the rippling rock, Ollie and Len at his elbows. As soon as they were all clear, the wall solidified again and Ollie's eyes widened as he glanced back.

'Seriously, how weird was that?' he asked.

'I think we would all like to know the answer to that question,' said an irritated voice.

Xander spun around to see Flint, Reeve and Petros standing by the small table, where Ollie's cards were still spread out; Flint with an expression to match his tone. Reeve was holding one of the cards in his hand, staring at the three teenagers with a stunned face. He threw the card aside and hurried over, running his hands across the wall inside the alcove. Then, with an explosive breath, he turned around.

'They let you in?' he demanded eagerly. 'They actually brought you through?'

Xander and Ollie exchanged glances, acutely aware of Flint's annoyance and the fact they had not exactly done as they were instructed.

'They were pretty insistent, actually,' said Ollie apologetically, as Xander remained silent.

'That's amazing,' burst out Reeve, his eyes wide. 'They haven't let anyone in there for years, not since –' he cut that thought off. 'It's astounding though, isn't it? Incredible. They used to train some of us engineers, back before –'

His voice trailed off again, a pained look crossing his face.

'So what exactly did they want you for?' broke in Flint. Xander did not think it was his imagination that the 'you' sounded rather accusatory, as Flint's cool blue eyes settled on him.

'There was this really old hobgoblin,' explained Ollie. 'He was sitting on this throne thing and he wanted to see Xander.'

All of the adults were now staring at Xander in astonishment.

'The Elder Goblin,' said Reeve in a choked voice. 'The Elder Goblin wanted to see you?'

'Why?' demanded Flint, as ever straight to the point. 'What did the Elder want with you?' The unspoken 'of all people' hung in the air, and Xander thought he might have been offended if he did not secretly feel the same way.

'He told us about all of the sickness and how they were so few now, and then he said that I could speak to the stones and that I might be related to someone who could do that a long time ago, something about a bloodline,' said Xander, rather incoherently. 'I have no idea what he was talking about but he wouldn't listen.'

'Then they took us to the centre of their Core,' burst out Ollie, as though he could not hold it in any more. 'It was seriously funky-looking, all dark and broken up. They said it was humans' fault. They *really* don't like Thorne.'

'Are you sure?' said Reeve, leaning forward in his interest. 'They think the damage started here? What do they think caused it?'

Suddenly Petros, who had been silent up to now, began flapping one hand urgently. A moment later, a loud voice rang out.

'They're here, sir. Doing nothing useful at all, it would appear.'

Latchet, the owner of that voice, sidled around the corner and Xander was surprised to notice that his former striding and arm-waving had been replaced with an obsequious air.

Then, emerging from behind Latchet, a personage appeared who made Xander blink his eyes in wonder. He was soft-looking, with thinning blonde hair and bulbous eyes, but it was his clothes that were most striking; the man looked quite extraordinary. His long jacket and wide trousers were pin-striped in a garish shade of pink on blue, and he wore a velvety waistcoat in a clashing shade of pink. Completing his outfit was a striped silk cravat and highly polished black boots, heeled to give him additional height. He wore an extremely self-satisfied expression and Latchet was gazing eagerly at him for approval, like some particularly unattractive lapdog. Confronted with this startling vision, Xander almost did not notice the small, nondescript looking man standing quietly behind them, preoccupied with checking off some papers on a clipboard. He did not look up at Xander or the others.

'What in Haven are you doing back here, Reeve?' demanded the peacock, in a shrill voice. 'You're supposed to be Chief Engineer and you're gossiping with Travellers,' his protuberant eyes rested with disfavour on Flint, 'and children. Have you found the source of the contamination yet?'

Reeve did not react.

'Narrowing it down, I think,' he said, in a calm voice. 'Although something interesting has come up. I'll let you know when there's anything definitive. I'm not going to jump to conclusions, Simm, no matter how much he yaps.' Reeve sent a contemptuous look at Latchet, who bristled with indignation, and then jerked his head to Flint and the others. 'Come on, we're done here. I'll walk you out.'

Simm looked most dissatisfied, and his mouth twisted petulantly.

'Make sure that you do, Reeve. I'm a very busy man, and I don't have time to keep running over here every time you engineers miscalculate and blow a section. When you have an answer, let Latchet here know. He'll get it straight over to me.' Latchet swelled up with pride, but Simm had already turned away. 'I shall be over at the Council Chamber if I am required.'

He spun around on his high heels, long jacket flaring out behind him, and swept away, his exit only slightly marred by the fact that he had headed off the wrong way and had to be discreetly steered by his quiet shadow. Xander frowned as his eyes followed the small, unremarkable figure of the third man, still unnamed.

'Funny,' he murmured to Ollie. 'There's something a bit weird about that guy.'

'Who, Simm?' said Ollie, with an incredulous look. 'You think?'

Xander did not have a chance to correct him as Reeve and Flint indicated firmly that it was time to go, leaving Latchet glaring impotently after them. Filled with relief he was going to get out of this place and back to fresh air and sunlight, Xander decided that it was probably not that important and hurried after them as they headed through the looming crystal slabs.

CHAPTER SIX

Xander had half-expected a further interrogation by Flint about the events in the Core once they had emerged from the echoing vestibule at the Nexus, but the Traveller appeared to be deep in thought and said nothing further to any of them. He hurried them through the gates and then back up the winding lane to Woodside, the forbidding frown on his face discouraging Xander from raising questions of his own. The faint rumble of many voices in the kitchen was discernible as soon as they entered the house and Flint strode ahead of them, pushing open the heavy door.

Xander, Ollie and Len paused in the hallway to exchange glances.

'Communicative as ever,' said Len and Xander nodded in agreement, that sense of frustration rising again.

'Might as well see what's causing all the bother this time,' suggested Ollie, before adding with a hopeful expression, 'and it has to be lunchtime by now. I'm starving after all that.'

Xander realised that his stomach was also feeling empty, not to mention rather uneasy after the events of that morning. It was a feeling that was becoming all too common for him. Following on behind Ollie, he saw that once again the kitchen was full of Travellers, and Flint was already deep in conversation with someone that Xander had not seen before, a tall and strikingly handsome man, with tousled black hair and grey eyes. Len had wandered into the kitchen behind Xander and her eyes fell on the man talking with Flint. Xander saw her stiffen and, for just a moment, a hopeful expression crossed her face. As if sensing her eyes on him, the man glanced over and saw Len standing by the door. His flinch was almost imperceptible but Xander saw it and so, it seemed, did Len. Her face shifted immediately into its usual unconcerned look and her mouth tightened. Without another glance at the man, she walked over to the sink and poured herself a glass of water.

The man hesitated and then walked over.

'How are you, Len?' he asked stiffly.

'Fine,' said Len, without turning around. She paused, then reluctantly, 'you?'

'Yes, good,' he said 'I mean, I'm fine.'

'Good,' replied Len. There was another awkward silence. Len drank her water and then rinsed the glass and put it to drain. Without another word, she turned and left the kitchen. The man stood for a moment, staring at the glass that Len had left on the draining board, and then turned and walked back to the fireplace.

Xander's gaze followed him curiously and so he caught Mrs Stanton also watching, with an exasperated expression on her face. She glanced around in time to meet Xander's stare and then bustled over to where he and Ollie stood, lifting a large jar down from the dresser as she came.

'Lunch isn't ready yet,' she said. She thrust the jar at Ollie, who was very obviously trying to overhear the quiet conversations at the fireplace. 'If you have nothing better to do than hang around here, you two had better take this and feed those nixies. I can't remember when you last did it and Katie will be devastated if they leave.'

She shooed them outside, ignoring Ollie's mutinous mutterings, and shut the back door after them. Ollie paused, eying the kitchen window, but a moment later Mrs Stanton's face appeared as she pulled it closed. She gave him a knowing look and insistently flipped her hand.

Ollie heaved a sigh. 'She's always so untrusting,' he said dolefully. 'I suppose we'd better feed the repulsive things.'

After a final reproachful glower over his shoulder he began to trudge down the garden. Xander followed him across the smooth lawn.

'What are niskies?' he asked.

'Nixies,' corrected Ollie, gloomily. 'They're Katie's idea of a pet. They're nasty, they bite and they generally have no redeeming qualities whatsoever, other than being 'sparkly'. Unfortunately, they're the latest craze, so Katie has to have some – and now we're stuck with the foul little things. And by 'we', of course, I mean me; Len claims she's allergic to them.'

Ollie sighed again, looking thoroughly ill-used. Xander, on the other hand, was keen to see what passed for a pet in Haven, and he looked around for some sign of them. They headed down to the far end of the garden, walked past a group of flowering shrubs, and stopped in front of a large, rather murky-looking pond.

'Don't get too close,' warned Ollie as he twisted the top off the jar, and then grimaced as he pulled out a handful of what looked like blue rubber worms. 'They can jump right out of the water.' He threw his handful of worms into the pond, where they floated for a moment before slowly sinking.

Xander watched from a safe distance, but he couldn't see anything moving. Ollie leaned slightly further out. 'Maybe they've all cleared off,' he said hopefully, scattering another handful of worms. With barely a splash, a glittering shape launched itself out of the pond, its teeth snapping inches from Ollie's fingers. He jerked his hand back with a furious yell but the thing had already disappeared again, slapping its tail maliciously on the surface so that Ollie was showered with pond water.

'Ugh,' he said, wiping his face and glaring at the nixie that had just re-surfaced. 'I told you they were foul.'

Several other heads broke the surface, and they all stared avidly at Ollie, mouths agape to reveal hundreds of tiny serrated teeth.

Xander prudently backed up several more paces from the water and stared at the strange creatures; they did not look like anything he had ever seen before in a garden pond. Their bodies were lizard like, with long spindly limbs and thin webbed fingers that paddled the surface of the water. The most disturbing thing about them, however, were their large, round heads with vaguely humanoid features – wide, unblinking eyes, thin blue lips and no nose. As Ollie had said, their only redeeming feature was their glittering skin, shading through rich jewel tones and overlaid with a faint golden sheen so they appeared to sparkle in the water. They snapped at each other and stared at the jar in Ollie's hand with a voracious hunger in their flat green eyes. Xander grimaced. Sparkly or not, they were quite repulsive.

'They're horrible,' he said in disgust.

'Told you,' said Ollie grimly. 'I cannot believe that Katie actually thinks they're *cute*. She must be completely deranged.' The nixies snapped their jaws at him as if they understood what he was saying and Ollie chucked another handful of worms to them. They flung themselves about in a frenzy of snapping teeth, clawing at each other with their webbed hands as they fought over the food.

'Ollie, who was that man in the kitchen?' asked Xander, with one eye on the nixies in case they tried to savage him instead. 'The one who spoke with Len at the sink.'

'You mean Uncle Jasper?' asked Ollie. 'Len's father.'

Xander swivelled to stare at him.

'You're kidding,' he said. 'Why do they act like that to each other?'

'Dunno, really,' replied Ollie, after some thought. 'They're always like that, so I don't notice it anymore. I suppose it was a bit awkward.'

Xander thought that was the understatement of the year.

'A bit?' he said incredulously.

Ollie shrugged. 'It's not like he's around that much, being a Traveller and all.' He didn't seem to think there was anything else to add. Xander shook his head but decided to change the subject.

'Did you hear what they were talking about in there? What's got everyone all riled up now?' he asked.

'Nope,' said Ollie, answering the first question. 'They were all talking too quietly. Something must have kicked off though; maybe there's been another breach?'

A moment later, Xander was grateful that they had changed the subject, as Len herself emerged from around the flowering shrubs. Up to this point, she had rather held herself aloof from Xander but this time she favoured him with a quick grin.

'You got kicked out, I assume,' she said, reaching over to take a handful of the nixie food.

'Thought they gave you hives?' Ollie said acidly.

Len threw him an amused look.

'Please,' she said. 'I just didn't want to get stuck looking after the little fiends when Katie inevitably gets bored with them.'

She threw the worms one by one into the pool. The nixies

snatched at the food but Xander noticed in surprise that they were suddenly more restrained. They also watched Len warily, making no attempt to snap at her even when she leaned right over the pond.

Len had also noticed their unusual behaviour. 'Weird,' she said. 'Maybe Katie's actually hit on a way to train nixies–this lot seem far less homicidal than usual.' Losing interest, she rubbed her hands clean on her trousers. 'Food's gone. You can clear off now,' she told the nixies. Without a sound, every one of them promptly dived under the water and disappeared. Len's eyebrows shot up, and she looked around at Xander and Ollie.

'Well, that's unexpected,' she said and then shook her head, dismissing the nixies' odd behaviour. 'Anyway, the coast is clear and Gran says you can come back and help with lunch.'

With a last wary glance back at the now quiet pond, Xander hurried after Len as she marched back up the garden.

Lunch was a quiet affair, the kitchen being deserted again when they returned. Despite Ollie's attempts to ask leading questions about what had prompted the meeting earlier, Mrs Stanton resisted all of his attempts to probe and refused to give anything away, finally losing her patience and packing him off upstairs to tidy his room. Len pulled a mocking face at him and was unfortunate enough to get caught by her grandmother.

'You needn't act so superior,' Mrs Stanton said tartly. 'It may not be in the same league but your room is hardly pristine either. Up you go and sort it out, and then you may be in a position to judge your cousin.'

Len rolled her eyes at that.

'Where are the brownies, anyway?' she grumbled. 'Honestly, what's the point of being plagued by weird little oddities with body image issues and a cleaning fetish if they don't even tidy our rooms?'

'Not another word,' said Mrs Stanton ominously, with a wary glance around the kitchen. She glared at Len. 'They don't do your rooms because you have two arms and two legs and are more than capable – and I don't want to hear you speaking about them like that ever again.'

Mrs Stanton rose from the table and eyed Len with that look of awful majesty she could, on occasion, draw around herself. Len was certainly not equal to it and slid out of the kitchen without another word of complaint. Xander also stood, feeling rather awkward and wondering whether he should go upstairs to help Ollie, but Mrs Stanton turned to him with her charming smile and laid a gentle hand on his arm.

'Sorry, Xander,' she said. 'Please don't leave – actually I rather wanted to have a word with you.'

Xander eyed her worriedly, and she laughed and shook her head at him.

'No need to look so terrified.'

She slipped an arm through his and led him down the hall and into one of the sitting rooms. The big windows were open wide, and it was light and airy in there, with colourful flowers peeping over the sill and pouring their fresh scents into the room, along with the soft hum from the bees at work in the garden. A large clock ticked away in the corner and there were clear signs of Jenna's handiwork in the pots of richly green plants and bowls of flowering bulbs sitting among the many photographs scattered through the room, in delicate silver frames. It was a restful place and Xander sank down amongst the plentiful cushions on the big sofa, Mrs Stanton settling beside him with a grateful sigh.

'It's good to sit down for a moment, it's been quite a hectic morning,' she said, and then turned so she could see Xander better. 'I just wanted a quick chat because I saw you noticed that ridiculous scene between Len and her father earlier.'

Xander was not sure what he was supposed to say to this, so he nodded wordlessly. Mrs Stanton did not seem to expect any comment and continued on.

'Len seems to have taken to you and I'm grateful for that, as she doesn't make friends very easily. I realise that she can be a bit spiky and stand-offish but whether or not she wants to admit it, she needs more people in her life than just her cousin. I wanted to explain about her before she manages to chase you away as well.'

As she spoke, Mrs Stanton reached over to a side table and opened the drawer, lifting out a framed photograph and laying it face down on her knee, before continuing.

'Jasper is my younger son, and he's always been the quieter of the two. To be honest, it worried us when we realised that he'd inherited his father's Traveller abilities while James didn't, but James never let that drive a wedge between them. He was always keen on following in my footsteps and passionate about working with animals; he never once resented Jasper's abilities. Jasper was away from home more and more as he grew older, spending time at the Lodges and training. Then, when he was twenty, he went away for around three months and when he returned, he brought a girl back with him.'

She smiled in recollection, her fingers idly stroking the photograph frame.

'We'd never seen him so lit up, so happy, like he'd transformed from the inside out. Her name was Vivian.'

Mrs Stanton paused and then turned over the photograph and offered it to Xander. Xander recognised Len's father, his handsome face alight with laughter as he looked down at the woman beside him. She had the same pale blonde hair as Len, although hers rippled down her back in waves and curls, and her skin had that same golden tinge, but there the similarities ended; her expression was bright and filled with happiness, making her look very different to her daughter's habitual coolness. Mrs Stanton smiled sadly.

'They were both young, but we all knew that they were right for each other; they got married shortly afterwards. Everyone loved Vivian. She was one of those people who lit up every room she entered. She was sweet and thoughtful, and she brought such joy to our family and to Jasper; he would have done anything for her.' She glanced around the room as if she could see Len's mother right there, before she continued on. 'James had married Jenna the year before, and both Vivian and Jenna became pregnant together. Woodside was filled with happiness and excitement; we felt blessed beyond measure, until the sickness came.'

She looked down and sighed.

'Flint said that the hobs told you about that this morning, Xander, but they weren't the only victims. Humans were less susceptible, it's true, but it was no less lethal to us. James fell ill first and then, while Jenna and I were frantically trying to nurse him, Vivian was struck down too. It was a bad case from the beginning. She held on for a while, a few weeks, until she had given birth to Len but then we lost her.'

Mrs Stanton pressed her lips together, looking at the photograph, as if there was something else she wanted to say but she just shook her head again, her expression bereft.

'We lost our Vivian, and it broke Jasper. James was recovering and luckily Jenna never caught it, but all the stress and strain brought the baby early. Oliver was incredibly tiny and fragile, and we weren't even sure at the time that he would survive. Jasper had already left; he couldn't bear to be here, in the place where his life had fallen apart. And then, just as I thought we had hit our lowest ebb, the border failed and shades struck, catching a group of Travellers completely unaware.'

Xander looked up at her sharply, and Mrs Stanton nodded.

'Yes, I know that Ari took you to see poor Alvin Tavish, and that she told you that there were two others with him who didn't survive.' She hesitated and smoothed out her skirt with hands that shook a little. 'One of those two was my husband, Max.'

Xander did not know quite what to say; he cleared his throat awkwardly.

'I'm really sorry,' he said quietly.

Mrs Stanton patted him on the knee. 'That's very kind,' she said, and then sighed again. 'It was a long time ago now, but I still remember how desperate things were. Max and Vivian were gone, Jenna was exhausted with a terribly frail baby, James could barely get out of bed after that awful sickness and Len was a motherless newborn, with Jasper who knew where. Everything was falling apart and sometimes I didn't know how I could go on, I felt so shattered.'

She looked up at Xander, her expression bleak and then, unexpectedly, a little smile tugged at her lips. 'That's when something amazing happened. One morning, I came down-stairs to the kitchen and found it immaculate. The floor was shining, every pot, dish and pan was gleaming, all the laundry was done and a fresh loaf of bread was waiting for us on the side. I could scarcely believe my eyes, but Brolly and Spike kept coming every day, washing, cleaning and keeping us going until we had the strength to begin again. Those 'little oddities' that Len is so dismissive of brought us through the worst time in our lives, and I will never stop being grateful to them. It's funny though,' she added pensively. 'We didn't see them for many years, once we were back on our feet, but then they turned up again, a few months ago, as if they were checking in to make sure we're okay.' She fell silent, her expression thoughtful.

Xander tried to take all of this in, turning it over in his mind. 'So what happened with Len's father?' he asked hesitantly. 'Is it weird between them because he left her?'

Mrs Stanton took a deep breath.

'Not entirely,' she said. 'Jasper came back when the news reached him about his father. That didn't help, of course, because he was racked with guilt about not being there. Ben Flint is just as bad – Max was his mentor and trainer when he was a young Traveller.' She huffed. 'As if there was anything either of them could have done if they had been there. Anyway, Jasper came back but there was no heart left in him. He did try with Len, but the older she got the more she reminded him of her mother. Her expressions, her mannerisms, sometimes it's like seeing Vivian all over again. Maybe for some people, it would have been a comfort to see reminders of the person they loved, but not Jasper. I would see him flinch when he looked at her, just like today, and Len was quite sharp enough to pick up on it as she grew older. Jasper began to stay away more, and the distance between them has kept on growing.' She turned an exasperated look on Xander. 'If I thought it would do any good, I would bang both their stubborn heads together,' she said tartly.

'Have you talked to Len about it?' asked Xander.

Mrs Stanton laughed.

'Ha! Have you tried talking to Len about something she doesn't want to discuss? Brick walls are more receptive! Len doesn't want to hear any of it and she refuses to discuss her mother.' She looked down again at the picture on her knee and then laid it face down in the drawer and shut it away with a soft sigh. 'I have to keep this photo hidden. Len doesn't want to see it and it hurts Jasper to remember those times. It's been nice to talk to you about her though. I loved Vivian very much, and I miss her every day.' She patted Xander on the knee. 'You've been very kind to listen to me ramble on, but I wanted you to understand about why Len is so prickly sometimes. You seem a nice young man and it would do Len so much good to have a friend she could count on, other than just Ollie. Don't let her push you away.'

She was looking at Xander so hopefully that he felt like he must give her some kind of reassurance and he nodded, with an awkward smile. She beamed back at him and then stood up briskly.

'Wonderful,' she said. 'Now, if you don't mind, you had better pop upstairs and give Ollie a hand. That boy is absolutely incapable of tidying anything and I dread to think what he's doing up there.' With another quick smile, she led Xander out of the room and headed back to the kitchen, leaving Xander to walk slowly up the stairs, his thoughts busy with everything he had heard.

Sprawled out on the beds in the boys' room that night, with Len joining them for the first time, they talked over what had happened in the Core that afternoon and how it might fit in with the other information they had. It turned into a minor argument between the cousins, Len proving to be rather sceptical about the hobs as a source for any further infor-mation. She suggested sardonically that the brownies were likely to be more forthcoming, while Ollie remained adamant that they clearly knew things they were not telling Xander, and his best hope was returning to the little shop near Fountain Square to ask Hob for his help.

'Fine,' conceded Len, eventually. 'But if you come away with yet more mysterious warnings and absolutely no concrete information, don't blame me.'

Xander made no reply to this as he thought Len was most likely correct, but as he went to bed that night, it was with the memory of the hobgoblin's creaking voice telling him they would be waiting. His sleep was not very restful.

The next morning, Ollie was hopeful that classes would be cancelled after the Nexus power outage but he was swiftly disabused of this by his parents, who both laughed at his disappointed expression.

'You'll be lucky,' said James, shaking his head. 'Why do you think they have secondary nodes and backups? The likelihood of the Academy being disrupted by power outages is about the same as a nixie being appointed Chief Engineer at the Nexus.'

Ollie pulled a disappointed face at Xander as he and Len headed out for the day. Mrs Stanton, with an eye to Xander's slightly lost expression, immediately claimed his help and kept him busy most of the morning with baking bread, roasting a ham and chopping up fruit for jellies. Xander had done very little cooking before, having viewed the kitchen as a health hazard and a place to be avoided, and he found himself rather enjoying the process and even planning to have a try himself, when he got home again.

After lunch, he fetched the reference book down and sat in the dappled shade in the orchard, munching apples and reading about the Mining Guild and their ongoing payment disputes with bluecaps. According to the book, the tiny figures which frequented the deep mines like blue flames were particularly sensitive to impending cave-ins, and they charged the Guild handsomely for their services in providing warnings. Several times in Guild history however, members had become suspicious that the somewhat taciturn bluecaps were actually setting up the collapses themselves to extort further payment; prolonged standoffs had then occurred, only for the relationship to be re-kindled again amidst mutual distrust and general hostility. Xander shook his head in disbelief and smiled wryly as he flicked through the pages and imagined exam questions on this subject.

When his watch told him it was near enough to the time that classes finished for him to leave without suspicion, he took the book back inside and asked Mrs Stanton if he could meet Ollie and Len. She was distracted at the time in repairing a large bowl which Katie had progressed sufficiently with her orb to explode in a spectacular fashion that morning, and Xander got an absent nod and a query about whether he was sure he knew where he was going.

With a quick affirmation and a wave, Xander headed out of Woodside and down towards the gate in Wykeham. It was rather an odd feeling to realise that this was the first time he had gone anywhere alone since he had arrived in Haven, and he strode through the carved stone arch with a sudden grin on his face, entirely certain that Flint would have been extremely disapproving if he knew.

Despite the fact that he had only done it a couple of times, the route already seemed familiar to Xander and he was even starting to become inured to the strange sights and inhabitants. A small clutch of fauns wearing what appeared to be large sandwich boards, dragging placards behind them, got barely a glance from him now as they emerged from another of the gates, and he made a point to smile warmly at a rather startled-looking giant who crossed the street in front of him.

Walking at a brisk pace that Mrs Stanton would have been proud of, Xander rapidly drew level with the bright lights of the Thorne Store and all of its shimmering orbs, and then turned his back on the glittering windows and looked down the little side street, where the old wooden sign creaked in the light breeze. He was not feeling very positive about yet another encounter with hobgoblins, but he knew that Ollie was right; he needed to get some answers.

With a deep breath, and before he could change his mind, Xander pushed open the door; the bell chimed out, just as he remembered. The shop was unchanged from his previous visit, still dimly lit and dusty, but this time Hob was sitting at his cluttered desk, sorting through a jumbled pile of rocks. He looked up as Xander entered and stared at him, with no sign of welcome. There was an uncomfortable silence.

Xander cleared his throat. 'Hello,' he said awkwardly.

As if he had passed some unspoken test, Hob put down the rock he was holding and gestured towards the armchairs by the hearth. Not sure whether he was relieved that he had not been thrown out immediately, Xander walked over to the nearest chair. His eyes had been slow to adjust to the dim light, and he realised with a small start of surprise as he sat down, that one seat was already occupied. This hobgoblin was not as ancient-looking as the one they had met yesterday at the Core, who Reeve had referred to as the Elder Goblin, but he had grey hair, with long wrinkles creasing his pale, papery skin. He stared at Xander, his spidery fingers clutching a small cloth-wrapped bundle. The faint glimmer of the glowstones in the fireplace glittered in his eyes.

'We have expected you.' The voice was dusty, as if it was rarely used. 'The conditions have been met.'

Xander had had a long list of questions on the tip of his tongue but after that disquieting announcement, there was a brand new one, right at the top of the list. 'I don't understand,' he said, his voice rising a little. 'What conditions? What does that even mean?'

The hobgoblin stared at him, his expression closed. 'That is not your concern. It is a matter for goblin-kind, not you.' His mouth snapped shut, and he stared forbiddingly into the distance.

Xander swallowed. Clearly that line of questioning was not going to get him anywhere and, with a sudden remembrance of Len's scepticism, he tried another.

'I was just wondering,' he said haltingly. 'I don't know why I'm here or why weird things keep happening to me, like yesterday. I thought maybe you might know something about it? I just want to know why.' The last words came out more plaintively than Xander intended and he fell silent, his hands clutching the arms of his chair.

The hobgoblin sat rigid, the only movement that of his fingers stroking the bundle in his lap. Suddenly his head slowly swivelled so he could look directly at Xander, examining him as if he were some strange kind of insect. There was a long pause, when all Xander could hear was the sound of his own breathing. Finally, the hobgoblin looked away with a sigh.

'We do not have all the answers you seek, Xander King,' he whispered. 'Your story is not ours to know, we who have lost all but fragments of our own. What we have left warns us of an ancient foe, an eternal enemy who strikes without warning, a destroyer.'

Leaning forward, the hobgoblin reached out and took Xander's hand in his own, turning it in his cold fingers so that the palm was visible, then hovering his fingertips over the scar.

He paused for a moment, lost in thought, and the room seemed to get darker and colder. Xander waited, eyes fixed on the old hobgoblin until he glanced up, a small smile flickering over his thin lips, and then continued.

'The darkness has marked you here, where you met it and threw it back but that is not all. Our oldest traditions speak of the ancient blood which stood against the enemy once, to defy him. The trace of that blood is also here in you, down through all the ages. But is it enough? That we do not know.' His dusty voice trailed away.

A dozen questions jostled for room in Xander's mind and he blurted out the first one.

'What ancient blood? What does that mean?'

'The ancient blood was once a shield for us, more than that we cannot recall,' replied the hobgoblin. 'I told you we have lost much, and are left with only the shattered pieces of our knowledge, our history. We have the memories to detect the bloodline when it returns, no more. The hand of the enemy has weighed heavily upon us, our fortunes have turned and we are diminished, almost gone.' The hobgoblin spoke without emotion, his voice as dry as death.

Xander swallowed. 'Who is the enemy?' he asked.

'He has many faces but only one desire, to destroy and tear down. He does not sleep or relent in this thirst, and the powers of darkness are his to command.' The hobgoblin's strange eyes glittered again as he stared at Xander. 'This is what we know of our enemy; perhaps you will learn more.'

Xander had a very bad feeling about that. He opened his mouth to ask another question, but the hobgoblin made a sharp gesture with his hand, cutting him off.

'It is enough. We have no more answers for you, Xander King; you must walk your own path. However, tradition demands one more thing of us: something we have held since time immemorial, waiting.'

The hobgoblin began to unwrap the bundle on his knee with exquisite care, and Xander's eyes widened as the soft material was drawn away to reveal a silver band. It was strangely twisted and engraved, and set within it was a black jewel, glimmering in the dim light. Xander had seen many orbs since he had arrived in Haven, but none of them had looked like this. He swallowed as the hobgoblin held it out to him.

'Um, the last time I touched an orb, it didn't go too well,' he said.

There was a snort from behind him and Xander jumped. He had quite forgotten Hob, standing silently through all of this exchange.

'Piece of rubbish, that was,' Hob said contemptuously. 'Thorne's tat, far too weak to contain the power you are capable of commanding. This is hob-made, and it's unique. This stone was passed down to us along with the old knowledge of how to prepare it, for when the blood returned again. It took many of our kind to craft it.' His lip curled in disdain. 'What you will do with it, of course, is another matter.'

The old hobgoblin was still holding out the orb to Xander and, tentatively, he reached out and took it. The stone felt warm to Xander's fingers and as he looked more closely, he saw tiny flickers deep within it, sparking like lightning as they burst up to the surface. It was mesmerising.

Suddenly realising that both hobgoblins were watching him intently, Xander laid the band on his left wrist and fastened it, tensing a little despite Hob's assurances, just in case history repeated itself. The orb didn't show any signs of shooting out destructive beams of light, although for an instant he had felt a tingle in his left palm. He held up his hand and admired the glimmering stone. Strangely, it felt absolutely right, as though he had been missing something that had unexpectedly been restored to him.

'Wow,' he said, without thinking, turning it to admire the way the light chased along the silvery band.

'That remains to be seen,' whispered the old hobgoblin. 'Try to use it well, Xander King.' He stood up, staring coldly at Xander, who rose awkwardly to his feet at the brusque dismissal.

'Thank you so much for this,' he blurted, trying to express his gratitude for the beautiful orb.

The old hobgoblin paused, with a sharp look at Xander.

'We will be watching,' was all he said, which sounded vaguely ominous, before disappearing through a small door that Xander had not noticed before. In the meantime, Hob had walked back over to his desk and sat down at his pile of stones. Xander looked at his bent head, which did not invite any further conversation, but he had one more question and he blurted it out before he lost the nerve.

'What would have happened if I hadn't come back here?'

Hob didn't even bother to look up. He picked up a large stone and began to examine it.

'Then the conditions would not have been met,' he grated out, and flicked his fingers at Xander in an obvious, if unsubtle, indication he should leave.

A moment later, standing out in the warm sunshine, and even with the reassuring weight of the orb on his wrist, Xander still could not quite believe what had just happened. He held the orb up, staring at the beautiful band and the unusual black stone, and suddenly couldn't wait to show Ollie and Len. Suppressing the urge to run, he pulled his sleeve down over the orb and turned left, heading for Fountain Square and the Academy steps.

The square was busy, as always, with the usual collection of strange and unusual figures passing through. A giant, walking ahead of Xander past a large, pastel-flowering bush, sneezed violently and a cloud of fairies shot up from the bush, swirling in agitated circles in the air until they gradually began to descend back to the leafy branches. The giant looked very apologetic, grimacing repentantly at Xander and the other people nearby, while a couple of the tiny, winged figures drifted over to Xander. He picked up his pace, really not keen to find out whether they would settle on him as well.

He hurried across the square, past the fountain in the centre, and dodged out of the way of a harried-looking little woman who was shepherding a small flock of shopping bags before her. Xander thought back to his astonishment of just a few days ago, when he had first seen this sight, and smiled again at how quickly the strangeness of Haven had become commonplace to him.

Following Mrs Stanton's previous instructions, Xander crossed over to stand at the foot of a broad set of stairs leading up to one of the massive, official-looking buildings that surrounded the square. From Ollie's descriptions he knew that inside that building were not only classrooms, and halls but also gates, which carried the pupils off to the various Guild training locations for their apprenticeship options. Xander privately considered that, Ollie to the contrary, the Academy sounded like much better fun than his own schooling. The doors at the top of the steps were still closed, but groups of adults, mainly women, were gathering along the bottom stair, and the sound of laughter and chat floated over to Xander as he stood there, his hands in his pockets, trying to look unobtrusive.

A huge clock set atop the Academy chimed the hour and immediately all the doors along the base of the building burst open; within moments, the staircase was boiling over with pupils of all ages. Younger children were shepherded over to their waiting parents but most of the older ones rapidly dispersed, individually and in cheerful groups, although some stood in small gaggles on the steps, garnering annoyed looks as they blocked the way for others trying to get home. In all the noise and bustle Xander almost missed Ollie jogging forward, his backpack slung over one shoulder. He grinned when he caught sight of Xander and angled over to meet up with him. The flood of people leaving the Academy had lessened but there was still no sign of Len's characteristic pale hair among the groups of girls coming down the steps. Xander did spot Katie, off on a play date and bouncing alongside another little girl of her own age, while the girl's mother led them both away with an indulgent smile for their antics.

'Planning on joining us after all?' asked Ollie, with a wave of his hand towards the building behind them.

Xander shook his head, with a wistful look. 'Nah,' he replied. 'I was just in the area and thought I would come and meet you guys.' He looked about with a frown. Most of the people had now gone, and the steps were almost empty. 'Did we miss Len?' he asked.

Ollie grimaced.

'Nope,' he said. 'She got put in detention again, over at the Halls.' He gestured towards another beautiful building, with huge stained-glass windows, across the square and then glanced at Xander, seeing his interested expression. 'Come on, we'll pop over there and see how long till she gets out.' He trotted down the rest of the steps and led the way.

Xander fell in beside him. The orb still felt heavy and

significant on his wrist but somehow he didn't feel that the middle of Fountain Square was the right place to reveal it to Ollie. He examined the impressive building as they drew nearer.

'What are the Halls?' he asked.

'The Halls of Records,' corrected Ollie. 'It's a massive library, with lots of rooms in it, hence 'Halls'. People do research there and a copy of pretty much every document in Haven is stored there somewhere. We're not allowed into the parts with the oldest stuff, of course, but students can use the main part; that's generally where they send people to do detention. You get Primilla Pennicott breathing down your neck and between her, the dust and the musty smell, it's a pretty horrific punishment.' Ollie shuddered expressively.

That name rang a bell for Xander; he frowned a moment until he suddenly recalled the pinch-faced woman with the carping voice who had left the complaining message on the day he had arrived in Haven. The two boys walked together up the shallow, foot-worn steps leading up to the Halls. The wooden doors were enormous up close and were closed, looking like they had not been opened for a very long time, however within one of them was a much smaller door, standing open. It looked small by comparison but in fact, as Xander passed through, the top of it was high above his head.

Inside the entrance was a dim reception hall lit by glow-stone lamps, where old wooden-framed notice boards lined the bare stone walls, covered with various yellowing notices, timetables and announcements. There was also the distinctive, slightly stale smell of an ancient building and an over-powering silence, like a long-deserted church. Directly ahead of them was another set of large wooden doors.

Ollie put his fingers to his lips. 'Follow me and don't

speak. If we make a row, we'll get thrown out and we don't want to attract the old dragon.'

Xander nodded to show he had heard, and Ollie turned the old brass doorknob, easing the big door open just a crack, enough to let the two boys squeeze in. While Ollie closed the door carefully behind them, Xander looked around the room curiously.

It was massive, with a vaulted ceiling supported by many huge beams, all intricately carved. Hanging down from the high ceiling on lengthy chains were several chandeliers, filled with glittering white glowstones, while the enormous stained-glass windows that Xander had noticed from outside sent their soft, multi-coloured beams to paint the bookcases with jewelled light. The shelves along the back walls were set in tiers, rising almost up to the ceiling, with balconies to access them lined with wrought-iron railings and lit with ornate lamp-posts set at intervals along the galleries.

More huge bookcases criss-crossed the central space, each with a carved wooden ladder to roll along it and allow the highest shelves to be accessed. Tables were tucked away throughout the space, large and small, which were evidently meant as workspaces for those who came here to study. Some of them were equipped with the same terminals that Xander had seen in the Stanton's kitchen, with neat screens rising out of the surfaces. People were sitting at some of the tables, and others were standing, consulting books. There was no sign of Len anywhere.

Ollie elbowed him gently in the ribs.

'Keep your head down,' he murmured, with a wary glance over his shoulder. 'She's on her perch. Come on, before she spots us.'

Ollie ducked off to his right but Xander risked a quick

glance before following. Behind him to his left was a raised dais with a high, imposing-looking desk set atop it, and sitting at the desk on a tall, spindly chair was a gaunt, sour-faced woman with a rabbity mouth. She appeared engrossed in a large, dusty catalogue but every moment or so, her pinched face rose and scanned the central aisles of the library, seeking anyone who dared to disturb the sanctity of her domain. She had not yet looked in their direction, and Xander bent his head and hurried after Ollie who was already vanishing behind one of the stacks.

It took a little while for them to find Len, as the library was something of a labyrinth but eventually they ran her down in a little dusty nook by the golden stone wall, her pale head bent over a thick, leather-bound book. She was scribbling rapidly and, while one of the stained-glass windows decorated her table and the wall in cheerful patterns of coloured light, it did nothing to lighten her furious scowl. As Ollie and Xander turned the corner, she glanced up with a glower that disappeared as she recognised them.

'Is this prisoner's visiting hour?' she asked with a quick grin, dropping her pen and flexing her fingers. Ollie slid into the seat opposite her while Xander leant against the wall, propped up on a handy stone ledge.

'We'd break you out but I'm afraid there be dragons,' Ollie replied, with a grimace over his shoulder in the vague direction of Primilla Pennicott's platform. 'What's she got you doing this time?'

Len shoved the decrepit old tome towards him across the table and Ollie flipped through some pages, wrinkling his nose at the dust that floated out.

'Since I apparently have *no respect for our heritage*,' she said, imitating Primilla's carping voice, 'I have to write out the lineage of the Founding Families, along with their terms of office on the Council. To call it a total waste of my life would be an understatement.'

Ollie pulled a face in sympathy.

'How long's she got you for?' he asked.

'Until she feels I've suffered enough, which probably means forever,' grumbled Len. Her eyebrows shot up as Xander lurched away from the wall and turned to stare at it in surprise. As he had been leaning back, a sudden bloom of warmth had flared against his hip and now little flashes of light were sputtering across a square of pale, smooth stone set in the wall, just above the little shelf. Xander backed away warily; the memory of the last time a stone tablet started unexpectedly flickering was only too vivid in his mind.

'What's happening?' he asked, glancing at Ollie and Len. They both looked perplexed.

'No idea,' said Len. 'I've never seen that before. I thought it was just part of the wall.'

Ollie reached out a curious hand towards the little flickers on the stone and Xander hurriedly batted it to one side. 'I wouldn't,' he said, in an incautiously loud voice. From the distance came the abrupt scrape of a chair.

'Better get out of here,' hissed Len, dragging the book back towards her. 'You don't want to get caught. I'll catch up with you later at home.'

The clack of high heels was rapidly approaching and both boys dived towards the thick stack of bookcases leading to the entranceway. In a final, quick glance over his shoulder, Xander saw that the stone in the wall had returned to its previous appearance, blank and worn.

By unspoken agreement, Ollie and Xander headed straight back to the Wykeham Gate. Ollie was frowning, obviously still thinking about the strange behaviour of the stone in the Halls but Xander had other things on his mind, in particular the new and unaccustomed weight on his wrist. One more weird stone flashing at him felt far less urgent than telling Ollie about what had happened in Hob's shop and showing him the black orb, and Xander was eager to get back to Woodside as quickly as possible.

The front door, as usual, was standing wide open and as they went in Xander was about to ask Ollie to come upstairs for a minute; he was distracted, however, by the truly appalling stench floating down the hallway. In Xander's previous life he had been accustomed to the kitchen being the source of culinary tragedy and unspeakable smells, but since his arrival in Woodside he had adjusted to a new reality of fresh, homemade food and appetising aromas. This horrible odour and the blue haze that appeared to be accompanying it was therefore an unwelcome surprise. It did not appear to come as any shock to Ollie however, who pulled a face.

'Not again,' he muttered, and then marched down the hallway. Xander trailed behind him, trying to breathe as little as possible.

The kitchen was filled with even more of the blue haze and the terrible smell was far more concentrated here. Ollie glared accusingly at the two indistinct figures bending over the stove, stirring the contents of a large pot.

'You know that Mum is going to murder both of you,' he said darkly. 'She told you that you were only allowed to do that at the Institute because the stink kills her plants, not to mention *all the rest of us*.'

Mrs Stanton and Ollie's father both swung around, looking as guilty as two people with watering eyes and damp table napkins tied over their noses could appear.

'She's not back yet, is she?' asked James, looking worried.

'No,' replied Ollie, 'unless she's already been knocked out by the stench and is unconscious somewhere.'

'Oh, good,' James said in relief, ignoring the sarcasm. 'It's a treatment we've been developing for skin sores that has applications for humans and animals, but it's turned out to be a bit more pungent than we expected. We thought we'd be done before any of you got home.' He looked thoughtfully at the blue fog hanging over everything. 'Do us a favour and open the back door, would you? A bit of fresh air will blow it all out.'

Ollie snorted in disbelief, but picked his way through the haze and pushed at the back door. 'You'll be lucky,' he said, his voice muffled through the shirt sleeve pressed to his mouth and nose. 'Nothing short of a tornado is likely to blow this lot out before Mum gets home.'

'Nonsense,' said Mrs Stanton, although her tone lacked some of her usual certainty. 'We're all finished now. You two pop upstairs and we'll have supper ready in no time.' She blotted her watering eyes with the back of one hand and added, 'I think maybe we should eat outside though.'

The stench was somewhat less overpowering upstairs and Ollie shut their bedroom door with a sigh of relief. 'That is truly disgusting,' he said, pulling a face. 'And if they think Mum isn't going to know immediately–'

His voice trailed off as he shook his head in disbelief at that folly.

'Never mind the smell,' said Xander, unable to hold in his news any more. 'I've got something to show you.'

He tugged up his sleeve and held out his wrist. Ollie froze, his eyes wide, as he took in the intricately chased silver of the band and the black stone set in it, glinting as it caught the light.

'What? I mean, where –? What?' he said, incoherently.

Xander grinned at him. 'I know,' he said.

Ollie sat down on his bed and gestured to Xander to do the same. 'Speak to me,' he said, still staring at the orb on Xander's wrist. 'What is that thing? I'm assuming that your visit to that hobgoblin has something to do with it?'

Xander nodded.

'Got it in one,' he said, and then related everything he could remember about the strange encounter in Hob's Orbs, including the little information the hobs had passed on about his blood, and the enemy they blamed for all their misfortune. Ollie listened carefully, although his eyes kept wandering back to the glittering black orb, and Xander waited anxiously for his reaction.

Ollie did not speak for a moment, chewing on his lip. Finally he looked up.

'Are they expecting you to do something for them with that thing?' he asked. 'You said they kept talking about this blood shielding them before from their enemy – is that what they want you to do?'

Xander shrugged. 'I have no idea. You know what they're like.' For just a moment the utter absurdity of a serious discussion on the foibles of hobgoblins struck him, but then he mentally shrugged; this was apparently his life now. 'They gave me a few bits of information and then basically told me to have at it, whilst making quite clear that they have zero faith in my ability to do anything.'

'Sounds about right,' agreed Ollie, with a grimace. 'So, what now?'

Xander looked doubtfully over at the dully opaque orb on

Ollie's wrist. 'Do you think you could show me how to use this?' he asked.

Ollie hesitated.

'I don't think that's a good idea,' he said. 'I mean, I'm not exactly skilled with this one and it's not in the same league as yours.' He thought for a moment. 'I've never seen a black one before, but that's essentially a Traveller orb you're wearing. To be honest, I think they're your best bet.'

Xander pulled a face at the thought of Flint's likely reaction to this latest development, but he knew that Ollie was probably right. Before he could say anything else, there was a knock at their bedroom door, followed by James Stanton's face peeking around the doorframe.

'Suppertime,' he announced, and then sniffed cautiously. 'Not bad at all now,' he said in a satisfied voice.

'You're joking, right?' Ollie called after him and then looked over at Xander. 'You'd best tell my dad tonight and he'll get hold of Flint. There's no point you having that thing if you can't use it.'

Xander nodded. 'I s'pose,' he said reluctantly, before following Ollie as he headed for the stairs.

Just as they reached the downstairs hallway, Jenna and Len came in through the front door, the latter with a quick wink and knowing grin for the two boys. Jenna took two steps into the house and then stopped abruptly, sniffing. Ollie stifled a smirk.

'James Stanton,' she called out irately. 'Have you and your mother been trying to exterminate us all with toxic fumes again?'

There was a guilty silence from the kitchen and Jenna rolled her eyes before marching down the hallway to the kitchen door. Ollie's snigger finally broke loose.

'I can't believe he thought she wouldn't smell it,' he said, shaking his head. 'But while she's busy in there, show Len what you got up to this afternoon.' He sent a meaningful look at Xander's wrist, where the orb was once more concealed under his sleeve.

Len's expression of surprise was almost comical as Xander held up the orb for her perusal. 'Where d'you get that from?' she asked as she stared at the two boys. Xander repeated the gist of what he had told Ollie upstairs, and she frowned as she listened to him intently.

'What do you think?' Xander asked when he had finished.

Len eyed him thoughtfully.

'Well, for a start I don't think it's a good idea to tell Gran about mystic enemies and ancient blood. She tends to think that sort of thing is hogwash,' she said crisply, sounding very much like her grandmother. 'Secondly, I think Ollie is right. You need to talk to the Travellers.'

Mrs Stanton's voice came floating down the hallway from the kitchen. 'Where on earth are those children?' The kitchen door opened, and she poked her head out. 'Are you lot rooted to the spot down there?' she demanded.

'Coming,' said Ollie quickly.

The smell had dissipated somewhat in the kitchen, but a faint blue haze remained in the corners of the room and Len looked around with a puzzled air.

'What's all that?' she asked, wrinkling her nose in distaste.

'You may well ask,' said Jenna tartly. 'Your grandmother and your uncle have been creating noxious brews again.'

'Medicine,' replied Mrs Stanton and James, both at the same time and with the exact same injured look. Len glanced between the two of them and laughed.

'Nope,' she said. 'Aunt Jenna is definitely right.'

'Oh, sit down, all of you,' said Mrs Stanton. 'We won't hear you complaining when you have skin sores, now will we?'

'Really?' said Ollie disgustedly. 'We're going to discuss skin sores at the supper table. It's enough to put people off their food.'

Jenna laughed.

'If by people you mean you, then that's a miracle I've never seen before. Sit down, for goodness' sake.'

Despite the lingering smell, the food was as tasty as always and Xander was happy to enjoy it before broaching the subject of his new possession. As the meal was winding down however, Len sent Xander several meaningful looks and finally Mrs Stanton spotted her.

'Is there any reason why you're grimacing like that?' she asked Len, who just turned and raised her eyebrows at Xander. He realised that there was no point in putting it off any further and tugged up his sleeve, holding his wrist out self-consciously in front of him. There was a moment of stunned surprise.

'Good gracious.' Mrs Stanton's eyes were wide, and she looked over at her son, who looked completely nonplussed.

'Where did that come from?' asked James, his voice rather worried.

Xander looked straight at him. 'They gave it to me at Hob's Orb shop,' he explained. 'They said that they had had it for a long time, waiting for the right person to come along, and they seem to think that's me.' He took a breath. 'I don't really know why, to be honest.'

James, Jenna, and Mrs Stanton exchanged quick glances across the table, as Ollie chimed in. 'I said to Xander that it would be best to talk to the Travellers about it. I mean, it looks kind of like one of their orbs.'

James nodded slowly, sitting back in his chair.

'That's not a bad idea,' he said. 'I'll get in touch with Flint tonight. See if he can come over tomorrow morning and have a look at it.' He hesitated a moment. 'In the meantime Xander, if you don't mind, it would probably be best if you took it off and stuck it in your pocket or something. You haven't had any training and we don't want any accidents; Traveller orbs are pretty powerful things.'

Xander felt strangely reluctant to remove the orb from its gentle clasp around his wrist but seeing how anxious the adults looked, he nodded in agreement and ran his finger around the silver band, looking for the release mechanism. After a moment of futile searching, he turned his wrist over for a closer examination but to no avail; it appeared that there was no way of removing the band.

'I don't think it comes off,' he said.

'Okay,' said James reassuringly, seeing Xander's anxious expression. 'Don't worry about it; I'm sure Flint will sort it out. In the meantime, just try to ignore it.' With another quick glance between them, the adults stood up from the table and began to clear away the dishes.

'Dad,' said Ollie casually, as he passed over some plates. 'You know the Halls of Records?'

'Hmm?' replied James, still looking deep in thought.

'On the wall under the stained-glass windows there's this little ledge sticking out, with a funny pale stone square above it. Do you know what that's for?'

James frowned for a moment, trying to visualise the place Ollie had described. 'Oh, you mean one of the old terminals,' he said.

'Terminals?' said Len, sounding sceptical. 'That didn't look like any terminal I've ever seen.'

James smiled. 'They wouldn't,' he said. 'They're relics;

ancient artefacts, really. They were installed with the original Hall, but they're all broken now. They're left in place for their historical value.'

'*Ancient* relics?' repeated Len quietly, looking between Xander and Ollie. 'That's interesting, isn't it?'

Xander nodded as they all headed out of the kitchen. Ancient blood, ancient enemy and now ancient terminals; that couldn't be a coincidence. As he climbed the stairs after Ollie, he thought optimistically that at least some of the answers he needed right now might be found in the records of Haven's distant past.

CHAPTER SEVEN

Xander woke up early the next morning, a small knot of excitement and anticipation in his stomach, and it took a moment or two before he remembered the reason for it. The orb was still on his wrist, the dark stone glinting in the morning sunlight, and Xander wondered how it would feel to actually use it. Unsure what time Flint might turn up this morning, and too keyed up to stay in bed, Xander rolled over and glanced at his watch. It was definitely not too early to get up, and he poked Ollie's shoulder on the way to the bathroom, eliciting a groan.

'Flint could get here any time,' he explained, and shot out to the bathroom. By the time he returned, Ollie was already up and dressed, keen not to miss out on any excitement. However, when they got downstairs, the sound of raised voices from the kitchen brought them both to a sudden halt in the hallway, Ollie with his hand still on the door handle.

'You aren't seriously considering dragging us all to that thing?' Len's voice was higher-pitched than usual with outrage. 'Spending the whole night with that bunch of uptight, snobby, waste of space –'

'Family, Len, whether you like it or not,' Mrs Stanton interrupted crisply.

'They may be your family but they're certainly not mine,' Len retorted. 'It'll be full of spiteful little monsters like Larissa Larcius-Thorne and her hangers-on, all out in force and feeding off their own self-importance. No way am I going.'

'This is not up for discussion, Len,' Mrs Stanton said, a steely note in her voice. 'You *are* going and, what's more, you can dress like a girl for once. I picked this up for you yesterday.' There was a rustling noise, and then a moment of silence.

'Are you joking?' Len said flatly.

Xander and Ollie, still hovering outside the door, exchanged identical grins.

'It's a lovely dress, and you'll look beautiful in it. And while I remember, I also want you to do something with your hair.' Len made an inarticulate noise but Mrs Stanton continued adamantly. 'There is absolutely no point looking at me like that, Len. You're going tonight and that's the end of it.'

There was an ominous silence and then the door handle ripped out of Ollie's hand as the door was yanked inwards. Already slightly off-balance, Ollie was knocked sideways by Len's storming form. She did not even glance at them, and Xander dived to one side as she stomped past, her unruly hair actually seeming to crackle with the intensity of her fury. She thudded up the stairs and then there was a loud slam. Xander and Ollie exchanged looks again and then both of them hurried into the kitchen.

Mrs Stanton was standing with an implacable expression on her face and her hand still resting on a dress spread out on the table. Ollie took one look, and then doubled over laughing. His grandmother glared at him.

'I really don't see what is so shocking about a simple evening dress,' she said huffily.

'It has flowers on it,' choked Ollie. 'And they're *pink*.' Words failed him as he looked at the dress again and he collapsed on a chair laughing.

Mrs Stanton just shook her head in exasperation.

'When you've quite finished cackling like a hyena, I have evening wear for you two boys as well,' she said and, as Ollie looked up with a grimace, she pinned him with a dangerous stare. 'Don't *you* start.'

'Where exactly are we going?' asked Xander cautiously, wary of incurring any further wrath from the irate lady with her hands on her hips.

'To the ultimate horror,' Ollie informed him with a dark look. 'We may not make it back out again.'

Mrs Stanton rolled her eyes.

'Oh, for goodness' sake, don't over-dramatise. I've had quite enough of that from your cousin this morning.' She turned to Xander. 'It's a long tradition that the Twelve Families host a summer ball on the Solstice. I had some wonderful times there when I was younger, but of course I haven't been for some time,' for a moment her voice trailed away, then she continued firmly, 'but as a Peverell I am always invited and *this* year my grandchildren will attend with me.' The steel had re-entered her voice, and she turned a pointed stare on Ollie.

He held up his hands in mock defeat.

'Fine, but *I'm* not wearing pink flowers.'

Mrs Stanton snorted in exasperation. 'You're being ridiculous,' she said. 'Just get your breakfast before Ben Flint gets here. He told James he was coming by early and he won't be impressed if you two are messing around.'

That was enough to galvanise Xander into grabbing some toast and a mug of tea. He slid a plate in front of Ollie, who still had a tendency to snigger whenever his gaze rested on the dress lying forlornly over the end of the table. Eventually, with a disgusted roll of her eyes, Mrs Stanton swept it over her arm and marched out of the room.

Before Ollie had the chance to make any further comments, they both heard the rumble of Flint's voice from the front hall. A moment later he walked into the kitchen and pinned Xander with disapproving blue eyes. His gaze dropped to Xander's left wrist, where the orb was clearly visible, and there was a moment of deep silence.

'Unbelievable,' he said finally, shaking his head. 'Those hobs are absolutely unbelievable.'

He pulled out the chair next to Xander, gesturing for him to extend his arm on the table, and examined the orb without touching it.

'James said that it doesn't come off,' he said quietly.

Xander turned his wrist over, running his finger under the smooth band to demonstrate the lack of any clasp or other means of undoing it.

'Do you know how to take it off?' he asked Flint, offering it to him.

Flint pulled back immediately, holding up his hands.

'It's not a good idea to touch another person's orb,' he said. 'At least orbs like ours. There are certain defences that might be triggered and you have no idea what you're doing.' He looked utterly exasperated. 'Did those hobs give you any idea why they decided to land you with this? Did they even tell you how it works?'

Xander shook his head. 'They said that they'd been keeping it for a long time, but they thought I should have it because of my blood. They were worried about some enemy attacking them.'

He looked at Flint for his reaction, wondering whether any of this would make sense to him, but Flint just rolled his eyes and let out another explosive breath.

'So, just their usual paranoid clap-trap, then. Typical!' He stared at Xander for a moment, frowning. 'Have you tried to use it?'

'I wouldn't know how,' said Xander. 'I haven't tried anything yet.'

'Yet?' repeated Flint wryly, and stood up. 'Come with me.'

Xander exchanged swift glances with Ollie, who had been listening avidly, and then followed Flint out onto the terrace. The tall Traveller indicated that Xander should stand in front of him.

'I want you to try something in a minute, and I'll be ready to ward you, so don't panic,' he said brusquely. 'I want you to concentrate on the orb and try to lean into it. Don't think too much about what that means; just do it.'

Xander swallowed. He had no idea what Flint meant by 'lean into' his orb, but he took a deep breath and stared down at it, trying to do what Flint wanted. He felt the response immediately, a strange sensation as if his strength had been magnified, and focussed through the stone. All at once, the depths of the crystal began to spark with the contained lightning that Xander had seen before in the Travellers' orbs, and his eyes widened with amazement as he looked back up at Flint.

'Okay, stop now,' Flint said. 'Well, you definitely seem to have Traveller abilities or that stone would just have stayed inert.' He looked away, down the garden with a frown and then glanced back at Xander. 'As long as that orb's on your wrist you'll need training, for your own safety as well as those around you. I can't stay right now but I'll send Ari over to start you off, and in the meantime,' his voice hardened as he eyed Xander sternly, 'you are *absolutely* not to try anything by yourself. We don't know how powerful that orb is and you've had no training. Do you understand?'

Xander nodded, and Flint swung around and walked away. 'Unbelievable,' he muttered again as he disappeared in through the kitchen door, and Xander was left to wonder whether he was talking about the hobs, the orb or Xander himself. The next moment, Ollie shot out onto the terrace, staring at the orb on Xander's wrist.

'I saw it light up from the window,' he burst out. 'That was incredible. What did Flint say to you?'

Xander grinned at him, feeling a rush of excitement as he remembered the sensation of the orb activating.

'He says I have to train, and he's sending Ari over to do it. Also, I think he's going to kill the hobs for giving it to me.'

Having activated his orb once, Xander found it very hard to wait for Ari to come and give him some training, although Flint's dire warnings prevented any temptation to try again without her. However, Ari appeared at Woodside soon afterwards and met him with a wry look and an amused shake of her head.

'You do like to keep life interesting, don't you?' she said. 'It's driving Flint to distraction.'

Xander just grinned back at her.

'He'll have to take that up with the hobs,' he returned unrepentantly. 'This is all their doing, not mine.'

'Oh, believe me, he is,' Ari replied, and then jerked her chin at Xander's wrist. 'Go on, then. Show me the cause of all the fuss.'

Xander offered his wrist to Ari. He noticed that, like Flint, she kept a careful distance while examining the orb. She looked up at him after a moment, her eyes thoughtful. 'I've never seen a black one before,' she said. 'Flint says he thinks it's similar to ours though, so we'd better get training you before anything else happens.'

Xander beamed at her, and she shook her head in warning. 'Don't get too excited. Like I told you before, you need to start small with fine control before moving onto anything bigger.'

She led the way onto the grass and sat down, plucking daisies and dropping them into a small pile. With a strong suspicion of what she intended to have him do, Xander sat in front of her, his orb hand resting on his knee where he could see it.

Ari glanced up at him with a grin.

'You know what's coming,' she confirmed and gestured at the pile of flowers. 'Lean into your orb, like Flint showed you, and try to lift them up into the air. Don't worry if it doesn't work immediately; these things take time and practice.'

Xander took a breath and then did what she told him, seeing the orb bloom into gentle light as he bit his lip and focussed on the flowers. The pile of daisies floated serenely up and hung in the air just in front of his face. As Xander followed them up with wide eyes, he caught sight of Ari with her mouth hanging open.

'*Huh*,' she said, looking completely thrown. 'Have you been taught this before?'

'No,' said Xander quickly. 'This is the first time.'

He turned back to the self-supporting flowers and, on a whim, gave them a little nudge with his thoughts. They began to weave in and out of each other, whirling faster and faster into a blur of white, green, and yellow. A huge grin stretched across his face and he looked at Ari in delight.

'This is amazing.'

'Okay, stop now,' said Ari, looking baffled. 'Apparently you're a natural, but it's still a good idea to practice until you have complete control over each individual flower. It hones your precision and makes it second nature, so you won't have to even think about the mechanics.' She shook her head again, huffing a little laugh. 'You are certainly full of surprises.'

Xander let the daisies float down to the ground again, arranging them in little patterns on the grass. He grinned up at Ari, feeling a sense of exhilaration surge through him. He had never thought of himself as having a particular talent for anything, and it felt wonderful to see her obvious astonishment.

'Can you show me something else, like how you blasted those shades?' he asked eagerly.

Ari laughed out loud at that and rolled her eyes.

'Let's not get ahead of ourselves,' she said firmly. 'You definitely have an aptitude for this, but you still need to master the basics before I train you in lethal force.' Seeing his disappointed look, she stood up and pulled him to his feet. 'Come on,' she said with a quick grin. 'I'll show you a defensive ward. It's always useful and you can't get into any trouble with that.'

She stood alongside Xander and lifted her wrist, the orb glinting in the sunshine. 'You need to visualise a shield pushing in front of you, protecting you. I always think of an impenetrable glass barrier, but other people have different techniques. Watch, I'll show you.'

Ari's orb flared and a shining barrier burst out in front of her, a vivid reminder of the last time he had seen her do that in the museum. A moment later, it had gone and Ari turned to him with a quick smile.

'Your turn,' she said. 'I'll throw these daisies at you and I want you to repel them, okay?'

Xander nodded, staring in front of him as some of the flowers shot up in the air again and hovered. There was a moment's pause, and then the flowers showered all over him and he blinked in surprise. Ari just grinned.

'Well, that's rather a relief. If you mastered everything at the very first try, I might start feeling inadequate.'

Xander grimaced, frowning as he tried to understand what she had meant. 'Am I supposed to be pushing them away?' he asked.

'Sort of,' she replied. 'You don't want to get hold of individual flowers. It's more that you're shielding and pushing; imagine that the daisies are really dangerous to you. Do you want to try again?'

Xander nodded, trying to visualise the bright ward Ari had thrown up. The rest of the daisies shot up to hover in a little arrow head a short distance away from him, and then they all launched at him again. This time, Xander immediately shoved forward his mental image of a shield and the air flared into brightness, sending all the daisies flying in a wide semi-circle around him. He laughed out loud in delight and turned to Ari, who was once more shaking her head ruefully.

'Okay,' she said, with a little grin. 'I officially feel inadequate. You're definitely a natural at this.'

'What else can we do?' begged Xander, a huge smile on his face.

'Practice, practice, practice,' said Ari firmly. 'I'm serious about mastering the basics, Xander. It's very important and you don't want to be hampered later by a lack of preparation. Keep practicing what I've showed you and I'll check when I come by again, before we move onto anything else. All right?'

Xander nodded. He had just decided that he would practice every moment he could when Ari chimed in again, as if she could read his thoughts.

'Don't overdo it, okay? You can exhaust yourself doing this

too much, particularly if you're inexperienced.' She gave him a knowing look and Xander grinned back at her.

'All right, but when's my next lesson?' he asked.

Ari just smiled and turned back towards the house.

'Don't worry, I'll make time. It'll be worth it just to see the expression on Flint's face.'

As soon as Ari had left, Ollie was keen to see what Xander had learnt and amazed at his progress.

'That's incredible,' he said, gazing up at the whirling objects above his head. Xander had gathered up the rather wilted-looking daisies again, and augmented them with some tall stems of grass and the cores of several apples he and Ollie had eaten. 'It usually takes years to get that kind of control. *I* still struggle to hold things level and I've been doing this for ages.'

Xander grinned at him and sent his mini tornado of objects weaving in and out of the trees in the orchard. 'Maybe it's the orb that the hobs gave me,' he said. 'They might have designed it to be easier to control.'

'Hmm,' said Ollie, thinking it over. 'Being helpful and making things easy for you? That doesn't exactly sound like them.'

Xander smiled wryly, acknowledging the truth of that and brought his little whirlwind to settle down on the grass next to them. He sighed and leant back on his elbows, looking up at the clear blue sky. 'I just wish I knew what all this was about,' he said.

'Well, we'll think about that tomorrow,' returned Ollie with a quick grin. 'First we have to survive Len's entry into high society tonight, and I have a sneaking feeling that it isn't going to go well.'

Xander laughed at that and lay back in the cool grass, closing his eyes. If the evening was as eventful as the time he had already spent in Haven, he thought he could probably do with the rest.

Mrs Stanton had been most insistent that both boys cleaned themselves up before donning the formal wear which she had laid out for them, and so it was not until he had finished towelling his hair that Xander turned to the rather curious looking clothes spread out on his bed. The plain grey trousers looked familiar enough but the white shirt had a strange collar, and the deep grey jacket buttoned up one side, with dull silver buttons. It also had an embroidered, high neck, rather like the mandarin's robes in Xander's history books; a wide silky sash, in rich dark silver completed the outfit. It was very different to the evening wear that Xander was familiar with at home, but it had a rather stately grandeur to his eyes. He was just struggling with the stiff button fastenings on the jacket when Ollie came into the room, also with wet hair. He sent a sympathetic grimace to Xander and began to rub his own hair dry.

'We'd better get a move on or Gran is likely to do her nut. I think she's still expecting Len to throw a last-minute wobbly,' Ollie said, his voice muffled under the towel.

Xander glanced towards Len's room. There had been a rather menacing silence from that quarter since they had come upstairs. Ollie had knocked but there had been no reply and the door, when he tried it, was locked.

'Bit ominous, isn't it?' he said.

'Nah, she'll go,' said Ollie with certainty. 'Len knows it's not worth the hassle of getting Gran really wound up.'

Xander finished buttoning the high collar of his jacket with some difficulty and turned to pick up his sash, turning it over helplessly. Ollie, who had thrown on his own clothes at high speed, reached over to take it out of Xander's hands. He had already fastened his own sash around his waist, and Xander noticed the fine-drawn lines of a strange, ornate-looking symbol embroidered in glittering thread on the dark silver sash where it fell down Ollie's leg.

'It goes on like this,' explained Ollie, twisting it around Xander's waist and hooking up fasteners which were so well concealed that Xander had missed them earlier. Ollie tugged the sash slightly so that the fastening sat just above Xander's hip and the slight flare of material trailed down his left leg; his was plain silver, with no symbols on it.

'Thanks,' said Xander. He nodded towards Ollie's sash. 'Does that mean anything?' he asked.

'It's the Peverell family sigil,' explained Ollie. 'Members of the family wear it on formal occasions. All the Families have them – you'll see them on display tonight; anyone with the least connection to a Family will be out flaunting it.'

He pulled a face as he glanced down at his sash.

'The sigils are part of the family crests. It's tradition, Oliver, and that is not such a terrible thing,' came Mrs Stanton's voice from the doorway where she stood framed in the light from the hall in an elegant green dress, jewels glittering in her upswept hair. 'You boys look so handsome,' she said, the briskness with which she adjusted both their sashes belied by a certain mistiness in her voice.

'We scrub up all right,' said Ollie, admiring himself with an exaggerated swagger in the mirror. 'You look amazing, Gran.'

'Yes, dear,' she said calmly. 'I know. Now for goodness' sake, let's get going before one of you spills something down yourselves.' She hustled them both out of the room and then paused on the landing. 'We're leaving, Len. Are you ready?' she called.

There was a silence and then Len's voice floated back, unnaturally sweet.

'I'll be right down.'

Xander and Ollie glanced at one another, eyebrows raised.

They had all been waiting in the downstairs hallway for several minutes before Mrs Stanton made an impatient noise and moved back towards the stairs. She stopped as they heard Len's door shutting, and then careful footsteps along the upstairs hall. Mrs Stanton clasped her hands together, her face lighting up as she got her first glimpse of the long flowing dress, softly shimmering, with an elegant waist and creamy bodice.

'Oh Len, you look beau-'

Her voice cut off as Len's face came into view, innocent smile firmly in place and her hair standing out in a multi-coloured halo around her head, the vivid streaks of midnight blue and shocking violet all the more startling amid her natural silvery pale.

'You told me to do something about my hair, Gran,' Len reminded her. 'You didn't specify what.'

Mrs Stanton stared speechlessly at Len for a moment and then swung around to the front door. 'Let's just go before I have a nervous breakdown,' she sighed.

Once her back was turned, Len caught Xander's eye and looked meaningfully towards her feet; Xander followed her gaze. Len had hitched her long skirt several inches off the floor, far enough to reveal that, rather than the delicate little sandals Mrs Stanton had bought, Len was in fact wearing her usual, favourite boots hidden under the length of the dress. Xander smothered a laugh as Len winked at him and then clumped noisily down the rest of the stairs.

Xander felt rather conspicuous as they all walked down the lane towards the Wykeham Gate in their elegant clothes, but Mrs Stanton swept along in front as if she wore nothing else. Once they had passed through the gate, Xander began to see others wearing formal wear, heading in the same direction along the narrow street to a courtyard filled with smartly dressed people, all off to the Solstice Ball. Many of them seemed to know each other, greeting newcomers with loud voices and enthusiastic waves as they inched forwards. Standing alone in the centre of the courtyard was a large archway set atop a flight of stone stairs.

'Where exactly are we going?' whispered Xander, as they moved forward to join the queue.

'No-one knows,' replied Ollie, with a twinkle in his eyes as Xander turned to stare at him. He laughed at the reaction. 'It's all part of the mystery, you see. This place is only used once a year during the Solstice, to hold the ball, and no one knows where it is. It's supposed to be bad luck to find out.' He grinned and rolled his eyes. 'That's what they say, anyway.'

Mrs Stanton glanced back at them as they climbed the steps. 'Keep up, you three. Don't dawdle.' She disappeared through the giant archway and, walking in line with Ollie, Xander passed through the gate after her.

As usual, there was only the faintest tug to indicate that anything more than the obvious two steps had occurred. As Xander looked around, the first thing he saw was a steep grassy mound, up the centre of which ascended a wide stone staircase. Steady streams of people were already heading up, the women carefully lifting long skirts as they walked. Xander noticed that the men, while all wearing the same style of formal wear, wore a myriad of different colours with equally varied sashes, some of which had stylised sigils while others were plain.

Once Len had cleared the gate, muttering darkly under her breath, Mrs Stanton led the way up. Elegant lamp-posts flanked the steps, with the glowstones already glimmering although the evening sky was still light, while the faint sound of music and the hum of many voices grew louder and more distinct as they climbed. When they reached the top of the mound, Mrs Stanton took Xander's arm and drew him to one side so they could pause without blocking the way for the many people following behind.

'The Pavilions,' she said, glancing sideways to see his reaction. She was not disappointed. Xander had never seen anything like it and his eyes were wide as he gazed in awe.

Rising before him were three enormous stone edifices, the lower two set back into the rising slope while the uppermost sat on the top of the large hill itself. Xander stared in awe at the wonderfully carved archways and tall, fluted columns which looked almost too slender to support the weight of the vast stone ceilings of the buildings. The most striking thing of all, however, was the stone itself: it glowed and shimmered with its own soft light, making the whole structure look like it was carved out of the moon. On the far side of the hill the slope fell away steeply, and just past a copse of trees Xander could see the clear waters of a wide lake, gleaming in the soft evening light. It was, without a doubt, the most beautiful place Xander had ever seen.

'It's amazing,' he said in a soft voice, and Mrs Stanton smiled at his obvious sincerity.

'Isn't it?' she replied, her eyes slightly misty as she gazed up at the glimmering buildings. 'I remember my first time at the Solstice Ball. My mother had finally agreed that I was old enough to go, and I was so excited to climb these steps and see the Pavilions for the first time.'

Mrs Stanton turned to include Ollie and Len in her memories. Her granddaughter's mutinous expression promptly shattered any illusions concerning Len's reaction to her own first visit. Mrs Stanton sighed in resignation.

'Well,' she said briskly, leading the way back onto the path. 'Let's not block the way.'

As Xander got closer, he could better appreciate the precision and detail of the stonework, and the effort that must have gone into creating this place. Each delicate-looking pillar was precisely placed, supporting the concentric circles of stone which made up the levels, and the glimmering stone itself provided some of the soft illumination inside the Pavilions, augmented by a thousand tiny glowstones suspended from the ceiling. The result was breathtaking.

The lower level appeared to function as a reception area, and was absolutely packed with people, although Xander could see a steady stream climbing the sweeping staircase to the next level. Mrs Stanton was seized upon by half a dozen ladies, all exclaiming in delight at her entrance while trying very hard to pretend that they did not notice Len's hair. Ollie, Xander and Len were repeatedly introduced – Xander as a friend of the family, although which family was left unsaid.

Xander tried to pay attention but was distracted by the sight of glowing glass trays hanging in mid-air and slowly circulating among the guests, each carrying a variety of drinks. Particularly intriguing was a tray full of glasses of a bright blue liquid which appeared to emit tiny silver sparks, and Xander's eyes followed it as it floated towards a prominent-looking group of people. In the centre stood a large, heavy-set man with thick, slicked-back hair, a pale corpulent face and moist red lips. He oozed self-satisfaction and Xander felt a sudden, visceral wave of intense dislike.

'I see that the Larcius-Thornes are holding court as usual.'

Xander glanced over to see one of Mrs Stanton's friends nodding towards the group he had been watching. The ladies exchanged meaningful looks.

'I imagine that Thorne thinks the Council is pretty much stitched up now,' murmured one. 'Everyone knows poor old Barton Ferrars won't go on much longer, and Thorne has his brother-in-law neatly lined up to take over the leadership.'

'Can you imagine having the triumvirate of Felix Larcius, Irini Latimer and Marcus Melville controlling the Council?' said another lady, with a delicate shiver of horror. 'If you get one of them, you get them all. Those Families are so inter-married now it's almost impossible to untwine all the connections.'

'The role is largely ceremonial of course, and one wouldn't mind too much, but they are such dreadful snobs,' chimed in a third, and all the surrounding ladies nodded solemnly.

Conversation then veered off onto another subject and Xander was left to consider, once again, how little he really knew about this place. The crowds shifted slightly and Xander got a better look at the group surrounding Perrin Larcius-Thorne. Standing erect and immobile by his side was a tall, elegant blonde woman with an undeniably beautiful face, wearing a glittering white dress. The crowd was in constant flux as new arrivals came to greet her; most she acknowledged with a slight nod or tilt of the head, but the favoured few were graced with a cool smile and a few words. His wife's chilly poise provided a sharp contrast to Thorne's more effusive greetings to those who stopped to speak to him; he was clearly revelling in the attention. Xander spotted Primilla Pennicott, hovering behind the woman's shoulder, with a sycophantic smile on her face.

After ten minutes, Mrs Stanton relented and gave them permission to look around. 'But I want to see you in the Middle Tier when you hear the supper gong,' she warned.

'Finally,' said Len, once they were out of earshot. 'I thought we'd never get out of there. Her friends are a nightmare – all they did was stare at us.'

'No, they were staring at *you*,' Ollie pointed out mildly. 'Not really surprising, considering. What did you expect?'

'Actually, I was rather hoping that Gran might change her mind about dragging me along,' grumbled Len.

Ollie just snorted in derision.

'Fat chance.'

By this time they had climbed to the next level, where long white tables stood along each side of the room. Currently the only things adorning the tables were elaborate flower arrangements and there was nothing else interesting here, so by common accord they all headed up to the top.

As they stepped out onto the floor on the Upper Tier, Xander found it hard to hide his awe at the space before him. It was at least twice as large as the two lower levels, and the stone ceiling was so high that the small group of giants, all gathered self-consciously at one end of the room, seemed almost normal height. Round tables stood everywhere, each with a pristine white tablecloth and lit by intricately carved glowstone lanterns, while elaborate stone balustrades, low and wide enough to sit upon, enclosed the entire space. As Xander had noticed from his first glimpse of the Pavilions, there was a sheer drop from where he stood on the upper level, down to the lake shore, and the view over the lake to the trees beyond was breathtaking. As Xander watched, tiny lights began to glimmer in the trees along the shoreline opposite.

'The Committee has spared no expense this year, it appears,' said a familiar voice from over Xander's shoulder. He turned to see Callan Reeve standing behind him, his hands stuffed in his pockets and his hair unbrushed as ever.

Reeve had clearly tried to conform somewhat to the formality of the occasion, but his rumpled dress clothes looked as though he had slept in them for a week. Beaming at his elbow was Petros, looking far more dapper, although his frequent tugging at his outfit betrayed his discomfort at being out of his normal attire. Xander smiled back at them both, very relieved to see at least two familiar and friendly faces amongst the vast crowd of people.

'It's amazing,' Xander replied, waving his hand at everything around them.

'I see that Lester Simm has brought his usual date,' said Reeve, with an amused twitch of his lips.

Xander followed his gaze and saw the garishly dressed man from the Nexus tottering up the stairs on his high heels. This time he had dressed in an ostentatious electric blue jacket and a sash so liberally adorned with peacock feathers it looked like he had denuded a large flock of their tails. Heeling him was the stocky, bullish-eyed figure of Alan Latchet, wearing a clashing shade of pea green and glaring belligerently at anyone who he considered was showing insufficient respect to Simm.

Reeve drew back slightly behind a pillar, a wry expression on his face. 'I don't want to attract their attention,' he explained to Xander with a grin. 'We see quite enough of those two at work.'

'I wouldn't worry,' said Petros. 'They're far too busy making up to the great and the good. Felix Larcius and Marcus Melville are over there, looking down their noses at everyone else as usual, so Simm isn't going to notice the likes of us.'

He nodded over towards the far side of the room, where Simm was making a beeline for two tall men in the centre of another animated group. One of them was enough like the haughty woman downstairs to identify him as another of the Larcius family, although his hair was dark as opposed to her bright blonde, and so Xander assumed that the arrogant-looking pale-haired man next to him was Marcus Melville.

'Who are they?' Xander asked.

Reeve eyed him thoughtfully and Xander wondered whether he was revealing his status as an outlander again. 'They're the current heads of two of the Founding Families,' he said. 'They sit on the Council and spend their time interfering and creating unnecessary bureaucracy.' He pulled a face. 'Felix Larcius is brother-in-law to Perrin Thorne, who owns the Nexus. Despite knowing nothing about the technology, he tends to feel that that gives him the expertise to advise me how to do my job.'

As if he knew that he was being spoken about, Larcius looked over in their direction, his icy gaze sweeping across the crowds in the Upper Tier. Reeve ducked further into hiding before turning to Petros. 'Let's go find where your wife and her friends have tucked themselves away,' he suggested with a grin. 'We may need the protection.'

With a quick lift of his hand, Reeve and Petros disappeared back down the crowded staircase and Ollie pointed over to the balustrades. 'Let's have a look. I heard that they hired night-glowing pixies to light up the lake.'

Xander followed him, rather glad to get out of the line of sight of the cold-eyed Larcius, and hung over the wide stone balustrade. The lake rippled softly just beneath them, and the lights he had noticed glimmering on the opposite shore were moving in gentle swirls in the growing dusk under the trees. Somewhere behind them, soft music had begun to play and Xander caught his breath as he took in the beauty of this strange place.

A chiming noise cut across the hum of chatter and laughter, and Ollie turned around with a grimace as he saw the large number of people between him and the staircase.

'I knew we should have stayed by the food tables,' he groaned as they headed over to join the queue forming by the stairs.

However, despite Ollie's pessimism, it was not long before they were picking their way down the long white-clothed tables, now covered with delicious-looking food. Len was still garnering startled looks, and she kept behind Ollie and Xander as much as possible. This tactic did not prove sufficient to protect her from several of her grandmother's relatives, who insisted on greeting her with hugs and barely concealed curiosity about her choice in hair styling. Among them was a courtly-looking man with silver hair and a judicious air, who shook hands with Ollie and regarded Len with twinkling eyes.

'I've heard all about it from Thea,' he said and then gave her an approving wink. 'Good on you, keep the old girl on her toes.'

'Believe me, she doesn't need any encouragement in that, Horace,' came a tart voice as Mrs Stanton appeared, and the man turned to talk to her, with another quick smile at Len.

'Who's that?' asked Xander as he moved down the line filling up his plate.

'That's Gran's cousin, Horace Peverell,' replied Ollie, frowning slightly as he tried to balance an extra slice of quiche on the top of his pile of food. 'He's the head of the family and he sits on the Council, so he's pretty important, but he's actually really nice.'

Their plates now loaded up, the three of them headed back up the stairs. 'Grab the first table you see,' suggested Ollie in a muffled voice, having obviously made an early start on his food. However, when they reached the upper level it became immediately clear that every table was already occupied.

'Doesn't matter,' said Xander quickly. 'Why don't we sit over there?'

He gestured with his roll towards one of the wide stone balustrades, narrowly avoiding poking an elegant woman passing in front of him. Luckily she did not notice his mishap, but Xander heard Len's snicker from behind him. Flushing, he led the way over to a clear area away from the crowded tables and overlooking the lake. He hitched himself up to sit on the balustrade and leant back against one of the pillars, his plate propped on his lap. They were all hungry by this time, and for several minutes conversation languished as they dived into the food. Eventually, however, Xander began to look around him.

Not far away, four tables had been pushed together, and were overflowing with what were obviously the younger members of the Families. In the centre, and clearly holding court, sat a vivacious blonde girl with sparkling eyes and perfect features. As if drawn by Xander's gaze the blonde girl glanced over, her eyes flickering over them and then away in apparent disinterest. He felt his cheeks heat. He had never been great at talking to girls, particularly ones who looked like her, and he glanced away awkwardly, only to meet Len's knowing stare.

'What?' he demanded, as Len continued to eye him.

'Please,' she said with a withering look, and Xander felt himself flushing again. 'I really wouldn't bother. You have no chance and believe me, that's a good thing. She's a nightmare.'

Xander risked a glance back at the crowded table, and saw

that the girl was leaning forward, whispering something to a rapt group of her friends. 'Who is she?' he asked.

It was Ollie who answered, after hastily swallowing his mouthful.

'That's Larissa Larcius-Thorne. I don't really know her ('lucky for you', interjected Len) but her father is Perrin Thorne.' Ollie flicked another quick glance over to the table and added, 'That tall, dark bloke is her brother Roran, I think.'

'Half-brother,' muttered Len.

'Really?' grinned Ollie. 'I stand corrected. Have you been delving into the society gossip pages again? Gran will be pleased.'

'Don't be ridiculous,' snapped Len, her face darkening with annoyance. 'It's common knowledge. That's why his surname is Thorne. Larissa gets the Larcius from her mother, along with her delightful personality.'

Ollie laughed and leant forward, intent on continuing his teasing, but he was cut off by his cousin.

'Great,' hissed Len. 'Now she's coming over.'

Xander's head jerked around to see that the blonde girl was indeed walking straight towards them, a cool little smile tugging at her lips. Following behind her was a gaggle of girls, all whispering and giggling. Xander looked away hastily, feeling his ears burning and hoping that his face was not as red as it felt.

'Why, Len Stanton, I didn't see you tucked away back here,' said Larissa, in a precise voice like cut glass. She smiled sweetly, revealing perfectly even white teeth and a dimple that flickered in her left cheek. 'You mustn't feel awkward, you know. These little mishaps do happen.' There was a wave of tittering from the assembled girls behind her.

'What mishaps?' said Len in a flat, hostile voice.

'Your hair, of course,' Larissa replied, in mock surprise. 'You can't mean you actually did that *on purpose*?' She half-turned and called out over her shoulder. 'Roran, do come and see Len Stanton's hair. Isn't it interesting?'

Her light, poisonous tone made the word 'interesting' sound like a horrible insult. The tall, dark boy glanced up at her appeal and then sauntered over. Although he did not immediately recognise the boy's striking features or vividly blue eyes, Xander had a nagging feeling of familiarity and he frowned, trying to pin it down. Larissa's entourage was fluttering as the boy approached, but his gaze flicked over them coolly, before settling on Len.

'It's certainly – different,' he allowed in a bored drawl, and then looked away in clear dismissal. Xander felt Len stiffen in annoyance beside him, although her contemptuous expression did not change.

'Isn't it?' Larissa agreed, smirking. She leant forward, her voice dripping fake sincerity. 'I'm just so glad you were able to come to a Family occasion at all. I mean, you barely qualify.'

Len made a sudden movement, hostility rolling off her in waves, but Ollie was faster, gripping her arm firmly. Larissa just smirked at the success of her jab and opened her mouth again, no doubt to say something even more venomous, but before she could do so, a tall blonde woman swept up to the group. Xander recognised the beautiful, aloof woman from downstairs. Her mouth twisted into a sneer as she reached Len, the haughty contempt quite evident, before turning to Larissa.

'Darling,' she said, the endearment ice cold as it fell from her lips. 'Your father is looking for you. I believe that there are some people he would like you to meet.'

Larissa smirked at Len, then turned with a swirl of her filmy dress and walked off. Immediately, Mrs Larcius-Thorne glanced at the tall, dark boy. 'Roran dear, the dance floor is woefully unpopulated. Shall we set an example?'

'Certainly,' Thorne replied, extending his arm courteously to his step-mother. He escorted her over to the dance floor where, Mrs Larcius-Thorne to the contrary, there did not appear to be a shortage of dancers. There was an immediate stampede of girls to grab partners and join the dancing, all too obviously hoping for a dance with Thorne.

Left alone once more in their corner, Ollie grinned wryly at Len and Xander.

'Couldn't get her precious children away from us fast enough, could she?' he said. 'Wouldn't want them contaminated by mixing with the likes of us.'

Xander was not listening. The nagging sense of familiarity he had felt on seeing Roran Thorne had sharpened into a certainty as Roran had offered his arm for his step-mother's hand. On the middle finger of Roran Thorne's left hand was an intricately twisted silver ring.

'It was him,' he blurted out.

Len and Ollie both looked at him with confused expressions.

'Huh?' asked Ollie.

'It was him – the one that Flint sent to meet me when I first arrived here – it was Roran Thorne.' Xander knew that he wasn't making very much sense, but he was caught up in the sudden clarity. The only question that still confused him was –

'Why on earth would Roran Thorne help *you* or do favours for Flint, of all people?' Len's sceptical voice exactly echoed the questions circling in Xander's own mind.

'I don't know,' said Xander slowly. 'But I intend to find out.'

'Great,' grumbled Ollie. 'We'll just add it to the list of

things we have absolutely no idea about.'

Len huffed in agreement, but Xander could see by the slightly absent look on her face that she was already turning the problem over in her head. She looked up suddenly and met Xander's eyes, her smile pointed.

'Told you she was a nightmare,' she said.

Not long after that, Len disappeared, muttering something that Xander couldn't make out, and Ollie decided to see whether there was any food left. Xander abandoned his plate on a handy table and began to wander around the enormous Upper Tier. He found all the more exotic inhabitants of Haven endlessly fascinating and was just angling around to get a better view of the giants when he bumped into Callan Reeve again. The engineer gave him a rather knowing look, and Xander wondered whether he had spoken with Mrs Stanton.

'Interested in our large friends over there?' he asked genially. 'I see that everyone else is keeping a careful distance from them, as always. I doubt whether most of the people here have ever exchanged a single word with a giant.'

'So why are they invited then, if no-one talks to them?' asked Xander, confused.

'The Families like to be seen as socially inclusive,' replied Reeve. 'Pressure is put on various representatives of the old races to be trotted out at high-profile events, to 'send the right message'. Doesn't mean that anyone would be seen dead actually socialising with them.'

Xander frowned. 'That seems a bit –'

He paused to search for the proper word.

'Offensive? Dishonest?' suggested Reeve helpfully.

'Pointless,' Xander finished. 'I mean, if everyone knows the truth.'

Reeve chuckled. 'Well, now you have a thorough grasp of

the politics, would you like to come and meet them?'

'You know them?' asked Xander, although he realised that actually he wasn't surprised. Reeve might give the impression of being oblivious to social conventions, but it was clear that, in reality, he simply chose to ignore them.

'I do,' he confirmed. 'Quite well, actually. Come on.'

Reeve led the way across the crowded space towards the corner where the giants loomed awkwardly, speaking amongst themselves. As he drew nearer, Xander realised that there was a wide circle of empty space separating the giants from the rest of the circulating crowd. Just as they were about to step out into that space, Reeve suddenly put a hand on Xander's arm and drew him back.

'Hang on a minute,' he said, sounding slightly choked. 'This should be good.'

Looking around to see what had drawn Reeve's attention, Xander spotted the gaunt figure of Primilla Pennicott, walking primly towards the small group of giants while firmly shooing one of the floating trays in front of her. She wore the determinedly bright expression some people adopt when addressing very small children.

'There you are,' she said in a treacly tone, although Xander noticed that she avoided looking directly at any of the giants. 'I do hope you're enjoying yourselves.'

There was a slight pause, and then one of the giants cleared his throat with a sound like granite being crushed. 'Thank you, yes,' he replied politely in his gravelly voice. He had a strange accent, seeming to swallow some of the sounds in the back of his throat.

The other giants nodded, their eyes all fixed on the contents of a large bowl sitting on the glass tray. It seemed to be filled with odd, globular things which Xander did not recognise, and he stood up on tiptoes to see better; a moment later he wished fervently that he had not. Piled high and quivering slightly as the tray revolved in the air, was a mass of pale, blood-shot eyeballs.

Primilla gestured to her tray, with a self-satisfied expression.

'*Such* an oversight that these weren't served with the norm-, I mean with the *other* food. I thought I really should bring them over to you myself,' she said in the same sickly, patronising voice. 'The Committee does pride itself on trying to make our *special* guests feel quite welcome among us, and we were delighted to prepare your cultural delicacy. Do tuck in.'

Reeve let out a muffled squeak and Xander realised that he was actually shaking with laughter, his hand crammed against his mouth to stifle the sound. Xander himself could barely look away from the uncomfortable scene unfolding before him. Primilla, clearly mistaking the giants' stunned disbelief for delighted astonishment, propelled her tray with its macabre offering directly in front of the giants, where it revolved slowly, the eyeballs glowing in the tray's soft illumination.

There was an awkward pause, and then the giant who had spoken earlier reluctantly reached out his shovel-sized hand towards the bowl of glistening eyeballs. Xander, who unlike Primilla was looking at the giant's face, clearly saw the moment when his expression lightened. Instead of reaching into the bowl, he picked it up and thrust it out to Primilla.

'Please, have one,' he rumbled.

Primilla looked like she might faint. 'Oh, really … I couldn't … they're for you,' she stuttered. Her voice was more shrill than treacly now.

The giant jiggled the bowl, making the pile of eyeballs wobble and roll around.

'Is traditional,' he stated firmly. 'Always must share with host first.' He stared at her expectantly.

Primilla reached out a shaking hand and gingerly picked up the top-most eyeball in the very tips of her fingers. With a final, appalled look, she put it in her mouth and slowly bit down.

'Mmm,' she said with a feigned smile of appreciation, her cheek bulging, and then abruptly spun around and tottered away, covering her mouth with her hand as soon as she was out of sight of the giants. Reeve was doubled over by this point, almost choking with the effort of holding in his laughter. He looked up at Xander, his eyes watering.

'And the woman actually works in a library,' he sputtered. 'Where does she get this stuff from?' Finally, he drew in a deep, shaking breath and pulled himself together. 'Come on, let's go over before she comes back with any more cultural insights.'

Xander followed behind Reeve as he walked across the empty space and looked up at the group of giants.

'I'm sorry, guys,' he said, in a deadpan voice. 'I'm afraid that I didn't bring any body parts to share with you today, but I'll definitely rectify that oversight next time.'

One giant let out a harsh sounding chuckle, his rough features crinkling into a smile.

'Cal, old friend. Do not joke too loudly or else they may bring us more eyeballs than we can eat.' He rolled his eyes at the bowl with its grisly contents and shook his head, looking perplexed. 'I do not understand why anyone would think we would wish for such things.'

Reeve just snorted and then gestured to Xander. 'I have someone who would like to meet you,' he said. 'This is Xander King. Xander, meet Tyr, Alf, Jak, Orvar and Njord.'

Xander stared up at the group of huge figures.

'Hello,' he said.

The giant Reeve had introduced as Jak beamed at him, the rough skin creasing on his brow ridge.

'How do you do, Xander King? Is this your first visit to the Pavilions?' he asked, in his harsh voice.

Xander nodded and then swallowed. 'It's very beautiful. I've never seen anything like it before.'

The giants all beamed down at him as if he had said something particularly pleasing. 'Did you know that giants helped to build it?' asked Njord ponderously. 'The Wall of Constellations here is one of our finest works. Beautiful indeed, I think.'

'Why don't you show him?' put in Reeve, with a quick encouraging smile at Xander. 'It's pretty spectacular, and I'm sure he'd love to see it.'

'That would be great,' said Xander politely, and the giants looked delighted again.

They led the way between the pillars and out into a dimly lit passageway. At the far end, Xander saw that there were a couple of staircases leading down to the lake shore below. The giants turned to walk in the opposite direction, where the passageway turned to the left and then paused, gesturing to Reeve and Xander to go first. Not knowing what to expect, Xander turned the corner and gasped in amazement as he saw a massive stone wall twinkling with thousands of lights, as if it were a window into deep space. He took a few steps closer to examine it more closely and noticed a few constellations he recognised, like Orion and the soft lights of the Pleiades.

'Amazing, isn't it?' said Reeve quietly from behind him.

'It's incredible,' agreed Xander. He wondered why such a beautiful display was hidden away here, where so few people would see it, but was rather wary of asking any more questions which might draw attention to the fact he was an outlander.

'It's like being in the night sky.'

'The Constellation Wall is ancient,' ground out one of the giants behind Xander. 'We cannot make such things now but still, it speaks to us of what we once were.'

There was a rumble of agreement from the other giants, and then Reeve drew Xander back with him into the passage-way. 'Thank you for sharing this with us, my friends,' he said warmly. 'We've both appreciated seeing such artistry.'

'Definitely,' said Xander. 'Thank you.'

'It was our pleasure,' said Jak. 'It has been good to meet you, Xander King and to see our friend Cal, but I think we have done our duty now and will leave before we are presented with any other unexpected offerings.'

Reeve eyed him thoughtfully. 'Actually, I may join you, while I'm still ahead in avoiding unpleasant Family members and their hangers-on.' With a wry grin at Xander, he and the giants led the way back into the Upper Tier and disappeared towards the staircase.

Xander had just decided to go and look for the other two when Ollie himself appeared at his side, a worried frown on his face. 'There you are,' he said, sounding relieved. 'Where've you been? Is Len with you?'

Xander shook his head. 'No, I haven't seen her for ages. Have you looked downstairs?'

Ollie sighed. 'I did, but let's check again. I know that she doesn't really enjoy social events, but it's not like her to completely disappear.'

They both turned towards the staircase and almost bumped into a man who was staggering, clearly rather the worse for wear. He grabbed at Ollie, his breathing laboured, and peered into his face.

'S'traordinary thing,' he said solemnly. 'Never saw a girl do that with water before. Strange girl though,' he added, his eyes crossing as Ollie twisted away.

'Some people just don't know when they've had enough,' Ollie muttered irritably, as they continued down the stairs. When they had combed all three levels and drawn a blank, Xander looked at Ollie and saw the same concern reflected in his frown. 'You don't think she's gone home, do you?' he asked.

'No way,' said Ollie positively. 'Gran would be furious and even Len knows that it's not worth the row.'

Looking about for inspiration, Xander caught sight of the lake between the stone pillars, glimmering serenely in the moonlight. A vivid recollection of the words of the staggering man from by the stairs hit him. 'Could she have gone down there?' Xander pointed over towards the water. Ollie followed his gaze and his worried face brightened.

'Maybe,' he said. 'Let's go look.'

Xander and Ollie headed for the steep staircase that led down to the lake shore, hurriedly descending the worn stone steps to the wide terrace at the bottom. To their right, twinkling lights illuminated the shore, which was full of people. Couples strolled along by the water's edge, and there were several groups sitting in the soft sand, their laughter and loud conversations travelling in the still night air.

'She won't be over there,' Xander said with certainty. He turned away from the lights and noticed a narrow stair on their left, leading down to the other part of the lake shore, lit only by moonlight. 'Let's try this side.'

He and Ollie had only descended a few steps when their suspicions were proven correct. Len herself appeared out of the darkness and the two boys stopped dead, gaping at her. She was dripping wet from head to foot, her elegant dress clinging to her legs as she stomped up the stairs. Obviously whatever she had used to colour her hair did not simply wash out because it now resembled a mass of multi-coloured rats' tails. She looked thoroughly irritated.

'What happened to you?' asked Ollie, quite clearly torn between concern and amusement.

Len marched past him, her nose in the air.

'I don't want to discuss it,' she snapped.

Xander and Ollie exchanged glances and then turned to follow her up the steps.

'You realise that Gran probably will want to discuss it,' Ollie suggested diplomatically.

Len just sniffed, although Xander wasn't entirely sure whether it was in response to Ollie's remark or to the water still streaming down her face. As they reached the top, their way was blocked by a number of older boys, standing in a cluster on the steps; Xander recognised several of them from Larissa Larcius-Thorne's group earlier. Among the boys was the tall figure of Roran Thorne, leaning back against a pillar with his hands in his pockets, faintly illuminated by the glowstones above. He was eying Len with his head tilted arrogantly and an amused smile quirking his lips.

'Drowned rat,' he drawled. 'Yet another unusual look.'

The surrounding boys broke out in loud sniggers but Len completely disregarded them, sweeping past with a poise unmarred by the steady flow of water from her dress or the faint squelching noise from her boots. Xander was strongly reminded of her grandmother in that moment.

Thorne just laughed. 'You've got weeds in your hair,' he called mockingly after her, to another burst of laughter from his friends. He met Xander's gaze and immediately looked away with no sign of recognition, but Xander was more sure than ever that Thorne was the boy who had met him that first day. He scowled and pushed his way through the group of boys, who made no effort to move out of his way; Ollie shoved through beside him, muttering 'prats'. Finally, they made it past and hurried forward to catch up with Len. Ollie caught at her arm when they reached her.

'Look, why don't you just go down to the front and wait. We'll find Gran,' he suggested reasonably. 'You really don't want to walk around like that.'

Len paused to consider, and then nodded when she noticed the murmurs from people who had already spotted her. 'Okay, but don't be too long,' she said with a shiver. 'It's freezing in this thing.' She tugged distastefully at her dress, which hung forlornly, dripping onto the stone floor.

'I'll come with you,' offered Xander. He felt suddenly exhausted and reluctant to push his way through the still ample crowds of people.

'Thanks,' replied Len, whose teeth had begun to chatter.

Ollie disappeared into the crowd to find his grandmother, while Xander unbuttoned his jacket, shrugged it off and silently offered it to Len. She smiled gratefully at him and pulled it on, wrapping her arms about herself for warmth as they both began the descent to the lower level.

When Mrs Stanton arrived to meet them it was clear that Ollie had already briefed her on what to expect because she merely raised an eyebrow as she took in Len's tangled wet hair and the pitiful sogginess of her dress under Xander's jacket.

'I suppose I should have expected something like this,' she said in resignation, leading the way back down the lantern-lit stone steps. Xander turned at the top, for one last glimpse of the Pavilions glimmering against the starry sky, before hurrying after Mrs Stanton to the gate and home.

CHAPTER EIGHT

They were all up late the next morning, and breakfast turned into brunch. On hearing about Len's late-night dunking in the lake, James laid a hand on her forehead, even as she continued to pile honey onto a piece of toast.

'You feel cool enough,' he said, frowning. 'But it can't be good for you, getting soaked in the middle of the night and then standing around in a sopping wet dress. I'm amazed you haven't caught your death of cold.'

Mrs Stanton snorted.

'Not she,' she said. 'Your niece may be an absolute menace but apparently she's a very healthy one.'

Len beamed at her, tipping her piece of toast in a silent salute, and her grandmother rolled her eyes.

When they had cleared the table, the three of them headed out for the sun-warmed grass under the trees in the orchard to discuss their next steps. After going around in circles for several minutes, Len sat back decisively.

'There's only one place where you'll find the answers, Xander,' she told him. 'Like you said, you're talking about history and that's all kept in the Halls of Records. If we want to find out about ancient blood and enemies,' she ticked them off on her fingers, 'that's the place to go.'

Xander nodded slowly. It seemed obvious now that Len had pointed it out. However, there was still one problem and Ollie promptly articulated it.

'That means trying to get past Primilla Pennicott in her den, which is never a good thing.'

'Len's right, though,' said Xander.

'Of course I am,' replied Len airily.

Ollie shook his head. 'Why do I feel like this isn't going to end well?' he asked no one in particular and then got to his feet with a sigh. 'Well, we might as well get started. The quicker we get there, the quicker we'll get thrown out.'

Twenty minutes later, they were walking through the imposing doors of the Halls of Records and Xander felt a sense of excitement bubble up inside him. Finally, they might be close to getting some answers to the questions that had been dogging him since his life had changed irrevocably in the British Museum, as the impossible had unfolded before him. Len nudged him and gestured off to the right.

'The research terminals are over here,' she whispered. 'We can't search blind – there are literally millions of records here.'

Xander nodded and followed her. Ollie remained a few paces behind them, glancing up at the big desk on the dais which, ominously, was empty.

'She's loose in here somewhere,' he muttered under his breath, looking around him with a hunted air.

'Less chat, more hurrying then,' replied Len. She led them towards a terminal, tucked away between stacks of shelves, and then sat down and swiftly brought up a series of menus. 'What shall we search for first?' she asked, her fingers hovering over the keypad.

Xander thought for a moment. 'Try 'ancient blood',' he said.

With a few keystrokes, Len brought up list after list on the terminal screen. She muttered under her breath as she scrolled through them so fast that Xander could only catch a few words.

'Lots about healing, livestock breeding lines, some fairly disturbing accident reports,' her voice trailed off as the lists kept coming. 'Uh, this may take longer than we thought.'

'Try 'ancient blood' and 'enemy' together,' suggested Ollie, leaning over her shoulder. Len poked him irritably.

'Don't breathe down my neck,' she complained, as her fingers flew over the keys again. Ollie ignored her and then groaned as the screen once more filled up with records, most of which appeared completely irrelevant. 'We'll be here for days, sorting through this list,' he said despondently. 'Why can't things be simple for once?'

'I think we want the earliest records,' said Xander thoughtfully. 'The hobs kept talking about lost histories and memories, which probably means really old.'

'Good idea,' said Len, and reduced the number of records on the screen dramatically. She rooted in her pocket, pulled out a little pad and stub of pencil, and scribbled down the references left. 'We'll start with these,' she said, and then cleared the screen. 'We don't want anyone else seeing this and wondering what it's about,' she explained. Consulting her notes, she rose to her feet. 'This way,' she said firmly.

Feeling buoyed by Len's optimistic determination, Xander hurried after her. As they crossed one of the open spaces in the Halls, he was struck by the late morning sunshine streaming in through the beautiful stained-glass window up above. It turned the painted glass into jewels, and illuminated the striking image in the centre of the window, a tall rock surrounded by white-tipped waves under a brilliantly starry night. As he paused, gazing upwards in awe, he felt Ollie's insistent tug on his arm to hurry him along.

'Don't stand out in the open,' he muttered. 'We'll get caught.'

Reluctantly, Xander turned away and followed Ollie around the corner of another giant stack. They found Len on tiptoes, trying to nudge a large tome out of a shelf high above her head. 'You took your time,' she hissed over her shoulder.

'Sorry, Xander was just admiring the scenery,' replied Ollie with a grin, reaching up and lifting down the book.

Len did not answer, as she double-checked it against her notebook before putting it on the small table. 'You two check this one out, while I get the others,' she instructed, and then disappeared between the stacks.

Ollie and Xander looked at one another, then at the thick book with its tiny print. 'How about you skim the left page and I'll do the right?' suggested Ollie with a shrug. Xander nodded and the next several minutes were spent silently flipping pages as Len flitted back and forth, adding to a growing stack of books for checking. Finally, she settled down next to them and picked up the topmost.

Silence reigned for another ten minutes, and then Len glanced up with a frustrated grimace. 'The indexing in these things is hopeless and most of the references are pointing back to even older records, in one of the archives. If we want to track back to the right ones, we're going to have to *live* here for a week.'

'I know that your life is fairly tragic, but that really is a whole new level of sad,' said a scornful voice. The cut-glass tones were unmistakable.

Xander looked up with a sinking feeling. He had been so caught up in the books he had not even noticed Larissa Larcius-Thorne and her group of avid hangers-on come around the corner, staring at them with contemptuous little smirks.

Len rolled her eyes.

'Seriously?' she demanded. 'Do you not have anything better to do?'

'Oh, *we* definitely do,' returned Larissa, with one of her nasty little smiles. 'What on earth are you doing messing around with all these mouldy old books?' She stepped forward next to Xander, and he felt the cool swish of her hair as she leaned over the table with a hint of expensive—smelling perfume. She flipped the cover closed and read the title. 'No *wonder* you're so interesting, Len,' she said in her poisonous little voice. 'What fun hobbies you have.' She turned back to her entourage, who all tittered appreciatively. 'This must be why you have *so many* friends.' She sneered at Xander and Ollie and then pulled away as if they might contaminate her.

'Oh, why don't you just shove off,' retorted Ollie. 'If you keep hanging round us, people might talk.'

'Please,' scoffed Larissa, dropping the superior act and glaring at him. 'As if anyone would think I'd spend time with losers like you. Blown up anything good lately? I'm surprised they still let you wear that thing.' She glanced disdainfully at the discoloured orb on Ollie's wrist. 'I should tell my father not to let you get another one – it would be a blessing for the rest of us.'

Ollie flushed a dull red and Len threw an indignant glare at Larissa, her chair scraping as she jumped to her feet. Larissa took several prudent steps back to the safety of her little gaggle but, undeterred, Len squared up to her.

'Get lost,' she snapped, 'or maybe he'll blow you up next. It would certainly be no loss.'

As if things could not get any worse, there was a sudden clacking of high heels and a moment later Primilla Pennicott tip-tapped into their midst, her narrowed eyes sweeping across the little group. Len rolled her eyes as Larissa immediately turned to the pinch-faced woman.

'Oh Miss Pennicott, thank goodness' you're here,' she

gushed, grasping at the woman's bony hand with wide eyes and a pitiful expression. 'I was looking for you with a message from Mother, and Len Stanton actually threatened me for no reason. Didn't she?'

Larissa appealed to her friends who all nodded, putting on shocked expressions.

'Larissa didn't do anything, Miss Pennicott,' one of them chimed in quickly, 'and Len threatened to blow her up in the library.'

Larissa let out a little fake sob and Miss Pennicott put a protective arm around her, while turning an awful expression on the three around the table.

'How dare you come into my Halls and behave like savages,' she hissed, and then her eyes fell on the table. 'And who gave you permission to touch those books? Damaging ancient records, threatening innocent students – you wait until I speak with your grandmother. Out! Out!' She gestured at them furiously, her rabbity mouth twisting with anger. 'You will not be permitted back in here until I am satisfied that you can behave in a civilised manner, which I don't imagine will be anytime soon.'

After one more comforting pat on Larissa's shoulder, Miss Pennicott marched Ollie, Len and Xander off towards the exit. Xander didn't look back, reluctant to see the triumphant smirk on Larissa's face, although he couldn't block out the tittering noise from behind him. They were no closer to figuring out any of the mysteries, and now they had actually been banned from the one place where they might find the answers. All in all, it had been a far from successful morning.

Standing out on the front steps of the Halls, they exchanged despairing looks.

'We'll never get back in there now,' said Len glumly.

'She'll be on the look-out.'

'We need that information,' said Xander, as the frustration swam up inside him. 'It has to be there somewhere.'

'That's all very well,' grumbled Ollie, 'but we'll never get to see it. That old dragon will be guarding it from dawn till dusk.'

There was another depressed silence as they all absorbed the truth of that statement, and then suddenly Xander looked up as a thought occurred to him.

'She's not there at night, though, is she?' he said. 'If we go then, we'd have plenty of time to search without any more interruptions.'

Len's eyes began to sparkle.

'Excellent,' she breathed approvingly.

Ollie looked less pleased.

'Um, Xander? You don't think breaking into a government building is maybe taking all this a little far?'

'Do you have a better idea?' demanded Len.

Ollie stared at his feet for a moment before looking up and rolling his eyes at her.

'No,' he said. 'But that still doesn't mean that this is a good one.' He eyed them both and then shrugged. 'Fine, I'm in, but don't forget that I said so when this inevitably ends in disaster.'

Back at Woodside, an exhaustive discussion began as to how they would actually pull this off, given that the Halls were likely to be securely locked-down out of hours. It went on for some time. Finally, Mrs Stanton called them in from the garden, after some rather suspicious looks out of the window at their little huddle in the middle of the lawn; a location chosen by Len so that no-one could overhear them. At least they had come up with the beginnings of an idea, involving finding the plans for the Halls and then examining them for likely vulnerabilities in security. Ollie was still rather doubtful about the whole thing but Len's enthusiasm for the 'mission', as she had promptly dubbed it, overrode his qualms and he was left to console himself with the thought that she probably wouldn't be able to find a way in anyway.

As agreed, after supper Len gathered up a pile of folders and stalked over to the little terminal in the kitchen, slumping into the seat with an ostentatious sigh. Mrs Stanton glanced over as she wiped down the kitchen table.

'*Now* what's wrong?' she asked.

Len gestured dramatically to the folders.

'Cruelty to children is what's wrong,' she said darkly. 'They must believe that we don't need sleep if they think we can do all this homework.'

Mrs Stanton rolled her eyes. 'For Haven's sake, don't be so histrionic. We all survived our schooling and I think you probably will, too.' She turned to Ollie and Xander, who were hovering behind Len. 'And you two can find something useful to do and stop distracting her. If Len has the kitchen to herself, then I'm sure that the work will get done in no time.'

She flapped her hands insistently at the two boys, following them out and shutting the door, but not before Xander got a quick glimpse of Len's exultant grin as she was left alone at the terminal. It was a long wait after that, nearly an hour and a half, before the door to their bedroom was pushed open and Len sauntered in.

'So?' Ollie asked, eying his cousin's deadpan expression. 'Is there no way in?' His voice sounded faintly hopeful. There was a moment's silence, and then Len beamed triumphantly at both of them, pulling a folded piece of paper out of her pocket.

'Oh, ye of little faith,' she said. 'It's simple. We're going in via the fire-escape at the back of the building onto the roof and then through the air duct system. It's a bit of a maze, but I managed to acquire the plans, and I have the directions to get to the main Hall.' She waved her piece of paper at them with a superior smile.

Xander swallowed. Along with the sight of blood, enclosed spaces were definitely not one of his favourite things and he wished silently that Len had found another way into the building. Ollie, however, had a different objection.

'You 'acquired' the plans?' he said in a sceptical voice. 'Do we want to know how you 'acquired' them?'

Len rolled her eyes. 'Details, details,' she said airily. 'Just be ready to leave after midnight, okay? Everyone should be asleep then. And also, don't forget to wear dark clothes; it's stealthier.'

With another quick grin, Len disappeared back into the corridor and the two boys were left to exchange rueful glances.

'She's getting way too into this,' muttered Ollie and Xander nodded, although he couldn't deny the little surge of excitement at finally getting some answers.

So far, the midnight trip to the Halls of Records had gone as successfully as Len had predicted. No-one stirred as they crept through the house and out into the lane, and there was enough moonlight to illuminate their way down to Wykeham and then through the broad thoroughfare from the South Gates to Fountain Square. It was rather eerie to see the city so empty, and they kept to the shadows as much as possible as they hurried onwards. With one accord, they skirted around the outside of the square, rather than cutting across it in the open, but when Xander glanced over at the fountain, his eyes widened in surprise. Ringing the near side of the fountain pool were at least two dozen nixies, silhouetted in the faint light, with their glittering eyes staring intently over at them.

Xander paused.

'Do you see that?' he whispered, with a shiver at the uncanny sight. 'Is that usual?'

Len shrugged, her expression unconcerned. 'They're nixies, it's not like they're going to tell anyone they saw us. Come on, the fire escape is at the back.'

With a deep breath and a last apprehensive glance back at the silent witnesses, Xander followed her around the building and began the long climb up the metal fire escape. When they reached the enormous flat roof, Len led them confidently over to a large metal grate, set in the wall ahead.

'It's screwed shut,' whispered Ollie, leaning over to examine it. 'How are we going to get in?'

Len pushed him out of the way and reached into her pocket.

'With a screwdriver, genius,' she replied tartly.

'All right,' said Ollie, with an easy shrug. 'No need to be sarcastic.' There were several moments of silence as Len struggled with the screws. 'Need a hand?'

'No,' snapped Len, and then, 'Fine! You do it.'

Xander suppressed a grin as Ollie edged forward and took the screwdriver from Len, wisely making no comment. After several minutes of hard work, the rusty screws gave way and Xander helped Ollie to lower the metal grille to the roof. Revealed before them was a large cavity, pitch black against the paler stone.

Xander eyed it reluctantly.

'Are you sure that this will take us all the way in?' he asked Len. 'I wouldn't want to get stuck in there, or find it's a dead-end.'

Len shook her head firmly, a shadowy figure in the gloom. 'I've checked and double-checked the schematics. This will bring us out in the central hall.' She crouched down to enter the hole.

'Hang on a minute,' objected Xander. 'Don't you think Ollie or I should go first?'

'Why?' asked Len blankly.

'Well, in case there's something in there,' Xander muttered awkwardly, as both Ollie and Len turned to stare at him.

Len snorted in amusement. 'I think if there was a monster living in the air duct system at the Halls, we would probably know about it by now. Also, you don't actually know the way.' Xander saw her roll her eyes, before clambering into the hole.

Ollie sniggered.

'Good one, mate,' he said, before following Len.

Xander took a deep breath. The idea of climbing into a dark, enclosed space was even less attractive now they were actually here. As he hesitated, Len's impatient voice broke into his thoughts, sounding hollow and distant as it echoed out of the vent. 'Come on, Xander, and don't forget to replace the grate. We don't want to draw any attention.'

With a wry glance around the rooftop, shadowy and empty, Xander took another deep breath and climbed into the hole. After balancing the grate against the exit, Xander turned and crawled forward until he bumped into the soles of Ollie's shoes.

'Okay,' he whispered. 'I'm here. Let's get this over with.'

'Hold on,' said Len.

A moment later the dim light of a glowstone bloomed in the darkness, revealing Len and Ollie's backs and legs, and they all began to crawl. The tunnel itself was not quite as bad as Xander had imagined. There was at least room to move in moderate comfort and the walls were smooth and fairly clean, although they all sneezed from time to time as they disturbed the thin layers of dust. However, as they began to reach intersections of tunnels, with Len choosing each turning without hesitation, a deep sense of unease began to grow in Xander as he became increasingly aware of the labyrinth of vents around him. Sweat broke out over his body, and it was not because of the physical effort.

'We'd better not get separated,' he muttered to Ollie's legs. 'We'd be stuck in here forever.'

'Shush,' said Len, from in front. 'I'm trying to keep count. Now, where was I?'

Xander groaned, but Len crawled forward again, and he had no choice but to follow her. After ten interminable minutes, she finally came to a halt and there was a moment's silence.

'Are we lost?' Xander demanded, hoping that his slight panic was not creeping into his voice.

'No, we're here, I think,' said Len. There was a pause. 'Only thing is, I'm not sure how we unscrew it from this side.' She sounded rather sheepish.

Xander groaned. 'You have got to be kidding me,' he said. 'We've crawled through miles of vents and *now* you say –'

'S'okay,' broke in Len cheerfully. 'This one isn't screwed on. It's got catches, and if I can just –'

Her voice faded away and there were two scraping clicks, then a tremendous clang.

'Oops,' she said.

'Stealthy,' remarked Ollie. 'Really stealthy.'

'Oh, shut up,' snapped Len. 'Move back so I can turn around.'

Awkwardly, Xander and Ollie both backed up a little to allow Len to twist around, and then lower herself backwards through the hole. There were scraping noises and then a soft thud. Len's voice floated up to them.

'The vent comes out quite high, but luckily there's a bookcase below it. Lower yourselves out and climb down. Be careful though,' she added. 'A couple of shelves are loose.'

Ollie twisted around and lowered himself out of the hole, and after a moment Xander followed, his way faintly illuminated by the glowstone Len was holding. He was halfway down the bookcase when the light flickered and went out. Xander froze in the thick blackness.

'Where's the light?' His voice sounded unnaturally loud.

'I'm so sorry,' Len said, sounding panicky. 'I dropped it, and now it's gone out and I can't find it.'

The dark was so intense Xander felt like it was pressing into his eyeballs as he stared blindly over his shoulder, trying to remember how far down the bookcase he had already climbed.

'Ollie, can't you make some light?' asked Len plaintively.

'I dunno. I s'pose I could,' said Ollie, sounding rather uncertain.

'Try!'

There was a pause, and then a flash of light so blinding that Xander reflexively threw up one hand to shield his eyes, thereby letting go of the shelf he was gripping. He toppled backwards and landed with a bone-jarring thud on the floor, thankfully only a few feet below.

'I said some light, not the *sun*,' hissed Len.

'Sorry,' muttered Ollie, and the light went out, plunging them into darkness again. Xander blinked rapidly; there were several glowing afterimages flickering in front of his eyeballs. One of them lifted and bobbed over towards them, and it took

Xander a couple more blinks to realise that it was Len's glowstone.

'Here,' said Ollie, sounding apologetic. 'I saw it on the floor.'

Len took it from him rather ungraciously. 'I'm just amazed that you weren't blinded like the rest of us,' she said waspishly.

Xander saw Ollie bristle and stepped in before they could start bickering again. 'Shouldn't we get on with it before someone comes to investigate the strange noises and lights?' he suggested.

Ollie satisfied himself by pulling a face at his cousin and then headed off towards the stairs. They had come out on one of the iron-railed balconies at the back of the hall and there were several spiral staircases to descend before they stood on the level again. Even trying hard to walk quietly, their footsteps on the metal stairs still rang out in the huge echoing hall. They couldn't see anything beyond the faint circle of light thrown by the glowstone, and subconsciously all three walked close together, their eyes straining into the darkness surrounding them.

'D'you think it would be faster if we separate?' whispered Len.

'Not really, since you have the only light,' retorted Ollie, obviously trying to retaliate after his cousin's earlier sarcasm.

Len turned and glared at him.

'Look!' she said, with incautious loudness. They all cringed as her voice re-echoed around the Hall. 'Look…look…look.'

'Let's just stick together and get through this as fast as possible,' said Xander, when the echoes had finally died away.

'Good idea,' said Len, sounding rather subdued. 'And I was thinking that actually we'd better find where that archive is; the one that holds the earliest records. The books we had before were full of footnotes referring back to older references.'

Xander nodded in agreement and Len led the way over to their left, to a little nook by the wall where a large search terminal rose from the desk. Someone had left a pile of folders next to the keyboard, and Len gathered them up and moved them to one side before sitting down before the terminal. She handed the glowstone to Ollie and then began to type, her fingers almost blurring over the keys. Again, Xander and Ollie leant over her shoulder as the screen flickered with words and figures, too quickly for them to keep up. Len paused, with a small huff of frustration, and then continued tapping away for another moment, before she sat back in her chair and glared at the screen.

'Is anything the matter?' asked Ollie, unnecessarily. It was more than clear that there was indeed something wrong.

Len gestured to the terminal with an aggravated frown.

'Unbelievable,' she said. 'Every single reference to 'ancient blood' and 'an enemy' together leads back to documents in the oldest collection of records, all of which were historically stored in Archive 6, which used to open out of the main Hall.'

'Used to?' asked Xander, with a bad feeling beginning to grow in his stomach.

'Used to,' confirmed Len gloomily. She scrolled the screen up to the start of an article and pointed. 'Read for yourself.'

Xander and Ollie both leant forward. '*The Halls of Records have remained largely intact for thousands of years, expanding whenever additional archiving was required and consistently well-funded by the Council of Twelve. However, it has not entirely escaped catastrophe. In a most unfortunate event, lightning struck the Halls during an unusually damaging July storm, causing Archive 6 to burn to the ground with the loss of many irreplaceable documents and records,*' read Ollie out loud. He looked up at

Len and Xander. 'You're kidding!'

Xander shook his head, disappointment pounding inside him. Everywhere they turned, access to the information he so desperately needed was withheld from him, if not by uncommunicative hobgoblins, then from inconvenient natural disasters.

'Unbelievable,' he growled in frustration. 'After all of this, we can't even get the records we need. They were all destroyed centuries ago. Now what do we do?'

'Xander, you're doing it again,' Len said sharply.

Xander looked at her and she gestured over his shoulder. Previously unnoticed in the dim light, and in their preoccupation with the research terminal, was another of those worn stone shelves butting out from the wall and above it was a smooth square of paler material. Lights were now flickering across the square, getting faster and faster until they almost began to look like letters.

'It's one of those old terminals,' said Ollie, as they all stared at what was clearly now a partially functioning screen. 'What's it doing?'

'I don't know,' said Xander, slowly. 'I didn't even touch this one.'

As if his voice was a trigger, the stone flickered even more wildly, and then suddenly blanked before brightening into pearlescent silver. Two words appeared and flashed in the middle of the square.

'Login accepted?' said Xander, blankly. He looked at Ollie and Len. 'What login?'

They both shook their heads, eyes glued to the stone. 'Look,' said Len. 'It's flickering again.'

'Maybe it's some kind of glitch?' suggested Ollie.

'Maybe,' said Len, but she did not sound convinced. 'It's

doing something else.'

The two words vanished, and the screen flickered again before resolving into more words.

'*Seed of the ancient blood stand forth,*' read out Len. She twisted to stare at Xander, her eyes wide. Xander just gazed at the screen, a chill running down his back as he looked at the words which were still shining faintly.

'It's talking about you, Xander,' Len said in a hushed voice.

Ollie fumbled in his pocket for a piece of paper as the screen flickered, and then hurriedly scribbled down the words. He was only just in time, as the screen flashed and went blank.

'What does that even mean?' he asked, but Len shushed him.

'Look,' she said, pointing. 'There's something else coming.'

Another sentence emerged from the flashes: '*Only the stars can lead the way.*'

They were hardly breathing now; the only sound was Ollie's pencil frantically scribbling on his paper. There was another flash from the stone, parts of letters appearing and disappearing, before words formed again across the stone: '*The marks of the kin stand guard eternal.*'

After another interminable moment of flickering, while Xander bit his lip with the tension, slowly one more sentence began to form: '*Rock upon the water where the power lies.*'

Even as Ollie finished scribbling the screen blanked, as if it could no longer maintain sufficient power to remain alight. All three of them stared at it, as if they expected it to switch back on again but it remained quiescent, just another worn-looking stone in the wall. Finally, Len let out a breath.

'What just happened?' she demanded.

Xander sat back limply in his chair, looking down at the piece of paper with those strange, enigmatic sentences. He shook his head.

'I have absolutely no idea,' he confessed.

In the silence, the sound of a chair scraping back was disconcertingly loud and both Xander and Len turned to stare at Ollie, as he stood up decisively.

'It must be about two o'clock in the morning,' he said in a quiet voice. 'I don't think any of us will figure it out tonight and we'll be dead tomorrow unless we get some sleep. C'mon, let's head back, and we'll try and work out what it all means when we're less sleep deprived.'

Rather reluctantly, Xander nodded. Ollie's words made sense, but he had an irrational fear that the ancient terminal might start spewing out more mysterious sentences while he was not there to see them. He glanced over at the terminal but it gave no sign it had ever been more than a pale stone in the ancient wall. He turned to follow Len back up to the balcony with a plaintive sigh. There was a great deal of vent crawling to get through before they got home.

CHAPTER NINE

None of them were up early the next morning, and Mrs Stanton eyed them all thoughtfully as they trailed one by one into the kitchen looking for breakfast.

'I would ask why you're all looking like something the cat dragged in, but I probably don't want to know, do I?' she asked crisply. Ollie looked up, his eyes wide with feigned incomprehension, and she shook her head at him. 'Don't even try, Oliver,' she said, and Ollie flushed guiltily.

Len was quiet, staring into space as she ate, and Xander was certain she was mulling over the strange messages from the ancient terminal. He himself had been unable to think about anything else from the moment he had woken, blearily blinking away the midmorning sunlight.

After their late breakfast, the three of them foregathered in the boys' room and bent over Ollie's scrap of paper, debating what it could mean.

'Well, the first part is obvious,' said Ollie again, after an hour of vigorous and rather repetitive discussions. 'The hobgoblins said they could feel the seed of the ancient blood in you, and you're 'standing forth' because you've come here to Haven.'

'Maybe,' allowed Xander. 'That sounds like it could make sense.'

Len lay on her back, staring up at the ceiling and tapping her lip with one finger. 'That's all very well, *for the umpteenth time*, but what about the rest of it? It makes no sense whatsoever.' She sat up with a sudden glint in her eyes. 'Maybe we need to head back to the Halls tonight to check the system using those sentences as search terms?'

Xander groaned at the idea of more crawling through vents, but before he could speak, Ollie chimed in. 'I don't think so,' he said firmly. 'Gran has definitely rumbled that we were doing something late last night. There's no way we'll get away with it again.'

Len pulled a face, but she didn't disagree with Ollie's assessment. Another long silence descended that was only interrupted by the sound of a bell clanging from downstairs.

'Lunch,' declared Ollie, rolling off his bed with an enthusiasm undimmed by only having had his breakfast an hour and a half before. 'Come on, we'll figure something out afterwards. It's always easier to work things out on a full stomach.'

'You would know,' put in Len, as they all headed downstairs.

They had intended to continue their discussion after lunch, but Mrs Stanton had other ideas.

'Neither of you two have finished your civics project this term, have you?' she said, in a tone that indicated that it was not really a question. 'You can do something useful this afternoon and get it done. Take Xander along with you,' she added. 'It would probably be interesting to him to see how Haven is governed.'

'If by *interesting* you mean utterly tedious and relentlessly boring, then yes it would,' muttered Len, then threw up both hands in surrender as her grandmother pinned her with a trenchant look. 'We're going, right now,' she muttered, and ducked out of the room.

Contrary to Len's opinion, the question of how this

strange place ran quite intrigued Xander and was a welcome break from impenetrable messages. They headed over to Fountain Square again, and Xander could not help staring wistfully over at the Halls of Records. It was frustrating being so close, but he was under no illusions about their chances of getting in again under Primilla Pennicott's glaring eye. Ollie pulled a sympathetic face at him, his thoughts obviously running along the same lines.

'Nothing we can do about it right now, mate,' he said with a shrug, before angling over to another of the massive, official-looking buildings that ringed the central square. 'C'mon. This is the Council Chamber. It's supposed to be one of the first places ever built here. Our civics instructor says it's at least five thousand years old, and that we're absolutely not to touch anything.' With a quick sideways grin at Xander, he led the way into the chamber.

As with so many of the stately edifices around the square, the Council Chamber sat atop a wide set of steps made from the same beautiful golden stone as the buildings, where the wear of many feet showed their antiquity. Following Ollie, and with Len trailing behind, Xander walked through the great doors into an ornate entrance hall. There was a large reception desk placed in the centre, manned by several people in formal green robes with wide silvery bands around the neck and sleeves. Each one wore a badge with their name on, pinned to the front of their robe. Two of them were busy with other people and so Ollie headed towards the third, a white-haired man with a wrinkled face and 'Pritchard' printed on his badge. As they approached, he looked up with a gap-toothed smile.

'Standing for office or here for civics class?' he asked them cheerfully, and his eyes twinkled as Ollie held up a lime green exercise book. 'Civics it is.'

Both Ollie and Len passed over their books, and he efficiently stamped them both, glancing at Xander as he passed them back to their owners, but not making any comment on his lack of a book. Ducking out from behind the desk, he pointed them towards a winding staircase in the back of the hall, tucked away in a corner next to the row of closed wooden double doors which ran along the wall. From behind them came a faint but continuous murmuring noise and Pritchard held up a hand in warning.

'The session has already started so you'll need to be quiet,' he said, with a wink. 'Head on up to the Visitors' Gallery, and you'll get a good view. You can leave whenever you want, as long as you don't disturb anyone.' With a friendly parting smile, he went back to the desk where someone else was now waiting for him.

The staircase was broad, but it wound sharply upwards and there were no other doors until they reached the top, where a lobby led them to another wooden door. Ollie edged it open, and they entered a large balcony, full of rows of chairs but empty today except for a small figure at the front, scribbling in a notebook with a stub of pencil. Xander smiled as he recognised Petros, the little engineer from the Nexus, who glanced up as they came in and beamed at them. As he edged his way along the row, Xander looked over the side of the balcony into the room below and stopped short, staring in awe.

The chamber spread out beneath him, its walls of rich golden stone inset with huge painted wooden panels. Some panels were decorated with intricate and beautiful designs, while others showed Haven's landscapes or what Xander assumed were historical scenes. Portraits of distinguished-looking men and women hung prominently around the walls, looking down on the chamber, and these were interspersed with several deep-set alcoves, each one holding a statue of a person in sumptuous robes. As Xander's gaze continued upwards, he saw that more painted panels and carved woodwork decorated the lofty ceiling.

The chamber itself was circular, with three quarters of the circumference laid out in an amphitheatre-like arrangement of rows of green leather benches, set behind narrow tables ringing each level. Half of that area was currently empty, and the rest was filled with groups of people wearing various guild insignias, some scribbling at paperwork while others appeared to be chatting.

The remainder of the chamber was taken up by a large stone dais on which sat an enormous, polished wooden table. Well-spaced along the length of the table were twelve chairs, each one with an ornately carved back rising above the head of the person sitting on it. The largest and most impressive was in the centre, occupied by an elderly man with thinning grey hair who was leaning to one side as an aide whispered in his ear. In front of each of the people sitting at the table was an elegant printed nameplate, and Xander's eyes flicked across each of the famous names of the Founding Families: Lisle, Larcher, Peverell, Angove, Ingram, Melville, Larcius, Latimer, Blount, Raynott and Hackett, with Ferrars in the centre before the grey-haired man.

Awed, Xander sat down in the nearest chair and gazed around him. There was something timeless about this beautiful and ancient building, a monument to a civilisation which stretched back into the dawn of history, and Xander leaned over the railing as he tried to take it all in. Ollie nudged him in the ribs, leaning forward to whisper.

'That's Barton Ferrars,' he said, pointing down to the centre chair. 'He's been Chief Councillor for ages now, almost twenty years.'

As Xander looked more closely, he began to recognise some faces from the Solstice Ball. The elegant pale-haired man with the nasty sneer was sitting behind a marker stating 'Melville', while next to him was Perrin Thorne's brother-in-law, dark-haired Felix Larcius. Xander also recognised the distinguished face and silver hair of Horace Peverell as he eyed Kirkland Blount, who appeared to be dozing. Several of the other councillors were taking the opportunity to confer with their staffs.

Suddenly, Ferrars leant forward and banged a gavel sharply down in front of him. Blount started and sat up, looking around him in some confusion. The crispness of the sound, even all the way up on the balcony, surprised Xander; the acoustics of this building were obviously remarkable.

'Back in session,' Ferrars boomed in a surprisingly loud voice for his frail figure.

Melville and Larcius ignored him for a moment, carrying on a quick, muttered conversation before deigning to turn back to the table. Ferrars continued on, announcing, 'Mr Simm will now address the Council.'

Petros stopped scribbling and peered over the edge of the balcony. Xander followed his gaze and instantly recognised Simm's over-dressed form strutting across the floor in front of the dais. He mounted a small podium and turned with a flourish to face the councillors at the table. His outfit today was burnt orange with a lemon yellow cravat and sparkling buttons which flashed every time he moved, finished off with another pair of high-heeled boots, and a self-important smirk. Just behind him stood the squat form of Alan Latchet, gripping a pile of folders and watching Simm with fixed attention.

Simm swept a low bow to the table, causing some Councillors to raise their eyebrows in surprise.

'Thank you for your kind invitation to address the Council,' he began. 'As you have entrusted me, I have now carried out a full and complete review of the Nexus upon which we all depend, with particular attention to the critical interfaces with the secondary Core which the hobs maintain.'

Next to him, Xander heard Petros snort at this, muttering, *'secondary?'* under his breath, and shaking his head. Simm continued on.

'As the honourable Councillors would expect, I have spared no time or effort in evaluating our vulnerabilities, as recently highlighted by the most regrettable recent failure of a new node which led to a temporary but deeply concerning downturn in supply.'

Simm carried on in this vein for several more minutes, congratulating himself with every other breath for his own hard work and attention. It was very distracting to watch him talk, as he waved his arms about to embellish his points, and the buttons on his sleeves sparkled and flashed with each gesticulation. Xander's eyes were glazing over and several of the Council members stirred impatiently. Finally a small, sharp-faced woman with grey hair pulled back into a no-nonsense bun, sitting just to the left of Barton Ferrars, cleared her throat loudly and pinned Simm with a firm gaze. He paused for a moment and she seized her opportunity.

'This is all terribly interesting, Mr Simm,' she said, in a tone that indicated that she thought quite the opposite, 'but the Council has a very busy schedule today. Could you please let us have the conclusions of your no-doubt thorough investigation?'

Petros grinned and leaned towards Xander again.

'That's Enid Ingram,' he murmured. 'Not one to suffer fools gladly.' His voice made quite clear who he thought was the fool.

Simm blinked in surprise and then recovered himself.

'Indeed, Councillor,' he said, with another little bow. 'In sum, after extensive investigation and analysis,' he caught Ingram's eye again, swallowed quickly and continued, 'it is my conclusion that the Council should consider the immediate, full and final integration of the Nexus as sole provider of power to Haven.'

Petros let out an explosive breath, but it was almost drowned out by the burst of comments from Council members and other people throughout the chamber. Chief Councillor Ferrars banged his gavel repeatedly until all noise ceased.

'Order! Order in the chamber,' he bellowed. Xander noticed that Melville and Larcius were once again deep in conversation, and the latter wore a smug smile.

'Mr Simm,' said the woman sitting on Felix Larcius' other side. She was slender and upright, with a coldly beautiful face that reminded Xander of Larissa Larcius-Thorne's mother. The marker in front of her named her as the representative of the Latimer family, and Xander inconsequentially remembered the comment at the Solstice Ball that the Melville, Larcius and Latimer families were so inter-married it was hard to separate them out. 'Do we understand that you recommend that we cease all further reliance on the Hob's Core, the traditional source of our power system on Haven?'

Simm nodded self-importantly.

'You are, as ever, entirely correct in your understanding, Councillor Latimer. It is my assessment that this is the only truly forward-looking approach for us to take. Invaluable as the hobs' contributions have undoubtedly been in the past, one must move with the times.' Simm's hands waved around like a demented windmill, as he warmed to his theme. 'Looked at objectively, impassionately, rationally and scientifically, the hobs' technology is out of date and has become a liability. One simply cannot be sentimental about these things, however respectful one may be to tradition.'

Next to Xander, Petros shook his head even as he scribbled frantically on his pad.

'This is not good,' he muttered. 'Cal will be furious. *Contributions*, indeed! Hobs created this technology and made it available to us for thousands of years. This is insane.'

At the Council table, Horace Peverell frowned heavily.

'What you are suggesting is unprecedented, Simm. Do you not think this is rather precipitous? We may do ourselves and our allies, the hobs, a grave disservice to take such a dramatic step over what only amounts to a few minor glitches. I generally distrust such hastiness.'

Several other Councillors began to nod at this and Simm leant forward, his face assuming what he meant to be a sympathetic look, but which actually just made him look faintly constipated.

'Oh, of course, Councillor Peverell, it is most natural and admirable to feel that way,' he oozed unctuously. 'One cannot but feel for the hobs in their unfortunate plight after such tragic losses, however one cannot hark back to a past long gone. It is our duty as engineers (Petros' head shot up at this, with a bemused *'him?'*) to look to the future, to be progressive and to offer solutions for our time.'

Simm clasped both hands together, overcome by his own rhetoric, and his buttons flashed blindingly again.

There was another stir around the chamber and this time Ferrars did not check it, instead making a quick motion which caused all of the Councillors to lean across the table for a brief, urgent consultation. Clearly the acoustics in the chamber could be manipulated, as all Xander could hear was a low murmuring, masked by the rushing sound of general conversation in the room.

After several minutes, during which Simm continued to preen up on his podium while Latchet stood guard, bristling with self-importance, Xander suddenly noticed a third person standing waiting just below Simm. It was the man he had seen at the Nexus, the quiet, brown-haired man clutching a clipboard who was so nondescript he seemed to fade back into the woodwork. As he stared, Xander realised that the man's lips were moving very slightly, and assumed that he was quietly addressing Simm in the interval.

Ferrars' gavel came down again. Looking back at the table, Xander noticed that Larcius was frowning, although Melville's face was smooth and expressionless.

'Four in favour of the proposition before the Council, four against and three undecided on preliminary consideration,' announced Ferrars. Whispering broke out across the chamber as he continued. 'Therefore, it is our decision that further monitoring shall be carried out by Mr Simm on our behalf and he will report back to this Council in one month's time or sooner if the circumstances warrant it. This matter is concluded.'

Petros leaned back in his chair and closed his notebook.

'Well,' he said, glancing sideways at Ollie, Len and Xander, 'I suppose that could have been worse. A brief reprieve in any event.' He slipped his notepad in his pocket and stood up. 'I need to get back to the Nexus and brief Cal. We'd better hope that there aren't any more outages or there'll be no stopping that buffoon.'

When he had gone, Xander exchanged glances with Len and Ollie.

'I have a feeling that the hobs aren't going to be too happy with this,' he said quietly.

Ollie nodded. 'You're not wrong,' he said. 'Maybe this is why they're pinning all their hopes on some ancient bloodline coming back to save them?'

Len, who had been silent until this point, looked up.

'Save them from what, though?' she asked. 'They talked about an enemy before. Who're the bad guys this time?'

They all looked at one another and then Xander leaned over the balcony again, only to meet the cold eyes of Felix Larcius as he glanced up and then away again dismissively.

'Who stands to benefit from their losses?' he asked shortly, and Len's eyes widened with quick understanding.

'Come on,' said Ollie, getting to his feet. 'I think we've seen enough.'

Silently, they all walked down the stairs to the reception hall again, only to be almost mown down by the flamboyant figure of Lester Simm. Latchet was staggering some distance behind, loaded down with folders, and Simm swept past without a glance at the three.

'Come Gage, we have much to do,' he declared to the quiet, brown-haired assistant walking at his side.

Xander's gaze idly followed them, wondering what it was about the plain-looking man that bothered him. He was startled when the man glanced up and then stared right back at him, his eyes intent, before disappearing into the crowd with Simm. The sense of malice and threat he left behind, however, lingered in Xander's mind for much longer.

When Xander came down to the kitchen the next morning, the screen on the wall was showing a news station, and he paused for a moment to listen as the presenter announced further minor power outages affecting several of the Guilds overnight. There was also coverage about the outcome of the Council session the day before, and the segment finished with dire predictions about what was likely to happen if the outages continued. Mrs Stanton was kneading dough at the table and she shook her head in exasperation.

'It would be more helpful if they confined their 'news' reporting to actual *news* rather than wild speculation,' she said to Xander with a quick roll of her eyes.

'Some of the Councillors seemed keen for Thorne's Nexus to take over everything,' Xander said. 'What would happen to the hobs if the Council decided to do that?'

Mrs Stanton paused. 'It's more about their access to their Core,' she said thoughtfully. 'To be honest, the Nexus already provides most of the power used these days by the Guilds and households; it's been expanding its infrastructure over the past twenty years. If Thorne decides that a contagion from the Core is affecting the Nexus, and persuades the Council of that, it may get difficult. The hobs aren't very inclined to co-operate these days.'

'The hobs think it's the other way around. They believe the Core is being damaged by Thorne's Nexus, though,' objected Xander. 'That's what they said to us the other day.'

'Well, I'm sure they'll all get to the bottom of it; Callan Reeve is incredibly talented, whatever I may think about his employer.' Mrs Stanton sniffed contemptuously at the mention of Perrin Thorne and returned to her kneading, while Xander turned to get some breakfast.

He was glad he had got up early when Ari appeared at the door for another training session a few minutes later. In his spare moments over the last couple of days he had practiced his control and his defensive warding, and he was keen to demonstrate his prowess and hopefully learn something new. Ari, however, looked rather more serious than usual and exchanged a few murmured words with Mrs Stanton before turning to Xander.

'It won't be a long lesson today,' she said. 'We've had more issues with border security overnight. Come on outside and I'll take you somewhere where you can stretch your abilities a bit.'

Once out on the terrace, Ari held out her arm and jumped them away with no further explanation. As usual, there was a sharp lurch as they arrived and Xander's knees sagged, before he looked around to see where she had brought him this time. They were in woodland again, near the ruins of a large tower, mostly now reduced to large blocks of stone scattered with an odd randomness amongst the undergrowth. It was a rather desolate-looking place and Xander looked curiously at Ari, wondering why they were here.

Ari beckoned him forward towards the ruins and smiled at his blank look.

'Welcome to the Folly,' she said, waving at the remnants of the old tower. 'It was built by a somewhat eccentric member of the Lisle family several hundred years ago but it's been derelict for ages. We're actually in London here, in one of the great parks.' She pointed across the glade to where an old track led away through the woods. 'If you follow that path, it will lead you pretty much straight through the South Gates. Normally I'd bring you here by the gate, but I don't have a lot of time today.'

'What's been happening with the border?' asked Xander.

Ari frowned. 'It's just not holding,' she said. 'Shades aren't yet breaking through completely like they did in the museum, but there've been some manifestations. It's concerning. Border security is tied somehow to the hobs' Core and we know that there are problems there.' She shook her head. 'Flint's at the Nexus now, trying to find out what's going on.'

'What *are* shades exactly?' asked Xander. He had never had a straight answer about this, although his memory of them was disturbingly vivid, and in some ways he was in two minds about finding out more about them.

'To be honest, no-one really knows,' Ari answered with a grimace. 'They seem to be pure expressions of chaos, terror and pain, but we don't know whether they're actually conscious themselves or where they come from. It's not like we can communicate with them, and anyone who gets too close ends up either dead or incapable of describing what they experienced. You saw poor old Alvin.'

Xander nodded.

Ari eyed his pale face and changed the subject.

'Anyway, we came here because it's used for young Travellers to practice and build their stamina and control. Watch.'

As Xander stood beside her, Ari lifted her hand and her orb flared. At once, one of the large stone blocks lying on the ground lifted into the air and hung unsupported in the middle of the clearing. A moment later, another block joined it, and then another and another. Xander gazed in awe as the enormous chunks of stone floated as lightly as dandelion seeds in the air, rotating gently before sinking back down to the ground. Xander suddenly understood why the scattering of stone blocks looked so random; they were not lying where they had toppled from the old tower, but where generations of young Travellers had dropped them.

Ari turned to him with one of her quick smiles, and a quirk of her brow.

'Come on then, prodigy,' she said with a hint of challenge.

'See how you do with those.'

Xander frowned at the massive blocks of rough stone and then focussed his attention on one of them, visualising lifting it up as easily as the daisies at Woodside. He raised his hand, and saw his orb flare into bright light, even as the block began to rise into the air. It trembled as Xander held it there, and he could feel a distinct strain on his muscles as if he was holding it up physically, although it was far too heavy for him ever to do that. He held his breath, trying to stabilise it, even as he reached for another of the blocks to lift. It was too much and both blocks dropped to the ground with solid thuds. Xander winced and glanced over at Ari, expecting to see her looking disappointed. Instead, she beamed at him and shook her head.

'Always a surprise, aren't you?' she said. 'Most people struggle to lift anything their first few times. That was brilliant, but maybe just try to hold one steady at a time before adding any extras. It's like using any new muscle – you need to build up your strength.'

Xander smiled, relieved at her encouragement, and focussed again on his first block. It floated up easily this time, and the resulting tension in his muscles felt more familiar as he just concentrated on supporting it in the air. A few moments later, he almost dropped it when Ari startled him by clapping.

'Very impressive,' she said, her eyes alight with approval, and then she laughed. 'You've certainly come a long way from the kid we picked up in a back alley in Fountain Square.'

Xander grinned at her.

'That was the maddest day of my life,' he confessed. 'Only beaten by every single day since then, of course.'

As his thoughts ran back to his arrival in Haven, he considered again the mystery surrounding Roran Thorne's assistance that day, and then eyed Ari speculatively. The red-headed

Traveller was generally friendly and approachable, and he wondered whether she would be more forthcoming than Flint.

'Ari?' he said casually, as the block revolved ponderously just in front of him. He glanced over to where she was sitting cross-legged on one of the larger stones. 'Why did Flint send Roran Thorne to collect me? He doesn't exactly seem friendly to the Travellers, and he was pretty rude about Flint.'

Ari's eyebrows shot up and she looked startled, before she shook her head with a quick, rueful smile.

'You don't miss much, do you?' she said wryly. 'We had no choice about the location you ended up. That Stone was unfamiliar and the only symbol any of us recognised was one that corresponded to an old civic building. It was sold off centuries ago, and went through a lot of different hands before Perrin Thorne bought it for his company twenty years ago. You came out of one of the back entrances of the building into that alley, but you've probably seen the Thorne Store at the front. Bright lights, very sparkly.'

Xander thought it over. 'But that still doesn't explain why Roran Thorne would do Flint a favour,' he said, with a frown. 'He didn't seem very happy about it either.'

Ari sighed. 'He wasn't exactly doing Flint a favour,' she said evasively, before giving Xander a straight look. 'I wouldn't normally talk about this, but I don't want you asking questions and raking over old hurts. Roran Thorne is Rafe's grandson.'

'Huh?'

This was the last thing that Xander had expected, and the large block thudded to the ground. He pulled a chagrined face as Ari shook her head at him, one eyebrow raised.

'Concentration is important, Xander,' she said pointedly, before sighing again and continuing. 'Rafe's daughter didn't take to Traveller life. I was too young to know her but supposedly she was limited in her abilities, and rather than stay on with us she went off and got involved with one of the Guilds. Anyway, that was how she met Perrin Thorne and they ended up getting married, against the wishes of her family, who really didn't like Thorne.'

Xander pulled a face. 'I can understand that,' he said.

Ari shrugged. 'Anyway, Roran was born and the family tried to make the best of it as Rafe didn't want to lose all contact with his only grandson. This went on for a few years and then that epidemic hit; Rafe's daughter was one of the people who died. Thorne had made his fortune by then, the Nexus was taking off and he didn't waste any time in marrying again, this time into a Founding Family. He claimed that he wanted Roran to have a mother but still, it was quick and there's no doubt he had his eye on moving up socially and politically. Venetia Larcius-Thorne is an unmitigated snob and the last thing she wanted was some socially-embarrassing Traveller grandfather hanging around. She cut him out of their lives as much as she could and influenced Roran to do the same.' She pulled a disgusted face and then looked over at Xander. 'Rafe has very limited contact with his grandson, and it wasn't easy for him to ask a favour like that. Don't talk about it round him, will you? No point in making it worse.'

Xander nodded, his opinion of the younger Thorne clear on his face.

'I won't say anything,' he promised.

Ari smiled. 'Tell you what,' she said, evidently relieved to be changing the subject. 'Since you've done so well with the basics, I'll show you an offensive ward. With these border breaches and your previous history as an unrestrained shade-magnet, it's probably not a bad thing for you to learn.'

Xander straightened up, his eagerness evident on his face

and Ari laughed. She jumped down from the stone and came to stand behind him, reaching out to take his left hand in hers.

'This type of ward is hard to describe,' she said, over his shoulder. 'I'll just do it and I want you to feel it through your own orb, okay?'

Xander nodded his head, and then felt her make a throwing motion with their joined hands. The sudden rush of energy reflected through his own orb startled him, and then made him smile with delight, as an arc of brilliant light illuminated the old tower in front of him, vividly highlighting every little crack and flaw in the stone. Ari let go of his hand and he turned to face her, his eyes alight.

'That was amazing,' he burst out. 'Can I try that?'

Ari grinned at him. 'You may, as long as you make sure you're directing the ward at inanimate objects, okay? This is for dealing with shades, not people that annoy you.' She gave him a mock severe look, and he laughed. He was about to attempt the warding technique for himself when Ari's orb chimed rapidly, and immediately her expression became serious.

'Sorry, Xander, I have to go,' she said. 'Hold on and I'll jump you back. You can feel how I do that, although don't try by yourself yet, for Haven's sake. You're not ready for it.'

Disappointed by the abrupt end of his lesson, Xander reached out to grip her outstretched arm again. This time however, with his new experience of feeling her orb in action, he tried to pay attention to what she was doing when she jumped, and felt again that faint reflection through his orb. Despite Ari's cautionary words, the technique felt quite clear to Xander and he wondered when he would be allowed to try for himself. A moment, and a sharp lurch, later they were back at Woodside and Ari was turning away, with a hasty goodbye before vanishing once again. With a wistful look at the empty space on the terrace where she had stood an instant ago, Xander turned towards the kitchen to find Ollie and Len, and update them on the latest information.

Over the next couple of days Xander trained hard, practicing all of the things that Ari had shown him, sometimes alone and other times accompanied by Ollie or Len. They endlessly re-hashed the few clues they had about why the hobs had given Xander the unusual orb, and the strange messages from the ancient terminal in the Halls. Ollie, inspired by the bright, powerful wards that Xander could now produce, had taken to practising himself with the more limited wards that synthetic orbs were capable of creating. Unfortunately his results were somewhat erratic, and Ollie's coding sometimes looked as though it would fizzle out entirely.

However, even as Xander's confidence grew in his new-found skills with his orb, the news continued to get worse on the stability of the border. The Travellers, who had hitherto enjoyed a fairly leisurely existence in terms of defending the border, were now rather stretched in finding people with the necessary skills to deploy to vulnerable areas. The few times that Xander saw Flint at Woodside, his demeanour was worried and forbidding, and he was even more unapproachable than usual.

Meanwhile, Xander was becoming increasingly convinced that the messages were referring to the hobs' Core, while Len absolutely disagreed with this conclusion.

'Think about it, Len,' Xander said to her, as they sat out in the garden after lunch while the adults spoke in worried undertones in the kitchen. 'You've been there. It's surrounded by water and the whole power core is made of crystal rock. The message said '*rock upon the water where the power lies*'; it's obvious that it means the Core.'

'It's not obvious at all,' retorted Len stubbornly. 'And what about the other clues? It's deep underground – how can stars lead the way there?'

Xander scowled at her, but Ollie suddenly sat bolt upright with the look of one who saw visions. 'The tunnel to the hobs' Core,' he blurted out. 'Don't you remember? When we walked through it, the glowstone made it look like the walls were covered in stars. Couldn't it be that?'

Xander beamed at him.

'You're right,' he said, filled with sudden certainty. 'We were led by the stars to the hobs' Core. That's brilliant, Ollie.'

Ollie grinned in pleasure at Xander's enthusiasm but Len shook her head, still unconvinced.

'That's a total stretch,' she said, with a mulish expression. 'And what about the other stuff? Where are 'the marks of the kin'?'

Xander brushed that away.

'Their 'kin' are goblin-kind,' he said firmly. 'They probably have marks all over the place that we don't recognise. They said I could heal the blight and speak to the stone, and that's why they gave me the orb. I think Thorne and Larcius want to take over using the Nexus, and they'll be able to if the hobs' Core is out of the way. Probably they're even involved in sabotaging it – the hobs did say that the contagion is coming from the Nexus.' Idly, he plucked some grass stems and sent them whirling up into the air, before showering them down on Len's head. 'Maybe you're just peeved because you didn't think of it yourself.'

Len rose to her feet with great dignity and stared down at him.

'Or *maybe* you're a show-off who doesn't know as much as he thinks he does.'

She stuck her nose in the air and stalked off, leaving Ollie and Xander to exchange quick grins.

Xander stood up as well, feeling a sudden sense of urgency in honing his skills with his orb. 'I'm just going to head over to the Folly to practice lifting and offensive warding,' he told Ollie. 'I'll be back before supper, okay?'

Ollie laughed. 'Wise decision,' he said. 'She might have calmed down by that time. Or, of course, she may have spent the afternoon stuffing your bed with frogs.'

His training session had proved very successful, and he could now handle several of the great stone blocks with ease, but Xander, frowning up at the darkening sky as he hurried back along the track, couldn't help wishing he had paid closer attention to the weather. Ominous-looking black clouds were massing heavily to the north and the temperature had plummeted. Clearly a storm was going to hit very soon, and the electric tension in the atmosphere made Xander shiver and pick up his pace even more. Just to add to his unease, shadows were beginning to shift and blur in the growing dusk under the thick canopy of leaves behind him, and there was a deep silence which Xander was determined to ignore, not wanting to think about the implications. His palm began to itch insistently and he rubbed it against his trouser leg.

'I'm just imagining things,' he told himself firmly, but if the last few weeks had taught him anything, it was that his imaginings were frequently far less alarming than reality.

He shivered as the temperature dropped even further and

then began to run, but it was already too late. Even as thunder growled in the distance and the first big drops of rain began to fall, the shadows under the trees stirred ominously. This was the first threat of border failure in the city that Xander was aware of but, as he threw worried glances over his shoulder, at least it didn't appear to be a full breach as the shades remained in place rather than coalescing. Xander glanced down at the orb on his wrist and wished that Ari had taught him how to communicate through it, as the Travellers did. He knew Flint would want to know that the border was weakening even here.

Finally, he reached the shelter of the first buildings and heaved a quick sigh of relief, casting a last glance at the dusky woodland behind him. He froze in shocked concern. Hurrying along the track was a tall boy, his shoulders hunched down away from the shifting shadows, while his orb glittered fitfully in an effort to maintain a rather anaemic-looking ward. Even as Xander watched, the shades were swelling in the dusk under the tree line too quickly to be outrun and the boy looked around him apprehensively, the faint light from his orb illuminating his face and making Xander's eyes widen in recognition; it was Roran Thorne.

Without giving himself too much time to think about it, Xander raced back down the path. He leant deeply into the orb just as Ari had instructed him and then threw out his arm, letting the energy surge out through his orb in a soaring arc of brilliant, sparkling light. It seared into the wavering shadows under the trees, crackling as it ignited them in an instant, and Xander felt a sense of total exhilaration, as if the pure force of it could lift him right off the ground and send him soaring. It felt more glorious than he could ever have imagined and he grinned with sheer joy; even the fat rain drops splashing down around him could not dampen his excitement.

Thorne had dropped into a half-crouch as Xander had unleashed the intensity of the orb strike into the trees behind him, but now he stood up again and looked around warily.

'It's okay,' said Xander. 'The shades are all gone.'

If Xander had expected any heartfelt thanks for his efforts, he was clearly doomed to disappointment. Thorne simply stared at him for a moment, his face expressionless, and then continued to walk along the track, brushing rudely past Xander without a word. Xander glared after him, feeling a surge of annoyance at the ingratitude, and then was hit with a sudden inspiration.

'We're even now, okay?' Xander called out.

Thorne stopped walking. 'I have no idea what you're talking about,' he said flatly, without turning or looking at Xander, but his tension was clear in the rigid set of his shoulders.

Xander suppressed a triumphant smile.

'Oh, I think you do,' he said lightly. 'I know that it was you Flint sent to meet me, even if you did try to blur your face. So thanks for that, I guess. It's nice to return the favour.'

Thorne stiffened and then spun around to face Xander, his fists clenched by his side and his eyes blazing. 'You don't know anything,' he snarled. 'And you certainly don't know anything about me. I didn't do you any *favours* and I didn't need your help just now. I was fine until you nearly blinded me.'

Xander's own temper began to rise at this and he opened his mouth to refute it, but Thorne rushed on, his voice cold and livid.

'Only idiots like Travellers, who know less than nothing, go around confronting those things and you're not even one of them, just a stupid nobody who apparently has a death wish.'

Thorne's eyes were icy blue, his face was twisted with contempt and the rain continued to beat down on both boys as they glared at each other.

'I think it's you who has the death wish,' Xander snapped back. 'Shades were manifesting everywhere, and what were you doing? Cringing along with barely a blip from daddy's orb to protect you. How exactly did you plan to drive them away?'

Thorne looked like he was about to hit Xander.

'Drive them away?' he spat. 'You could have lost control in a moment, you incompetent moron, and killed us both. For your information I was warding, which would've got me through quite safely without your stupid antics putting us both at risk. Next time, I suggest that you try to keep a grip on your delusions of grandeur, and ward and run like the rest of us, before you kill yourself and everyone around you.'

Thorne turned and stormed away up the track and into the city, leaving Xander open-mouthed and fuming on the path behind him. Thunder rolled ominously overhead and the first stab of lightning lit up the dark, northern sky. Abruptly aware that he was now absolutely drenched, Xander pushed the soaking hair off his face before turning to head back to the gate.

Len was rather distant with him when Xander returned, clearly still annoyed about his earlier comment, but Ollie was keen to hear about what had happened with Thorne and the shades, and flatteringly impressed with Xander's feat in driving them away.

'There's no point paying attention to what someone like him says,' he said. 'He was probably just embarrassed that you dealt with them, while he could barely do anything. He's a nasty piece of work.'

Xander agreed, but Thorne's implication that he was incompetent and stupid continued to nag at him. The next morning brought even more dire news about the state of the hobs' Core and Xander worried that he was running out of time to do anything. He and Ollie discussed the situation and decided that the best course of action was to go to see Hob at his shop, and get his opinion.

'They gave you the orb, after all,' Ollie had said. 'Not to mention, it's their Core that's in trouble. If you offer to help and they turn you down, at least you'll know that you've done everything you could.'

Len, who had overheard this, rolled her eyes with a theatrical sigh but Xander ignored her. 'You're right,' he replied to Ollie. 'If the whole thing goes down, then it'll be too late and we'll never know if I could've done something.'

Ollie nodded solemnly, while Len just walked away, shaking her head.

That afternoon, therefore, found Xander heading back to Hob's Orb shop with a sense of relief that he was finally doing something, mixed with slight apprehension at dealing with the hobgoblins again. The bell rang as he pushed the door open for the third time, and then stepped into the shop. Once more, Hob was at his desk and his strange eyes narrowed as Xander walked over to face him.

'You're back,' he grated, not sounding at all pleased about it.

Xander stood his ground, determined not to be intimidated this time.

'I need to talk to you about something,' he said. 'It's about the orb and what I'm supposed to do with it.'

Before the hobgoblin could interrupt or make any disparaging comments, Xander poured out his account of the mysterious messages from the ancient terminal and the conclusions he and Ollie had come to about what they could mean. When he had finished, he looked anxiously at the hobgoblin, wondering what his response would be.

Hob's yellow eyes were hooded and secretive as he stared at Xander.

'Interesting theory, human, but what makes you think you can do what we cannot?'

Xander swallowed, and then stared straight back at him.

'Your Elder Goblin said that I can heal the blight on Haven. Isn't that why you gave me this orb?'

'Foolish boy,' said the hob, dismissively. 'We gave the orb in response to an ancient imperative, not by our choice or opinion about our Core.' His face twisted for a moment, and then he stood up. 'However, this is not for me to judge. Come.'

The hobgoblin walked over to the door of the shop and Xander expected him to open it, but instead he turned a heavy key in the lock and then led the way over to the little doorway that the old hobgoblin had used after giving Xander his orb. He turned to glower at Xander.

'We do not take humans by our ways but in this case we will permit it.'

Looking at the shadowy space behind the door, Xander swallowed again but it seemed ridiculous to object now. He followed the hobgoblin through the doorway, bending his shoulders down to get through. When he stood up again, he was looking at a large, ornate rock formation in the middle of a beautiful landscaped garden, the sound of running water coming from his right. Blinking in confusion, he turned to see the unmistakable structure of the Nexus.

'Was that a gate?' he asked the hobgoblin, who just stared at him disdainfully.

'I told you, we have our own ways,' he growled, then turned and stumped away in the opposite direction to the Nexus.

Trying not to roll his eyes in exasperation at the hobgoblin's unrelenting unfriendliness, Xander followed him across the clipped green lawn to an area where the ground became rougher and less manicured. Just through a small belt of trees was an odd structure, like one of the stone alcoves Xander had seen in the Nexus itself, leading to the Core. It looked particularly out of place here, standing upright and alone in the middle of the rough grass. The hobgoblin stepped inside it and then turned and beckoned, in an eerie repetition of the previous visit to the Core. Xander took a deep breath and a final glance around, and that was when he spotted the shadow of a face moving out of sight just behind the alcove. He stiffened, and then ducked sideways so he could see the curving back of the edifice. There was no one there.

Hob stuck his head back out and glowered at him.

'If you have quite finished,' he grated out, 'I have better things to do with my afternoon than watch you play games.'

Xander opened his mouth to explain and then shut it again. He took a last uneasy look towards the place where he was sure that an ordinary, unremarkable face with menacing eyes had been watching him, and then walked into the alcove. The hobgoblin led the way through the rippling wall, back into the hobs' Core.

It was dark and hot, with a faint sulphuric smell he did not remember from before, and after a few breaths it coated his tongue and left a burning sensation on the back of his throat. Clearly things had got much worse since Xander had last been here a week before and he stared about, shocked by the change. Hob silently led Xander forward into the crystal mass, no longer pulsing with colourful light but now dimmed and opaque, with a sickly overtone of yellow and green.

The Elder Goblin was standing in front of a dark, shattered spire surrounded by a group of other hobs, their faces creased with worry, and he turned at Xander's entrance to look at him with cold yellow eyes. Hob stumped forward and bowed his head.

'The boy thinks he is getting secret directions to heal our Core, and that he has sufficiently mastered the orb to do so,' he grated, in a voice which clearly communicated his scepticism about both claims. All of the hobs stared at Xander, who shuffled his feet awkwardly and tried not to duck his head.

Finally, the Elder Goblin spoke. 'Why do you believe these things?' he asked, in his dry creaking voice.

Xander swallowed, and it sounded far too loud in the quiet. He was getting a little dizzy in the stifling heat of the Core and his throat felt raw. Trying not to breathe too deeply, he recounted again his theory about the messages, and attempted to inject his words with his previous certainty, although that was withering under the cold gaze of inhuman yellow eyes. When his voice trailed off, there was another long silence, and then the Elder Goblin sighed, as if he had been presented with a burden too great to carry.

'We will see,' he said, as his gaze travelled across the ruined surface of the Core, its sickly light reflected in his eyes. He shook his head. 'This corruption does not originate here, with us; of that, we are quite certain. Still, perhaps you can indeed drive it out. Perhaps –'

He turned to face Xander, gesturing for him to approach the Core, and Xander caught the faint glimmer of what almost looked like hopefulness.

The hobgoblins stood in a silent circle as Xander walked over to a stretch of crystal which looked a little less unhealthy than the rest, although that feeling of wrongness was equally strong. As he drew near, it seemed to beat at his face and his throat flamed in response. With another quick glance over at the hobs, all watching him intently, he forced himself to reach out with his orb hand and lay it on the wall.

He almost gagged as he touched it. The greasy feeling of last time had now become an overwhelming surge of putrid slime, coating his skin and running up his arm. His hand began to shake with the strain of holding it there against the rising tide of decay and the disgust he felt, and this time the crystal wall did not respond with even the faint light of before.

With a desperate effort, Xander leant into his orb, reaching for that powerful response but for the first time it did not bloom into light. His heart pounding, Xander tried again and the orb just flickered, and then went dark. Unable to hold on any longer, he lurched away from the wall and then doubled over, his stomach heaving as he tried to control his gagging. When he straightened up again it was to meet the cold, critical eyes of the circle of hobgoblins, all staring at him with the same bitter expression.

'Perhaps not,' came the creaking voice of the Elder Goblin. 'Perhaps we have placed our hopes foolishly and this is the end for us.'

Without another glance, he turned away and several hobs jumped forward to support him. One of the hobgoblins beckoned to Xander and then silently led him back through the stifling Core to the translucent entrance to the Nexus. As Xander stumbled through it, he was not sure whether it was the caustic smell of sulphur or the pain of failure that burned more fiercely in his throat.

CHAPTER TEN

Blurry-eyed and sick to his stomach, Xander blundered through the short passageway. He had been delusional, thinking he could sweep in and be the hero, and his face burned as he remembered his inability to help and the Elder Goblin's bitter words. In his misery, Xander hadn't even thought about how he could get out of the crippled Core but as he faltered on, he saw that the ward at the end was rippling again, with the cold light from Thorne's massive crystal slabs shining intrusively into the rocky passage. He stepped back out into the glare of the Nexus.

He had no idea how to get out but, right now, he didn't care if he wandered in here forever. It only took ten minutes of stumbling between the glittering aisles, however, before he bumped into a familiar figure. Petros looked at him in surprise, his bright brown eyes blinking behind his glasses.

'Xander?' he said, looking around him in mild confusion. 'What are you doing here? Is Flint with you?'

Xander cleared his throat.

'Um, no. I was with someone but they're busy now and I wanted to go home.'

He was relieved that he got this much out without his voice cracking, but Petros looked more puzzled.

'Well, they really shouldn't have left you wandering around by yourself. It's not safe.' When Xander just stood, staring at him, Petros peered closer and then smiled reassuringly. 'Never mind. I'll escort you out, okay?'

Petros trotted off at his usual energetic pace and Xander trudged along behind him, head hanging. He was never sure what made him glance up to see the neat figure of Gage, for once not in the shadow of Lester Simm, walking towards him with a large container tucked under one arm and the usual bland expression on his face. Petros didn't acknowledge him as they passed and Xander wondered whether the man was as despised here as Latchet. Despite his self-effacing air, there was a distinct sense of menace about him and Xander shivered at the thought of him lurking around the entrance to the hobs' Core. As if he could hear Xander's thoughts Gage looked over at him, lips twisting in contempt. For a moment, Xander's ears burned with a hot, roaring noise, until Gage looked away and cool air rushed in again.

Xander twisted to look over his shoulder but Gage had disappeared among the glowing rows of crystal, and a few moments later Petros led him over to the gated platform waiting at the lower level to whisk Xander away. He opened the gate and then patted Xander's shoulder.

'You don't look great,' he said in a sympathetic tone. 'Don't worry, you'll warm up as soon as you're topside. It's sunny today, I hear.'

Xander managed a shaky smile, although privately he thought the reason he was pale and shivering was unlikely to be helped by a bit of sunshine.

'Thanks for bringing me out,' he mumbled and Petros beamed at him again, before shutting the gate and reaching for the button. His hand froze in mid-air as the wail of a loud and discordant siren blared out over the Nexus, echoing and re-echoing in the enormous space.

For an instant, everyone was still and silent, staring at one another, and then they burst into action, racing off in every direction. Petros dashed off the platform and fixed Xander with an urgent stare.

'It's the emergency alert. Something's gone seriously wrong,' he exclaimed. 'Head straight home and let Flint know if you can, okay?' He leaned over the gate and stabbed at the button.

Before Xander could answer, the platform was sweeping upwards and he could see Petros pelting off down one of the aisles. As he soared up high above the Nexus, Xander's view was unimpeded across the enormous space and he caught his breath. A thick greenish-black haze was rising from the rear of the Nexus, the area where – Xander frantically tried to recall his bearings – the internal entrance to the hobs' Core lay. A sickly yellow light flickered in the depths of the dark haze and Xander shivered as the siren continued to blare out.

Trying not to see any more, he stumbled over to the lift, which carried him swiftly to the corridors above. They were boiling with people, all shouting to one another, and he was able to pass through unremarked to the lift back up to the atrium. The siren was still audible there, though much fainter, and people were thronging around the reception desk. In the turmoil and confusion, Xander made it across to the large revolving doors, through the metallic touch of the ward and out into the sunshine outside, with no-one to enquire what he had been doing there in the first place.

Xander squinted up at the sky. It didn't seem right for the afternoon to be so bright, as if it were just another carefree summer day, when everything was going wrong and Xander was responsible for the biggest failure of his life. With one final glance back at the Nexus, he crossed over the little bridge and began the journey back to Woodside to carry out Petros' request, although he did not look forward to telling Flint where he had been, and his stomach lurched again at the thought of what Ollie and Len would say when they heard how badly he had failed.

Head hanging, Xander trudged on with miserable, dark thoughts swirling relentlessly round in his mind and did not even look up as he passed through the first gate home.

As it turned out, Xander did not have to break the news himself. By the time he got back to Woodside, the kitchen was filled with people staring at the big screen on the wall, while the serious voice of a newscaster was recounting the details that were known so far about the calamity at the Core. Xander slid through the door and joined Ollie and Len, who were perched on the end of the table.

'You okay, mate?' murmured Ollie, with a quick sideways look.

That Ollie had clearly been sitting here worrying only made Xander feel worse, and he stared at the floor.

'It was a total disaster,' he muttered. He sensed Len's eyes burning into the side of his head and moved impatiently. 'And do *not* tell me you told me so, please,' he snapped. Unfortunately, his voice cracked as he spoke, and he gulped.

It turned out that the news service only had limited information thus far, which they repeated over and over again, interspersed with various 'experts' rounded up to come on and give their views. They seemed to be competing over who could give the most melodramatic opinion, and Xander reflected that the people who were genuine experts, like Reeve and Petros, were probably far too busy right now to waste time being interviewed.

After the fourth or fifth repetition, Mrs Stanton waved a hand and muted the sound. 'I think we've heard quite enough of that,' she said and then bustled about the kitchen while Flint, Jasper and a couple of the other Travellers drew off into a little group and spoke in low tones. There was no sign of Ari's bright red hair, and so no chance of any back-channel information.

Ollie eyed Xander cautiously. 'So, what happened?' he asked.

Xander shook his head.

'Nothing,' he said. 'Literally nothing.' He looked away and blinked rapidly. 'I've been kidding myself all along.'

Len made an impatient sound, but Xander did not want to hear it. He jumped up before she could say anything and walked out. Out of the corner of his eye he saw Ollie put a hand on her arm and murmur, 'Not now.'

It was early evening when Xander finally got off his bed and went back downstairs, drawn out partly because of the insistent growling of his stomach and partly due to the increasing volume of voices from the kitchen. Len was not among the large group of people there, but Ollie, clutching an armful of plates, looked up as he entered and sent him a quick, sympathetic grin. Xander smiled weakly back but his gaze was immediately drawn to the dishevelled-looking figure of Callan Reeve, who sat at the table with a cup of tea and an exhausted expression. He slid into a chair and listened to the conversation.

'So, what's the status of the hobs' Core now?' Flint asked.

Reeve pushed a hand through his untidy hair, dragging it back from his face and exposing a long scrape across his forehead.

'Status?' he repeated in a tired voice. 'It's a disaster. Most of the place is inaccessible now, and what we can see is burnt out.'

'Inaccessible?' asked James Stanton, with a worried look.

Reeve shrugged. He looked drained. 'When that amount of rock comes down, it's pretty hard to get through it. Oh, I'm not saying that there may not be areas that have survived, but I don't know how you'd get to them; it's completely unstable in there.'

Silence fell for a moment around the table and Xander's stomach twisted.

'Was anyone hurt?' It was Mrs Stanton's voice, quiet and concerned.

Reeve glanced over at her. 'As far as we know, everyone got out but you know how the hobs are about sharing information. They don't want anything to do with humans at the best of times.'

His voice trailed off, and he shook his head helplessly.

Xander stared at the table, wracked with guilt yet again. Ollie slid a plate in front of him and he ate mechanically, without tasting any of it. He was so engrossed in his own misery that he took a moment or so to realise that Callan Reeve had paused behind his chair.

'Petros said that you were at the Nexus today,' Reeve said quietly.

Xander looked up at him and nodded, bracing for the inevitable barrage of questions.

'Are you okay?'

This was not what Xander had expected to be asked, and

he was horrified to feel his throat burning again. He nodded mutely, and Reeve's hand clasped his shoulder for a moment before he moved away again. Before he could lose control and embarrass himself in the middle of the kitchen, Xander jumped up and slipped through the back door into the dusky garden beyond, hurrying into the darkness as if he could somehow outrun the sick sensation of failure in his stomach.

When he reached the end of the garden, he ducked behind the flowering shrubs and lowered himself to the grass near the soft gleam of Katie's nixie pond. It was a warm night, but he wrapped his arms around himself and hunched down; right at this moment, he wished that he could just disappear altogether. He had not been sitting there long before he heard footsteps heading over towards his refuge. He didn't have to turn around to identify their owners.

'I don't want to talk about it,' he growled, stiff-backed and staring straight ahead of him.

Predictably enough, he reflected with some bitterness, his pursuers ignored that. Ollie sank down on the grass next to him while Len circled around in front, a dark figure silhouetted against the pond.

'So, it wasn't a success,' Ollie began carefully.

Despite Xander's determination to remain silent, a snort of disbelief escaped him at the scale of this understatement.

'You think?' he said. 'It was a catastrophe.'

Ollie and Len just waited and suddenly Xander found words bursting out of him, as though a dam had burst.

'They were all just standing there, watching me and waiting for me to fix it and I couldn't. I couldn't do anything. My orb didn't even respond, just flickered and then went out. Nothing.' He took a shaky breath. 'I don't know what I was thinking, believing all of this rubbish. I shouldn't even be here – everyone knows I don't belong.'

'Well, that's total drivel.'

Len's voice cut straight across him, clear and concise.

Xander's head swung up. He glowered at her but she just stepped closer, her arms folded tightly. 'Saying you're not supposed to be here is pathetic. You can't throw everything away, everything we've seen and been through, simply because you're feeling sorry for yourself. You're the one who assumed that you were meant to resurrect the hobs' Core. Your problem is that your *conclusions* were wrong, not that *you* are. As I told you at the time.'

Len couldn't resist tacking on that last sentence, the superior little 'I told you so', and Xander's temper surged. He jumped up angrily to face her and saw Ollie scramble to his feet too, looking worriedly between the two of them.

'Well, if you're so brilliant and always so right, explain it to me then,' Xander snapped. Len tilted her chin and glared back at him but he didn't stop. 'Tell me, o wise one, why am I here and what am I supposed to be doing about all this?' Xander's hands were clenching convulsively as he threw the words at her like weapons, and he shook his head as she opened her mouth to respond and then shut it again.

'See,' he said triumphantly. 'You've got no more idea than the rest of us, so pack it in with the whole condescending act. You don't know *anything*.'

Len stared at him for a moment, then turned on her heel and walked off without a word, head high and back very straight. Watching her stalking away from him, Xander thought he ought to feel better for having got that off his chest, but all he really felt was guilt. Len could be truly annoying, but she hadn't deserved for him to take out his frustration and worry on her. He grimaced ruefully and saw Ollie watching him.

'You realise that she's going to make both of us pay for that,' Ollie said wryly, then grinned and shook his head. 'C'mon. Best to get the grovelling apology over with sooner rather than later. Believe me; you don't want to let her stew.'

With a weak smile, Xander turned and trudged back up the garden. On the whole, he reflected, this had not been one of his better days.

Another major power surge occurred at the Nexus overnight, and several more Guilds were now complaining of interrupted energy supplies and unpredictable orb outages. The presenter on the morning news programme disclosed these things in low, dramatic tones and dolefully predicted further disasters. There was some condemnation of the fact that the Core had been allowed to get into such a state without intervention by the Nexus management and finally, an emergency Council session was announced for that afternoon. Xander listened with a sinking sense of responsibility, as Mrs Stanton shook her head and exchanged looks with Jenna.

'Has anyone heard from the hobs?' asked Jenna, while Xander hovered quietly in the background.

Mrs Stanton sighed.

'Not according to Flint. He said that Cal and the other engineers have been trying to reach them, but they've disappeared. Apparently they're blaming us and said that they won't trust any more humans.' She shrugged. 'You know how they are.'

Jenna nodded gloomily and Xander slipped out of the kitchen, not wanting to hear any more.

The news of a Council meeting to discuss the situation

kept nagging at his thoughts however, and after lunch Xander asked if he could go. Mrs Stanton pursed her lips, with a quick glance out of the window as if checking to see whether shades were manifesting in the garden. As there had been no more reports about border breaches and the Academy had remained open, she agreed on the proviso that Xander go only to the Council chamber and come straight back.

The streets were a little emptier than usual as Xander hurried along, but the inhabitants of Haven that he passed did not yet seem too concerned about the disruption to the tenor of their lives. Xander wondered whether they were not aware of the effects yet, or if they had simply chosen not to believe the dire sensationalism of the news, but it was rather reassuring to see that life was continuing.

The reception hall at the Council chamber was full this time, and Xander waited in the queue before the main desk, listening to the hum of voices coming from behind the closed doors at the back. When it was his turn, he looked up to see the crinkled face and gap-toothed smile of the white-haired old man in his green robe who had greeted them on their last visit. He beamed at Xander.

'Ah, the young man standing for office,' he said with a wink. 'Never forget a face. Back again, eh? You picked a good day for it – lots happening. You'll need a pass, young sir, since you're not with your friends with the civics books today.' He pressed a small rectangle of paper into Xander's hand and pointed him off towards the door in the corner. 'You remember the way up, eh?'

Xander smiled weakly at him, rather thrown by the man's prodigious memory for people who had visited the Council chamber, and then hurried over to the stairs up to the visitor's gallery. This time, when he entered the gallery, every seat was taken, and he squeezed in at the edge of the balcony. The great chamber below was equally packed, with every one of the green benches full of Guild members. When he peered down, he was surprised to see the hulking figure of Perrin Thorne standing on the little podium, evidently in the middle of giving testimony. Barton Ferrars brought his gavel down several times.

'If everyone keeps interrupting every five minutes, this chamber will never get any decisions made,' he said crossly, and banged his gavel again for good measure.

'Mr Larcius-Thorne,' said Randall Hackett, leaning forward with a grave expression. 'You have updated us on the impact of the Core collapse on the integrity of the critical services which the Nexus provides. We have heard also from the honourable representatives of the Guilds, who are present today and have given their testimony. I realise that you are a busy man, particularly today, but would you please give us your professional opinion? Should we remove the interfaces with what's left of the hobs' Core and direct all of our energy requirements to the Nexus? Is that your recommendation and are you in fact able to support such a thing at this time?'

There was another burst of worried-sounding comments from the floor and Ferrars banged his gavel, glaring around.

Thorne waited until silence had fallen again before answering. He gazed back at the Council members with his cold, black eyes, the light gleaming on his thick, slicked-back hair.

'It is my professional opinion, and that of my engineers and technical staff, that the *only* way to guarantee the power supply on Haven at this point is by removing the now-defunct interfaces to make sure we have no further disruptions from the breakdown of the hobs' Core,' he said in a smooth and mellifluous voice. His tongue flickered out to moisten his lips as he shook his head in a show of regret. 'We remain deeply indebted to our little friends who guided our first tentative steps in this technology. Indeed, we are hopeful that we can now extend the hand of assistance to them in our turn as they work through their difficulties. However, our view at the Nexus is that we have a responsibility to the citizens of Haven to ensure that their lives and important work can continue without constant interruption, and we are standing ready and willing to guarantee that happens.'

The noise of many voices rose again in the chamber, but this time the general sound was approving. Xander saw Marcus Melville and Felix Larcius exchange smug-looking smiles, before Barton Ferrars banged his gavel again and called the councillors to consultation. While they whispered amongst themselves, Thorne tilted his head up to look idly at the portraits gazing down on them, his pale, corpulent face calm and confident. In a much shorter time than before, Ferrars was banging his gavel and everyone quieted to hear him speak.

'Eight in favour of the proposition before the Council, three against and one undecided on final consideration,' announced Ferrars, before bringing his gavel down again. 'It is the Council's decision that the immediate, full and final integration of the Nexus as sole provider of power to Haven is initiated.'

There was a roar of voices from the floor of the chamber and scattered clapping, while Thorne nodded his head in acknowledgement to the Council, his gaze lingering on his brother-in-law with a twitch of his thick lips. Enid Ingram and Horace Peverell had immediately leaned in to speak with Ferrars, with urgent expressions on their faces, and he listened for a moment and then nodded.

'Order, order,' he boomed. 'Given the unprecedented nature of this step, and to ensure its success, it is appropriate that the Council should establish an oversight committee to report on the progress made and any issues which need immediate action.'

Melville nodded, his eyes glittering in triumph.

'An excellent suggestion, as always,' he drawled. 'May I suggest that, given his familiarity with the work at the Nexus and his conscientious attention to detail, Mr Lester Simm is appointed as head of the oversight committee?'

Xander saw Horace Peverell and Enid Ingram exchange rueful looks but they did not object when it was put to a general vote, and Simm was duly appointed. Suddenly, Xander spotted him over on the far side of the chamber, wearing an eye-watering shade of violet, and repeatedly bowing with huge flourishes of his arm toward Larcius and Melville, who did not appear to have noticed his genuflections.

Xander sighed. Despite Thorne's claims that his engineers supported his earlier statements, Xander wondered about Reeve's opinion on all of this. Up on the balcony, he overheard some comments from people as they prepared to leave.

'Well, that's it then,' said one lady, pursing her lips. 'The Nexus running everything and next thing you know, Thorne's relatives running the Council as well. All a bit too cosy, if you ask me.'

'Hmm,' replied her neighbour. 'As long as they don't put the prices up or interfere with us, I don't really care who runs it. Those hobs always did give me the shivers, anyway.'

With a sinking feeling, Xander joined the queue of people now heading down the staircase and then went to hand in his pass at the desk, receiving another quick wave and wink from old Pritchard. Remembering his promise to Mrs Stanton, he headed across the square and back towards the South Gates but he could not resist a quick look down the little street to Hob's

Orb shop as he passed, wondering guiltily if he should apologise for his failure.

To his surprise, the little wooden sign was no longer hanging above the doorway and he hesitated for a moment, before curiosity and a hint of worry, brought him over to the door. The first thing he noticed was that the window was boarded up and when he tried the door handle, it was locked. Clearly, the hobgoblins had not just chosen to withdraw from their wrecked Core but from everywhere else, and Xander felt that tightening of guilt in his chest again. As he trudged back to the gates, it was with an ominous conviction that things were likely to get worse and there was nothing he could do about it.

By the next morning, his gloomy prediction seemed to be well on the way to coming true. There had been more breaches on the border and they were becoming more unpredictable. The shades could not yet fully manifest but several people had been caught without adequate wards, and even a mild case of shade-strike was extremely unpleasant. In addition, and to his growing concern, he was struggling to use his orb with the same ease as before. Sometimes he could lift things and ward with his previous ease, but more often the orb barely responded and Xander's anxiety grew every time that happened. He might have discussed it with Ari but evidently she was too busy to spare any time to teach him now. Even the brownies had been missing for the past couple of days, and the house seemed strangely empty without their little forms darting about and hiding behind chair legs and plant stands.

On the third day after the hobs' Core collapse, the announcement came out mid-morning that the Academy was being temporarily closed, pending the full integration of the Nexus and hopefully the resuming of border security. Jasper and Flint had gone to collect Ollie and Len from the city, and Xander was helping Mrs Stanton lay the table for lunch, while in the background the sombre voice of the newscaster related the latest failure on the border and the hospitalisation of yet another person. Mrs Stanton paused a moment, listening with a worried face, and that bitter sense of responsibility flooded through Xander again.

'Can't they stop it?' he asked her. 'Travellers, I mean.'

Mrs Stanton took one look at his tense face and crossed the kitchen to put an arm around him, hugging him reassuringly. 'Of course they will,' she said quickly. She gestured at the screen and it blanked, the dolorous voice replaced with soft music. 'You know Flint. He'll have it under control in no time, don't you worry.'

Xander tried to be encouraged, but he couldn't help his voice shaking slightly as he asked the question he had been worrying over for days. 'Do they think that the hobs' Core going down is what caused all of these breaches?' He stared hard at the handful of forks he was clutching as he waited for her answer.

'Honestly, dear, I don't know. Callan thinks their Core has been failing for a long time now, but you know how they are, so secretive, holding themselves apart. They just don't trust us, so we really can't help them, unfortunately.'

'Failing for a long time now.' Xander tried to hold on to that thought, to believe that he wasn't responsible for the disaster unfolding on Haven. He kept his eyes down, carefully laying out the cutlery but Mrs Stanton, with her warm heart and sharp eyes, was not fooled.

'Xander?' she said gently. 'Is everything okay with you?'

Xander swallowed, but before he could decide whether or not he was going to answer that, the front door banged and the sound of many voices flooded down the hallway into the kitchen, followed a moment later by all the family, with several additions in the form of Ari, Flint and Callan Reeve, who looked absolutely shattered.

'Hey, Gran,' Ollie burst through the door and beamed at them both. 'That smells good. I'm starving.'

'When are you not?' retorted Mrs Stanton. She gave Xander's arm a squeeze and murmured, 'We can continue this later, if you like?'

Xander swallowed and then looked up at her with a bright smile. 'Oh, I'm fine,' he said hastily. Mrs Stanton looked unconvinced, but he hurried to put out the rest of the cutlery, avoiding her eyes.

Lunch was as delicious as ever, the good food and friendly faces around the table holding the worrying news from outside at bay, at least for a little while, but as the meal went on the atmosphere became quieter and more serious. Flint, Rafe and Jasper were talking with a couple of other Travellers, whose names Xander didn't know but who he recognised from Flint's circle. The tall dark Warden, Kirrin Ledger, turned up late and slipped in near Reeve, his face sober and concerned; and even Ari appeared more subdued than usual, as she sat next to Jasper with her usual twinkle entirely absent.

Xander listened intently to the conversation at the end of the table which had grown louder as people finished eating.

'So apparently Simm told the Oversight Committee earlier that there will have to be significant changes to secure the power supply again,' Jasper said.

'Yes, overriding every safety protocol we have ever established,' replied Reeve, his voice sharp with annoyance and frustration. 'There's a reason we've always implemented advancements cautiously and with careful risk assessments. To be honest, we still know far too little about this technology, and Thorne is over-confident about how well we understand the linkages to the underlying power sources in the deep earth. Of course, Simm is refusing to acknowledge any of this – the man's a complete idiot.'

'Tell us something we don't know,' interjected Ledger with an ironic lift of his eyebrow.

'I know, but now he's behaving really oddly,' said Reeve. 'His team is shutting us engineers out of whole areas of the Nexus where it physically interfaces with the hobs' Core. We've tried to speak to him, but he's just not listening. He's got Latchet running around threatening people, although that's hardly a change.'

'What are they trying to do at the interface?' asked Flint.

'I told you, I can't tell because we're not allowed anywhere near it,' replied Reeve, frustrated. 'From what we saw before they shut us out, they've forced their way into part of the Core. As you know, the damage is extensive there and the hobs seem to have completely abandoned it now. There's no sign of any of them.'

'What in Haven is Simm doing in there, then?' demanded Ledger.

Reeve shrugged and shook his head.

'I think he's looking for something but whatever it is, his team don't seem to be finding it. Simm just marches up and down talking to himself ten to the dozen. I swear, the man has cracked up.'

As Reeve stared at the table, his exasperation evident, Xander could not help but wonder whether Simm was talking to himself as Reeve assumed, or whether he was actually talking to the strange and disturbing man who had the knack of being overlooked.

'Can you try to reason with him?' asked Ari.

Reeve made an aggravated sound.

'How?' he asked with a roll of his eyes. 'It's like talking to an over-dressed brick wall, even if it's possible to get past Latchet. Simm doesn't listen to anyone.'

Xander suddenly had a vivid recollection of the nondescript man, his lips moving as he talked to Simm in the Council chamber. Without thinking, he blurted out, 'He listens to Gage.'

The adults around the table all turned around to stare at him, and he flinched. Clearly, most of them had forgotten that Xander, Ollie and Len were still at the table, and both Flint and Ledger frowned.

'Who did you say, Xander?' Reeve asked kindly, but his face looked tired and worried.

Xander flushed.

'Gage,' he repeated. 'You know, the guy who's always following Simm around with a clipboard. Brown hair, kind of,' he groped in his memory for a description, 'average-looking.' Xander was rather surprised at how difficult it was to recall an accurate image of the man; he was just so ordinary.

Reeve looked blank. 'Sorry, Xander,' he said, shaking his head. 'I can't think of anyone like that. The only person who's always hanging around Simm is Latchet.'

Xander gaped at him. He had never seen Simm without the silent figure of Gage walking behind him, and it was very odd that Reeve claimed never to have heard of him. Flint abruptly cleared his throat and Xander looked up to see him sending a meaningful look at Mrs Stanton. Immediately, she stood up from the table and the next moment the three of them were being ushered firmly out of the kitchen. She shooed them up the stairs.

'Go find something useful to do,' she said, before turning back to the kitchen.

At the top of the stairs, Ollie gestured towards the bathroom with a raised eyebrow. Xander just shook his head and went to lie on his bed, throwing an arm over his face. He felt thoroughly confused.

The next day the situation had deteriorated further, and in the early evening Flint came to request Mrs Stanton's help at the Lodge for a Traveller injured with shade-strike. She packed up her medical supplies with a worried face and then insisted that Ollie, Len and Xander should accompany them.

'James is out and Jenna has enough to do, and I'm not leaving them to get up to who knows what.' Her gaze rested most sharply on Len, who looked wounded at the implication.

Flint appeared thoroughly distracted and for once did not even put up an argument, simply jumping them straight to the guide-stone and then hurrying them along the path to the Lodge. It was quieter than it had been before, when they had come for the Gathering, with only a few hearths and one bonfire burning, but there were quite a few people milling around there, most of them looking tired and some clearly injured. After indicating that her two grandchildren and Xander should sit outside the Lodge, Mrs Stanton went inside.

Flint ignored them, also heading inside, and Len heaved a gusty sigh.

'Well, this is just perfect,' she muttered. 'What a way to spend an evening.'

Xander rested his elbows on his knees, staring at the ground and privately agreeing with her. He had caught several wary looks directed at him from a few of the Travellers moving about the glade, and he hung his head, letting his hair conceal his face. A moment later however, he looked up involuntarily as voices drifted out of the open window behind them.

'There is absolutely no reason to over-react.' It was Atherton's voice, sharp and precise, and sounding exasperated. 'We are assured that the Nexus will come fully online within the next few days and surely all of this disruption will calm down at that point.'

'I disagree.' Wooten's quavering tones were just as distinctive, and he snorted sceptically. 'We have no guarantee whatsoever that this new-fangled technology will adequately replace the Core. How do we know that our security is not linked to the original source of energy on Haven, eh?'

Another person chimed in and Xander recognised the calm, authoritative voice of Kirrin Ledger.

'Border security is not our only concern. There are reports that the Stones are unresponsive and, as it stands, we cannot cross the border. It appears likely that it's linked to the failures on the border generally and may suggest a deeper problem here.'

Wooten started to respond but Atherton cut straight across him.

'I hardly think our temporary inability to Travel over the border is a major concern at the moment. Until it's clear that this is anything more than an inconvenience, which will be alleviated in a couple of days, I refuse to flap around or make rash decisions.'

'Reeve is concerned that Thorne may be under-estimating the difficulty of fully replacing the Core with Nexus functionality.' Flint's resonant voice was equally recognisable. 'We should at least have contingency plans if things deteriorate further than they have in the last couple of weeks.'

'Oh, for Haven's sake –'

Atherton sounded thoroughly irritated, but Wooten now cut him off in turn. 'Speaking of which, where is that troublesome outlander boy you picked up, eh? He doesn't belong here, that's certain, and his arrival seems to have coincided with all of this chaos and disorder. Is that happenstance or should we be looking more closely at him?'

'I hardly think so,' said Ledger, in a sceptical tone and Flint snorted in agreement, but Xander did not wait to hear any more. With a sudden prickling feeling behind his eyes, he lurched to his feet and hurried away into the woodland surrounding the Lodge. It was bad enough to carry a sinking weight of responsibility, but for it to be expressed out loud in Wooten's accusing voice was unbearable.

When he was out of sight of the clearing Xander stopped and leant back against a tree, angrily shoving at the exposed root with his shoe. *'He doesn't belong here.'* The words he had over-heard wouldn't stop revolving around in his head; he'd been so stupid to think there was a place here for him, that he was wanted. Probably the Stantons were just waiting for Flint to take him back home, and they would all be relieved when he was gone. The Travellers certainly wanted him out of Haven, and the hobs would never forgive him. Xander felt a hot lump rise in his throat and his breath caught in something near to a sob.

'Mate, are you okay?' Ollie's voice rang out from nearby and Xander brushed a quick hand across his eyes.

'Fine,' he replied flatly. There was a moment's silence.

'It's not true, what he said, you know.' Len's voice was clear and sure, and for a moment Xander hated her for her certainty. 'He's trying to blame you because they have no idea how to handle things.'

'How could you possibly know that?' Xander snapped at her, as he swung around angrily. It felt good to shout at someone. 'Maybe it *is* my fault, have you thought of that? Maybe they're completely right and I shouldn't be here. It's not exactly been a raging success so far, has it?'

Len's eyes narrowed, and she opened her mouth to respond, but Ollie got in first. 'Look, things have been a bit rough, but there *is* something behind all this and we're close to figuring it out. Think of everything that's happened so far – it has to mean something.'

'Come on, we're just kidding ourselves,' snarled Xander, and Ollie looked taken aback by his vehemence. 'We've been running around achieving – what exactly? Nothing! I don't belong here, and I should leave. I'm only causing problems.'

'Well, wallowing in your own private pity party will definitely improve matters,' retorted Len. 'You're not the only person in the world who has problems, so drop the 'poor me' act.'

'Len –' warned Ollie, but Len rushed on.

'No, he needs to hear it. He's been moping around for days now and it's enough.'

Xander glared at her, his anger like a physical thing inside him, clawing to get out. 'Well, you're right about one thing,' he said furiously. 'It is enough.'

He wanted more than anything to be away from everyone and a sudden, stray thought came to him, an idea of where to find some peace so he could think. Before he could lose his nerve, he lifted his wrist and his orb flared. He just had time to see the surprise on Ollie's and Len's faces as he vanished.

CHAPTER ELEVEN

Even before opening his eyes again, he felt the change; the sudden absence of distant voices and the scent of bonfire smoke. This had been his first jump without a guide, and he looked over the grass to the dilapidated frontage of Mistleberry Lodge with a small sigh of relief that he had made it there. Sunset light still lingered faintly in the little clearing, illuminating the great wooden door to the Lodge, and Xander remembered, with a lurch of bitterness, when Ari had first brought him here. He had been so naive and so ready to believe in the wonders of this world, but it had just let him down and rejected him.

With another small sniff, Xander walked over towards the Lodge, his feet scuffing the short turf. He would stay here a while and think, he decided. Lodges were supposed to be a place of refuge – *for Travellers*, came the unwelcome thought, *which he was not*. He shook his head. It didn't matter. It wasn't like he belonged anywhere in Haven, and nobody would miss him.

He put his hand on the cold metal latch of the door and pushed. It didn't move. He shoved angrily at it but it remained immobile, as if it had never been meant to be opened. After a moment's thought, Xander channeled his desire to open the door through his orb, which flickered fitfully and then went out. The door remained shut. Even the Lodge was rejecting him now, he thought miserably. There was a sense of deep emptiness about the place, and suddenly Xander remembered an overheard conversation about the Tavishes being withdrawn from Mistleberry because they wouldn't stop complaining – about strange and unnerving noises around the place. A cold chill ran down Xander's spine and he spun around, turning his back to the solid wooden door.

It was utterly silent as his gaze darted about the clearing, but it no longer felt peaceful. The sun had set and pale twilight blurred the edges of the trees into looming shapes, menacing in their stillness. Something was very wrong here, he thought, his palms pressing back against the wood and his heart thumping painfully. It took several panicked breaths before he realised that they were wisping out before him in the rapidly chilling air.

'This is not happening,' he groaned, but the faint sound of rising static, crackling across the clearing, was unmistakable.

Desperately he lifted his hand before him and his orb lit, but the glow was muted and kept flickering out. On the far side of the clearing, Xander could see the ominous sight of shades moving, flowing and merging all around the tree line, fully manifested and surrounding the Lodge so he could not get beyond the ward to jump away again.

He panicked, looking for a way out and some remembered words, scornfully thrown at him, came back and echoed in his head, '*Ward and run, you idiot.*' He attempted to throw up the kind of solid ward that Ari had showed to him, which he had achieved so easily when the threat of shades seemed far away. To his despair, all he could produce now was a faint, amorphous glow, which dissipated with each fearful breath.

The shades were in the open now, looming high and ringing him slowly and deliberately, as if they knew there was nothing he could do. The sudden thought of Alvin Tavish, scarred and broken, flashed across his mind and he gave a terrified moan. As he leaned on trembling legs against the door behind him, it felt like the museum all over again, except this time he knew, only too well, his fate if the shades overcame him. All that had happened since then had only bought him a few more weeks and some strange experiences, none of which would help him now. Knowing it was pointless, he slammed both fists backwards against the door.

'Help,' he shouted, his voice cracking and breaking. 'Please, someone, help.'

The sound of his fists was muffled and the door remained closed. No-one was coming. The shades were so close now that his face was numbing, and he had a strange fancy that there were almost intelligible sounds in the crackling hiss. He cringed, sliding down the door onto the ground and throwing his arms up over his face. This was it then. He closed his eyes and waited for the end.

Unexpectedly, there was a sudden lessening of the cold, and then a flare of blazing light shone through Xander's tightly closed eyelids, penetrating the shield of his arms. The hiss of the shades rose to a sudden shriek. Terrified, his breath coming fast and hardly daring to look, Xander squinted into the glare and his mouth dropped open. Surrounding him, with their hands raised defiantly to the looming shades, stood a circle of brownies, their little forms glowing with brilliant light. They did not waver as the shades swayed and hissed in displeasure, their expressions set with utter determination as they drove back the darkness.

One of the little figures turned and held out a shining hand to Xander.

'Will come?' he asked, his voice tiny but firm. It was Brolly.

Xander felt the words rush out before even having to think. 'Yes,' he gasped. 'Yes, please.'

The screech of the shades was pure rage as the small, strong fingers closed around Xander's hand and Mistleberry Lodge vanished in a blink.

The relief of finding himself far away from shades and imminent death hit Xander like a punch in the gut. He remained doubled-up in a crouch, his arms wrapped around himself and his face between his knees while he breathed in and out slowly, and tried not to burst into tears. After a moment, when he felt like he had recovered some control, he lifted his head. The little circle of brownies still surrounded him, no longer glowing but all of them regarding him solemnly. With a sudden recollection of Ollie's warnings, he averted his gaze.

'Thank you,' he told the stone floor, shakily. A little hand reached over and tapped him on the knee, and he looked up, startled.

Brolly was smiling, his black eyes twinkling.

'You very welcome, Xander King,' he said. 'You come now, meet our people.'

Xander clambered to his feet, looking around himself for the first time. He was standing in a little stone chamber, the roof curving above his head and lit with glowstones set into alcoves. Surrounding him on all sides were simple pictures painted directly onto the walls, like cave paintings, depicting humans, giants, hobs, brownies and many other strange creatures Xander had seen in Haven. They were done in bright, vivid colours which almost seemed to move in the glimmering light of the glowstones. Xander followed the little procession of brownies as they led him out of the room and through a short passage, grey and undecorated. Xander had to duck his head, his shoulders hunched, as the ceiling began to slope downwards and he wondered whether he would end up crawling, brownie-height, into wherever they were taking him. A moment later, they stepped out of the passage through an archway and Xander straightened up to look around.

A huge, wide space opened out before him, many times his height and rising to a vaulted ceiling in a soft, misty blue. The curving wall ahead of him was a tapestry of little wooden staircases as high as he could see, painted in many colours, with twisting banisters and balustrades, and punctuated everywhere with tiny doors, some of which were standing open giving a glimpse of the rooms beyond. To his left was a blank wall, partially shrouded by a long curtain made of some pale gauzy material, billowing gently. From behind the veil swelled a soft chorus, rising and fading and occasionally falling silent, only to begin again, with a faint but insistent pulse weaving through it as a constant undertone. The sound blended into the general bustle, as brownies moved about everywhere, climbing the staircases, darting in and out of doors and sitting in groups across the open space in the middle of the vast chamber, busying themselves with various occupations from carpentry to painting. A few of them glanced over at Xander with smiles, but did not react otherwise to his presence.

There was a sudden stir in the chamber as two elderly brownies appeared and steadily descended the many staircases, one with her hand resting on the arm of the other. Her hair was pure white and twisted up in an intricate knot on her head, she had a little snub nose and skin like old parchment, but her dark eyes were wide and clear. She wore the same dark leggings he had seen on every other brownie but her tunic was longer, belted with a silvery chain and covered with embroidery, the rich colours of flowers and vines swirling all over it. The silver haired brownie on whose arm she leant wore a shorter tunic in a glowing green which perfectly matched her vines, and his pale, pointed ears drooped slightly, giving him a quizzical look. With respectful nods, the other brownies stepped aside as the pair passed by until, finally, they stood together before Xander, gazing up at him with serene smiles. Xander felt a strange urge to bow but a sudden scurrying of brownies, all dropping small cushions on the floor to make a colourful heap, distracted him.

'Please, sit,' said the female, as she sank cross-legged onto the cushions with an ease belying her apparent age.

Gratefully, Xander sank down in front of her, his legs still rather wobbly. Another brownie appeared at his elbow, offering a small, handle-less cup of sweet-smelling tea. With a murmur of thanks, Xander cupped it in his shaking hands and then took a sip, feeling a burst of warmth running through him as he swallowed.

'I apologise for our lack of facilities for you,' continued the female, in her soft voice. There was only the hint of an accent to tell Xander that this was not her own language. 'You are the first human who has ever been in our home.'

Xander's eyes widened in surprise and he realised that what he had taken to be a cup without a handle was actually a brownie-sized cooking bowl.

'You are most welcome here, Xander,' said the male brownie. His voice was a little deeper than his companion but he had the same ageless eyes and parchment skin. He smiled and his little face lit up with warmth. 'We are the Tan and the Tani of our people – you would perhaps say, Speakers.'

'Thank you,' said Xander. His voice cracked a little and he cleared his throat, flushing. 'For rescuing me, I mean. You saved my life.'

The Tani smiled at him enigmatically.

'You asked for help,' she reminded him.

'But I thought that you – that brownies – didn't speak to humans,' blurted Xander. 'I was told that you weren't visible to us. Not that I'm not grateful that you did,' he added hurriedly, in case he sounded unappreciative.

To cover his awkwardness, he took another drink from his bowl and felt the warmth sooth him again, running right down into his fingers and toes. The soft sound from behind the veil rose in a wistful harmony and then dropped into a whisper, a constant backdrop to the general murmuring of voices in the chamber. As Xander glanced over, he saw a brownie appear from behind the shimmering drape and trot up some stairs, while another immediately rose from a group of weavers and ducked out of sight through the veil. He looked back to see the Tan watching him with a smile.

'That is not exactly the case, Xander,' he said, 'but it is not strange that you should have been told so.' He glanced over at the Tani who nodded, her wide eyes fixed on Xander's face, and then he continued quietly. 'What you refer to, we call the Penance and its history is what you hear being sung, from the first light of the sun in the east to the last glimmer on the western horizon. Upon adulthood, we take our place behind the veil in our turn, our voices never ceasing and the words engraved on our hearts from our earliest memory.'

He paused and the Tani took up the thread.

'We atone, Xander,' she said. 'Our terrible failure must never be forgotten, lest we repeat it. When our time of testing came it found us lacking, pride was our downfall and we nearly destroyed the world with it. We atone so we will never again risk such destruction with our arrogance and conceit.'

Xander frowned, trying to view the two tiny figures before him, and the other brownies trotting cheerfully up and down the many staircases, in the light of these ominous statements. He smothered a little smile. It was impossible, comical even, to believe that they could possibly have had the ability to do as much damage as they claimed.

The Tan rose to his feet and held out a hand to Xander.

'Come and see for yourself,' he said. 'It is the best way for you to understand us.'

Clambering to his feet again, Xander followed the brownies across the chamber towards the gently swaying curtain. The voices from behind it were a soft murmur now, like running water. The Tan held a corner of the veil for Xander, who ducked low and followed him through. He saw a large, dim cavern, with a ceiling shrouded in darkness. Rugs were layered on the floor in bright, jewel-like colours and sitting in groups on them were many brownies, all singing. An enormous bronze lamp hung suspended from a thick chain, the length of which disappeared up into the shadows above. It was covered with a slowly revolving casing, allowing a single shaft of light to spill out in a narrow, circulating beam. The room was warm and dusky, and incense drifted through the air.

At a signal from the Tani, Xander sank down to the floor next to the cross-legged Tan who had joined in with the singing, his eyes closed. He felt the Tani settle by his other side and lay a gentle hand on his arm.

'We sing in our ancient language,' she murmured. 'I will translate for you, if you wish.'

Xander nodded speechlessly. His eyes had been drawn to the wall, which was being illuminated by the shaft of light from the hanging lantern. Painted upon it were more of the vivid pictures and as the beam passed over they seemed to leap out of the darkness, glowing with life and movement, before fading back into the shadows as the light travelled onwards.

A brownie's face shone out, startlingly unfamiliar in its twisted scorn, lips curled back and expression full of pride and hatred; and then a snake, lurid in poison green, leaning into the brownie's ear, bright red tongue flickering, flickering in the shifting light. The next image showed darkness spreading across the land, the unmistakable shapes of shades looming up over the bright figures of humans, giants and hobgoblins, and Xander could barely repress a shiver. A boy on a flying horse, glimmering pale against the storm clouds and surrounded by huge birds with golden, glittering eyes, jumped out next and then a huge stone platform enclosed by pillars, with a mirrored wall reflecting the starry sky, lightning striking into its heart. Next came an image of towering waves, foam-tipped, devouring the shores and it seemed to Xander that faces appeared and disappeared amidst the foam and water. A night sky appeared again, riven with lightning, until the light moved to reveal the clenching fingers of an enormous hand reaching out to seize the land below.

As the images appeared and faded, Xander's stomach twisted with fear at what he was seeing without comprehending. The sense of terror and menace was overwhelming and he fought the sudden urge to huddle down, and close his eyes. The soft voices of the brownies, rising and falling in their endless song, with a pulse like a heartbeat underscoring it, seemed to hold him up but also pin him in place; he was helpless to do anything but watch and listen, as the Tani spoke quietly into his ear and the Tan sang on, his voice blending with the rest.

'We envied those created bigger and more powerful. We were so sure that they looked down on us, took advantage of us and did not honour us as they should. Bitterness grew like a worm in our hearts and we were ripe for the words of one who told us we deserved so much more than we had: that what was not freely given to us, both in words and deeds, should be taken with force.' The image of the serpent with its flickering tongue, hissing into the ear of the cold-faced brownie glowed out again from the wall and Xander realised that the song itself had become sibilant and menacing. 'We deceived those who trusted us; our tongues were twisted with lies.'

The Tani's hand clasped his arm and then she joined in the lament. Xander found he could understand, as she translated the words as she sang:

> *'Grasp for more than hands can hold,*
> *eyes devouring, hearts stone-cold.*
> *Itching ears for serpent's tongue,*
> *turned from truth; deceitful song*
> *of power and might, the ancient wrong.'*

The Tani took a quick breath, as more terrible images leapt out from the wall, and then continued on as the song changed, becoming faster, more anguished.

> *'Following, pride-blinded, a pretty path of lies,*
> *wide the way, swift our feet, departing from the wise.*
> *Good for evil, evil good, up rose the twisted cry;*
> *walk into the darkness, do not question why.*
> *Until, too late, the power unleashed and boiled into the sky.'*

The song ceased for a moment of terrible quiet, as the light fell on an image of a night sky rent open with livid, lurid shades of yellow and green. Xander's eyes were wide as he stared at trees, buildings and hillsides lit up by the arcing, sickly light and then vaporised, brownies struck down alongside all of the other races. The music began again, a hushed moan, and the Tani's voice continued in his ear, pouring out their sadness and their failure.

'Star-struck, star-stone, blazing through the land,
earth rocked, air roiled, sea driven out from sand.
Too late for sorrow, too late our grief,
stunned, destroyed, in disbelief.
And then, unlooked for, came relief.'

The song rose in a hopeful note at the end and Xander's gaze was drawn up, up to the top of the wall where a picture gleamed out of a group of figures, some clearly human, some giant and others small like hobs. They were racing forward, one of the smaller ones with a hand held high, blazing with a blue-white flame, towards a large platform on a rock surrounded with turbulent water. The Tani fell silent and nodded her head quietly, the song continuing on as she turned to Xander.

'We were rescued from the darkness of our own making by those whom we had betrayed. We could not control what we had helped to unleash, but others stood forward at that dark hour and drove it back, saved us all. And then we, who least deserved it, were given a place in our world, and safety, by those we would have destroyed. We knew then that we must make amends, must repay the kindness and the courage. Most importantly, we knew that we must never allow this to happen again.'

The Tani bowed her head and Xander just sat, rooted to the spot, as the notes of the un-ending song flowed on and the strange, vivid images swam in and out of the moving light. It felt unreal; the terror at Mistleberry followed by this hypnotic moment in the dim light, with the sharp, strange smell of incense in his nose.

A small hand touching his shoulder brought him back to himself and he turned to see that the Tan and Tani had risen, and were waiting patiently behind him. He scrambled to his feet and followed them out, ducking beneath the veil with a final, dazed look back into the chamber.

The Tani led him back to the pile of cushions and drew him down to sit beside her. As if by an invisible signal, a group of brownies hurried over with trays of tiny cakes and little sweet-smelling pastries, and another richly scented bowlful of drink was pressed into his hand.

'Eat, before we talk further,' urged the Tan, as other brownies settled down around him on the cushions, eating and chatting together in soft voices.

Xander had not realised how hungry he was until the first pastries melted in his mouth, tasting of cheese and the tang of strange herbs, or how tense he had been until he met the gentle smiles of the little figures which gathered around him, and felt the peace of this place melt into his bones and muscles.

When Xander was sipping at his third bowl of tea, the Tan finally spoke again.

'Now that you understand our past, we can speak to you of our present. After we were saved, we knew that we must seek a different path. We were humbled by the gift we had received without merit.'

The Tani smiled and took up the story.

'From the depths of darkness we were called to freedom and our people knew that we must not take this gift to fulfil our own desires but first, through love, to serve others. In humility, we would count others more significant than ourselves, as a shield against the wickedness that had overcome us. So, we re-ordered our own society and in this spirit we reached out to humbly serve those who had shown us such grace.'

'However,' said the Tan with a wry look, 'it is never so simple in practice, is it? We went out to serve freely, and people tried to repay us in money, or goods or words of gratitude enough to turn our heads. We, who did not deserve these – no, not one – what could we do? Then, into our urgent counsels spoke the voice of a little one.' He turned to a tiny brownie who was sitting next to her parents, her huge eyes fastened on Xander with open curiosity. 'What did the child say?' he asked her gently.

The little brownie sat up, beaming at the Speakers.

'We could bless best if no-one saw,' she said in a small silvery voice.

'That's right,' said the Tani. 'And so it began. At first, we went to help others in the dark of night or when they were not there to see us, but as the centuries passed, the stories told in the world about our service shifted and transformed, until they bequeathed us invisibility itself. In this, we find freedom and the fulfilment of our ancient pledge.' She leant forward and placed a hand, soft as cobwebs, on Xander's arm as a smile lit up her gentle face. 'But we also found something unexpected, our great gift and joy. We learned that as we served in darkness, our own lives became illuminated.'

Xander blinked, trying to turn this over in his head and feeling rather overwhelmed, but the Speakers had not yet finished. The Tan rose to his feet. 'Now you understand all of what we are,' he said, 'but we have one more thing to show you.'

He beckoned to Xander to follow him and Xander got up,

towering once more over the brownies around him. He followed the erect little figure across the open space, to a wooden door so old and grey it blended into the stone wall. It was large by brownie standards, more than double the Tan's height, but Xander had to crouch down to go through it. As he straightened up he realised that he was standing on shale and rock, perched on a ledge jutting out of a great stony cliff which was lit by moonlight, gleaming out fitfully from behind skeins of cloud. Before him was a heavy, grey sea and down below long rolling waves crashed ceaselessly onto a shingle beach, sucking the stones backwards into the surf in a rhythm that Xander suddenly recognised; this was the continual pulse behind the music of the brownies' lament.

As he breathed in the cool, salty air, Xander realised that the Tan had not waited for him and was already a considerable way down the steep path that led to the beach below. He hurried after him, stepping carefully in the dusky light. When Xander reached the shingle beach, he glanced back up at the way he had come. The little door was almost invisible, but a stray gleam of moonlight reflected off tiny windows in the rock face and Xander realised that the whole of the brownies' home was actually built inside the cliff itself.

Still moving swiftly, the Tan led Xander along the beach, their feet crunching on the shingle mixed with fine sand and then paused, pointing upwards. 'This is our way now,' he said, and Xander could just make out another ledge, with the faint, dark gash of a cave or crevice in the rock face. 'Can you manage the climb?'

As Xander eyed the steep gradient, privately he considered that the old brownie should be more concerned about doing the climb himself; it looked well beyond the reach of the little figure. A few minutes later, Xander was ruefully re-thinking this estimation as he heaved himself up the cold, rough rock, while the brownie seemed to flit effortlessly before him. Finally, Xander dragged himself onto his stomach on the ledge and twisted around, the salt air burning in his throat. The Tan waited with patient composure while Xander caught his breath and then gestured to the cleft in the rock.

'In here,' he said, before vanishing into the dark space.

Xander heaved a sigh and then struggled to his feet. The cleft was not wide and the sharp rocks tugged at Xander's clothes and jabbed at his ribs as he squeezed through. The moonlight was barely sufficient for him to make out the brownie standing just in front of him with an expectant expression on his face, and Xander blinked as he peered around. Initially he saw nothing but a pile of jumbled stones to his left, but then he stiffened. Faint threads of light were flickering across one of the stones, roughly tablet-shaped and half buried beneath the other rocks, illuminating the worn symbols carved into its face. Xander gasped and dropped to his knees to look more closely at it.

'As I thought,' said the old brownie gently. 'It responds to your call.'

'It's a Traveller's Stone,' said Xander, his voice shocked. 'And it's still working! But – how is this possible?'

'That, I am afraid, I cannot tell you,' replied the Tan. 'We are not to be trusted with such knowledge, and so we buried our memories so deep that only the stars can remember. Our song speaks of this.'

'Only the stars can remember,' repeated Xander. 'That doesn't really help me because apparently they aren't talking.' He shook his head in frustration, as the fine filaments of light continued to shiver in the faint grooves on the stone.

The Tan moved to stand beside Xander. 'I did not bring

you here to give you yet more unanswered questions, but to give you the gift of choice.'

'What does that mean?' asked Xander, although he had an inkling of what was coming.

'There is a symbol upon this Stone which will take you home again, right back to where you began this journey, if you so choose,' the brownie said, his ageless eyes resting gently on Xander, before he turned to point out a glimmering mark on the second row. 'You could take your orb and your new found knowledge, and return. You have the ability to keep yourself and your home, your kin, safe now.'

'I didn't do too well at Mistleberry just now,' muttered Xander, feeling his ears burn. 'I wouldn't have made it at all if you hadn't rescued me.'

'You did not fail, Xander,' replied the Tan. 'You chose to give in to your fear and your doubt, and you chose to hide. When you have faith, and stand strong without wavering, you will overcome the darkness.'

'Maybe,' allowed Xander, rather doubtfully. Without thinking, his fingers stroked his orb and it blossomed into gentle light under his touch. In response, the Traveller's Stone blazed into brighter illumination, the symbols now clear and crisp on the stone. Xander stared at it and then back at the Tan, who was watching him with quiet sympathy.

'What do you think I should do?' asked Xander, suddenly desperate for some guidance. He felt like he had been stumbling through his time in Haven, unable to see or understand what was expected of him. 'Do you think I should leave? Is that why you brought me here?'

The old brownie smiled at him, his silvery hair gleaming in the dim cave and his eyes crinkling with affection, and shook his head.

'Oh no, Xander King,' he replied, his voice soft but firm. 'My people have learned our lesson; never again will we partake in the folly and evil of forcing actions on others, nor will we manipulate. The greatest and most important freedom we are given is that of making our own choices. This decision is for you to make, no other.'

'Yes, well, my choices haven't really been very good, so far,' muttered Xander, petulantly.

'Maybe, maybe not, but they have brought you here, to this place,' said the Tan. 'I will make you another gift, Xander; the gift of time. I will return to our home and the door will be left open for you. If you do not come back to us then we will know that you have chosen to go home and I will wish you well in your journey there. If you choose to stay, we will return you to your friends' home and you can follow your path here. The decision rests with you.'

With a little pat on Xander's hand, the brownie turned and slipped through the cleft in the rock out onto the ledge. Xander hesitated a moment, staring at the Stone and then jumped to his feet and squeezed his way through the gap. The ledge was empty and as he peered down there was no sign of the Tan, either on the rocks or the beach below.

'How fast can he move?' wondered Xander out loud, shaking his head in disbelief. He slumped down on the rocky shelf and dangled his legs over the edge. 'Well, this is just great, isn't it?' he growled. 'Make your decision, Xander. Catastrophe or disaster, the choice is yours.'

He glared out over the restless waves, grey and forbidding under the dark sky. He could just choose to go home, he thought. He didn't belong here anyway, and everyone would probably be glad that he was gone. With a sudden pang, the thought of Mrs Stanton's face popped into his mind – her warmth and the way she had welcomed him into her family. Wouldn't she worry if he just didn't come back? And Ollie and Len might blame themselves if he disappeared after that horrible fight with them. Were they still waiting for him and panicking that he hadn't come back? Maybe they had told Flint and Ari by now and everyone was looking for him. He shook his head.

'Well, they certainly won't find me here,' he said. He kicked his feet into the rock wall below and several pieces broke off and tumbled down to the beach below. As he looked out over the sea, it felt rather as though he was sitting on the edge of the world. The lines of white foam on the waves moved and ran into each other ceaselessly and, as his eyes followed them, he thought of the vivid image in the brownie's lament, the lines on the water shifting into the faces and bodies of mysterious creatures. He shivered, feeling the hypnotic strangeness of those pictures again, so vivid and unforgettable, particularly the pale, pillared platform with the mirror wall reflecting the night sky, while lightning arced and struck at it.

'Only the stars remember now,' muttered Xander, with an irritated snort. 'Why can't people just talk plainly here? *Only the stars remember* – so not helpful.'

His voice trailed away as his mind wandered down that train of thought and focussed on the vivid image of stars reflected in a mirrored wall. This blurred into another of the pictures he had seen, of a small group hurrying towards a stone platform on a rocky promontory surrounded by turbulent water. Many of the pillars had fallen and it was in ruins, but it was still unmistakable. It was the same place, Xander realised and then he stiffened, suddenly rigid as comprehension dawned.

'*Rock upon the water,*' he whispered. '*Stars will lead the way.*'

It had certainly changed, extra walls and levels had been added to it, but he could recollect clearly the beautiful shining structure and see the original shape within it, the ancient bones of a pillared platform with a wall of stars.

'It's the Pavilions,' he breathed. That was the place the people had been running so desperately to reach, to avert the great calamity that the brownies were still atoning for, and that was the place the mysterious messages were trying to direct him towards now. It hadn't been the hobs' Core at all that he was meant to restore, just as Len had said.

Xander scrambled to his feet, and then caught a sudden glimpse of glimmering light from inside the cleft, where the Traveller's Stone stood waiting for him. He hesitated a moment, realising that this was his real choice. He could stay in this place, with all of its dangers and uncertainties and fight on, or else he could go home and step back into his old life. In the end, his hesitation did not last long.

'This may be the stupidest thing I've ever done,' Xander said to the Traveller's Stone, just out of sight. 'But I'm staying.'

Without a second glance, he lowered himself over the edge of the little ledge and began to climb down, his feet scrabbling in the darkness for the notches and hollows he had used to get up there. He slid down the last few feet and stood on the beach again, only slightly out of breath. The cleft and its faint light were invisible now, blending into the rough cliff face. Hurriedly, Xander retraced his earlier route along the base of the cliff and then clambered up the steep path to the old grey door, waiting ajar for him. He bent over to get through it and almost bumped into the Tan, who was standing before him with a warm and approving smile on his parchment face.

'You knew what I would choose,' Xander said. It wasn't a question.

'We have watched you and seen who you are,' replied the old brownie. 'The only one who doubted your choice was you.'

The Tani appeared by his side and then reached up to grasp Xander's hand.

'You have found your path and we wish you well, Xander King. Remember that you are not alone on your journey, and step out in faith.'

Her words were oddly formal and both she and the Tan raised their right hands in the same gesture of farewell. Xander was struck again by the sudden urge to bow but just waved his hand back rather awkwardly. A moment later, hand still half-raised, he found himself standing in the lane outside the gate to Woodside with the small figures of Brolly and Spike beside him, barely visible in the dusk.

'Home again,' said Brolly, his cheerful grin so wide it looked like his cheeks might split. Spike's head bobbed up and down in animated agreement.

Xander smiled back at them both. 'Thank you,' he began, but Spike immediately put his finger to his lips and shook his head.

'All gone now,' he whispered.

Both brownies put their hands over their eyes and tiptoed to the hedge with exaggerated stealth, bumping into one another and crashing into several branches, before disappearing through into the garden beyond. Xander stared after them blankly, before realising that this was the brownies' way of wordlessly restoring the status quo. They were invisible again. He lifted one hand in a silent salute to them both, before opening the gate and hurrying down the path towards the lights of Woodside.

CHAPTER TWELVE

Xander slipped through the front door into the dimly lit hallway. There was a sliver of light shining out from under the kitchen door at the end of the hall and the rumbling sound of many voices. He hesitated a moment and then hurried up the stairs, two at a time. If he was missed and people had been worried then it was probably best to find out first from Ollie and Len. As he walked along the upstairs corridor, he could hear their voices coming from the bedroom.

'We can't just sit here forever, Ollie,' came Len's sharp voice. 'This could be serious.'

'And do what?' demanded Ollie.

Xander pushed the bedroom door open, feeling guilt sweep over him as he saw the two figures huddled on Ollie's bed, Len looking pale-faced and worried. They both glanced up as he entered the room, smiling sheepishly at them.

'Hi,' he got out before Len almost throttled him with the strength of her hug. She pulled away as quickly as she had launched herself at him and hit him on the arm. 'Don't ever just disappear like that again,' she said, her voice oddly choked. As she saw Xander looking guiltily at her red-rimmed eyes, she cleared her throat and glared at him. 'Ollie's been freaking out,' she snapped.

Xander looked over at Ollie, whose eyebrows had risen nearly into his hair.

'Um – no! I told Len she was over-reacting and that you'd

be fine. It's not like you've been gone that long,' he said.

Xander stared at him in surprise. With everything that had happened at Mistleberry and then his extraordinary experience at the brownies' home, it felt to him as if a lifetime had passed since their argument.

'So, where've you been, if you don't mind our asking?' asked Ollie, a little awkwardly and Xander realised that their fight, which seemed so long ago to him, was still at the forefront of Ollie's mind. He decided that the quickest thing to do was just to tell everything and try to straighten things out with the two of them.

'Well, you were both completely right,' he began.

Len walked back over to Ollie's bed and sat down, waving her hand imperiously for him to continue.

'We're listening,' she said primly. Ollie rolled his eyes and elbowed her in the ribs, whereupon Len's face creased into a grin and she dropped the pompous attitude. Xander felt the tension break, and he laughed, collapsing onto his own bed.

'When I left you I went to Mistleberry,' he said. He saw Len lean forward, ready to launch into some kind of speech, and he lifted his hand quickly. 'Just let me tell the whole thing and then you can say "I told you so" as much as you want. It's fair enough, as you did, and you were right.'

He recounted what he had found at Mistleberry, the attack of the shades and how he had been unable to stop them at all.

'What happened then?' demanded Ollie. 'Clearly you got out of it somehow.'

Xander hesitated. The brownies' secret was not his to tell. They had not said anything to forbid him but they had made clear they were reverting to their previous relationship with him, invisible again. He looked at the two people he trusted most, who had stood by him unflinchingly, and made a quick decision.

'I'll tell you what happened but you have to promise, to swear, that you won't tell anyone or act any different.' He stared at both of them, his face serious and they both nodded, equally solemn. Xander took a deep breath and plunged on. 'I didn't get out of it at all. The brownies rescued me. They held off all the shades and asked if I would accept their help, and then they got me out of there and took me to their home.'

'Huh?' said Ollie, his jaw slack with surprise.

'Asked you?' said Len. 'Brownies don't talk to people. They just don't. They think they're invisible and they don't speak. And how could *brownies* have stopped shades?'

'Yeah, about that – I can explain, but this is what you can't ever tell anyone.'

Xander recounted everything he could remember about the Penance, the brownies' home and what he had experienced and seen there. While Ollie and Len stared at him, for once entirely speechless, he told them about the cliff, the Stone and the choice he had been given. After he had finished, they both sat staring at him wide-eyed. The silence was just growing uncomfortable when Ollie finally spoke.

'Well, no one can say you don't know how to spend an evening, can they?'

There was a pause, and then Len spluttered. Suddenly all three of them were laughing so hard that Xander had to lay back across his bed, his stomach hurting and tears running down his face. Eventually they all fell quiet, with just the occasional hiccup from Len, and Xander rolled over, pushing his hair back off his face.

'So, what do you think?' he asked.

'Well, obviously we haven't seen those pictures that you did,' said Len thoughtfully, pulling her legs up and wrapping her arms around them. She rested her chin on her knees. 'But it

317

sounds right. The Pavilions can somehow stop the shades destroying everything, and the key is that star wall. If Xander is the seed of the ancient blood –'

'Whatever that means,' interjected Xander, but Len waved that away.

'– which the hobs seem to believe, then we still need to figure out how to get in there, unless Xander can just waggle his fingers at it or put his blood on it, or something.'

Xander screwed up his face in distaste at the thought of blood, but it was Ollie who spoke up.

'Well, before Xander starts randomly smearing walls with gore, how about we look at other options? I don't think it can mean literal blood, anyway. We never did figure out what that last bit means; the stuff about the 'marks of the kin'. That has to be relevant.'

'What exactly did it say?' asked Xander, frowning. Ollie fished under his bed for a moment and then produced a crumpled piece of paper, which he tried to smooth out before giving up and handing it over to Xander.

'The marks of the kin stand guard eternal,' Xander read out and then pulled a face. 'Well, we know what they are guarding now but what on earth are the marks of the kin?' He stared at the paper as if the words would re-arrange themselves into something that made sense by sheer willpower alone, then shoved it away with a disappointed sigh. 'I just don't get it.'

'What do we do now, then?' asked Ollie, leaning back on his bed.

'Well, while you think about it, you two could always spend a bit of time tidying up this dump,' remarked Len. 'Honestly, it's a complete tip. Don't you put anything away?'

Ollie just shrugged. 'It's easier to find stuff this way.'

'Yeah, right,' said Len. 'I'm sure that will convince Gran.

You're sitting on all that formal wear. It's totally messed up.'

'Since when do you care?' asked Ollie.

'Oh, I don't.'

Xander had tuned out the usual sound of Ollie and Len bickering as he stared in frustration into space, but something Len had said triggered a vagrant thought in his subconscious. He turned to look at Ollie who, as Len had correctly pointed out, was sitting on a pile of their formal wear, his sash dangling down with the Peverell family sigil half-obscured. He stared at it, his mind groping for something, running the words through his head: the symbol of the family, the *mark* of the family. The mark of the –

Xander lurched forward and grabbed at the sash, nearly dragging Ollie off the bed.

'Oi! You almost had me on the floor then,' spluttered Ollie. 'Don't let Len's sudden fetish for tidiness set you off.'

Xander ignored him, brandishing the sash in the air.

'This is it!' he burst out. 'Can't you see it? Your family *is* your kin. This is your kin mark, right here. Look!'

They both leant forward obediently, gazing at the sash.

'Could the Families really go back as far as that?' asked Ollie, chewing on his lip as he eyed the mark thoughtfully. 'The hobs were talking about something really ancient, weren't they? And it says the marks stand guard *eternally*.'

Len grinned. 'Gran would tell you that there *is* nothing older than the Families. Right back at the dawn of time they were there, informing the other cave people of the only socially acceptable way to carry a club.'

'So that must be it,' said Ollie, slowly. 'The marks of the kin are the Twelve Families' sigils.'

'Maybe we're supposed to look for them carved somewhere on the Pavilions, guarding something?' asked Xander.

Len had been eying the sash, deep in thought, but at this she looked up.

'They can't be there in plain sight,' she said with certainty. 'Don't you think that if they were, then the Families would have known about it after all these centuries? They would definitely make a big deal about it during the Solstice if their sigils were carved into the Pavilions themselves. Talk about feeding their self-importance. The marks *must* be disguised.'

'So, now we have the star wall leading the way, while the family sigils guard it,' said Ollie. 'Except we don't know what that actually means. It's like going two steps forward and one step back.' He rolled his eyes and then lay back on his bed, staring at the ceiling as if he might find inspiration there.

Xander stared down at the sash on his lap, biting his lip. They were so close, he could feel it. It was almost within his grasp and he screwed his eyes shut, wrestling with an idea which was dancing just out of reach. The Peverell family sigil floated before his mind's eye as he groped desperately, trying to visualise the glowing wall at the Pavilions with its scattering of stars. Stars grouped together in their familiar constellations, forming shapes on the wall. His eyes sprang open, and he stared down at the sigil again, his hands shaking in his excitement.

'It's Orion,' he exclaimed, wildly. 'You're Orion and the other Families must have matches too.'

Len leapt up without a word and dashed out of the door, while Ollie sat up and stared at Xander, comprehension dawning as he reached over to grab his sash. He smoothed it out to examine the sigil.

'You're right,' he said in an awed voice. 'I never thought about it before, but this does look a bit like Orion, with his belt in the middle and that slash through it as his sword.'

Len burst back into the room, waving a magazine at them both. Ollie's eyebrows shot up as he glimpsed the cover.

'Is this really the time to get caught up with your trashy reading?' he enquired.

'Idiot,' said Len breathlessly. 'Gran never buys this stuff normally, but she got this one because it has an article on the Solstice.'

She flipped through the pages until she found the headline, *'Solstice Ball kicks off the summer season'*. Several pages followed, filled with glossy pictures of the party, and Xander recognised many of the faces he had seen that night, of prominent Family members.

Ollie leant over her shoulder. 'You didn't make it, Len, I'm afraid,' he said, with mock sympathy.

'Haha,' said Len, sardonically. 'Look, you twit! All the Families are represented here, which means all of their sashes and sigils. Honestly, sometimes I struggle to believe we're actually related.'

Ollie elbowed her half-heartedly as he stared down at the pictures, then he made a long arm to grab a notebook and pencil from under the pile of shirts on his bedside table. After tearing out a couple of pages, he leant over Len to lay one over the first picture he could see where the sigil was clear and carefully traced it out, then wrote the Family name next to it in neat letters. For several minutes, they were all busy flipping through the magazine to find the best representations of each sigil and then tracing it out. In the end, they had six pages of the notebook, each with two sigils on it, and Len shoved the magazine to one side.

Ollie produced an atlas from his bookshelf and turned to the end where there were several pages representing the night skies. With one accord, they all dropped to the floor, putting the open atlas in the centre and spreading the pages of sigils out around it. They looked back and forth between the book and the pages, and for a few moments silence reigned in the bedroom. Then the arguing began. Most of the sigils were fairly obvious and easily matched to their corresponding constellations, but for two or three of them their stylised representations were not so straightforward to match, until Len flipped forward in the atlas and found that the southern hemisphere was represented separately. For once, she managed to restrain any sarcastic comments, and they found the final sigils.

'This has to be it,' said Len, speaking faster than usual in her excitement, as they all sat and regarded the fruits of their labour. 'We go to the star wall at the Pavilion, we find those constellations, Xander works his mojo and then we get in there and fix it.'

'Fix it how?' demanded Xander. 'The last time I tried to tinker with something that powerful it didn't go too well, remember.'

There was a small silence, and then Ollie just shrugged.

'Len was right then; it wasn't the proper place. This is different. I do think we need some help though. Mistleberry shows that the borders are weakening everywhere and who knows whether even the Pavilion is still safe. We should take some Travellers with us – we can't depend on the brownies to come fish Xander out twice in one day.'

'I doubt they impose a quota,' said Len. 'But I think Ollie's right. Also, I think we should ask Callan Reeve to come. There's no-one who understands more about the power in Haven than him, except for the hobs and they aren't talking to humans anymore.'

Xander turned all this over in his head but it was obvious

that Len and Ollie were right. There was only one issue.

'How are we going to persuade them to come with us, without confessing to breaking into government buildings by night and telling the brownies' secrets?' he asked.

Len rolled her eyes.

'Tactical truthfulness, of course,' she said. 'Suitable vagueness where necessary, innocent evasion and careful control of the narrative. Honestly, it's like you've never spoken with an adult.'

Ollie laughed. 'Yeah, right,' he sniggered. 'And the number of times that has actually worked on Gran is, oh, precisely zero.'

'We're telling the truth,' said Xander firmly. 'About our stuff, anyway. How can we expect anyone to believe us if we start out by lying to them?'

'And the brownies?' asked Ollie.

'I can't tell about them,' replied Xander. 'I'll just explain that I can't say.'

'Yeah, that'll go well,' muttered Len.

'What's all that noise?' asked Ollie suddenly, going to the bedroom door to listen. The volume of voices downstairs had been growing throughout their discussion and, as they stood listening, the front door banged again. 'What's going on?'

All three hurried for the stairs, following the sounds of many voices all talking at the same time. They paused just inside the kitchen door. The whole room was packed with people and Xander noticed many of the Travellers he had seen at the Gathering, standing in groups and deep in conversation. Through the open door of Mrs Stanton's dispensary, he could see her treating someone while James was busy seating several other casualties; with a shock, Xander recognised the pale burns of shade-strike.

At the other end of the room, near the hearth, stood Flint with Ari's bright hair visible beside him. With them were Jasper, and several of the Wardens, including Alwyn Atherton, Edric Wooten and Jory Bardolph, the latter's florid face drooping like a concerned bulldog. Atherton was alternately rubbing his tired face and then interjecting with decisive hand gestures. The back door into the dusky, warm garden stood open, and Xander felt Len's elbow in his side as she leant forward to whisper.

'There are giants in the garden. What in Haven's name is going on tonight?'

As if in answer to her question, Ari glanced over and spotted them standing hesitantly at the door. She slid around behind the arguing group and came over to join them. Her face was serious, the amused sparkle that generally danced in her clear eyes missing this evening. Before she could say anything, Ollie jumped in.

'What's going on, Ari? Why's everyone here and what happened to those people?' He jerked his head towards to the injured awaiting Mrs Stanton's care.

Ari frowned, fiddling absently with her orb.

'It's not very healthy out there tonight,' she said, her voice low. 'We're losing control and even the Wardens are beginning to realise it.' She glanced back over at the group around Flint where Atherton was now speaking, his face looking lined and old. Flint stood with his arms folded, frustration evident in the tension in his body and his heavy scowl. 'Of course, that doesn't mean they plan to listen,' she added wryly.

'We need to speak to Flint,' blurted Xander. 'We've figured out how to fix this.'

Ari shook her head. 'I don't think this is the time, Xander,' she said in a gentle voice, but her expression was firm. 'Flint will get it sorted, guys. Don't worry.'

Len opened her mouth to argue but as she did so, a sharp whistle cut through all the noise. Everyone turned to look as Flint walked into the centre of the room, Bardolph and Atherton behind him looking anxious and unsettled.

'Thank you all for coming,' said Flint, his voice loud enough to reach the giants leaning in at the door. 'You know the current situation. After much discussion and consideration, we believe that the best option open to us right now is to guard and aggressively ward all the known vulnerabilities on the border. We'll be mounting twenty-four hour warding schedules while we work out how to address the underlying weakness.'

Flint's eyes flicked towards the table and Xander recognised Callan Reeve sitting amidst a pile of papers and notebooks. He looked exhausted and did not look up from the diagrams of schematics and scrawled equations.

'We here who are uninjured will cover the first shifts,' continued Flint, 'while the Wardens will convene a Meet to draw up ongoing rotas for all Travellers trained and able to ward.'

At this point Wooten stepped forward, clearing his throat importantly.

'Everyone,' he said in a voice which wavered slightly. 'Please be assured that we will have everything under control very shortly and there is no reason to be alarmed. We are dealing with a slight aberration in Haven's defences –' he paused, and Xander saw Wooten's watery blue eyes rest momentarily on him, '– but you can trust your Wardens to bring it under control again, as we have done before in our long history. Please come and get your assignments, and we appreciate your assistance.'

The crowd around Flint began to thin, as people moved

over to the Wardens to get their duty assignments. Xander saw his opportunity and hurried over, dodging Ari's attempt to grab at his arm.

'Excuse me,' he said when he reached Flint, who was talking quietly to Rafe.

Flint turned and made an impatient noise when he saw Xander.

'What now?'

Xander knew that he had a very short time to get his point across.

'I know why the borders are failing,' he blurted, trying to get the words out before he was cut off. 'And I know how to fix it. I just need some help from you or a couple of Travellers in case we get more shades there.'

'I heard about your earlier attempts to 'fix things' at the hobs' Core,' said Flint. 'It wasn't too successful I hear, not to mention that we don't have anyone to spare on your antics tonight – you heard what we're dealing with here.' He shook his head in exasperation and began to turn away. Xander grabbed his arm desperately.

'Please, you have to listen. I got the wrong place before, but this time we're sure. It matches all the clues.'

'Clues?' Flint asked, his eyebrows rising.

Ollie stepped in. 'Clues from the ancient terminal in the Halls of Records,' he said. 'It lit up again and gave us the information we need.'

Callan Reeve had looked like he was miles away in thought, but at this he lifted his head abruptly, frowning.

'That's not possible, Ollie,' he said. 'Those terminals are dead and crumbling, they've been inert for literally a thousand years. They're not even attached to any power grid anymore. They're just historical artefacts.'

'But it did,' Ollie said stubbornly, and rather incoherently. 'It responded to Xander because he's an ancient seed, the hobs said so.'

Flint and Reeve exchanged looks.

'An ancient seed?' Flint repeated, his voice now thoroughly irritated. 'Look, kids, we just don't have time for this right now. If you haven't noticed, we're in the middle of a serious situation here and we don't need juvenile fantasies.'

Xander almost gave up but then he felt a warm pressure against his leg. Suze, Rafe's dog, had moved to stand by him and her silent support gave him the courage to press on.

'Flint,' he said again, loudly enough to make him turn back. 'It's the Pavilions. That's the whole key to this. It's 'the rock upon the water where the power lies' and 'only the stars remember'. The star wall will lead the way, but we have to go *now.*'

Flint heaved a sigh, clearly warring with his impatience and a careful effort not to explode.

'Compelling as that gibberish clearly is,' he said, sarcasm lacing his tone, 'maybe no-one has told you that the gate to the Pavilions will only open on the Solstice and it's impossible to jump there. I tell you what, you run along now, and I promise that I'll come with you next year when it opens again – if you still feel like an ancient seed then, that is.'

Xander glared at him, but Flint just turned away, shaking his head.

'Ari,' he said sharply over his shoulder. 'We're at Mistleberry.'

Ari looked at Xander, her expression worried. 'Sorry, Xander,' she said gently, but her eyes were already following Flint and she turned away to go.

'Wait,' said Xander. 'I was just at Mistleberry earlier. It was crawling with shades – they nearly got me.'

Ari swung back, her face shocked but Flint was already at the door.

'Come on, Ari,' he called impatiently.

Ari gave Xander's arm a swift squeeze as she turned to leave. 'We'll talk about this later. Don't worry, I'll warn Flint.' With that, she hurried off, calling to several other Travellers as she left.

Xander stood staring at the floor as the room emptied, blinking rapidly as frustration and panic swelled up inside. He had failed and he couldn't think how they would manage alone, with no adult help. Worn out and worried, he rubbed his face and finally looked up. Callan Reeve was standing in front of him, while Rafe had perched on the table behind, arms crossed and face expressionless but still there, waiting.

Reeve broke the silence.

'I tell you what,' he said. 'Since I seem to be at an impasse with the Core and I'm of no use to the Travellers, why don't you tell me about what has been going on with you three? What do the Pavilions have to do with anything, and what in the name of Haven is an 'ancient seed'?'

Xander heard Len's deep breath of relief before she and Ollie fell over themselves to fill in all the details of the events of the previous few weeks, occasionally talking over each other in their enthusiasm. Reeve's face grew more and more surprised as the tale unfolded, and he exchanged glances with Rafe a few times. When they had reached the events at Mistleberry in their re-telling, they both paused and looked over at Xander. To this point he had stood silent, letting the words flow over him as if they were referring to someone else.

'The shades were all around him and he thought he was a goner,' Len finished breathlessly.

All eyes turned to Xander. 'So, what happened then?' demanded Reeve. 'Obviously you did get away.'

Xander swallowed, the memory of terror still thick in his throat.

'I didn't,' he said slowly. 'I would have died if I hadn't been rescued.'

'By whom?' asked Rafe, leaning forward and speaking for the first time.

Xander stared straight back at him. 'I can't tell you.'

Rafe frowned and Xander spread his arms wide, appealing to him. 'I'm sorry, I would tell you if I could but it's not my secret. I'll say as much as I can but I can't betray them. They saved my life.'

There was a long pause.

'Fine,' said Rafe finally. 'We'll come back to that. Just tell us why you think the Pavilion is the key.'

Relieved by the respite, Xander described the images he had seen and how they illustrated a great and dreadful battle linked to Haven's past. He left out all mention of the brownies, but told about the Shades rearing up to devour the world, the terrible power in the sky and the vivid images of the pillared platform on a rock in the midst of water. The two men listened in silence as the story poured out and it was only when Xander reached the end of his tale that Rafe finally looked up, with an unreadable expression.

'You're expecting us to take an awful lot on trust here, Xander,' he said quietly. 'Tell you what – if you want our help, tell us who showed you these things.'

Xander clenched his fists, his nails biting into the palms of his hands in his frustration at failing again, but he knew that his path was clear. Always choices, as the Tan had told him.

'Then I'll have to manage without your help,' he said, with

a painful gulp. 'It's not my secret to tell.'

Xander was shocked to see a rare smile light up Rafe's face. He was even more surprised when Rafe stood up decisively.

'We had better get prepared,' Rafe said. 'Have you got what you need, Cal?'

Xander's jaw dropped in surprise.

'Huh?' he said stupidly. 'But, I thought you said –'

'I *said* that you were asking us to take a lot on trust,' interjected Rafe. 'I just needed to make sure you were trust-worthy.'

Xander grinned in pure relief, and then he caught sight of a flicker of motion. Ducking down behind one of Jenna's plant pots on the floor was a small, curly head, which lifted momentarily to show a pair of sparkling black eyes, one of which dropped in a quick but unmistakable wink, before whisking away. Xander looked down at his feet, smiling quietly.

A thump on his arm brought his attention back up to a beaming Ollie. 'Are you planning to stand grinning mysteriously at the floor all night, or are you coming?' he demanded.

'I suppose there's no chance of the hobs helping us?' Rafe asked.

Reeve shook his head, his expression sombre.

'They've all disappeared. I wouldn't even know how to get a message to them,' he said, regret shadowing his face. 'I know that they've always been secretive and untrusting of humans but I thought they knew that some of us at least have good intentions.' His voice trailed off and Xander could see his genuine sadness at the breach of their relationship.

'I'm really sorry,' he blurted out.

Reeve put a hand on his arm, shaking it to make Xander look up and meet his eyes.

'Not your fault,' he stated. 'The mistrust has run deep for a long time – evidently deeper than we knew. You did nothing wrong. You didn't poison their Core, and you certainly didn't cause the breakdown, okay?'

Xander nodded, still not entirely convinced but feeling better that Reeve at least did not blame him. A loud grinding noise from the back door made both of them turn around. A giant, bending over so he could poke his head through the door, smiled apologetically and cleared his throat again. All at once, Xander remembered him as one of the giants he had met at the Solstice Ball; he had been the one who had offered Primilla Pennicott's macabre bowl of eyeballs back to her.

'Alf, my friend,' said Reeve, walking over to speak to him. 'I'm afraid that I haven't been too successful in my research so far, so we are going to try another way.'

'I will come with you, brother,' the giant ground out, in his gravelly voice. 'Our oldest legends speak of our part in building the Pavilions. If that is so, perhaps a giant can help now, if you will have me.' He smiled diffidently as he made his offer, as if half-expecting to be turned away.

'I saw giants,' blurted Xander. 'In the old images, I mean. Humans, hobs and giants were all together at the rock.'

Alf beamed at him, his teeth gleaming like fresh-cut quartz.

'Then it is fitting that we stand together once again,' he said.

'Let's hope it's not critical though,' muttered Len darkly. 'As we can't seem to persuade the hobs to do the same.'

Xander had worried that someone would step in to stop them leaving, but in all the turmoil it was, in the end, easy enough to slip out of the front door. Rafe led the way and Suze ghosted ahead in and out of the shadows, her eyes gleaming pale in the darkness and her ears cocked alertly. Her calm watchfulness as they passed along the track was reassuring, confirming that there were no shades breaking through here to menace them or at least, not yet. Alf brought up the rear, walking along ponderously with Reeve, who was carrying a bulging backpack full of his technical gear. Now they were all on their way, Xander felt the weight of responsibility like a stone in his gut.

'I hope we're right about all this,' he muttered.

Ollie was characteristically cheerful.

'No point panicking about that now,' he said. 'Anyway, I'm sure we are.'

'And if we're not, then we won't be able to get in and we'll all just go home again,' added Len, with cool practicality.

'Yeah,' said Xander. 'I guess.' But he continued to worry as they hurried on through the Wykeham Gate and then passed through the silent streets of the city, until they reached the dusky courtyard where the Pavilion Gate loomed. It stood atop its flight of wide stone steps, faintly illuminated by the glowstone which Ollie pulled out of his pocket, and throwing a long shadow on the pavement behind it. Xander remembered it from before, brightly lit with the stairs filled with smartly dressed guests waiting their turn to pass through, and he shivered in the darkness and the silence.

Rafe glanced at Xander and then approached the gate and thrust one hand through the archway. It remained clearly visible and Rafe waggled his fingers before letting his arm fall and stepping back. There was an awkward silence.

'So,' he said. 'Obviously it's not working at the moment. Any thoughts?'

Xander inspected the inert gate. The strange carvings, weaving all over the worn grey stone, seemed to mock him for his lack of understanding.

'How do they usually turn it on at the Solstice?' he asked.

'They don't,' replied Rafe, evenly. 'It activates at sunrise on the morning of the Solstice and remains open until sunset the following day.'

Xander stared at the gate in utter frustration. He had been so certain about the Pavilions, it had never even occurred to him that he wouldn't be able to get there. Flint's sarcastic words rang in his ears and he tried to ignore them, casting about in his mind frantically, trying to remember if there was some clue or hint they had missed.

'Just try –' Len waved her wrist in front of Xander. 'You know, zapping it.'

'Zap it?' repeated Reeve, dubiously.

Ready at this point to try anything, Xander lifted his orb and concentrated hard on the image of the arch as he remembered it, alight and humming with power. His orb remained unresponsive, and the gate shut; after a moment he lowered his arm in defeat.

'Maybe it runs on some mystical power thingy from the alignment of the stars or something,' suggested Ollie in a worried voice.

'Mystical power thingy?' snapped a familiar grating voice from behind them. They all spun around and Xander's jaw dropped. Standing before them, scowling horribly, was Hob. 'You humans really are clueless.'

'I'm very relieved to see you, old friend,' said Reeve, delight clear on his face. Hob looked uncomfortable at this warm greeting and hunched his shoulders, glowering. Reeve just smiled at him. 'I've been trying to reach you for days but we didn't know where to start. How did you know we were here?'

Rafe stood silently, watching with a guarded expression,

and Hob stared back at him with glittering eyes before turning abruptly to Xander.

'Some friends of yours,' he snapped. 'They have some very irritating notions about choices.'

Xander heard Len's quick intake of breath beside him and he couldn't stop the little smile that pulled at his lips. Hob glared. 'We were minded to ignore it but, on balance,' he paused darkly, 'we decided to see what foolishness you were embroiled in now. You certainly don't disappoint. Zap it, indeed!' His face twisted in contempt.

Xander strangled a sudden urge to push the annoying hobgoblin down the stairs and took a deep breath. 'We need to get to the Pavilions, Hob. We think the ancient power to protect Haven is there, guarded behind the Constellation Wall, but we can't get past the gate.'

'Power at the Pavilions?' interrupted Hob testily. 'What rubbish is this now? There's no ancient power source there, or don't you think the hobgoblins would have known about it?'

Xander thought quickly.

'The Elder Goblin said that so much knowledge was lost to you,' he said. 'Don't you think it's possible that this might have been too?'

'Absolutely not,' growled Hob.

'But you do know how to open the gate,' said Rafe, finally breaking his silence. Hob pressed his lips together but Rafe continued, his voice quiet but relentless. 'You called us clueless about opening it, which would seem to indicate that you know how.'

There was a moment's silence, while Hob appeared to be wrestling with himself. 'Fine,' he snarled. He glared at Ollie. 'Mystical stars do not turn on the gate, foolish child. We do.'

'You?' said Reeve in surprise. 'But why don't we know this?

Why the secrecy?'

Hob eyed him coldly. 'It is just the way,' he said. 'The timings and the secrecy have been passed down our generations. It is not for us to question the wisdom of our Elders, of our traditions.' He looked very put out. 'A tradition which I have now betrayed. I suppose that it is too much to expect that you will respect our ways?'

Xander lifted his chin and stared back at Hob.

'You can trust us to keep your secret. We won't tell.'

Reeve nodded earnestly. 'Perhaps today can teach you some faith in your friends,' he said gently.

Hob just snorted.

'But doesn't this back up what Xander says?' said Ollie suddenly. 'Why else would the hobs have wanted to control the access to the Pavilions and keep it secret and secure? They wouldn't have done that for nothing.'

Xander felt the certainty tingle through him that Ollie had hit on the truth and he turned eagerly to the still scowling hobgoblin.

'So, how does the gate turn on?' he asked.

Hob paused and then growled something in a language which Xander did not understand, but which sent Reeve's eyebrows shooting up. 'We controlled it from the Core, obviously,' he said.

'But that's destroyed,' burst out Len.

'I am aware of that,' said Hob sarcastically. 'However, there is also a manual control on the gate itself, which a hob may activate.'

He stumped up the last few steps to the right-hand side of the gate and, after sending one final glower at Xander, fitted his fingers into a series of depressions which apparently only he could see in the surface of the carved stone. Immediately,

Xander could sense the difference. The gate itself had not changed, there had been no flare of light or dramatic sign, but it now seemed to hum with suppressed power. Xander felt a shiver run across his skin and the prod of a strange urgency. He had the strong feeling they should not linger here.

'Right then,' he said, trying to make his voice appear confident and certain. It sounded odd in his own ears. 'Let's get on with it.' Taking a deep breath, he walked forward through the gate.

CHAPTER THIRTEEN

It was noticeably cooler as they stepped out of the arch onto the hillside. The stars were brighter overhead and the huge green mound reared up before them, a darker shadow against the sky, with the steep stone staircase gleaming in the centre. Memories struck Xander again of when he had been here last, of the staircase lit up with many twinkling lanterns and filled with people, the sound of merry chatter filling the air. Now, the silence and the dark pressed down on him like a living thing and he looked anxiously at Suze. The animal was alert, her ears flicking back and forward, but she did not seem unduly concerned. Xander took a deep breath.

'Okay,' he said out loud and almost winced at how hollow his voice sounded.

He began to climb the stone steps and heard footsteps following behind him, the giant's only a little heavier than everyone else as he tried to move quietly. The Pavilions gradually came into view as they mounted the top of the stairs. No longer glowing with its own light, the building was an enormous, dark silhouette against the clear, starry sky and the columns which had twisted so elegantly now loomed up forbiddingly. Despite the creepy air about the great, empty place Xander felt a sudden rush of intense relief. Now that he was here and could see the structure again, outlined so starkly against the night, he could quite clearly make out the platforms and pillars of the original images from the brownies' painted memories. The structures had been carefully incorporated into the subsequent design of the building, but they were unmistakable enough to Xander that he turned, without hesitation, towards the Constellation Wall before the giant could point the way.

Their footsteps rang out once they had entered the Pavilion itself, echoing sharply between the stone walls, and Xander could feel his stomach clenching with the sudden tension. Evidently, he was not alone in his reaction as he heard Len's breathing becoming shallower. Another nervous glance at Suze showed her watching him, her pale eyes gleaming. As their eyes met, Xander's thoughts flashed back to the museum, when she had looked at him across a crowded atrium and somehow dared him to embark on this whole mad adventure. For a moment, Xander had the strong urge to tell Suze that all of this was her fault. Her jaw dropped, tongue lolling, and Xander had the oddest feeling that she was laughing at him. He gave himself an internal shake. This was definitely not the time to let his mind wander.

'Here it is,' came Alf's rumbling voice. Ahead of them was a wide stretch of stone wall, blank and with no sign of the glittering constellations. Xander frowned, confused.

'Where are all the stars?' asked Ollie plaintively.

Alf shook his head. 'I have never been here but for the Solstice when all the stone is alight. Perhaps the hobs –'

His rasping voice trailed off and they all turned to look at Hob, who glared back.

'Oh, so now you don't know how to do this either? Yet another great plan, human,' he sneered contemptuously at Xander. 'No, I don't have any idea how to switch on your wall. You're supposed to be the seed of the ancient blood, aren't you? Use what you were given or else let us all go home.' He gestured in annoyance to the orb on Xander's wrist.

Xander lifted his arm and stared into the dark crystal orb on his wrist. Deep inside it he could see the flickers of light, like contained lightning, and there was a slight tingling sensation in his palm, where the starburst scar of his shadow-strike was still clear and pale on his skin. Following a deep instinct, he placed his hand flat against the wall and closed his eyes, visualising the pale sparkle of stars in the sky being mirrored on the wall. A gasp from behind him snapped his eyes open again and he stepped back. The wall was alight with constellations and, in the darkness of the Pavilions, it was even more spectacular than Xander remembered. He glanced sideways at the hob, who was staring at him with hooded eyes, and felt a shiver run down his back.

A moment later there was a rustle as Len pulled the note-book pages out of her bag and began flicking through the names and images of the constellations they had matched to the Twelve Families.

'We need to find these as quickly as possible,' she said, handing the pages around. The piece of paper looked ludicrously tiny in the giant's enormous hand, as he carefully held it between the very tips of his thumb and forefinger. Hob had stepped away, his hands behind his back, when offered a page and Ollie rolled his eyes and grabbed it instead. There was a few moments' silence as they all consulted their sheets of paper in the dim light, looking back and forth between the diagrams and the wall.

'There's one,' said Reeve, pointing at a cluster of stars. 'That's Angove.'

'What now?' asked Alf, turning to Xander.

'Maybe I touch it?' said Xander, uncertainly. He felt less comfortable with their previous methods of trial and error in front of the three adults, not to mention Hob's unfriendly glower.

'We're all of us in the dark here, Xander,' Reeve said, seeming to understand Xander's hesitation. 'Just do your best, we can't ask any more.'

Relieved, Xander smiled and then stepped forward, reaching up to touch the star pattern that Reeve had identified. His orb began to glow by itself before his fingers even touched the wall, and the stars he had selected blazed into a brighter light as he brushed the stone. Xander let out a sigh of relief and everyone began hunting earnestly for the patterns on their papers, feeling encouraged that they appeared to be on the right track.

'Ingram.'

'Lisle.'

'Ferrars.'

The finds rang out one after the other and, as Xander touched each one, the intensity of the selected stars brightened. Finally, Ollie found the twisted constellation that belonged to the Melville family, right off to one side.

'Typical. Always difficult, that family,' he said with a wry grin.

Xander had to stand on his tip-toes to reach that pattern, but he managed to just brush the edge. As soon as he had touched it, every star illuminated on the wall blinked and then went out; the wall was once again dark and featureless. Despite a growing certainty that this was not what was supposed to happen, Xander pressed his hands against the wall and pushed. Nothing happened, the cold stone was as obdurate as ever, and he felt despair rise like a smothering cloud. He smacked both hands against the cold stone in futile frustration.

'This doesn't make sense,' he said, turning to Ollie and

Len. 'It was working, I'm sure of it. What went wrong?'

'I don't know,' said Ollie, slowly. 'We found the marks of the kin, like it said, and all of the patterns fit. We checked that.'

Reeve gathered up all of the pages of the notebook and examined them intently, comparing the Family sigils with the constellations. 'They seem right,' he said finally. 'Is there a step missing here? Maybe there's some information that we don't have.'

He glanced over at Alf and the hob, his expression questioning. Alf slowly shook his head, a ponderous frown lowering his brow even further.

'Our legends tell us that we built this wall but we have only fragments. If ever we knew anything more, that knowledge is lost,' he said in a downcast rumble, as if he felt he was letting everyone down.

Hob just folded his arms and half-turned away, his contempt for the process quite clear. It was evident that no help would come from his quarter.

'Shall we try again?' asked Ollie, hopefully. 'Maybe Xander accidentally touched one of the wrong patterns?'

'No, he didn't,' said Reeve, before Xander could object. 'I was checking.'

'Look, clearly this is the right track,' said Rafe, in his reasonable, calm voice. 'We got this far but maybe there was a mistake earlier. Are you sure that you copied the Family sigils correctly?'

Xander made an impatient movement, but it was Ollie who answered.

'We traced them really carefully and double-checked. We couldn't have –'

'Of course!' Len's voice cut straight through the discussion, high pitched and getting faster and faster in her excitement. 'It's so obvious I can't believe that I didn't realise it before. It was right there in front of me. So obv –'

'Len!' Xander had to almost shout to get her attention. 'What's obvious?'

Len turned to him, her eyes sparkling in the faint light.

'Do you remember when Primilla Prissy-pants gave me that detention, and made me write out all of those tedious old records of the Twelve Families and their boring histories?' she demanded.

'Yeah, I remember,' said Xander, feeling confused about where she was going with this.

'She dug out the oldest, dustiest, most mind-numbing records she could find, tracing the Families back in time. In those records however, I learnt that sometimes there isn't a direct male heir and the Family would continue through the female line.'

'Okay' said Ollie blankly. 'How does this help us?'

Reeve and Rafe looked at each other, smiling as comprehension dawned.

'Of course,' said Reeve quietly.

Len heaved a sigh of vindication. She turned back to Ollie and Xander.

'There have always been the Twelve Families and their history traces back to the beginning but they aren't the exact same Twelve as today. The Raynotts and the Hacketts aren't the original families. They replaced the,' she stopped and frowned a moment before continuing, 'the Helthons and the Walkers. They were the originals.'

'So that's why it didn't work?' Ollie burst out, having finally caught on. 'We had two of the original sigils wrong, so we picked the wrong star patterns.'

'Yep,' said Len. 'Exactly.'

Xander felt his hopes begin to rise again, but –

'We still don't know the kin marks of the original Families, their sigils. We'll have to go home and research them before we can get any further. We can't go on now.' Again, he felt that strange pull of urgency, the sense that it would be too late.

'In the hands of a lesser detention detainee that might be the case,' said Len airily, a smug smile pulling at her lips. 'I, however, can remember pretty much anything I have written down, given a minute or two.'

She shut her eyes and frowned in concentration as they all waited, then waved her hand imperatively.

'Paper and a pen,' she demanded.

Ollie shoved some notepaper towards her while Reeve fished a stubby piece of pencil out of his pocket. Len knelt down on the ground, while Ollie held his glowstone close so she could see the paper. Quickly, she drew two sigils, one above the other, and then handed the page up to Xander. Everyone crowded in to look except Hob, who still stood to one side. His air of disinterest was somewhat undermined by the quick glances he kept snatching at the paper.

'Are you sure these are accurate?' asked Reeve.

Len gave him an outraged look. 'Absolutely,' she said.

'They will be,' said Ollie, with a quick grin. 'This is why Len drives the instructors at the Academy insane – she remembers everything she's seen, even when she looks like she's not paying attention.'

'Really?' Reeve said, looking interested.

'Len, you're amazing,' said Xander.

'I know,' she replied nonchalantly, but Xander could see the genuine smile and her faint blush.

'We'll start again,' said Xander. 'Ollie, you help me with

the ones we did before, minus the wrong sigils, while the rest of you look for the star patterns which match the new kin marks. I'll light the wall back up so you can see.'

Strangely now, despite his earlier doubts, Xander had no fear that he could not activate the wall again. Confidently, he placed his hand against it and, with a quick flare of his orb, the stars glimmered once again within the stone. Now there was a real sense of purpose as he and Ollie worked to re-light the constellations matching each of the original correct sigils, while he could hear the faint murmur of discussion and disagreement from the group behind him, their heads bent closely together. Alf leaned over the top of them, his deep granite voice breaking in every now and again.

When the first ten constellations were glowing again, Xander turned around.

'How are you doing?' he asked. 'We need to hit the final two.'

'This one is the Helthon mark,' said Reeve, pointing down to the left while all the others nodded in agreement. Xander hurried over and activated the pattern.

'And the last one?' he asked.

They all looked at one another. 'We can't really agree on that,' said Len reluctantly.

Rafe pointed to two very similar patterns. 'It could be either of those, but neither one seems to fit perfectly.'

Xander's heart sank as he looked between the two choices. There was an abrupt shuffle and Hob pushed forward.

'No wonder I had to come along,' he said nastily. 'With both hands and a map, you couldn't find your own –'

He cut off under Rafe's disapproving gaze, glancing side-long at the younger members of the group. 'Bah,' he muttered and then pointed down at the bottom of the wall. 'There is your pattern.'

Xander leant down to see, and recognised immediately that the hobgoblin was correct. The match to the Walker kin mark was barely above floor level, but quite clear. His hand reached out, hesitated for just a second, and then touched the stone. All of the stars blinked and, for one desperate moment, Xander thought they had failed again. This time however, the stars in the chosen constellations did not fade away but grew brighter and more intense. The other stars dimmed until they disappeared, as the wall itself grew darker while becoming transparent. In just a moment, Xander was standing in front of a huge vista, deep and cold without measure, the patterns now transformed into constellations of blazing stars hanging in empty space. He took an uncertain step backwards.

'Unbelievable,' murmured Reeve.

'Now what?' said Ollie, his eyes wide and awestruck. 'How in Haven are we supposed to get past that?'

And suddenly, Xander knew. He took a deep breath.

'Faith,' he said quietly and, before he could talk himself out of it, he stepped out into space.

For a second, he was blinded by the flare of starlight, but he felt the slight, familiar prickle of a ward and a moment later he was standing in a stone corridor, dimly lit by the glow from his orb. Turning around, he saw the hazy figures of his companions on the other side of the star-speckled barrier; their voices were faint but it looked like absolute bedlam was breaking out. Rafe was dragging Ollie back from the barrier, while Len and Reeve shouted Xander's name and Alf loomed worriedly behind them. Even the hobgoblin looked shocked.

'It's okay,' yelled Xander, as loudly as he could. 'I'm fine. I can still see you all.'

There was a sudden, shocking silence on the other side of the barrier.

'Xander?' called Reeve. 'Where are you?'

'I'm right here,' said Xander. 'It's just an illusion, a ward. You can walk right through it.'

'*You* can walk right through it,' muttered the hob. 'Doesn't mean that we can.'

His voice cut off as, without any hesitation, Len stepped forward. From this side, Xander could see the flare of starlight, illuminating the barrier and making it ripple, before Len walked through into the corridor. She glanced back over her shoulder, with a quick smile of wonder, before taking two steps towards Xander and thumping him hard, on the arm.

'Ow,' Xander yelped. 'What was that for?'

'For scaring us like that, you idiot,' Len snapped.

The barrier flickered and rippled again as the rest of the group followed Len's example, the hobgoblin bringing up the rear muttering furiously. Xander was rubbing his arm ruefully and Rafe's eyes followed the motion.

'I see that Len has already expressed our feelings over the recklessness of that action,' he said evenly, 'so we'll leave it there.'

'Thanks,' grumbled Xander. Len had a very good arm when she was annoyed.

Reeve and Ollie both held up glowstones, and Alf was looking around with awed wonder on his rough-hewn face.

'This is our work,' he said, gesturing at the precise joinery of the soaring stone walls and arched ceiling up above them. He moved over to gaze at a beautifully carved niche in the wall, surrounded with decorative stone work. 'Such care, even on the smallest details. We cannot carve stone like lace any more. We have fallen so far.' Wistfully, he stroked the intricate carvings, oblivious to the spider webs which covered every surface and hung down in festoons from the high ceilings.

Ollie wrinkled his nose. 'It smells pretty bad in here though,' he said. 'Hopefully that ward will let in some fresh air now.'

Hob snorted. 'We are far from fresh air,' he growled. 'That ward does not just conceal. It has carried us deep underground. We'll probably all suffocate down here, but doubtless that's just another well-considered part of your grand plan.'

'How can we be deep underground?' demanded Len, with a sceptical expression. 'We can see straight out there to the Pavilions.'

Hob glared at her.

'Did humans develop a profound connection to the deep earth while we hobs weren't looking?' he asked sarcastically. 'The ward and your eyes deceive you – we are a long way below the Pavilions now.'

With a quick frown, Rafe examined the passageway, shining his light as far as it would reach. 'Given the dust on the floor, no-one has been here for many years, maybe centuries. We need to be careful – there may be some damage along the way.'

'No,' rumbled Alf. 'Our work has stood undisturbed for millennia in other places. Not a stone will have moved from its allotted place.'

'Hmm,' said Rafe, noncommittally. 'Even so, let's walk carefully. Better safe than sorry, eh?'

As they moved forward along the corridor, it grew more dank and musty smelling, and Xander could see the swirling dust that they had disturbed with their footsteps. The corridor continued on, with no openings or doors along its straight length, although it sloped subtly downwards. It was almost a shock when it terminated in a large door, big enough for Alf to pass through with room to spare. There was no obvious handle or control but when Xander touched it with his fingertips, his orb flared with warm light and it began to slide slowly and ponderously to the side, with a grating noise which reverberated in the enclosed space. It didn't open all of the way, wedging itself with a groan, but the gap was wide enough to admit everyone, even the giant who squeezed through with a grunt.

Rafe ignited his orb and it surged into a dazzling light. Xander gasped and heard similar intakes of breath all around him. They stood in a massive chamber, easily as large as the Nexus, the ceiling so high that it was lost in shadows. The fractal shapes of soaring crystal spires, like mountain peaks, glittered in the orb-light and filled the enormous space. For a moment, they all stood stunned and then Hob dived past them, almost knocking Ollie over in his haste and exclaiming rapidly in his own language. He stopped in front of the nearest spire, his expression reverent as he laid both hands on it and then pressed his cheek against the crystal, his eyes squeezed shut. Reeve had also taken a few steps forward, his face alight with wonder, but he paused to watch the hobgoblin. There were a few moments of silence when all Xander could hear was the sound of his own breathing. Hob lifted his head and turned to them.

'This is ancient beyond our imaginings. It is almost gone, but I sense a faint spark still in it.' He looked stunned, his eyes wide as they rested on Xander. 'You – you did it,' he said in a wondering voice. 'You found what we did not know we had lost, our ancient Core.'

His voice trailed off, as if he couldn't find the words and he turned to gaze around in awe. The next moment, and without a backwards glance, he was off and running in a swift, purposeful jog into the chamber. Reeve dashed after him and, after a startled pause, everyone else followed, their footsteps echoing in the stone and crystal maze.

Xander could see that the hobgoblin was trailing his fingers along the crystal as he hurried along, guiding them unerringly through the pathways. Rafe leaned over to Xander as they raced behind. 'Be wary and stay close,' he said quietly, his voice rough. 'There is something here that makes me uneasy.' Xander followed Rafe's sidelong glance at Suze, who was moving alongside them with tense ears and lips curling up, showing her white teeth. He nodded to Rafe to show that he had heard, but did not reply as Hob slowed and then stopped before a tall, delicate spire.

'Look,' he said, his harsh voice sounding choked with emotion. 'It is here.'

Xander looked up and saw the glimmer of a faint light, deep within the spire. It pulsed gently, like a heartbeat, and small shimmers of light radiated through the crystal in response to each beat. It was breath-taking, but somehow sorrowful, as if they were witnessing the last, laboured breaths of a wounded creature.

'This is incredible,' breathed Reeve. He held his glowstone high to illuminate as much as possible. 'The complexity of this is beyond anything I have ever seen. The power running through here when it was operational must have been immense.'

'Is this the place which powered the Travellers' Stones and the border that protected Haven?' asked Ollie. 'Are they failing because the power here is almost gone?'

'This is the heart of it all,' came the harsh voice of the hobgoblin, although he didn't look up from where he crouched on the floor, examining the base of the structure. 'How could we have abandoned it? How could we have forgotten?' The deep bitterness in his voice left an uncomfortable silence.

'Is the better question not 'how' but 'why'?' Alf's rumble broke in. He looked at the floor awkwardly when everyone turned to look at him. 'With apologies, my friend, but hobs are not known for deserting their creations. Even when the whole structure was collapsing, the hobs did not want to leave their Core. They were shielding the ruins from the Council's people and their snooping. Why would you have left all of this?'

Hob scowled up at him.

'I don't know. We would protect a place such as this with our lives.'

'Maybe that's it,' said Xander slowly, thinking out loud. 'It *was* protected. Protected from people who might try to harm it, protected from exactly what has happened to your old Core. If no-one knew about it, then they couldn't destroy it.'

'That would make sense if the hobs had just kept the secret from everyone else, but what would be the point of forgetting it themselves?' Ollie demanded. 'This would have needed maintenance, wouldn't it?' He appealed to Reeve, who was staring at his feet, thinking hard. Reeve glanced up.

'It would and this must have been a massive work over the centuries, but don't forget that goblin-kind were decimated by sickness a hundred years ago, as well as more recently. Perhaps this was a closely held secret among the Elders; they were the most susceptible to the epidemic, the first to fall. The secret could have been lost without the hobs who survived even realising that it ever existed. The only thing that remained was the traditional control of the Pavilion Gate leading here, but with no memory of why they controlled it in the first place.'

There was a profound silence.

'Secrets,' said Rafe quietly, shaking his head.

'Indeed,' rumbled Alf. 'It is always the way. So much knowledge lost rather than shared. We all lose. I wonder whether we will ever regain all that we have lost.'

'Very philosophical,' Hob growled. 'Some secrets are kept for a reason and some knowledge is too dangerous to be freed. We remember that, even if we have forgotten much else.'

Alf looked concerned, but before he could continue the argument Len broke in.

'Seriously? Is everyone just going to stand about wittering on?' she demanded. 'Can't we do whatever it is we're supposed to do here, like turn it back on again? This place is making me itch.' She scratched her arm ostentatiously.

'Just turn it on again?' snapped Hob. 'I don't have time for this ignorant rubbish.'

Len looked offended but the hobgoblin ignored her, turning his back and pressing his hands against the crystal, his forehead resting against the spire. Clearly his awe at the discovery of the great core had not overtaken his usual sour disposition. He paid no further attention to them, seemingly in a trance.

Rafe turned to Xander. 'Did those clues of yours indicate what you were supposed to do, once you got here? If the failure of this core is affecting the Stones and the border, then we need to do something about it.'

Xander glanced at Ollie and Len, and then shrugged helplessly.

'They weren't exactly clear instructions,' he said.

'Maybe we should fan out,' Rafe said. 'See if we're missing something. Ollie, you go with Alf, Len with Reeve and Xander, you come with me.' He glanced over at the hobgoblin, but he remained oblivious and Rafe shrugged. 'We'll leave him here, see what he can come up with. Don't go far and give a shout if you find anything, otherwise we'll meet back here.'

It was a strange and eerie experience, walking through the

opaque, twisting crystal as Suze padded at Rafe's heel, radiating alertness. Their footsteps rang hollowly and an air of desertion hung over the place, but Xander was beginning to feel uneasy. He kept seeing sparkling inclusions in the crystal out of the corner of his eyes, but whenever he looked directly at the spot, the crystal was lifeless and opaque. He tried to persuade himself that he was only glimpsing reflections from Rafe's orb-light but it wasn't convincing. His shoulders felt tight with tension and his stomach knotted.

When the shout came from their left, Xander flinched. Rafe eyed him thoughtfully but said nothing, just turning to move towards the call.

'Over here.'

It came again and this time Xander recognised Reeve's voice. A moment later he and Rafe were standing in a wide-open area, between the peaks of crystal and a bare stone wall. One section of the wall, where Reeve and Len were standing, was quite different.

A large, roughly oval section was not the same plain grey stone as the rest of the wall; instead it was woven through with the same crystal as the matrix. It glimmered softly, illuminating several veins of crystal set into the floor, joining the strange structure with the core behind them. Xander realised that he was standing on one of the veins and quickly moved his feet as a faint pulse of light passed through it.

'What *is* that?' demanded Ollie, in a hushed voice. He and Alf had also joined the group from the other side, and he stared blankly at the wall and then at the floor under him. He shifted his feet. 'It feels weird.'

Reeve shook his head in wonderment, tracing the veins on the floor with his eyes. 'I have no idea,' he acknowledged. 'I've never seen anything like this before.'

'Why not ask him?' asked Len, furiously itching her hand.

They all turned to look where she was gesturing. Moving slowly, like a bloodhound on the track, Hob was making his way towards them, bent over with his eyes closed and his fingers trailing just above one of the crystal veins. His eyes sprang open at Len's loud question, and he glowered at her before his eyes widened on seeing the wall behind her. He hurried forward, astonishment clear on his face, and stopped in front of the great tapestry of crystal filaments.

'Incredible, incredible,' he said, awe gentling even his harsh voice. 'We had theorised that it was possible but that it actually exists –'

His words trailed away as he gazed upwards, his eyes wide with wonder.

'What is it?' asked Rafe.

The hobgoblin hesitated, clearly wrestling with the desire to keep the information to himself, and then his eyes flicked to Alf.

'It's a cloaked link,' he said. 'A remote interface, if you will. It connects our former Core to this original, to act as a protection and a disguise, while all along it was here that the real power was generated to secure Haven.'

Reeve frowned, as a thought occurred to him. 'Is this what the Council's crew were looking for then, when they were so desperate to search your ruined Core?' he asked.

Hob spun about to stare at him, his expression twisting in sudden comprehension.

'Simm,' he spat. 'Breaking into our places and poking through the remnants. They were searching for this link.'

'That's not all,' said Xander, certainty filling his voice. 'They had to get the hobs out of their Core otherwise they knew they would never get in there. I don't think the damage and the failure were an accident.' He could almost see Gage's face as he spoke, wearing a twisted smirk as he slipped back towards the hobs' Core.

'But why?' demanded Reeve. 'Why risk so much destruction?'

'That's obvious. Thorne wants to control all the power,' said Len immediately. 'He's greedy and wants his technology to take over everything. The hobs were in his way, so he got rid of their Core and then he realised that there had to be something else providing power, and he wants to find it so he can take it out as well.'

'Len's right,' said Xander. 'He probably paid off Simm to find the hidden core for him.'

'You know what Simm is like,' added Ollie. 'He'd do anything to crawl up to people like Larcius and Melville. They're both related to Thorne and it would give them control on the Council.'

Rafe and Reeve exchanged quick glances.

'Look,' said Rafe. 'You'll get no argument from me that Perrin Thorne is a nasty piece of work and certainly he's greedy, but I just can't see him actively sabotaging the hobs' Core.'

'A lot of the difficulties with the Core result from them losing population so tragically,' agreed Reeve. 'Thorne isn't responsible for the epidemics; he lost his first wife in the last one.' He glanced apologetically at Rafe, who remained expressionless.

'But Xander saw that man who worked for Simm hanging around the hobs' Core,' argued Len. 'He was even there the day of the explosion.'

Reeve shook his head. 'The man that apparently only Xander has ever seen,' he said quietly. 'Sorry guys, but you'll need more evidence than this if you're planning to blame Thorne. You can't prove that he knew that there was an additional, hidden core – not even the hobs who built it remembered that.'

'Then why were Simm, Latchet and their people so obsessed with getting into the ruined Core and poking around?' demanded Len. 'I don't know how they knew, but they must have. You said yourself that they were looking for something and being secretive about it.'

Reeve frowned, but before he could answer Hob hissed at them.

'Be quiet,' he snapped. 'I am sensing something but I cannot hear myself think with all of your incessant yammering.' They all quieted under the ferocity of his glare, although Len rolled her eyes and muttered 'drama queen'.

'There's some kind of feedback,' he said, hunching down toward the crystal wall. Reeve hurried over to him, pulling equipment out of his backpack and settling on the floor; one device immediately began beeping, and the panel on another was flashing with rapidly changing numbers. There was a tense silence while the hob and the human worked side by side.

'I'm picking it up too,' said Reeve. He glanced sideways at Hob. 'Could it be some kind of back-wash from what's left of the Core or is someone interfering?'

Xander was looking away, still frowning in annoyance at the summary dismissal of their case against Thorne, so he was the first to see Suze go from quietly alert to tense aggression, her lips rippling in a furious snarl.

'Get back,' yelled Rafe, grabbing Reeve and yanking him backwards. His orb flared and the hob shot back across the floor, away from the wall. He was almost fast enough.

Sickly green light, writhing like snakes, flickered through

the tapestry of crystal channels for just an instant, before the wall blew outwards in a soundless explosion. The force of the blast lifted the hob off the floor and he flew back into Len and Ollie, sending all three tumbling far across the floor. Alf, moving with unexpected speed, grabbed Rafe and Reeve and twisted around to use his broad back to protect them from the shattered crystal which splintered outwards in tiny shards.

All of this Xander seemed to see in slow motion, as once again his arm rose without conscious thought, his orb flaring out a protective shield before himself and Suze. Crystal splinters rebounded from his ward, falling to the floor with a faint tinkling sound. The pressure of the explosion beating in his eardrums, Xander stood before the huge cavity in the wall watching as Simm, followed by Latchet and Gage, picked their way over the debris. He heard the low rumble of Suze's growl and realised that her pale eyes were fixed, not on the three walking into the chamber, but on the darkness which followed them. It seethed and hissed menacingly, and Xander felt the terror of it swelling in the back of his throat, sharp and suffocating.

Simm held up his glowstone and Xander got a clear view of his face. His pale, bulging eyes were shining with a mad intensity, and he was staring around with a strange mixture of triumph and fear.

'Knew it was there, didn't I? Knew they hid it there all along. Hobs lie, don't they, Latchet? Sneaking around, keeping it to themselves, keeping it hidden. But I knew, I knew we would find it. Can't hide it from me.' His muttering voice broke off as his gaze fell on Xander, standing frozen with shock. His face twisted in sudden fury. 'It's the boy, isn't it, Latchet? That spying boy, always creeping around with the deceitful hobs, always where he's not supposed to be. Grab the sneaking boy, Latchet. The Council will hear about this. *Grab him!*

His voice rose into a shriek and Xander backed away, with a worried look at Latchet who stood several steps behind Simm, his face completely vacant. There was clearly something very wrong with both of them. The silent figure of Gage stood behind them, a faint smirk twisting his lips. Latchet began to walk forward, his eyes fixed on Xander, but a light suddenly flared and Rafe's calm voice rang out.

'No-one is grabbing the boy,' he called. 'Step back and we can sort this out.'

Simm shrieked again, a shocking sound that echoed off the crystal spires around them, as the orb-light illuminated all the people in the chamber. 'Fools, all of you,' he hissed, and Xander could see flecks of spit bursting out with every word. 'Sort it out? You can do nothing to stop it. We claim this place and the darkness will take it and the roaring lion will devour it. You will never leave here.' His voice dropped to a menacing snarl. 'You will be entombed in here forever.'

'He's completely barking,' said Reeve quietly to Rafe. He glanced back at Alf. 'We'll have to contain both of them, and get them out of here before they hurt themselves or someone else.'

Horrified, Xander realised that, yet again, no-one else appeared able to see Gage standing in plain sight. He could see Gage's lips moving continually and soundlessly, and felt a pang of fear. Then, with appalling suddenness, Simm threw himself at Rafe, clawing at his face. At the same moment, Xander saw Gage gesture with one hand and the darkness swelling behind him grew liquid, flowing across the floor and then congealing into the rearing shapes of multiple shades. Latchet charged straight at Xander but Reeve dived forward to intercept him, throwing Xander out of the way. As he fell, Xander got a glimpse of Ollie over by the far wall, his orb flaring frantically as he tried to protect himself and Len, who was bent over the hob lying limp on the floor.

As if all this chaos and fear was not enough, there was a sharp cracking sound and a large facet of the nearest crystal spire began to shear off, right over the top of Reeve and Latchet. Alf shouted a warning and clambered up towards the fracturing matrix, bracing his shoulders against it in a desperate attempt to stop it falling.

Xander lay sprawled on the ground, stunned amid this pandemonium, with his orb still glowing enough to illuminate his panicky breaths in the rapidly chilling air. Mist was rising from the floor and rolling off the walls, as the shades gathered to strike.

'The servants of darkness have come for you all,' shrieked Simm, but Xander's eyes were drawn to Gage, as he walked towards the Core itself. As he approached, a sickly green light began to ripple through the crystal matrix, lighting up Gage's face into an inhuman mask and reflecting off his shining teeth as he smiled triumphantly.

'Xander,' yelled Rafe as he struggled with Simm, while throwing a powerful ward out towards the massing shades. 'If you're planning to do something, now might be a good moment.'

As if Rafe's shout had released him, Xander scrambled to his feet and ran to block Gage's way.

'I see you,' he gasped. 'I know it's you who is doing all this.'

Gage halted, his eyes pinning Xander like an insignificant insect.

'You see me, do you?' he said, his voice surprisingly soft, with just the hint of a hiss. He looked at Xander with contempt. 'You see nothing. You know nothing.'

'I know that you and Thorne are behind all this,' Xander retorted, his lips numbing in the cold. 'You're working with him so he can control all of the power.'

Gage laughed scornfully.

'You know nothing,' he repeated, cold amusement in his voice. 'You are a stupid, insignificant child who should have just left when you had the chance. You don't belong here. Go back and fall with your foolish friends – there is no place here for you.'

Despite himself, Xander felt that familiar pang of doubt as he stared at Gage's face, twisted with contempt. Maybe Gage was right and he didn't belong here. What could he possibly do against all this? He swallowed, feeling terror and hopelessness rising inexorably inside him. Then, off to his left in the growing darkness, he saw the desperate flare of Ollie's orb and a sudden remembrance came to him of another time light had come to drive back the fear, in the small, indomitable forms of the brownies who had come for him, to give him choices.

Xander straightened up.

'I decide where I belong,' he said sharply. 'Not you.'

Gage snarled, the green crystal light sparking in his eyes, and lunged towards him. A wall of shades reared menacingly over his shoulder but, with the clarity that the memory had brought to Xander, had come another certainty. He had to get to the faint spark of light before Gage got there and destroyed it. He spun around and ran. His orb seemed to tug on his wrist, leading him through the crystal matrix so he took each turn decisively, his heart pounding as he heard Gage's footsteps racing behind him.

With a desperate effort, Xander threw himself around a corner and there before him was the twisted spire, its faint light still feebly pulsing at its heart. Without thinking, without hesitation, he pressed both hands against the crystal.

'Whatever you need to do, please do it,' he begged his orb as he saw Gage slide to a halt a few paces away, his face demonic with fury. For an instant, for a couple of pounding heart beats, nothing happened and Xander could not breathe with the desperation of it.

Then, power ripped through the spire, illuminating it so brightly that Xander was dazed by the light, and warmth flowed through him like a torrent of water, beating through his orb and rippling out through the matrix of crystal nodes around him in a thousand different colours, sparkling like sunlight on drops of water. It was the most beautiful thing that Xander had ever seen and it was blinding in its intensity.

For just a moment, Xander caught a glimpse of Gage's face, his expression shocked and furious, before he was swallowed up in the dazzling radiance and Xander had to blink his watering eyes. Suddenly, he felt himself rising into the air as the spire soared upwards with the power within it and he could see over the top of the rest of the matrix, spread out in a pulsing web below him. He heard a frantic yell and saw Ollie and Len over by the wall, cringing back from the onslaught of shades rearing over them. Instinctively, Xander threw out his hand towards them and a glittering lightning storm erupted from his orb, streams of power that bounced off the walls and floor and obliterated every shade they touched. His jaw dropped in shock at what he had just done, and still the light continued to surge through the crystalline structures with a soft chiming sound, until every part of the great chamber was lit up.

Finally, there was silence. Xander took a deep, shuddering breath and then climbed carefully down, using small footholds which seemed to have been placed there for his convenience. The crystal spire glowed softly, its pulsing beat steady, and Xander laid a gentle hand on it.

'I'm not really sure what just happened, but thank you,' he said quietly.

There was no sign of Gage; he had vanished without a trace. Filled with concern for his friends, Xander turned and ran back through the maze of pathways. His orb was no longer guiding him and so he took several wrong turns before he burst out into the space in front of the former link, where he had left the others. As he got there, he heard an odd, high-pitched noise and stopped abruptly. The scene before him was a strange one. Rafe was straightening up, his face scratched and battered, while Simm lay curled up in a ball on the ground with Suze standing over him watchfully. Reeve was massaging one hand, Latchet spread-eagled at his feet with his nose bleeding profusely, while Ollie and Len stood to the side, apparently unhurt. Everyone, however, was staring at Hob.

The hobgoblin was leaping and prancing around in a mad dance next to one of the crystal nodes, cackling and whooping in glee. He spun around again and his gaze fell on Xander, standing watching him open-mouthed. With another wild whoop, he raced over and flung his arms around Xander's waist, then actually picked him up and began twirling him round and round.

'You did it,' he burst out gleefully. 'You gave us back our Core.' Finally, he put Xander down and then reached up to yank on his shoulder. His strange, slitted yellow eyes stared straight into Xander's with a meaningful look. 'I offer you my true name in honour and thanks.'

Xander blinked at the unintelligible stream of syllables that followed but, as the hob pulled back and beamed at him, he smiled.

'Thank you,' he said, feeling that he needed to acknowledge this momentous tribute, although he was entirely certain that he could never remember, much less pronounce, the hob's name. 'I am truly honoured.'

Evidently it was the right thing to say as the hobgoblin beamed at him again, the expression rather unnerving on his usually dour face.

'Is everyone okay?' Xander asked, turning to the others who had been watching the scene with bemused expressions. The next moment he was wrapped in a bear hug by Ollie.

'I knew you wouldn't let us die,' he said, with another squeeze which made Xander grunt.

'Although you needn't have cut it quite so close,' said Len in a voice that attempted to be nonchalant, despite her hand shaking as she pushed her hair back off her face. 'It got a little hairy over here, what with all the shades and the lunatics.'

She looked over towards where Simm lay, muttering under his breath and making no move to uncurl from his position on the floor. Xander was surprised to realise that he could feel a distinct sense of wrongness rolling off the man as he lay there, his expensive clothes dusty and ripped. His eyes travelled over to Latchet, still unconscious, then up to Reeve who grinned at him, while lightly massaging his hand.

'I've been wanting an excuse to do that for a very long time,' he said unrepentantly. 'It felt good.'

Xander laughed, feeling the knot of tension relax as he looked around at everyone. Alf was standing alone, stretching and rolling his shoulders, while above him loomed the enormous node that Xander had last seen cracking, about to fall down to crush the people below. Evidently the crystal had been healed by the pulsing energy, as there was no sign now of any fissures in its soft glow.

'Alf, you were amazing,' said Xander. 'I still can't believe that you held up that thing by yourself.'

'Oh, it was nothing,' said Alf bashfully, his coarse skin reddening in an awkward blush, but he looked very pleased.

'So, what actually happened in there?' demanded Ollie, turning to Xander.

'It was Gage,' said Xander. 'He was here. He wanted to destroy the Core, and he almost got there before me.' Xander shuddered as he remembered the green light flickering across Gage's face, twisted in hatred and malice, and the sound of his footsteps pounding behind him. 'He was controlling the shades; they answered to him.'

There was a brief silence.

'Gage?' said Rafe. 'I don't mean to doubt you, Xander, but I didn't see anyone else here. I saw you talking to yourself, and then running into the Core.' He glanced around and then shrugged, his expression calm. 'However, if you say someone was here then I believe you. There was clearly more going on than we realise.'

His gaze dropped to Simm, now rocking gently on the floor.

'What happened after that?' demanded Len. 'The next thing we saw was you up on a crystal spire hurling lightning bolts around, which, by the way, you'd better not tell the Wardens. They're already worried about you being another Zeus – this would tip them right over the edge!'

Xander laughed.

'I have no idea how I did that. The orb guided me straight to the spire, and I put my hands on it because I didn't know what else to do. Believe me, I was as shocked as everyone else.'

'So, is the Core fixed now?' asked Ollie curiously, looking

in awe at the glowing crystal soaring over them.

Reeve stepped over Latchet and went to retrieve as much of his gear as he could salvage from under the shattered wall. 'I'll have a look,' he said.

Hob turned around, glaring in disapproval at Reeve.

'Have a look?' he snorted. 'Can you not feel the Core yet without your foolish instruments?'

'Ah,' said Reeve, an impish expression crossing his face. 'All finished with the dancing then?' His voice was teasing and the hobgoblin glowered at him. He was obviously embarrassed by his earlier abandon, and as a result looked even more grumpy than usual.

'I was not dancing,' he snapped.

'Twirling, then? Leaping?' asked Reeve innocently. 'There was definitely cavorting. Sorry, my friend, but I am unlikely to ever forget that sight.'

Hob turned his back with great dignity, growling furiously under his breath, and Xander smothered a smile. Clearly, things were now right back to normal.

'Since the disaster appears to have been averted, is there any chance that we could leave now?' demanded Len, plaintively. 'We've been down in this dusty cavern so long that I'm breaking out into hives. I need some fresh air.'

'Leave?' said Hob, looking around with disbelief. 'What do you mean – leave? There is much to do here, ancient secrets to uncover. I am staying.' He rested his hand on the crystal matrix in a caressing gesture. It was quite clear that nothing would induce the hobgoblin to go, probably for a very long time.

Reeve waved them on. 'He's right. We've got a lot of work to do and we'll need to get some teams down here – both hob and human.'

Hob eyed him darkly for a moment, his face wreathed in

suspicion and hostility. Then, once again, his gaze flickered to Alf and, rather reluctantly, he nodded.

'We will work together – if the Elders permit it. It is time to let some of the secrets be told.'

Reeve's face lit up with pleasure and the hobgoblin grimaced. 'Don't get carried away, human,' he growled quickly. 'I only said *some*.'

The engineer just grinned at him.

'*Some* is a good place to start,' he said cheerfully. '*Some* we can build from, together.'

With a suppressed smile at Hob's obvious misgivings, Xander turned to Rafe.

'Shall we head up?' he asked, and then glanced at Latchet and Simm. 'What about them?'

'No problem,' rumbled Alf and bent down to scoop up Latchet and then Simm, dangling one over each shoulder. Latchet was still limp, while Simm muttered continually but made no further movement.

Xander waved to Hob and Reeve.

'See you upstairs,' he said with a quick grin, and then turned with relief to head for the way out.

CHAPTER FOURTEEN

Xander felt the exit before he saw it, a sudden touch of cooler air, and he hurried forward. The ward glittered with stars as he approached and he began to run, relief and exultation sweeping through him as he burst through the shimmering barrier and out into the night air.

They had actually done it! He spun around to face the others as they emerged, a huge grin on his face, and then took a step backwards in awe. The constellation wall was ablaze, and the Pavilions were glowing, lit up from within as if the building itself was aware and celebrating the events of the night. Xander heard Ollie and Len gasp as they came out after him, staring about in wonderment. Alf was more phlegmatic, as he lumbered through the ward with Latchet and Simm slung over his shoulders like sacks of flour. Xander could see the darkening of a spectacular black eye on Latchet, where Reeve had punched him, and Simm hung limp now, his eyes blank. The giant grunted when he saw the beautiful glow of the Pavilions and carefully laid his burdens on the stone floor.

Struck by a sudden urge, Xander's feet carried him forward, away from the constellation wall and down to the long stone veranda overlooking the lake. After all the struggle and emotion of the past few days, he felt an overwhelming need for stillness. The shining Pavilions were reflected in the quiet waters of the lake like an underwater palace, the soft ripples making it appear unreal. Looking up, the sky was as black as the lake water and Xander caught his breath at the millions of pinpoints of light, blazing brighter than he could ever remember before. He gazed wide-eyed, standing there in the silence, and thought he would remember this exact moment for all of his life.

'It is beautiful, no?'

The deep, rumbling voice from behind him made Xander jump. He turned, surprised at how silently the giant could move when he chose and then nodded, with a smile.

'I've never seen the stars so bright,' he answered quietly. 'But maybe I've just never looked properly before.'

'Tonight is special,' said Alf, with a smile. 'It will be remembered for a long time.'

There was a pause and Xander almost turned to leave, when he heard Alf's voice rumbling out of the darkness again.

'And let them be for signs, and for seasons and for days and years.'

Xander stared at the giant and Alf cleared his throat like a gravel slide, looking down.

'We have forgotten so much of the old lore,' he said wistfully. 'But maybe we will find it again, our old knowing. We built wonders together, once.' His eyes swept over the Pavilions again, but this time there was a light in them and he stood a little straighter.

Xander patted him on the elbow, which was as high as he could reach, and then turned as Ollie appeared around the corner.

'Amazing isn't it?' he said cheerfully, his eyes bright. 'Although Hob might have to work out how to turn it down a bit for parties or else we'll all be walking around squinting.'

Xander laughed out loud, feeling normality beginning to settle down like a comfortable blanket around his shoulders.

Ollie's practical, matter-of-fact cheerfulness was the perfect antidote to the high drama of the evening.

'Are you guys coming?' Ollie continued. 'Rafe and Suze are guarding the prisoners, but he thinks we should get back and brief Flint.'

Xander nodded, with one last glance at the starlit lake.

'Sounds like a good idea,' he said. 'Is Len there too?'

Ollie looked surprised.

'Len? I thought she came with you.'

Xander shook his head but in an echo of an earlier time, there was a distinct splashing noise from the shallow steps down to the lake. A moment later Len herself appeared, trudging up the steps with her clothes dripping and her hair plastered across her face. She lifted her head as she noticed them all standing staring at her and pressed her lips firmly together. Xander opened his mouth to say something and Len pinned him with that familiar look, scraping her hair out of her mouth with a defiant tilt of her head. Xander closed his mouth again and exchanged a rueful look with Ollie.

'We know,' Ollie said, a small smile tugging at his mouth. 'Don't ask.'

Len nodded tartly and attempted to sweep past them in dignified silence, her shoes squelching noisily with every step.

Their triumphant return turned out to be rather more dramatic than Xander had hoped. They were met at the front door by a harried-looking Mrs Stanton, who swept all three of them into a tight hug, murmuring something Xander couldn't hear, although he could feel her shaking. Then she pulled back and glared at them, before spotting Rafe with his scratched and battered face and behind him Alf, lurking in the darkness and holding out Simm and Latchet like some bizarre offering. She took a deep breath and then summoned her characteristic poise.

'Please, could you bring those two to the back door?' she asked Alf, and then turned to the others. 'Kitchen, now.'

There was still a crowd in the kitchen when they entered it again, although it was quieter than the frantic bustle of earlier. As Ollie went in first, there was the sound of a chair scraping back and Jenna, her face tired and her hair rumpled, launched herself forward to hug him.

'Honestly, I'm fine, Mum,' muttered Ollie, his face flushing with embarrassment although Xander saw that he was hugging her back. Out of the corner of his eye, he noticed Jasper Stanton standing by the other end of the table, his eyes fixed on Len.

'Where on earth were you all?' Jenna demanded, reverting to maternal annoyance after a quick, relieved glance at Len and Xander. 'And what possessed you to go out tonight of all nights? You knew it was dangerous. You could have been killed.'

'I would also like to know where you were,' Flint interjected, stepping out from the group near the hearth and interrupting Jenna's increasingly high-pitched interrogation. His gaze rested on Rafe, standing behind them, and then his eyes widened as Alf appeared, bending awkwardly through the back door. The giant deposited Latchet and Simm on the kitchen floor, Latchet looking dazed as he began to come around.

'Please excuse, but I think these two need a healer,' he rumbled apologetically, but Xander saw the quick flicker of amusement in his eyes as he straightened.

It was quite satisfying to see Flint rendered speechless. Mrs Stanton and James hurried forward to bend over the two prone figures, while Flint swung around to stare at Xander.

'Any chance of an explanation here?' he demanded, his eyes flicking between Xander and Rafe, who was suppressing a smile. He pulled out a chair by the table and gestured abruptly to the other side. They all sat, and Xander glanced at Rafe.

'Oh no,' said Rafe, with a wry grin. 'This is definitely your story to tell.'

A small crowd gathered around them as Xander, Ollie and Len once again poured out the story of the last couple of weeks, culminating in the events of tonight. They were incoherent, and fairly obvious in their avoidance of naming Xander's rescuers, but Flint just sat back in his chair, listening without interrupting, although his eyebrows shot up at several points in the story. After they had finished, there was a short silence, and then Flint let out a long breath and stared at the ceiling. Xander felt the tension pinning him to his chair.

'Well,' said Flint finally, in an even voice. 'I would suggest that you appear to have an absolute genius for trouble, but that wouldn't take into account the apparent determination of trouble to seek you out.'

He shook his head and then, to Xander's shock, started to laugh, his eyes crinkling. Rafe's lips quirked as well and Xander stared blankly at them both. Amusement was definitely not the response he had expected.

'Right, if you're all quite finished,' said Mrs Stanton, bustling up with a stern expression on her face. 'It's very late and these three children need to be in bed. Any further discussion can be postponed until the morning, which is almost here.'

'But Gran,' protested Ollie, but she would have none of it.

Xander did not object, admitting to himself that the only

place he wanted to be right now was in bed. The re-telling of the story to Flint had brought home to him how much had happened in the past day, and he felt heavy with exhaustion. He stood up, swaying slightly, and then felt a firm grip on his shoulder. Flint had come around the table and was standing in front of him, his intense blue eyes warmer than Xander ever remembered.

'Having said all that,' he said quietly, ignoring Mrs Stanton's tutting, 'you've done us proud. I still don't know what brought you here but, whatever it was, I'm grateful for it.'

Xander was embarrassed to feel tears suddenly pricking at the back of his eyes, but Flint seemed to understand, squeezing his shoulder again before turning away to speak to Rafe. Xander barely remembered stumbling upstairs or kicking off his shoes before falling into bed, too exhausted to do anything else, but as he plunged down into deep sleep, it was buoyed with the memory of Flint's approving look.

The sun was shining brightly through the window, filling the room with golden light, when Xander woke up. He could hear heavy breathing coming from Ollie's corner and for a moment, as he shifted uncomfortably, he wondered why he was wearing his trousers in bed. He sat up, groggily pushing the hair out of his face, and his eyes fell on the papers scattered across the floor, covered in sigils and star patterns. Memory shot through him like an electric current, bringing him upright with his feet on the floor in a moment, staring wide-eyed around the room. The events of the day before had a dream-like quality, and he needed some confirmation that it had all actually happened. He grabbed a pillow and hurled it into the back of Ollie's head.

'Wha –?' Ollie's voice was thick with sleep. 'Why does ever'one keep doing that?'

'Wake up,' said Xander. 'I need to talk to you.'

'What's up?' Ollie was never quick to wake up at the best of times and now he rolled over reluctantly, his sandy hair standing on end, before looking down at himself in confusion. 'I'm dressed?'

His eyes suddenly widened, and he sat up abruptly.

'There it is,' grinned Xander, as he tugged on his shoes.

'I can't believe all that really happened,' said Ollie, before leaping up and diving for the door. 'Bathroom first,' he threw over his shoulder.

Five minutes later, both boys, looking rather rumpled, were pounding down the stairs. After all the turmoil and crowds of yesterday, the house was peaceful and warm sunshine poured in at every window. The kitchen door stood ajar and Xander pushed it open. The room was almost deserted, with only the solitary figure of Len at the table, eating a bowl of cereal. She glanced up as they came in and smiled condescendingly.

'Finally up, are we?' she said.

'Yeah, right,' retorted Ollie. 'Pull the other one. You've only just got up yourself, haven't you?'

Len grinned, dropping the superior air. 'You don't know that.'

'Yes, I do,' returned Ollie. 'You've still got pillow creases on your face.'

'Where is everyone?' asked Xander, interrupting before they could progress to bickering. The kitchen looked so normal and peaceful it was hard to believe that only a few hours ago Latchet and Simm had been lying unconscious on the floor.

'No idea,' said Len, shrugging. 'Haven't seen anyone yet.'

The front door banged, and they all turned to see who was home. There were swift footsteps on the stone floor and then Mrs Stanton swept into the kitchen, looking as immaculate as ever and certainly not as if she had been up half of the night. Her eyes took in the three of them and she smiled.

'Good,' she said briskly. 'I hoped you were all up by now. You were flat out when I checked on you an hour ago.'

Ollie pulled a face at Len, who grimaced cheerfully back at him.

'What's been happening while we were asleep?' asked Xander, anxiously.

Mrs Stanton began filling up the kettle.

'Well, it's been quite a morning, I can tell you,' she said, but her tart tone was softened by a surprisingly mischievous smile. 'The Council is in emergency session, mostly flapping like flummoxed chickens and achieving very little, but that's pretty much expected. The only thing that they seem to have firmly determined is that none of them are responsible in any way.' She sniffed contemptuously and then glanced over at Xander. 'They do want to speak to you, dear.'

'Me?'

Xander felt a lurch of fear and it must have shown on his face because Mrs Stanton gave him a reassuring look.

'Don't worry, you won't be going there alone. Flint and some other Travellers will be with you, and Reeve as well if we can drag him out of the Pavilions.'

Xander offered her a wavering smile, but he felt ill at the thought of standing before all those people in the enormous Council chamber.

'What about Simm and Latchet?' asked Ollie, around a mouthful of bread and honey.

'Ah,' said Mrs Stanton, a slight hesitation in her voice.

'Well, Latchet only had a mild concussion and was suffering from shade exposure. He's recovering, although he may soon wish that he was not. The list of charges against him is mounting, and I don't think the investigation will treat him very kindly. He claims to have no memory of what happened in the Pavilions and that he was just following Simm's orders. We'll see how that pans out for him.'

'And Simm?' asked Len.

Mrs Stanton looked evasive. 'He appears physically fine,' she said.

'He completely lost it last night,' said Ollie, rolling his eyes. 'I mean, he was always a bit weird, but he was ranting and raving like a nutcase. Pretty freaky, actually.'

Mrs Stanton ignored this, putting a sandwich in front of Xander with a swift look at his pale face. 'Eat up,' she said gently. 'We need to leave in a minute.'

Under her firm gaze, Xander choked down some food and a cup of strong tea. Mrs Stanton also insisted that he shower, and change into something less wrinkled. Anxiety continued to gnaw in Xander's stomach, but he had to admit that he felt better when he was clean and dressed in fresh clothes. They all headed out together, walking down to the Wykeham Gate. Len nudged him with her elbow as they went, and he glanced over at her. Mrs Stanton had sent Ollie and Len to wash as well and her damp hair, smelling strongly of lavender shampoo, swung over her face. She smiled at him.

'Don't worry,' she murmured. 'It's not like they can do anything to you. You're not even from Haven. Maybe they just want to say thanks.'

'Maybe,' muttered Xander, but he was not reassured. She was right about the fact that Haven was not his home and he didn't have a place here, however welcoming the Stantons were, and however much he had grown to like it. This whole episode had caused a lot of damage and expense, and Xander was gloomily certain that he would be blamed for at least some of it. He didn't think they could actually lock him up, but they could decide to banish him from Haven and he felt sick at the thought of never seeing it again.

All in all, Xander was feeling thoroughly pessimistic by the time they reached Fountain Square and the steps of the Council chamber. He felt a twinge of relief as he spotted Flint, Rafe and Reeve waiting for him in front of the door. Rafe gave him a reassuring smile, but Xander was shocked to see the damage to his face in the clear sunlight. He was still bruised and scraped, despite the clear evidence of Mrs Stanton's healing work, and Xander remembered with a shiver how Simm had launched himself at the Traveller, shrieking and ranting. Callan Reeve looked absolutely exhausted, his untidy black hair even more of a contrast with his pale, tired face, but his eyes were glowing with satisfaction and he was the first to speak.

'You've got to come and see,' he said to them, without even a greeting. 'It's all coming back online and it's breathtaking. The complexity is something I have never seen before – it'll take a lifetime to study, maybe more.'

'Save it for inside,' broke in Flint, characteristically impatient. 'Come on, they're all waiting for us.'

Far too quickly for Xander's jangled nerves, they passed through the atrium to the security point where Pritchard was on duty again. He tipped his cap to Xander with a gap-toothed grin.

'We'll have to be getting you a permanent access card soon,' he said with a wink.

Flint looked sharply at Xander, one eyebrow raised quizzically, but didn't comment. The noise from the chamber had been evident from the moment they had entered the building, muffled by the great doors into a loud hum, like a busy hive full of bees. When they walked into the chamber it reached a sudden peak and then died down to a low, whispering murmur.

It seemed to Xander, his heart thumping rapidly, that the place had never been so full and that every eye there was burning into him as he walked between Flint and Rafe. He ducked his head and was grateful when they reached the small group, which had evidently been waiting for him to the left of the main dais. Ari's red hair was a beacon among them and Xander edged his way through to stand beside her, insulated by the others from the staring eyes. She turned to him with a grin and Xander noticed that she had a bandage on her arm.

'Finally decided to re-join the living then?' she said in an amused voice. 'You've missed some real fun and games here.'

'What happened to you?' asked Xander.

Ari shrugged. 'Got a bit exciting at Mistleberry,' she said casually. 'Thanks for the warning, by the way. We took extra people there, which was lucky because the place was literally crawling with shades. It was starting to get pretty bad, but then the air started shimmering like a rainbow and all the shades disappeared. Apparently that was your handiwork?'

Xander flushed but Ari just gave him a mock pout.

'I can't believe after all the time I spent training you, that you upped and left me out of all the fun,' she said, teasingly. 'Most unfair.'

'We clearly have different definitions of the word *fun*,' retorted Xander. He paused and then asked in a rush. 'Will I have to stand up there and tell about everything?' His throat tightened as he asked and his fingernails dug into his palms.

Ari smiled and shook her head.

'It's okay,' she said. 'Rafe and Flint already briefed them this morning.'

Xander's head shot up. 'What? About everything?'

'Hardly,' replied Ari, with a roll of her eyes. 'Need to know only. Flint is good at skating where necessary.'

Why am I here, then? Xander wondered silently. He wished he could have heard what they had said, so he didn't disclose anything he shouldn't when it was his turn. Suddenly, he heard Callan Reeve's voice, calmly replying to a question, and realised that he was already up on the podium. Reeve did not appear at all concerned by the formality of the occasion and was answering with all the enthusiasm of a professor lecturing on his favourite subject. Judging from the somewhat perplexed looks of several Council members, Reeve's explanations were more detailed than they expected. Xander smiled, despite his worry about his own summons.

Enid Ingram finally leant forward, her eyes bright behind her spectacles.

'Young man, we are unfortunately not all blessed with your technical expertise,' she said in her precise voice. 'Are we to understand that what your team activated last night is in fact the original Core on Haven, of which our current power sources are merely adjuncts?'

Reeve beamed at her. 'That is correct, Councillor.'

'And are we further correct in thinking the power from this restored Core will now rectify all the recent, regrettable incidents with border integrity and power surges?' she continued.

'That is our current belief, Councillor,' replied Reeve. 'Hopefully, the joint team working there will confirm this shortly, but it appears that the incursions disappeared the moment that the Core came back on line.'

'Well,' said Ingram, sitting back in her chair with an air of relief and eying Melville and Larcius sharply. 'It seems all has been resolved to our satisfaction then.'

Barton Ferrars harrumphed in agreement. 'Hear, hear,' he said happily. 'It's also most fitting that this enterprise should have healed the painful divisions between humans and hobs. Joint team, eh? Most gratifying indeed.' He beamed around at everyone.

Felix Larcius' face looked like he had bitten into something particularly sour, but Melville's expression was as smooth as ever, his smile silky and condescending.

'Oh, quite,' Melville drawled, his gaze flickering over to where Xander stood, half-hidden behind Flint's broad back. 'However, I find myself still curious on a number of matters, including how that boy came to acquire the key to reactivate the original Core, not to mention the knowledge of its location, which we are led to believe had been lost for at least a century.' A malicious smile flickered over his face as his cold grey eyes met Xander's own worried ones. 'How fortunate that he is here now. No doubt he will be able to provide explanations to us. I summon the outlander boy to the stand.'

Xander's throat tightened as Melville gestured to him, and it felt like every eye was once more staring at him. He stumbled towards the podium, which seemed to rear up above him ready to expose him like a sacrifice. Reeve passed him on the way down and briefly squeezed his arm.

'Don't worry,' he murmured. 'It'll be fine.'

Xander strongly doubted that as he climbed up the steps, his eyes on the floor while he wished fervently that he was anywhere but here. All too soon, he reached the top and reluctantly looked up at the Council members but, to his surprise, none of them were looking at him and Melville had an annoyed frown on his face.

Xander shot a look over his shoulder and felt a surge of relief. Flint was standing there behind him, hands in his pockets and wearing a bland smile as he gazed back at the Council.

Irini Latimer spoke first, her beautiful features cold and her lips thin with irritation. 'I believe that we have already heard from you today, Mr Flint,' she snapped. 'It is the boy's testimony that we require now.'

Flint continued to smile.

'And you shall have it, Councillor. Xander is, however, a minor and therefore he is entitled to an Advocate. I'm quite certain that none of us would wish for a breach of the Council's protocols here.'

Latimer's eyes narrowed but Barton Ferrars leant forward over the table, flapping his hands reassuringly.

'Of course, of course. Quite right, entirely appropriate. We shouldn't be questioning the young fellow without an Advocate,' he said, nodding in affirmation.

Xander noticed that not only did Melville, Larcius and Latimer look put out, but that a frown also chased across the pleasant face of Randall Hackett. Enid Ingram looked at him with her piercing eyes, but her face was not unkind.

'I understand that you are not from Haven? You are in fact an outlander?' Ingram said. Xander nodded, and she continued. 'We further understand that you had no knowledge of Haven before you used the Stone to travel here?'

Xander nodded again.

'In that case, may I ask why the hobgoblins gifted you, a stranger here, with such a significant artefact as the orb which you wear on your wrist?'

Xander swallowed and then cleared his throat awkwardly.

'They said something about it being in my blood and that they had been waiting for me,' he said, his voice sounding high and unnatural in the silence. 'I didn't really understand it myself. The hobs don't tend to explain their reasoning.'

A flicker of a smile crossed Ingram's face, and she nodded, but Melville leant forward, his expression twisted with disbelief.

'Oh, come now,' he sneered. 'You cannot expect us to believe that they handed over such a powerful and significant stone to a strange boy for this garbled explanation.' He glared at Xander.

Before Xander could muster a reply, Flint's firm voice rang out from behind him.

'I believe, Councillor, that the point is the hobs themselves were unaware of the actual significance of the stone. Its origins were lost in time and only a fragment of an instruction survived to hand it over when the right person came along. In their minds, Xander was that person. They certainly had no idea that it would be instrumental in re-activating their ancient Core, since they didn't know that it existed.'

'How can you possibly know that?' snapped Melville. 'We want to hear from the boy, not your speculations.'

'No speculation,' replied Flint evenly. 'I discussed the matter with the hobs when they first gave Xander the orb.'

Melville's eyes flashed with annoyance, before he returned to the attack. 'And how is it that you, having barely arrived in Haven, knew exactly where to find this long-lost Core? It took months of painstaking work for Simm and his team to identify and access this place, while you simply waltzed in the front door. How do you explain this?'

To Melville's evident fury, it was once again Flint who calmly responded.

'As I explained this morning, we believe that the power in

Xander's orb when he wore it into the Hall of Records temporarily reactivated an obsolete terminal, giving him enough information to find his way to the Core. Clearly, it was an ancient program, keyed to that particular stone being worn by an appropriate individual, but given the age of the system it could only pass on fragments.'

'That certainly sounds plausible,' said Horace Peverell, interjecting for the first time. His usual air of quiet gravitas had many of the Council members nodding along with him. Xander stood very still, trying to keep his face expressionless, as Reeve's opinion about the unlikelihood of that theory ran through his mind. Knowing the engineer's propensity to correct technical mistakes, he braced himself for an objection, but there was only silence behind him.

Melville and Larcius were whispering furiously as Latimer spoke up again in her clipped voice.

'The Council's Nexus liaison, Mr Simm, is currently unable to address this chamber and his deputy, Mr Latchet, is claiming to have no memory of the events of last evening.' She stared beadily down at Xander and her accusing look seemed to indicate that she held him personally responsible. 'Can you shed any light on what may have caused their unfortunate incapacity?'

Xander opened his mouth and then shut it again firmly. He was certain that he knew what or, more accurately, *who* was responsible and he shivered at the memory of Gage's twisted face, lit up with malice in the sickly green light. There was no point even mentioning him however, as there wasn't a single other person who could confirm his existence. Xander stared back steadily at Latimer.

'I don't know,' he said. 'Mr Simm was already –' he hesitated, searching for the right words. 'Totally nuts' didn't seem like an appropriate description to give to the Council. 'He seemed a bit disturbed when he came through from the Nexus. He wasn't really making any sense and then he attacked Rafe. The shades came next and everything got a bit confusing.'

'Indeed,' interjected Enid Ingram. 'I'm sure that it was a most disturbing incident.'

She continued talking, but Xander's attention was distracted by Marcus Melville and Felix Larcius. To his shock, Perrin Thorne was now standing behind them, leaning down to whisper while his cold black eyes remained fixed on Xander. Xander felt a queasy feeling in his stomach at the sheer hatred in that stare; it meant nothing good for him, he was quite certain. He only just caught Enid Ingram's final words.

'If no-one else has anything to add, then I think we can dismiss the young lad.'

Melville raised a languid hand.

'Actually, I believe that there are a few more unanswered questions but I quite agree that we should allow the boy to step out of the full glare of a Council hearing. We can much more conveniently explore all the parameters of this case in a private setting. Since the boy is not from Haven and has no guardianship arrangements, it would be most appropriate if we on the Council take responsibility for him and his disposition. We wouldn't want to overlook proper protocols.'

His eyes glittered triumphantly as he looked at Flint and Xander stiffened, his throat dry, as he heard the whispers rising again across the chamber. Perrin Thorne was smiling in satisfaction, his thick lips glistening moistly.

Flint strode forward to Xander's side. 'He belongs with us. He doesn't require Council guardianship,' he snapped.

Melville's mouth stretched into a mirthless grin.

'I'm afraid that you have no authority to claim him, Flint.'

At least half of the Council members were nodding in agreement and Xander felt sick.

'You are quite correct,' said a cool voice from behind the podium. 'However, you will find that *we* do have that authority.'

Xander risked a quick glance backwards and his jaw dropped. Stepping out from among the crowd, and moving forward to surround the base of the podium were Alwyn Atherton, Gerrold Stavish, Edric Wooten, Kirrin Ledger and the rest of the Wardens. Jory Bardolph caught Xander's eye and winked at him. Atherton fixed steely eyes upon the Council members, his gaze particularly lingering on Melville.

'Xander King is a Traveller and therefore does not require your kind offer of guardianship.'

Xander's eyes widened at this, his heart pounding in shock and surprise, as the sound of whispering swept through the chamber behind him like a rushing wind.

Melville snorted. 'The boy is an outlander,' he said with a dismissive wave of his hand. 'Can anyone claim to be a Traveller now?'

Gerrold Stavish tipped his head back and regarded Melville with an amused air. 'If one can control a Traveller's Stone to cross Haven's border, use all the capabilities of a hob-orb and strike down shades then, yes,' he replied dryly, 'I believe that one could accurately be termed a Traveller.'

While Melville scowled furiously, obviously casting about for another argument, Atherton gestured to what had now become a large crowd of Travellers, many of them sporting bandages or other evidence of shade-strike.

'The boy is one of us and is therefore not subject to your jurisdiction. He has been courteous enough to come and answer your questions, as have others of us,' his glance flickered to Rafe and Flint. 'However, Travellers do not answer to the Council of Twelve, and we are outside your power to command or detain. We will withdraw now and leave you to your deliberations.'

He nodded solemnly to Barton Ferrars, while Melville spluttered audibly. Ferrars rose to the occasion, bowing his head politely.

'Absolutely right. The Council is most grateful to the Wardens for their kind co-operation and to the Travellers for their service in defence of Haven. We have just had a timely reminder of our debt to them.'

Flint nudged Xander's arm. 'Time to go,' was all he said, although a little grin tugged at his lips.

Xander's knees felt wobbly with relief and he concentrated carefully on his footing as he stumbled down the stairs. At the bottom he found himself face to face with the phalanx of Wardens. Atherton, his usually stern face lightened by an unaccustomed twinkle in his pale blue eyes, put an arm around Xander with a rather theatrical flourish and drew him into the group.

'Oh, I do enjoy tweaking the Council's collective noses,' he murmured in Xander's ear.

In a matter of moments, the whole group of Travellers had closed ranks around Xander and they walked out of the Council chamber together. The noise behind him was rising to a hubbub, but Xander's feet seemed to carry him forward without conscious thought, as his head swirled with emotions. Only when they had reached the steps outside, and he felt the warm sunshine on his face, did he take a deep breath. All around him, he heard laughter and warm words, while many hands patted him on the back or squeezed his arm.

Atherton, who was still standing next to Xander with a

genial smile, turned to face him.

'Welcome to the Travellers, Xander. But,' he said, lifting a cautionary finger, 'be aware that as one of us, you are under the Wardens' authority now. Next time you feel the urge to up-end the power dynamics of Haven, do come and run it by us first, old chap.' His expression was still amused, but his tone was serious and Xander nodded.

'Yes, sir,' he said politely. He still couldn't quite believe what had just happened.

Wooten, who looked as put out as usual, snorted cantankerously.

'Ha! I'll believe that when I see it,' he grouched.

Ollie bounded up, his hair standing on end, and Xander knew that his friend had been clutching it in worry for him. 'How amazing is this?' Ollie declared, a huge smile splitting his face. 'Did you see Thorne's face? It was epic when he realised that you were untouchable. And Melville looked like he was going to start chewing on the furniture. I bet him and Larcius are howling right now.'

'I'm just glad that it's over,' replied Xander honestly.

'Well, you're officially a Traveller now,' said Ollie. 'You belong here, just like I told you.'

You belong here. The words seemed to dance in front of Xander and then settle into the deepest part of him. He couldn't control the enormous smile which spread across his face.

'Well, are you coming or are you going to just stand there grinning like a nutter?'

Ari's light voice came from behind him and the next moment, she had caught him in a swift hug. She released him quickly, her nose wrinkling at Xander in an amused smile as he looked at her in confusion.

'Coming where?' he asked.

'To Whittlewood Lodge, of course. We're having a Gathering to celebrate. Are you ready?'

Xander opened his mouth to agree and then caught a glimpse of Mrs Stanton's elegant form crossing the square. Suddenly, he was certain that he knew where she was going.

'Can I catch up to you?' he asked Ari. 'There's just something I need to do.'

Ari grinned at him. 'As long as it's not something that the Wardens ought to know about,' she said warningly.

'Don't worry,' said Xander with a grin. 'I'm all out of mysterious messages.'

Ari laughed. 'Good,' she said. 'See you there later, then.' With a quick lift of her hand, she vanished.

'What do you need to do?' Ollie wanted to know, following Xander as he hurried across the square after Mrs Stanton. She was walking briskly and Xander only caught up to her as she turned into a small side street. She stopped as Xander and Ollie came abreast of her and turned to face them, one eyebrow raised in query.

'I thought you two would be off to the Gathering,' she said. 'It's largely being held in your honour.'

'Are you going to see Simm?' Xander blurted out.

'I am,' Mrs Stanton replied quietly.

'Can I come with you?'

Mrs Stanton eyed him thoughtfully, but she didn't seem overly surprised. 'Why do you want to do that?' she asked.

'I just –'

Xander hesitated. The memory of Simm's face as he came through into the Core was still vivid, but it was his words that had really stuck in Xander's mind. The others clearly thought Simm had just lost his mind but Xander had a strong feeling that there was something underlying what he had said, some meaning that he was not grasping. Simm had also been the only other person who had seen Gage, and he felt that had to be significant. The fact that the strange and malevolent man had apparently been invisible to everyone else was increasingly bothering Xander, and he really wanted to see if Simm remembered him.

'I just wanted to ask him something about last night,' he finished, rather lamely.

Mrs Stanton paused, and then nodded. 'Very well,' was all she said.

She led them a short distance along the narrow street and then climbed the steps to a large front door, deeply recessed and set between white columns. There was a discreet Institute of Healers sign set into the wall next to the door. She did not knock, simply placing her hand on the door and, as the coding in her orb flickered, it swung open smoothly and quietly.

Before them was a large entrance hall, with white-painted walls and a chequered floor in pristine black and white squares. A few paintings of peaceful pastoral scenes hung around the walls, while a white marble staircase with crisp black banisters rose from the middle of the hall. Everything was spotlessly clean. To the right of the staircase was a black marble desk, two tall pot plants standing on either side of it like sentinels, and sitting at the desk was a young woman in a crisp grey and white uniform. She glanced up from her screen as they entered.

'Hello, Healer Stanton,' she said, while her eyes flicked curiously to Xander and Ollie. 'Your patient was moved upstairs a few hours ago. He's on the second floor, room 212.'

'Thank you, Polly dear,' said Mrs Stanton. 'Has Healer Embert seen him yet?'

Polly nodded, still eying the two boys, but she didn't make

any objection as they followed behind Mrs Stanton. Xander looked around curiously as they went up the stairs. Long hallways opened off each landing that they passed, each one neutrally decorated and pristinely neat, and he saw figures moving along them, all dressed in either the white and grey uniform, or long white coats. There was an oddly muffled sense about the building, as if all sound was deadened, and even their footsteps on the marble staircase were muted. It made for a rather disquieting atmosphere and Xander shivered.

'Is this a hospital?' he asked Mrs Stanton in a whisper, because it felt wrong to speak too loudly in this place.

Mrs Stanton was evidently not affected in the same way, as she replied in her usual crisp tones. 'Not in the way you mean, Xander. It's not where you come when you are sick in your body. This is the Intuit Centre for mind healing. The healers here are at the top of their field and Embert is one of the best.'

'It's creepy, is what it is,' muttered Ollie.

His grandmother looked sharply at him. 'If you would prefer to wait downstairs, then I'm sure that Polly will find you a chair,' she said, but her voice was understanding.

Ollie shook his head. 'S'okay,' he said.

Mrs Stanton glanced at them both as they continued to climb.

'The Centre is kept quiet and calm to aid in the healing process,' she said. 'When peoples' minds are vulnerable, loud noises or voices can distress them. Each individual room has a noise-disrupting ward so that patients aren't disturbed if they need peace and quiet.'

She turned off into a hallway and began to walk down it. Xander noticed the same type of artwork as downstairs, set at precise distances along walls punctuated with wide doors made of an opaque, cloudy material, each with a number on it; they stopped at the door marked 212. Xander stared at the nearest picture, a bland still life of a bowl of apples, and wondered whether he was doing the right thing to come here. The image of Simm's face last night flashed through his mind, the man's mouth flecked with his own saliva and his high-pitched, furious shrieks. Suddenly, Xander felt very certain that he did not want to see Simm again.

Before he could say anything, he heard swift footsteps approaching from his right, and a small, rotund man in a white coat walked towards them with a welcoming smile. He was balding, with short grey hair, round glasses and the kindest face Xander had ever seen. His brown eyes twinkled irrepressibly, with laughter lines fanning out from their corners, and his smile was so reassuring that Xander felt his uncertainty melt away; the little man seemed to shine comfort and reassurance around him like a lamp. He beamed at Mrs Stanton.

'Come to check on our patient, Thea?' he said, and his warm voice matched his appearance. He winked at Xander and Ollie. 'Are these apprentices then?' he asked.

Mrs Stanton's lips twitched.

'Not exactly,' she said. 'This is my grandson, Oliver. Xander here is a Traveller. They were both with Mr Simm during his episode last night.'

'Ah, I see,' said Embert and, as he looked at them with those penetrating eyes, Xander got the strange impression that the healer really did see right into his thoughts. 'That must have been rather distressing for you. Hopefully, we can put your minds at rest. A most unusual case, to be sure.'

'How is he settling?' asked Mrs Stanton.

'Oh, less agitated now,' replied Embert. 'He calmed down once we provided him with something to write with; as you know, art can be very therapeutic and give us insights into a patient's state of mind. In his case, certainly, it is a rather strange manifestation but I'm sure that we'll figure it out.'

He lifted a hand towards the door, then paused and looked at the two boys.

'Our doors are made of a very special material. It can be opaque, as you see here, or else I can de-polarise it and we will be able to see through it. It will continue to appear opaque on the patient's side, so we won't disturb them. You'll see Mr Simm but he won't be able to see or hear you, okay?'

With a reassuring nod, Embert touched the door. The coding on his orb flickered, and the door disappeared, or so it seemed, leaving the little black numerals hanging apparently unsupported in the air.

The room looked warm and comfortable, with calm blue walls and bright coloured cushions on the bed, but Xander's eyes were immediately drawn to the man within it. In total contrast to his usual flamboyant appearance, Simm was wearing soft green trousers and a plain top in the same colour. Crouching barefoot on the floor near one wall with his back turned to the door, he hummed a soft repetitive sound which made the hair on Xander's neck prickle uncomfortably. He was drawing intently on the wall with a crayon and had already covered the whole of the lower portion with the same symbol drawn over and over again, a figure eight at every conceivable angle, some tiny and others drawn with great sweeps of the crayon. That sense of wrongness still hung about Simm like a cloud and, with a shudder, Xander felt the absolute certainty that whatever this all meant, it was nothing good.

'As yet, we don't know the significance to him of the number eight but hopefully we can get to the bottom of that in therapy,' said Embert. 'He hasn't said very much except for some ramblings about 'dark powers', possibly a reaction to shade exposure.'

'Hmm,' said Mrs Stanton thoughtfully. 'This may be quite deep-seated. When the Council retrieved his files from his office this morning, the Nexus Liaison folders were filled with sheets of paper covered with eights, drawn over and over, the same as he is doing here. The Council was quite put out by it, I believe.'

'Fascinating,' said Embert. 'We'll need to explore when this behaviour first manifested itself and hopefully we can then find out what triggered it.'

I know what triggered it, thought Xander, or rather *who* was the trigger; the man that only he and Simm could see. He watched as Simm shifted position to draw on a different section of wall.

'Weird,' said Ollie suddenly. 'Look at where he was before. If you look at it sideways, it almost looks like you can make out a face in all that scribbling.'

He lifted a hand to point, but Xander had already seen it and a sudden chill prickled his spine. Perfectly represented out of hundreds of number eights was Gage's face, staring out of the wall with that familiar malevolent look. Xander flinched and looked away, only to meet the perceptive gaze of Healer Embert.

'You recognise him,' he said gently.

Xander nodded. 'He was always with Simm but no-one else could see him. He brought the shades last night, and I think he did this to Simm.' He looked down at the floor, not wanting to see the predictable disbelief. Embert reached over and touched his arm.

'He frightened you, this man you saw?'

Xander's head jerked up to find the kind brown eyes regarding him with quiet compassion. 'You believe me?' he said, surprised that he knew with certainty this was true.

'I do,' said the healer. 'In the course of my practice I have seen too many strange things to put all of my faith in the material world.'

Mrs Stanton looked sceptical and Embert grinned at her, as if he was acknowledging a long-standing debate between them.

'My dear Thea, you are a most excellent healer, combating issues of flesh and blood and successfully knitting them back into good working order. On our side however, we frequently wrestle with matters of the soul and the spirit. Less tangible but, in the end, no less real.'

Mrs Stanton rolled her eyes good-humouredly at him but didn't argue further.

Xander took a breath.

'If it helps, the man's name is Gage.'

In the room, the humming stopped. Simm froze and then slowly pivoted on his heels, still in a crouch on the floor. He stared straight at Xander as if the door was not there, with eyes that burned with sudden intensity, and then hissed, a shockingly loud sound. Xander took a hurried step backwards.

'I thought you said that he couldn't see or hear us?' said Ollie, shakily.

'He can't,' said Embert, his voice puzzled. 'Although this is certainly very strange.'

As abruptly as he had turned, Simm went back to his drawing, his fingers moving ceaselessly, round and round in figures of eight. The humming started up again. Xander took a shuddering breath and decided that he would be very happy if he never laid eyes on Simm again.

'Very odd,' repeated Embert, then seemed to recall himself and smiled at Mrs Stanton. 'I hope that your mind is at rest on his physical health. I'll be delighted to keep you updated on his progress, if you would like.' As he spoke, he touched the door again, and it reverted back to its previous opaque appearance; the humming cut off. Xander's shoulders sagged in relief.

Mrs Stanton said something in response and the two healers turned back towards the staircase, chatting easily. Xander hurried after them, wanting to get far away from room 212 and this strange, muffled building where the silence seemed suddenly deafening.

'That was seriously weird,' muttered Ollie.

'Yep,' said Xander shortly. He really didn't want to talk about it. Ollie appeared to get the hint and didn't make any further comments.

Healer Embert bade them a cheerful goodbye at the top of the stairs, and then turned away as another healer waved a clipboard at him. Xander hurried down the stairs, his steps getting faster and faster, dashed through the reception hall and practically burst out of the large front door into the sunny street outside. He took several deep breaths.

A moment later, Mrs Stanton emerged, Ollie just behind, and she looked sympathetically at Xander before slipping an arm through his and steering them away from the Centre.

'It is a strange place,' she said gently. 'They do incredible work there, but it's understandable to feel a little uncomfortable. Many people do.'

Xander felt warmed by her obvious concern for him.

'I'm okay,' he said, and Mrs Stanton squeezed his arm.

'Good,' she said, resuming her usual brisk tone, 'because it's high time that we got to your party. Flint will be fretting that you're getting into adventures again. Will you do the honours?'

'Huh?' said Xander, looking baffled.

'We need to get there, and I believe that you are the only

Traveller in the vicinity,' replied Mrs Stanton in an amused voice.

Xander felt a sudden flush of happiness and a huge smile spread across his face. With a small flourish, he offered an arm to Ollie and Mrs Stanton. 'My pleasure,' he said and, as they laid a hand each on his forearm, he leant confidently into the power of his orb and felt the now familiar lurch of his stomach as space bent itself around him.

CHAPTER FIFTEEN

That evening was one of the best that Xander had ever spent. From the moment they arrived at the Lodge, where the bonfires were already ablaze, he was greeted with welcoming shouts and warm smiles from the many Travellers who were already there. Xander saw that quite a number of them had suffered injuries from the shade incursions, but everyone joined in the festivities with the same air of happiness and relief. Mouth-watering smells were drifting over from the cooking station, while the sounds of assorted instruments arose from near the Lodge as musicians experimented with various tunes, some gently melodic and others more swinging. Children dashed around, shouting to each other while the adults smiled indulgently. Many of the children gazed wide-eyed at Xander and the bolder ones called out 'Hi, Xander' to him, to the obvious admiration of their shyer companions. Xander smiled at them all, feeling a deep well of happiness brimming up inside him.

Zach, Milo and the other younger Travellers hurried forward to meet them and Milo flung a friendly arm around Xander's shoulders, drawing him into their group as they all clamoured eagerly for inside information.

'How d'you know where to go?'

'Did those two Liaison blokes really lose their minds and try to kill you?'

'Were there seriously thousands of shades there waiting for you?'

Xander suddenly noticed that Ollie was hanging back a little, swept aside by the press of numbers, and he paused.

'If you want to know about shades,' he said firmly to them all, turning around to gesture to Ollie, 'you need to talk to this guy. He held off a wall of them from him and Len, all by himself with only a busted synthetic orb.'

'Seriously?' asked Tomas in surprise, while they all turned to stare at Ollie who flushed, shuffling his feet, before nodding awkwardly. 'Wow, that's amazing.'

Ollie's face broke into a grin.

'Terrifying, is what it was,' he said frankly. 'I thought we were goners, for sure.'

'Wow,' repeated Zach, sounding awed and rather envious of the near-death experience. The group immediately shifted to encompass Ollie as well, bombarding him with questions, and Xander smiled to himself.

Food was pressed on them from all sides, and everyone was keen to hear about how the Wardens had faced down the Council. There was general amusement about Melville, Larcius and Thorne and how they had been out-smarted, and then they all wanted the details of the events at the Pavilions and how the Core had been reactivated. Xander felt rather shy about recounting it all, but Ollie had no such reticence and told the story with great relish several times over. He did not linger on, or embellish, the part about the lightning storm from Xander's orb obliterating the shades, but Xander caught several thoughtful looks from the Wardens at this point, and tried to look as innocuous as possible. He really didn't need them worrying about whether he had any ambitions to move to Mount Olympus and set himself up as a god on his return.

As he sat cross-legged in the middle of the group, the light and warmth of the fire washing over his face, Xander could hardly believe that only a few weeks ago he had been a stranger here, the Traveller community closed to him as to any other outsider. In the Council chamber they had come for him, accepted and defended him as one of their own, and Xander could not stop himself from smiling in the warm glow of belonging.

Later, when a group of enthusiastic singers had joined the musicians and people were reduced to picking at the left-overs of the feast, Xander wandered over to a big old log and sat down. He was flanked by Ollie and Len, who in her usual manner had only reappeared once the initial hubbub had died down, and he warmed his feet by the flickering flames of the bonfire. Len was gazing up at the starry sky thoughtfully.

'I can't believe we actually did it,' she said suddenly. 'It's a bit sad, really.'

Xander swivelled around to gape at her, open-mouthed.

'Seriously?' he said incredulously.

'Well, not exactly sad,' allowed Len, and then shrugged. 'It was all just really exciting, and now everything will go back to being boring and normal.'

Xander sputtered with disbelief. 'I'm quite happy with boring and normal, thank you very much,' he said fervently. 'Getting chased around by shades and nearly dying isn't my idea of great fun.'

Ollie swallowed his latest mouthful with some effort.

'Too right,' he said but then added pensively, 'I have a feeling that it isn't exactly over though. There are still a lot of unexplained things on our list.'

Len sat up immediately, her eyes bright, but Xander just laughed.

'Maybe,' he said. 'But not tonight, okay?'

'Not plotting any more wild adventures, I hope,' said a jolly voice from behind them. All three jumped slightly and turned, a little guiltily, to see the beaming face of Jory Bardolph, his white hair glowing in the firelight and looking wilder than ever. With him were Ari, Rafe, the neat dark figure of Kirrin Ledger and Flint, while a group of the younger Travellers gathered to sprawl around the fire.

'What's not tonight?' Flint demanded, a suspicious tone creeping into his voice.

'Nothing,' replied Xander and Ollie at the same time, and then grinned at one another.

'I hope so,' growled Flint, but Jory Bardolph just chuckled.

'Budge up, kids and let a little one squeeze in there,' he said, plumping himself down on the log between Xander and Ollie with a grunt. 'Don't you listen to Flint. He's one to talk. Have I ever told you about what an unruly young man he was when he was your age? Never knew where we had him, always in the thick of trouble.'

Bardolph's eyes twinkled as he looked around the younger ones, who all leaned towards him eagerly.

'Why, no, you haven't told us,' said Len, with a wicked grin. 'We'd love to hear about it.'

Flint sent an exasperated look at the laughing Warden and then shrugged. 'If you want to believe a word of it,' he snorted. 'He's getting a bit confused in his old age.'

Bardolph just laughed harder.

'You wish,' he chortled, and Flint rolled his eyes and gave up the argument.

From his place in the centre of the lively group, while Bardolph spun a wildly embellished tale of how Flint and his fellow mischief-makers had used their newfound abilities with their orbs to switch the guide-stones of the six most-used Lodges, causing absolute havoc, Xander once more found himself wishing that he could stay in this moment forever.

The next couple of days passed in a blur for Xander. They had all been far more exhausted by their efforts than they had realised at the time and Mrs Stanton, with an eye to pale faces and tired eyes, insisted that they rested and avoided doing anything strenuous. It was a mark of how right she was that even Len could not muster much objection.

As ever, Woodside was a hub for all the comings and goings, and news continued to trickle in about the repercussions of what was becoming known as the Great Border Breach. Despite Xander's deep suspicion of the man and his motives, Perrin Thorne successfully claimed ignorance of any involvement. He had even offered manpower and any equipment that the hobs might need in their full re-activation of the Pavilions. To Xander's relief, Callan Reeve assured him that the hobs had refused any Thorne equipment and were extremely picky about which humans were allowed on site, limiting them to Reeve himself, the ever faithful Petros and a few others all hand-picked by Reeve who had transferred out of Thorne Industries to work with the hobs.

There had been no further shade incursions, and the border appeared, once more, to be secure so Traveller life was resuming its usual quiet tenor. Xander, however, was still bothered by the discrepancy between the story that Flint had told the Council about how his orb had triggered latent information in the old terminal, and Reeve's insistence that it could not possibly have worked. In a quiet moment, when

Xander was alone with the engineer, he brought up his concern. Reeve frowned, pushing back his rumpled hair.

'No,' he said, after a long pause. 'What Flint described is just not technically possible.'

'Then how come you –'

Xander paused, wondering how to phrase it.

Reeve just grinned. 'How come I didn't correct this assumption at the Council hearing?' he asked and Xander nodded. 'Well, I have literally no alternative explanation and, more importantly, I didn't think they were asking because they actually wanted to know. It seemed to me that they were just looking for someone to blame for what happened and I didn't think it was fair for them to pin it on you.' Reeve's eyes twinkled at Xander. 'You had, after all, just handed me a lifelong dream.'

Xander had grinned back at him but the enigma of the inexplicable messages on the terminal continued to nag at him. After lunch and the clearing up that followed, Mrs Stanton having obviously decided they were all recovered sufficiently to help, Xander called Ollie and Len out to the garden and unloaded his concern.

'It just doesn't make any sense,' he finished. 'I want to go back to the Halls and see if the terminal will activate again.'

Len perked up immediately, an excited gleam in her eyes.

'Excellent,' she said brightly. 'Do we go openly, or shall we break in tonight?'

She looked far too pleased at the prospect.

Ollie, who had received several lectures from his parents on the iniquities of sneaking around by night, shook his head. 'No more breaking and entering,' he said, decisively. 'We'll just go there in the daytime like normal people.'

Len looked disappointed, but she got up gamely enough.

'Come on, then. I was going mad with boredom, anyway. It'll be good to get out.'

Mrs Stanton was baking bread in the kitchen, smears of flour once more adorning her apron, and Xander was reminded of the day that he had arrived at the Stantons' house, confused and overwhelmed. That boy seemed a million miles away from who he was now.

'Going to Halls?' she repeated. 'I don't see why not, but do try not to get into any more trouble with Primilla Pennicott.' Her eyes lingered on Len, who beamed at her.

'Who, us?' she said, with her most innocent expression.

Mrs Stanton sighed and shook her head ruefully.

'Just be back by six for supper, okay?'

They all agreed and shot out of the door before Mrs Stanton could have second thoughts.

After passing through the Wykeham Gate, they strolled up the wide street to Fountain Square. The sky was cloudless, and the beautiful, pale gold buildings of the old city were luminous against the clear, lucent blue. It was not a day for hurrying and even the fairy swarms were lethargic, fluttering up from the trees in slow, mesmerising swirls of colour before sinking back to their leaves to doze. The square was almost empty, and the sunlight sent rainbows shivering through the jets of the fountains.

The entranceway of the Halls of Records felt even cooler than usual and Xander had to blink several times before his vision adjusted to the dimmer light. They slipped in through the great doors and then paused, looking warily over at the raised platform where Primilla Pennicott was usually enthroned. The desk was empty.

'We'll have to be careful,' whispered Ollie. 'She's loose somewhere in here.'

Xander grimaced, but Len had stiffened as her sharp ears caught a breath of sound. She tiptoed over to the platform, despite Ollie's frantic hand signals for her to come back. When she reached the base of the dais, she peered around it and then hurried back, an impish smile on her face.

'It's okay,' she murmured. 'She's tucked in a chair back there, with a handkerchief over her face, totally flat out.'

'Let's be quick then,' said Xander. 'Hopefully we can get in and out without her even knowing about it.' He looked about him at the apparently impenetrable labyrinth of bookshelves and then turned to Len. 'Do you remember where that terminal was?'

Len managed to refrain from making any superior remarks and led them confidently into the maze. It was an odd feeling to be back here, Xander reflected five minutes later, as they stood in front of what was left of the ancient terminal. This time it was lit by daylight as the sunshine poured through the enormous painted window above, each beam of jewel-coloured light sending a million dust motes dancing along its length. Xander reached out a tentative hand and rested his palm in the centre of the cool stone. The faintest flicker ignited in his orb as he reached out for any sign of energy within the terminal but there was no reaction. Gently, he reversed the power, trying to feed it into the stone to see whether that would trigger a response but his palm began to tingle and itch as the power built there, with no way to dissipate. He lifted his hand from the stone with a sigh. Just as Reeve had said, there was nothing left here to activate. He glanced at the faint lights that danced along the starburst lines of his scar and then rubbed his palm reflexively on his trouser leg.

Len and Ollie had stood watching him in silence and he looked over at them, shaking his head ruefully. 'I don't understand it,' he said. 'There's nothing here, just like Reeve said. How could this ever have activated or sent us those messages? It's just not possible.'

Ollie frowned but Len turned and perched herself on the desk, legs swinging blithely. 'You're not looking at this right,' she said, with certainty. 'We all three of us saw it, so we know that it *did* happen. Someone or something made sure that you got that message, so the more interesting question is, who or what are they, and why did they send it to you? The 'how' is not really relevant.'

Xander took a moment to consider this and then looked up at her.

'You're right,' he said slowly.

Len smirked at him. 'Of course I'm right,' she retorted. 'I'm always right.'

Ollie rolled his eyes.

'Let's not get carried away,' he said wryly, 'unless you plan to supply us with the answers as well.' He fished in his pocket and pulled out a much-folded and grubby piece of paper. 'We'll add it to the list,' he said, scrawling a couple of words beneath several crossed-out items. He looked up to see Xander and Len suppressing grins. 'What?' he said defensively, as he returned the paper to his pocket. 'I just like to keep track of where we are.'

'Come on,' said Xander. 'We'd better get out of here before we get found and thrown out.'

'That would be an interesting first for us,' agreed Len, jumping down from her perch.

Heat seared up from the stone steps as they left the Halls and the sunlight momentarily dazzled their eyes. When Xander stopped squinting, he realised that the square was no longer deserted.

'Oh, great,' muttered Len, with heavy sarcasm. 'That's just perfect.'

Directly before the steps, lounging indolently on the low stone walls enclosing the fountain pool, was a small group of teenagers and in the centre of them all were Larissa Larcius-Thorne and her brother, Roran. Larissa did not spot them straight away. She was sitting with her face tipped back to catch the sun, her long blonde hair almost tumbling into the pool behind her, but one of her friends glanced over and then nudged her, whispering something in her ear. Larissa's eyes opened and focussed on the three standing on the wide stone steps.

'Just walk past and ignore them,' said Xander. 'Who cares what they say?'

He led the way down the steps, his face colouring slightly as he felt Larissa watching him intently. He tried to ignore all the whispering and giggling, knowing that they were only doing it to make him feel uncomfortable. They had almost got past when Larissa's mocking voice finally rang out.

'And for his next heroic feat,' she said, in that poisonous little drawl, 'he's taking the freaks out for walky-time.'

The whole group burst out laughing, except for Roran who stood glowering at them, his face disdainful.

'Just ignore them,' said Xander, between gritted teeth. 'Keep walking.' Ollie marched on doggedly next to him and Len tilted her chin, putting her nose in the air.

Larissa did not like being ignored. She stood up and called out loudly enough for the whole square to hear. 'Half of the Council say that you're nothing more than vandals. My father should sue you for damages for what you did.'

Xander's jaw dropped and, despite himself, he spun around to face her. She smirked in triumph at having got a reaction.

'Damages?' he said, in furious disbelief. 'Your father was behind all the destruction at the hobs' Core. He's corrupt and evil. He may think he can slither out of responsibility but I know that it was him and his friend Gage who did it all.'

Larissa bristled, but it was Roran who responded, stepping in front of her and looking at Xander with that familiar, arrogant stare.

'Prove it, why don't you?' he said coolly. 'Oh, yes – you can't!'

'Not yet, but I will,' Xander snapped back.

'Please,' Roran said contemptuously. 'Why don't you just gather up your little band of losers and misfits, and go home before you embarrass yourself further.' Larissa sniggered, quickly followed by the rest of the group.

Xander felt Len stiffen beside him and saw a dull flush stain her cheeks before she ducked her head down to let her hair fall over her face. Anger bubbled up inside him and he blurted out, without thinking, 'Maybe if you tried to be a bit more like your mother's side of the family, *you'd* embarrass yourself less.'

Roran's eyes blazed and his face twisted with fury, the supercilious air dropped in a moment.

'You know nothing about my family,' he snarled.

Larissa laid a hand on his arm, drawing him back. 'Of course they don't,' she said, with a spiteful look at Xander. 'They're just pathetic freaks and no-one who actually matters in Haven could care less what they think.'

She turned her back ostentatiously, with a flick of her glossy hair.

Xander took a deep breath, anger at her and her obnoxious brother boiling up inside him. His orb started to flicker in response to his surging emotions and Ollie's hand clamped on his arm, tugging him away.

'Not worth it, mate,' he muttered. 'They're just looking for you to give them an excuse to complain. Keep walking.'

Xander let himself be pulled away and tried to concentrate on breathing slowly in and out. The rage that had triggered a response from his orb was still simmering, but he knew Ollie was right; blasting a hole in the middle of the square and dropping them all into it would not be a good idea, however satisfying the thought. They had almost made it out of the square before the first scream rang out behind them, followed by hysterical screeching and yelling. Xander swung around to see absolute chaos erupting around the fountain pool.

All of Larissa's group were dripping wet, some of them actually sprawling in the water, while others batted at their hair with frantic squeals. Xander's jaw dropped in astonishment. The previously tranquil pool was now seething with many-coloured nixies, splashing water and pulling on hair and clothes indiscriminately. Their mouths were open in a disturbing approximation of grins and their sharp teeth glinted in the sunlight. For several minutes, mayhem reigned around the pool. Then, as suddenly as they had appeared, all the nixies turned and dived back under the water, with only ripples to show where they had been. The group fled away from the pool, shrieking, and a moment later the square was peaceful again, with just a few passers-by left to stand staring at the fountain pool in bemusement.

Xander realised that his mouth was hanging open, and he shut it again quickly.

'What just happened?' he asked.

Len shrugged, a secretive smile playing about her lips.

'Just desserts, I would say,' she said airily.

Ollie's snigger turned into a roar of laughter.

'Did you see that?' he choked, when he could breathe again. 'That was awesome. There were actually three hanging off Larissa's hair and she looked like she was going to wet herself. I may have to change my mind about nixies. It was a beautiful, beautiful thing.'

Xander felt his own lips quirk, but he turned to eye Len thoughtfully.

'What?' she asked in her most innocent voice, which immediately made him even more sceptical.

'I know you had something to do with that,' he said finally.

'Oh, please. Everyone knows that nixies aren't trainable and besides, I was right across the square,' Len replied, with a smirk which just confirmed Xander's suspicions.

'Fine,' he said, calmly. 'But at some point you're going to have to come clean about all this. Maybe we should add it to the list?'

Len just grinned at him, her eyes dancing, before turning to head home and, with a last look back at the quiet square, Xander followed her.

✕

That evening there was the usual Saturday get-together at the Stantons' house. Mrs Stanton took one look at the number of people congregating in her kitchen and decreed they should all eat outside on the terrace. This turned out to be a lucky decision as shortly afterwards, Reeve appeared with Alf and another of the giants in tow, Alf beaming bashfully around as he was welcomed with great acclaim.

Ari and Jasper handled the moving of the heavy kitchen table to join onto the one outside, while Ollie jumped in to help move chairs with great enthusiasm and alarmingly poor aim. After the events at the Pavilions, his parents had replaced his battered orb with a shiny new one and its coding flickered erratically as he attempted to control the moving furniture. He had a distinct tendency to shoot them unexpectedly skywards but managed not to blow any up, to Mrs Stanton's evident relief. Xander himself and Len were loaded with handfuls of cutlery and stacks of plates and told to lay the table.

Before long everything was ready, the table was covered with delicious food and everyone grabbed seats. The giants sat on the ground at the end of the table, so tall that their heads still loomed over the rest of the party, and talk and laughter rang out. Looking up and down the happy rows of faces, Xander felt that sense of warmth and belonging again. Twilight had fallen gradually, and the glowstones scattered down the table and hanging from the trees round about cast their soft light over everyone's faces, while the warmth of the day lingered and drew out the rich scents of the flowers. The sky was a deep crystal blue and the first stars were just beginning to glimmer over the gabled roof of the old house. It was a perfect evening.

Xander smiled as he watched Jenna poke Ollie in the side in response to some joke and then hug him, her affection clear on her face. Unexpectedly, a vivid recollection of his own mother came to him; his absent-minded, frequently distracted mother who couldn't always be trusted to remember to eat a meal, but who never failed to poke her head around his door to check on him before she went to bed. Her soft murmur of 'love you' in the night was one of his earliest memories. There was a momentary lull in the conversation, and Xander suddenly knew that it was time.

'I think I should go home,' he said softly, but they all turned to look at him.

Mrs Stanton was the first to respond, leaning forward to clasp his hand firmly in her own.

'I hope you will also consider this your home, Xander,' she said warmly, 'but I do understand that you must miss your family.'

Ollie pulled a face.

'When will you come back?' he demanded.

'Regularly,' put in Flint. 'You have an orb, which is a responsibility, not a toy. As long as you are wearing it you need the same training as any other young Traveller. Of course, if you want to give it up?' He let his voice trail off, raising an eyebrow. Xander grinned and shook his head. 'Thought not,' Flint said with a grimace, but his voice was amused.

'You'll stay tonight though,' asked Ollie anxiously. 'You're not leaving right this minute?'

'No,' said Xander. 'I'll leave tomorrow.' He wanted to savour this moment, surrounded by all the people he had grown to care about.

At the end of the evening, as the guests were taking their leave, Ari popped up behind Xander with that familiar grin that wrinkled up her nose.

'Do you want me to come to the Stone with you tomorrow?' she asked. 'Make sure you don't accidentally zap yourself across the world?'

Xander just laughed.

'I think I can manage,' he said and Ari grinned. She also pressed a piece of paper into his hand and when he glanced down at it, he saw that she had drawn the mark for a Stone she had told him about, not far from the British Museum, and a second symbol which she had labelled '*Haven – come back soon*'.

Xander hugged her.

'Thanks, Ari,' he said, and he meant more than just the note.

Ari seemed to understand. 'See you soon,' she promised, with a smile and a quick wink.

Flint had been standing back, as ever on the edge of the group. He met Xander's look with an unaccustomed smile tugging at his lips.

'Good journey back,' he said. 'Do me a favour and try to stay out of trouble.'

Xander felt a laugh break loose.

'I've been trying to do that ever since I met you guys.'

Flint shook his head, the wry smile widening. 'Try harder,' he advised.

Xander's last night was spent talking and laughing in the room he had shared with Ollie since his arrival in Haven, Len sprawled across the end of Ollie's bed, until Jenna came in and insisted on them getting some sleep. After breakfast the next morning, Xander hugged everyone while Ollie made up wilder and wilder excuses why he had to stay longer. Mrs Stanton finally rounded on him in exasperation.

'For Haven's sake, Oliver,' she said, rolling her eyes. 'You'd think that you were never going to see him again. The sooner you let him go, the quicker he can come back.' She turned and kissed Xander on the cheek, then enfolded him in a tight hug. Unexpectedly, Xander blinked back a faint prickling in his eyes.

When she pulled back, she looked firmly at him.

'Don't forget, we're family now,' she said with her beautiful smile.

Xander just nodded, his throat a little thick. 'I'll remember,' he got out, and then stepped back. Suddenly, he knew exactly where he wanted to go. With a last look around, he leant into his orb and vanished from the kitchen, a faint glimmer of light from his wrist winking for a moment behind him.

He reappeared an instant later, precisely where he had visualised. He was facing out towards the sea, standing on a narrow ledge with the dark entrance to a small hollow gaping open in the cliff behind him. This time, the sky was a clear, pale blue, and the sea sparkled merrily, while the white foam on the tips of the waves glistened in the sunshine. Overhead, a few seagulls circled lazily and their faint cries drifted down to where Xander stood. He took a deep breath of the rich, salty air and smiled, enjoying the peace and solitude.

'Welcome back, Xander King,' said a voice from behind him.

Xander started so violently that he almost plunged over the edge. Wobbling slightly, he swung around to see the Tan sitting cross-legged by the cleft, his parchment face wreathed with amusement.

'You made me jump,' gasped Xander unnecessarily, and then – 'How did you know I would be here? I only just decided myself to use this Stone.'

'You are here because it is now the time for you to choose to go home,' replied the Tan. 'This is the place of your choice, so of course you would return here.'

Xander stared at him blankly and then shook his head, thinking that of all the strange things he had encountered in Haven, the brownies might just be the most mysterious. The Tan continued to smile at him, as if he knew exactly what

Xander was thinking and it amused him.

'We did it, by the way,' Xander blurted out. 'We put all the clues together and found the ancient Core where the power saved Haven last time, like in your song. But you probably already know that,' he finished lamely.

The Tan smiled at him. 'It brought us great joy,' he said simply and Xander felt all of his awkwardness melting away.

Gracefully, the Tan rose to his feet and reached up to clasp Xander's hand in both of his small ones. 'Good journey, Xander King,' he said in a clear, formal voice. 'May you always find a light for your path.'

He vanished, and the ledge was empty once more.

Xander cast a last look out over the sea and then turned to squeeze through the cleft in the rock face. Immediately to his left, the Stone still stood just as he had remembered, half buried in the pile of tumbled rocks. As he drew near, faint filaments of light flickered through the symbols as the Stone recognised his power as a Traveller. In the centre of the second row was the glimmering outline of the symbol the Tan had once shown him, which would take him back to the British Museum. With a last deep breath, and only a moment's hesitation, Xander reached forward and firmly pressed his fingers to the Stone.

The symbol flared into incandescent light and, for the second time in his life, Xander felt the world wrench sideways around him, exploding colours whirling behind his tightly shut eyelids. An instant later the sensation stopped and Xander felt the ground firm once more under his feet. He dropped his arm and opened his eyes.

Hanging in front of him on the wall was an old stone tablet, cracked at the top and protected behind a thick perspex sheet. People were wandering past him, a couple of tourists standing a few feet away examining one of the other tablets. None of them seemed to have noticed that someone had just appeared out of thin air in their midst. For a moment, Xander wondered whether he had dreamt the whole thing and he would turn to see his classmates there, and his friend Will, muttering about cakes. He glanced down and saw the edge of his orb band peeking out from his jumper, the weight of it a solid reassurance on his wrist, and his lips twitched at the sight of his gleaming trainers. It had all really happened.

Xander turned and re-traced the path he had taken, in what seemed like a lifetime ago, through the hall and into the central atrium. He paused in the middle of it, the beautifully intricate glass ceiling soaring overhead, seeing again that moment when he had first watched the Travellers walking through, their wards casting the rest of the world into dull shades of grey, muted and lifeless. He had just stood and stared as they passed by, an outsider.

'I'm one now,' he said, in wonderment and satisfaction. He blushed as a passing lady gave him a funny look, realising that he had once again spoken out loud. With a quick grin, Xander headed out of the museum and ran to catch his bus home. This time, the shadows stayed exactly where the sun had pinned them.

The hallway was silent and dark as Xander let himself in and closed the door behind him, leaning back against it for a moment. He was home again, and it looked strange to him, but he knew that was not because it had changed; he was not the same person who had fled out of here in a panic only a few weeks before. He dropped his keys in the bowl on the hall table.

'How was the museum?'

Mrs King's voice rang out of the quiet and Xander felt a smile tug at his lips as he walked into the sitting room, to find her curled up on the sofa surrounded by papers. Her hair was piled into a lop-sided bun on top of her head, precariously secured with a couple of pencils, and with wild tendrils escaping everywhere. She had a long streak of blue on her nose where she had been pushing up her glasses with an ink-stained finger, odd socks on her feet, and a warm smile on her face, just for him. She stood up, scattering papers onto the floor and enveloped him in an unexpected hug.

'It's funny,' she said lightly. 'I feel like I've hardly seen you lately, I've been working so hard. I missed you, Xand.'

Xander swallowed and hugged her back.

'I've missed you too, Mum,' he said.

Mrs King squeezed him and then pulled back with a cheerful smile. 'I've got lunch cooking,' she announced.

Xander eyed her warily.

'Really?' he asked, trying not to sound too sceptical.

'I'll just clear this up a bit – I don't know how they all get scattered about like this,' she said, beginning to scoop up her papers. 'Lunch should be ready soon.'

Xander gave her what he hoped looked like an enthusiastic smile, before heading up to his bedroom. There didn't appear to be any smoke coming from the kitchen but it still seemed wise to put off the moment of truth about whatever his mother had decided to incinerate today. He took the stairs two at a time, noticing that the lamps were back on their side tables, and then hesitated for a moment outside his bedroom door. Now that he was back, the memory of the night when shades had manifested all over his house was still very vivid and he shivered before pushing the door open.

The room was tidy, his bed neatly made, and sunshine was pouring in through the window. His school bag sat next to his desk, as if he had just dropped it there, and his blazer hung over the back of his desk chair. Everything looked utterly ordinary. Xander sat on the end of his bed and looked down at his open palm, where the pale mark from his shade-strike glistened. He shook his head.

'Back to normal,' he said quietly, with a wry smile.

A small head popped up from behind the bed.

'All clear, Xander,' it said brightly.

Xander fell sideways off the bed, landing on the floor on his hands and knees, with his mouth open in shock. The face peered cautiously around the side of bed, eyes staring curiously at him. It was Brolly.

'You!' Xander spluttered. 'How are you here?'

Brolly beamed at him.

'Tan wanted to make sure all was now well in your home, and all secure,' he explained helpfully.

'But how can you even cross the border?' asked Xander, completely thrown by the sight of a brownie standing in the middle of his bedroom. 'I didn't think you could use the Stones.'

'Brownies don't need Stones, silly Xander,' said Brolly serenely. 'Only checking all is clear.'

Xander just stared at him. There was a small shuffling noise from the cupboard and his eyes immediately shot over that way, body tensing.

'What was that?'

Brolly looked evasive.

'Nothing,' he said, but it wasn't convincing.

Xander rolled to his feet, marched over to the cupboard and threw both doors open. On the floor, a tatty shoe in each hand, sat Spike with a guilty expression on his face; he sent a wavering smile up at Xander.

Brolly hurried forward.

'Can explain,' he said quickly. 'Tan said to check and return, but we checked cupboard and found *all this*.' He gestured to Xander's untidy shoe and clothes pile as if it were a treasure trove, then clasped his hands and gazed beseechingly up at Xander. 'Will be very quiet,' he begged.

Spike clutched a scuffed school shoe to his chest, with wide, pleading eyes.

'Oh, fine,' Xander surrendered, with a roll of his eyes. 'Just don't let anyone hear you.'

Both brownies dived forward to hug him around the knees and then settled down in his cupboard to root through their tool bags with beatific expressions on their faces. With a wry smile, Xander swung the cupboard doors partially closed to conceal them and headed back downstairs.

There was still no smell of burning coming from the kitchen and Xander was pleasantly surprised to find that his mother had actually got a couple of baked potatoes in the oven.

'Almost like a normal family,' Xander said with a grin and a quick glance upstairs, where the brownies were managing to remain quiet so far.

The kitchen table was, as usual, piled up high with files, old mail and shopping that hadn't yet been put away. Looking around as if he was seeing it for the first time, Xander could almost see Mrs Stanton pushing up her sleeves and hear her brisk voice saying, 'it's not going to clear itself'.

'I know, I know,' he muttered under his breath and gathered up an armful of papers.

Ten minutes later, the table was clear, the shopping put away and Xander was laying out cutlery and plates of food. He had unearthed a large colourful bowl to put the fruit in and it brightened up the centre of the slightly battered table.

'Lunch, Mum,' he called.

Mrs King looked slightly surprised as she came into the kitchen, to find her plate and her son awaiting her at a neatly scrubbed table. 'Oh, this is nice,' she said appreciatively. 'We should do this more often.' She searched for the television remote, to turn off the news programme that was flickering away on the television, but then paused. 'Oh, look. That's Dominic Bayle. His company is funding some of our work at the university.'

Xander glanced over and saw a tall, extremely handsome man, with dark hair threaded with silver and wearing an elegant suit, standing behind a glittering steel and glass lectern. Across the bottom of the screen ran the words, 'CEO of Infinity Inc, Dominic Bayle, opening a new marine research facility.'

'He's an amazing man,' said Mrs King, cutting into her potato. 'He runs one of the biggest global companies in the world with so many different divisions, from media to pharmaceuticals to mining, but he still finds time to support research and community outreach. I actually got to meet him once.' Her eyes glazed slightly as she gazed at the screen, her face flushed.

Xander reached for the remote control and turned up the volume. Dominic Bayle's voice filled the room, warm and resonant as he stared into the cameras.

'I'm proud that Infinity continues to embrace the future,

and that when we are confronted with impossible dreams, we stand together to declare, *'Why not?'* I hope that you will all join us in our journey, as we grasp today's possibilities and turn them into tomorrow's realities.'

'Such an inspiring man,' said Mrs King, admiringly.

The camera view panned backwards as applause rang out and Xander froze, his fork partway to his mouth as the lower half of the lectern was revealed. On it was a screen showing the company name and, below it, the logo; the infinity symbol spun over and around, looping like a twisted figure of eight. Xander followed it with his eyes, with an all too vivid memory of the hunched figure in room 212, drawing this same symbol over and over again on the wall.

'Could it be infinity, not eight?' he wondered, under his breath.

'What's that?' asked Mrs King, her eyes still glued to Dominic Bayle who was smiling and waving to the applauding crowds.

Xander shook his head and then stiffened again, this time with cold prickles running down his back like ice water and his heart pounding. The camera had been circling Bayle, looking for a different angle. Standing to one side of the lectern, holding a steel clipboard with the Infinity company logo on the front, and motionless but for his eyes alertly sweeping the crowds, was Gage. Xander heard his own breath come out unevenly as he gaped at the television screen.

The news programme moved on to a different story and Mrs King reached for the remote and flicked the television off. She paused, as she took in Xander's shocked expression, still immobile with a forkful of potato.

'Xander?' she said. 'Are you okay?'

Xander took a deep breath, smiled deliberately at his

mother and ate his potato.

'Absolutely fine,' he said a moment later, his voice slightly muffled. 'I think I just need to get a friend to add something to a list.'

His mother smiled vaguely at him.

'Lists are good,' she said, nodding her head. 'Break things down into small steps and that'll get you where you need to go. I use them all the time.' She patted her pockets absently, as if she had just remembered a list tucked in there.

Xander smiled and carried on eating his lunch. There was no particular hurry. He had a feeling that he knew exactly where those steps would take him, and Haven wasn't going anywhere.

AVTHOR'S NOTE

As a writer, the most exciting part of publishing your book is finally getting to hear from the people for whom you wrote it – the readers. I would love to hear what you think about the world of Haven and the characters who live in it, so please leave your thoughts for me by posting a review at Amazon. Even one quick sentence is perfect, and it also really helps other readers to decide whether my book is for them. Many thanks to all of you who have done so – it is much appreciated.

Join my VIP Haven group to receive Part I of the *Illustrated Guide to Haven,* free in ebook form, and advance notice of future releases.
Join here: www.sjhowland.com

The Traveller's Stone is the first book of a five-part series. The second book, *The Lore of the Sea* will be released in early 2020. Further details about the series can be found on my website.

As well as the wonderful readers, there are many other people for whose support I am immensely grateful: my husband and children – first, last and always – as well as all of the friends who have cheered and, occasionally, prodded me on and offered their time and opinions. Also, a huge thank you to the amazing Cakamura Designs who has the magical gift of seeing into my mind and then creating book covers which are a hundred times better than I imagined.

Made in the USA
Las Vegas, NV
26 May 2021

23679551R00249